Tara Pammi can't remember a moment when she wasn't lost in a book—especially a romance, which was much more exciting than a mathematics textbook at school. Years later, Tara's wild imagination and love for the written word revealed what she really wanted to do. Now she pairs alpha males who think they know everything with strong women who knock that theory *and* them off their feet!

New York Times and *USA TODAY* bestselling author **Jane Porter** has written forty romances and eleven women's fiction novels since her first sale to Mills & Boon in 2000. A five-time RITA® Award finalist, Jane is known for her passionate, emotional and sensual novels, and loves nothing more than alpha heroes, exotic locations and happy-ever-afters. Today Jane lives in sunny San Clemente, California, with her surfer husband and three sons. Visit janeporter.com.

Also by Tara Pammi

Blackmailed by the Greek's Vows
Sicilian's Bride for a Price

Bound to the Desert King collection

Sheikh's Baby of Revenge

Brides for Billionaires collection

Married for the Sheikh's Duty

The Scandalous Brunetti Brothers miniseries

An Innocent to Tame the Italian

Also by Jane Porter

Bought to Carry His Heir
His Merciless Marriage Bargain
The Prince's Scandalous Wedding Vow

Passion in Paradise collection

His Shock Marriage in Greece

Stolen Brides collection

Kidnapped for His Royal Duty

Discover more at millsandboon.co.uk.

A DEAL TO CARRY THE ITALIAN'S HEIR

TARA PAMMI

CHRISTMAS CONTRACT FOR HIS CINDERELLA

JANE PORTER

MILLS & BOON

First Published in Great Britain 2019
by Mills & Boon, an imprint of HarperCollins*Publishers*
1 London Bridge Street, London, SE1 9GF

ISBN: 978-0-263-27370-0

MIX
Paper from responsible sources
FSC™ C007454

This book is produced from independently certified FSC™ paper
to ensure responsible forest management.
For more information visit www.harpercollins.co.uk/green.

Printed and bound in Spain
by CPI, Barcelona

A DEAL TO CARRY THE ITALIAN'S HEIR

TARA PAMMI

To my endlessly patient and brilliant editor: Laurie.
Thank you so much for your guidance
on a super-fun but complex Modern.

CHAPTER ONE

"ARE WE REALLY supposed to think he's given up his twisted revenge scheme?"

Leonardo Brunetti, CEO of Brunetti Finances Inc., asked the question of his younger brother, Massimo, about the man who had done too much damage over the last few months to both BFI and Massimo's brainchild, Brunetti Cyber Securities.

Contracts had fallen through at the last minute, their father Silvio Brunetti's embezzlement from BFI and his corruption—everything Leonardo had cleaned up in the last decade since he'd taken over as CEO of BFI—was being recycled in the news again and again, and even worse, Vincenzo Cavalli had hired a consortium of hackers from the dark net to hit Massimo and his wife Natalie's multilayered security design for a billion-dollar contract for BCS.

They had almost lost that contract, too, except Natalie's genius had saved it at the last minute. And now, Vincenzo had disappeared. They both knew better than to think the man was done, not after his brutal tactics to bring everything related to the Brunettis down.

"What happened to the financial trail that Natalie gave us?"

"The investigator found only one small nugget of information. That account has ties to Mario Fenelli."

Mario Fenelli was one of the oldest members on the board of BFI, one of the old guard, a relic left over from when their father, Silvio, had ruled the board, and the staunchest, most vocal opponent of Leo.

While Leo, with his grandmother Greta's and Massimo's help, had cleaned up Silvio's corruption and ousted him from the board, BFI's founding board were members of Milan's upper echelons of society. Old money, old power—men who didn't want to give up what they had in the name of Leo's financial reform and ethics that he'd brought to the firm.

Vincenzo's actions had already had far-reaching consequences.

Contracts falling through, the cyber-attack on financial information of BFI's clients, leaving BFI's and BCS's cybersecurity vulnerable, and then leaking the information to the board—Mario had been one step behind with his accusations that Leonardo was following in Silvio's footsteps, creating an atmosphere of doubt and confusion among their clients, breathing rumors that Leo was just as corrupted.

It was because of the unprecedented growth and revenue BFI had seen under his leadership and the fact that the Brunettis—Greta, Leo, Massimo and their father, Silvio—still held the majority of stock in BFI that Leo hadn't been forced to step down.

With the financial connection between Mario and Vincenzo, it was clear that Mario had been bought.

"Mario Fenelli is a greedy bastard," said Massimo with a bite to his words.

"There has to be something in the old man's history that we can use against him," Leo said. "And if we can find Vincenzo through him, we can finally put an end to this."

"Ms. Fernandez is here," came his assistant's voice through the intercom.

"Neha is here to see you?" said Massimo, his brow tied. Neha Fernandez, Leo's oldest friend, was Mario's stepdaughter. "You're not involving her in this thing with Mario, are you?"

Leo wasn't insulted by Massimo's accusation. If he'd turned into the man that Silvio had brainwashed him to be, he wouldn't have hesitated to use Neha.

Massimo and he had made a pact to run BFI with ethical and clean practices—basically, to be the opposite of what their father had been.

But Massimo had had the influence of a mother who had tried her hardest to fight their father's corrosive and toxic influence on her weak son. A mother who'd strived to make sure that Massimo understood what was right and what was wrong. A mother who'd put up with an abusive husband because to leave would've been to give up on her son. Massimo's ill health, while making him the subject of Silvio's vicious rants, had also kept his father away.

Leo, on the other hand, had worshipped his father until he'd learned what Silvio was capable of. His mind had been filled with bitter poison against the woman who had walked out on her young son in the middle of the night by an infuriated Silvio.

"No, I'm not," he finally said.

Neha was the one woman with whom Leo's association spanned the longest. The one woman he respected and admired. The one woman he'd always been intensely attracted to but hadn't pursued because he wasn't a relationship kind of man.

The tentative friendship had built the first day when Mario, a new board member of BFI, had brought Neha with him on his trip to Milan, and Silvio had brought Leo.

While her mother and stepfather had postured about their wealth and connections, Neha—even then a quiet, sharp, pretty girl—had arrested his attention. She'd already been running her late father's bakery single-handed, and had been full of ideas for new branches. Leo, meanwhile, had been roiling with anger and rage—he'd discovered that week that not only was BFI in ruins, but that Silvio had been abusing Massimo emotionally for years, and that the man he'd worshipped for all his life was nothing but a bully all around.

Neha had listened to him rage about his father, the devastation he'd felt. She'd clasped his hand shyly and said, "But all you have to do is tell your brother that you're sorry. That you do care about him. That… You love him." He'd vowed that when he returned home with Silvio, he'd do just that.

In the meantime, he'd distracted himself by offering Neha ideas about how to raise seed money to expand her business.

And through the meteoric rise of her fame, from winning a local English village baking show contest at sixteen to transforming a chain of baking goods she'd created into a multi-million-pound business, Neha had come to him for advice and Leo had given it to the best of his ability.

Mario had spotted the extraordinary talent and work ethic his stepdaughter had possessed even at that young age and monetized it so fast that within just a few years of Neha winning the contest and creating the first line of confectionary goods, Mario had launched her as a child prodigy that created delicious confections. He'd made her into an international brand, franchised her talents so far and so wide that So Sweet Inc. had become a world-renowned business.

"Why is she here, then?" Massimo asked, pulling Leo from the past to the present.

"She asked to see me. As soon as possible."

Massimo waggled his brows, doing quite a good imitation of a schoolgirl. "Is it really business, though? I've always sensed something more between you two."

Leo kept his expression implacable. Neha was forbidden to him, would always be. "It's pathetic to see you act like a matchmaker just because you are blissfully in love." He strode to the door and opened it. "Now, go back to Nat and leave me to my business."

Mouth twitching mischievously, Massimo walked over to where Neha waited, and hugged her with all the easy energy of a man who didn't have the complication of wanting her and keeping her at a distance, as Leo had done all these years.

Through the open doorway, Leo could only see the clean lines of Neha's profile: her long neck, her brown hair tied back in a braid that highlighted those cheekbones, the elegant white sheath dress draped over her curvaceous body and the yellow pop of her pumps. It was her public persona. White dress, yellow pumps and a strand of pearls at her neck. Red lipstick that made her lush mouth look like one of her delicious creations. A dimple in one cheek and laughter in those light brown eyes.

All that creativity and passion wrapped in unruffled composure, all those voluptuous curves with the hidden sensuality buried in the elegant, girl-next-door package she presented to the world. That subtle lure of wanting to delve beneath the elegant persona she showed the world, to ruffle all that composure… It had started on the eve of her twenty-first birthday party.

Overnight, she had transformed from a shy, pretty teenager into a gorgeously sexy woman. The urge to undo all that elegance, to reach the woman beneath, was as fresh and urgent and intense as it had been that day. For a man who went after his goals with single-minded ruthlessness, Neha was the one thing Leonardo had had to deny himself.

Their relationship, as much as it had stayed inside the unsaid boundaries they'd both set, and as much as it defied the media's incessant efforts to label, was important to him. Against all the odds for a man who had problems with trusting the opposite sex, Neha had become the one genuine friend he possessed.

He could never risk that.

Massimo asked her how long she meant to stay in Milan, because he wanted to introduce her to Natalie. Neha's gaze flew to his.

Leo stilled; every bit of his attention arrested at something inexplicable that flashed in her eyes. He frowned.

She turned back to Massimo. And gave him a circular non-answer. Thanked Massimo with a graceful smile before saying goodbye.

Leo's curiosity deepened as he drank the sight of her in with a greed he knew was useless to try to curb. She stood there, framed by the arch of his door, her lower lip caught beneath her two front teeth.

Afternoon sunlight from the high windows behind him gilded her in golden light, tracing the curvy contours of her body with the same delight and thoroughness that he wanted to. He'd seen her in a million variations of the same color scheme and makeup. And yet the white dress ending a couple of inches above her knees, the high-necked bodice that showed off the swell of her breasts, the tight dip of her waist…everything that was familiar about her spiked his awareness.

So thoroughly mesmerized was he that it took him a few moments to notice the hesitation in her gaze. The rigid set of her shoulders. The tension emanating from her.

"Neha…" he said softly, and she snapped into the present. "Do you plan to stand there for the rest of the day?"

She entered his office without answer, closed the door behind her, still not quite meeting his gaze.

In the wake of Massimo's jokes, the silence was thick, awkward.

She walked toward the sitting area of his office, poured herself a glass of water from the carafe. Her knuckles showed white on the glass while her gaze stayed on the streets of Milan's business district rendered colorful on a bright afternoon.

They had always been courteous to each other through the years, close without getting personal. He'd been there when she'd called her wedding off eight years ago—calm, quiet and yet somehow devastated. He'd never asked her why, only given his support when she'd asked for his help to curtail the media swarming in like locusts at the prospect of drama and tragedy beneath the elegant, sweet public persona of hers.

He'd never let on that she was the one woman he wanted with a desire that seemed to span years, when usually his lovers had a shelf life of maybe six months.

As she grew older, she'd become even more irresistible. More beautiful, more elegant, more composed, which taunted his base impulses because he wanted to see beneath that perfection. He wanted to see her undone. In his hands.

"Thank you for agreeing to see me on such short notice. I know how busy you are," she finally said, turning to him.

"Why are you being so formal?" he countered. "Is everything all right?"

"Everything's fine," she said, raising her brown gaze to his, not quite smiling, not quite serious. She studied his features with something almost bordering on desperation, searching, as if she meant to see through to his soul. It was unnerving, and yet not…unwelcome.

"Sorry, I'm just… I don't know where to begin."

"Take your time, then."

She put away the empty glass, dropped her white clutch down on the coffee table and then rubbed her palms up and down her hips. Inadvertently calling his gaze to the thoroughly feminine swell.

His gaze traveled from where her hands rested, up, up, up her hips, to the thrust and fall of her breasts, the pulse beating away at her neck to the plump, glossed lips, to collide with her stunned brown gaze.

A sudden shimmer of awareness—bright as a bolt of lightning in a dark sky, sizzled through the air around them. Condensing the expansive room, the world, to just the two of them. Her gaze dropped to his mouth, for an infinitesimal second, before she pulled it back up. The moment was weighted, tangible, as if she'd pressed her mouth to his. But it was enough.

Enough for him to know that the attraction he'd denied for years wasn't just one-sided. Enough for his muscles to jerk and tighten in anticipation, in need. Enough for the rational side of him to issue warnings.

"I came to ask you something. Something very important." The words rushed out of her. "It's a big thing."

"Bene," he said, reaching for her, but she jerked back.

"No, it's a huge thing. Don't laugh at me, yeah? No, wait, I don't care if you laugh at me. Just don't dismiss it immediately, okay? Please, Leo." Desperation filled her words. "I went through every means available to me and I come to you after a lot of thought. Please promise me you will consider it."

"Neha…"

"I mean, you know me, yeah? For what? Sixteen… No, seventeen years! I've never done anything impulsive or rash or reckless. Head down, I worked just as hard as you. Harder even, because life's not easy for women in the business world. I've never…" When her breath became shallow and her eyes filled with an alarming combination of panic and fear, he grabbed her hands and tugged her toward him.

"Calm down, *bella*," he said, keeping his own tone steady.

She was the most levelheaded woman he knew. This panic, this anxiety…was bizarre. Alarm bells went off in his head. Was she in some kind of trouble? Not financial, because he would've heard of it. He had a huge stake in So Sweet Inc.

Was it...a man? The thought jarred him on too many levels.

"Make me that promise first," she said in a demanding, petulant, possessive voice that was completely uncharacteristic of her.

"I can't make a promise without knowing what you're asking me for." His words were clipped, curt, tangled up in his own reaction. It had always surprised him that after her broken engagement, Neha had never been involved again with another man. Or at least he hadn't heard about it. He shouldn't be this shocked that she was involved with a man now.

"All I'm asking is for you to consider my request first. I have gone over all of my other options. Coming to you is the right choice." She sounded like she was convincing herself, too. "This is what I want."

"Fine, *bella*. I promise to consider your request. Now, out with it. All the suspense is giving me a headache."

"Whatever your answer, will you please keep this whole thing from Mario? This is personal, this is about my future."

Leo nodded, shoving away the flicker of distaste.

It was about a man.

Why else would she not want her mom or stepfather to know? Was he good enough for her? Had he already deceived her? Did she know what kind of fortune hunters her wealth could attract?

She slumped down onto the sofa with a harsh exhale. The afternoon light caught glints of copper and gold in the thick, silky strands of her hair. Fingers, clasped tightly together, rested in her lap. "I thought it through, looked at it from all sides, and I've decided that this is the right thing for me. For my life. For the life I want." She licked her lips, a fine line of sweat beading about her upper lip. Then she looked up with the defiant tilt of her chin. “I’m going to have a child.”

It was the last thing he’d expected for her to say. For a few seconds, he stared at her, his brain trying to catch up.

She was pregnant? Had the man ditched her?

“What is it that you want from me, then?” he said, shock making his question curt.

Her teeth dug into that plump lower lip, her tongue flicked over it, demanding, and getting an unbidden reaction from his tense body. She tucked a wayward lock from her braid behind her ear, each movement so feminine, so utterly taunting.

“Out with it, Neha,” he said, corralling his own rioting reactions with a ruthless warning. He’d wasted enough time indulging an unlikely scenario between them that he would never turn into a reality.

She stood up and met his gaze head-on. “I would like you to father my child.”

CHAPTER TWO

IF ALL HER hopes and dreams hadn't been hanging on his response, Neha would have laughed at the astonishment on Leonardo's face. Like a typical man, he looked baffled by the concept of pregnancy. Or was it the forthrightness of her strange request?

Unlike any other man, however, he recovered fast and pinned her with his penetrating gaze.

"You're not pregnant already?"

"What? No!" She looked away, refusing to let her imagination conjure a quality to his question that wasn't there. "Of course I'm not pregnant. I haven't been with a man since..." She flushed at the sudden gleam of male interest in his eyes.

Clearing her throat, she slowly unlaced her fingers, forced herself to look up at him. "I'm not pregnant. But I want to be. That's why I'm asking you to... Be the father. To my child. So that I can be a mum. I want to build the family that I've always wanted. So that I can be...happy," she finished softly.

She grabbed her clutch and pulled a tissue out of it. Just to have something to do. He kept looking down at her, unblinking. Not betraying his thoughts. A stranger for all that she'd known him for so long.

Lord, she'd appeared on network shows, giving speeches at conferences with CEOs and entrepreneurs, and this, the most important thing of her life... She was making a total mess of this.

Even the practice sessions she'd done in front of the mirror in her bedroom didn't help. Because she couldn't recreate the most important facet of their relationship by herself in front of the mirror.

This pent-up, unwise attraction of hers that had taken root years ago. Leonardo was the one man who teased and taunted her dreams for so long, who made her want to break down hard-won defenses she'd built, for one taste of that carved, sinful mouth.

It didn't matter…it didn't seem to matter to her body how many times she told herself that Leonardo was out of reach.

For one thing, even if she could come out and ask him outright if he was attracted to her—and he amazingly said yes, Neha couldn't take him on because he was too…*important* to her.

For another, she knew what Leonardo thought of women in general and how far down his priorities romantic relationships were. He didn't believe in love and marriage any more than she believed that another man like her papa had been—loving, warm, unconditional in his love for her—existed.

In short, Leonardo was the last man on earth for a woman to build her future around. Not that he wasn't a good man. He was the alpha in any situation—a protector at heart—and he extended that protection and care to maybe two other people in the world.

She desperately wanted to be counted among them.

That first day when they'd met she'd still been grieving over her papa, and he'd been…ragingly angry about how his father had emotionally abused Massimo for so long. That regret and pain in his eyes that he hadn't protected Massimo… Neha had never forgotten that.

For a gorgeously striking young man with the world at his feet, there had been such dissolution in his eyes when he had to face the stark reality that his father was a brute who crushed weaker people. That he'd worshipped a man who was so far from being a hero that he'd have to question everything he knew of himself.

Wondering how many lies the foundation of his life had been built on.

It was the only time Neha had seen that vulnerability in him. The only time she'd seen beneath the ruthlessness, the arrogance, the aura of power that surrounded Leonardo Brunetti.

Once their careers had taken off, they had met a few times each year. In the beginning it had been accidental—bumping into each other at some conference, traveling at the same time. She'd started using him as a sounding board for her own business ideas. As the years went by, he'd started asking her to dinner every time he was in London. She'd begun stopping in Milan whenever she had the chance.

She had obsessively followed his relationships from that first day on social media, and in glossy magazines, feeding her addiction about his life, wondering if between all the women he seemed to sleep with and dump eventually, he remembered her existence. But whoever the current woman in his life, Leonardo Brunetti, CEO of BFI, would meet his close friend Neha Fernandez, CEO of So Sweet Inc., on his every trip to London.

For a confirmed bachelor, who couldn't be pinned down by even the most beautiful woman on earth, Neha had become a permanent fixture in his life.

Their friendship had deepened while morphing into a legend with the media. Their relationship had been analyzed and criticized and praised and "shipped" by some of Neha's fans.

And she was putting all that on the line. But her resolve didn't falter.

"You want me to…make you pregnant, so that you can

have a baby, which in turn will make you…happy?" Leo finally said, every word enunciated in a biting tone.

She held her composure, barely.

"That is the request you want me to consider before I reject it outright, *sì*?"

"Yes," she replied, squaring her shoulders.

A violent energy imbued his movements as he raked a hand through his hair and stepped away from her. "An innocent life is not a thing you go looking for because you're bored, or because you're unhappy, or because it's the latest celebrity bandwagon to jump on—"

"You've got every right to question the sanity of my decision. Every right to be shocked," Neha cut in, determined to make her point. His concern for a hypothetical child told her how right she was in her choice.

When it came to protecting an innocent life, Leonardo would always be a protector at heart.

"But don't think I came to this decision lightly. Or that it's some biological-clock-induced crisis I'm acting on without thought. And you know me better than to think it's for a publicity stunt." Her voice rose on the last and she took a deep breath to calm down. "I've always wanted a family. A man I'd respect and love, children, a house with a backyard and a huge kitchen while I do my best to be a good mum and run a bakery." A lump sat in her throat.

"Sometimes I wonder if I fell so fast and hard for John because he came with a ready-made family. His daughters, so young, needed a mum and I bought into the fantasy without knowing what kind of a man he was. The dream of fitting into that family blinded me to what I should've seen from that first day." She took a deep breath. "My dream has become impossible to achieve. One—" a bitter laugh fell from her mouth "—I can't afford for all the millions I've made." She'd morphed from a young girl, full of dreams, to a cautious, burned-out shadow of herself.

The anxiety attack had come out of nowhere but had been years in the making. Once she'd gotten over the shock and fear, she'd seen it for what it could be—a much needed wake-up call to fix her life.

It had given her the kick she'd needed to do something about getting the life she wanted.

"You never told me why you called off the wedding," inserted Leo, pulling her away from the whirlpool of her troubled thoughts.

Everything in her protested at having to share the shame of her naiveté, of her desperation.

But telling him why she'd called off her wedding was important now. For the most important decision she'd ever taken in her life. She had to strip her armor and bare herself. To a man who'd never be vulnerable in front of her, or anyone else, for anything in the world.

"John told me the night before the wedding that Mario had been pulling his strings all along."

Leonardo's pithy curse did nothing to salvage the pain of that meeting. The wound it had left in her. "What did the bastard tell you?"

His anger on her behalf sent heat prickling behind her eyes. Made her weak. And she'd promised herself that she would never be weak again. That she would never tangle herself up in fantasy so badly that she couldn't see the truth in front of her.

"Exactly five weeks to the day before I met John, Mario and I had a huge row.

"The company's IP hadn't been public yet. That first chain of bakeries we opened…it had become such a success in such a small span of time that I couldn't believe it. Mario's investment had come at the exact time. After the third bakery I'd opened, I was stretched to the max financially. I couldn't believe that he shared the same vision that I had had. It snowballed into a monster I couldn't keep grasp of soon after.

"Before I knew it, we were franchising my brand. New lines of goods were launched, only half of which I had designed. I signed with an agent, who in hindsight never shared my vision. I started to appear on network shows and then we released a line of baking tools. More and more things that I hadn't approved of. There were days when I hardly had any time out of meetings. But business was booming, and Mum was deliriously happy for me and so I let Mario steer the ship.

"I didn't quite have the guts to face up to him when I couldn't exactly pinpoint the source of my own frustration.

"Then I got a call from the CEO of a small American bakery goods company. He'd seen me on one of my shows and asked me to come take over his company's European branch. Offered me carte blanche—the vision, the line of the goods, a new bakery chain, everything would be up to me. It was exactly the break I needed from…" She looked away from him, refusing to share the complex relationship she had with her mum. "Anyway, it was the perfect time for me to start it.

"I gave myself six weeks to start tying up things with So Sweet Inc. before I accepted the offer. One week in, John joined my division. I found out later that Mario had appointed him to work exclusively with me. He seemed to be the perfect man—funny, kind, a wonderful father to his girls, and he believed in love. He wanted to settle down, get married and have more kids. Tailor-made for me because Mario had designed him like that.

"He'd been coaching him, pulling his strings, playing with my dreams and fears all along. John proposed within a month and I was more than happy to say no to the American's offer, to put everything I wanted on the line for the life we'd build. Mario got what he wanted.

"But the deceit turned too much for John. He came up to my suite the night before our wedding and came clean. Apparently, he'd been in dire need of funds since his wife had passed away and the medical bills had piled up. Mario offered him the position of chief of division if he played the part of my husband."

Leo cursed again. "Why the hell didn't you confront Mario? Why continue to work with him?"

"Mario and I had a nasty argument after everyone left. I told him I was walking away from So Sweet Inc. after his manipulations."

She looked away, the pain of the blow that had come after still echoing within.

Her mum had refused to walk away from Mario. She hadn't seen what was wrong with what Mario had done with John to keep Neha home. "It's not easy to break those ties," she added softly.

"I'm the last man a woman with your…dreams should proposition."

Neha moved to stand in front of him, letting him see her conviction. "I'm not that naive to think a man and love are needed for happiness. I don't think I can even trust a man to have my best interests at heart anymore.

"Success is a double-edged weapon, yeah? I've enjoyed all the perks it's given me. But I'm ready for the next stage. I want to share my life with a child. I want to give him or her my love, nurture it, build a relationship like the one I used to have with my papa. I want more than I have now and I'm going after it the best way I know."

The space around them reverberated with pain and hope and sincerity.

He sat down on the opposite sofa, his right ankle propped on his left knee, his face thoughtful. "Why not an anonymous donor?"

Even having been prepared for that question, the quality of his tone sidetracked her. Distrust? Suspicion?

"Why me? What do you want from me?"

Neha forgot all her resolution to present a rational, cohesive argument. "For goodness' sake, Leo, you can't think I'm out to trap you.

"I might not be the heir of some centuries-long aristocratic Italian family, but I've got a fortune of my own. You know I've invested wisely. I can stop working tomorrow to have the baby and live comfortably for the rest of our lives.

"Granted, I won't be able to fly to Milan on a private jet or afford a chauffeur-driven car or live in a mansion in the middle of London, but I never needed those things."

"So you're not after my wealth. What do you think is the one thing that most women that I have had a relationship with hope for?"

Sheer outrage filled her. "You think I want to marry you?"

He shrugged. The man's arrogance apparently knew no bounds.

"Your romantic relationships are designed to last no more than three months at the most. Massimo cares more for those hounds of his than you do women. You think I want a piece of that?

"And not every woman's dying to marry you, Leo. I definitely remember the scientist, and who's the other one…? The CEO who publicly quoted her outrage when the trashy article implied that you'd dumped her," she finished with savage satisfaction.

His blue gaze danced with amusement. "A good thing you keep such good track of my love life, *bella*."

So he knew she was obsessed with his love life. So what?

Rugged masculinity, charming smile, unlimited wealth

and power and a smoldering sex appeal meant half the women on the planet were obsessed with Leonardo Brunetti.

"So we've crossed off my wealth and my suitability as a husband. Maybe all this is a ruse to gauge my interest in you. To lure me into bed with you."

Lure me into bed with you...

A veritable cornucopia of images downloaded into her brain. Bare limbs all tangled up on pristine white sheets, of him bending that arrogant head to taste her lips, of him driving that rip-cord-lean body into her over and over again, of touching him intimately, of kissing that hard chest and lower, driving him crazy... Her skin prickled, her breasts swelling with an unspoken ache.

She couldn't look away from him, from the dawning desire in his eyes, from the acknowledgment curving his sinful, arrogant mouth, from the heat radiating from his powerful body. Her chest rose and fell as she forced herself to breathe in a long gulp. "If a red-hot affair's what I really wanted, I would've proposed that."

His eyes gleamed with a fire she'd never seen before. "Would you, truly?"

"No," Neha said, swallowing the *yes* that rose to her lips.

A flicker of disappointment in his eyes.

How had they arrived here, of all places? How did such a small thing that Leonardo was attracted to her send her sensible nature off running into the clouds?

For years she'd kept a lid on all her fantasies starring him, locked away all the feelings he'd evoked in her again and again, and now, when it came to the most important thing in her life, she wasn't going to let them create an obstacle for her.

"Don't mock this. Please."

"Why ask me and put yourself in this vulnerable position?"

When she'd ever been anything but...with him especially.

The ugly truth of her burnout, her inability to walk away from So Sweet Inc. all these years, the shame of her complex relationship with her mum… All these were vulnerabilities she loathed baring in front of him.

But Leo would not settle for half-truths. That he was a man who'd do anything to protect the people he cared about also meant that he'd strip her bare and leave her defenseless if she wasn't careful.

"You're the one man that Mario's always been wary of," she said. "My mum…she's the tether that keeps me tied to Mario and So Sweet Inc.

"In all these years, I haven't been able to figure out how to save my relationship with her, and walk away from his toxic presence. Mario rules my life—my day, my social life, my vision, my work, even how I dress and what I say outside the walls of the office…"

She rubbed her fingers over her temple, even talking about it bringing on a pounding behind her eyes. That powerlessness gave birth to anxiety that could choke her breath.

Hand on her tummy, she forced herself to breathe deeply, to anchor herself on one point in the room to focus on. To fight the wave that could overwhelm her so easily.

His hands as they poured a glass of water for her…she focused on them. Large, square tipped, and yet she knew, if he touched her, they'd be gentle.

And just like that, the encroaching darkness got pushed back. Knowing that she could control it, knowing what triggered it, made it less scary than that terrifying first time.

Knowing that she was taking the right steps to wrest her life back under her control, knowing that she was building a future she wanted helped.

"This last year…it's become imperative that I have to prioritize what's important to me.

"The pace that Mario sets for me, I can't continue and be sane. The entire board is in his pocket, even though I'm the CEO. Even though I own the IP to that first line of products that launched So Sweet.

"If I have a child with an anonymous donor, not only am I leaving myself more vulnerable to Mario's passive-aggressive tactics, but my child becomes a new weapon to manipulate me.

"Because, believe me—" a hysterical laugh left her mouth as she imagined the aftermath of the bomb she was going to drop on Mario soon "—he's going to try and come at me with everything he's got over the next few months. I refuse to let my child become a pawn."

"Are you sure you're not overestimating the threat he might pose?"

"Said every man who claims he's a friend to a woman in distress." The bitter words rushed out of her on a wave.

Leo raised his brows and waited.

Neha flushed at the infinite patience reflected in his gaze. "I'm sorry. That was uncalled for."

Leo waved it away. "I shouldn't have doubted you. You would not concoct fantastic scenarios."

His fingers landed on her shoulder and squeezed, concern expressed in an ephemeral second and then gone. As if he couldn't let the contact deepen. As if he couldn't linger even for a moment.

"There is more, *sì*?"

She nodded, not surprised at the depth of his perception. "I plan to retire soon. I have a legal team going over a million little things so that it can be a painless process. I plan to make a public announcement in a week or two."

"What?" He sat forward in his seat. "That soon? Don't make an emotional decision."

"I'm not."

"If this is about being a good mother—" admiration

glinted in his eyes "—I have no doubt you can do both, Neha. And well."

Her entire being warmed at his words. It felt immensely good to hear another person talk about her future with a child in it as a real possibility. "Thank you for the vote of confidence. I want to be a hands-on mum. But this pace I've been working at for the last decade, I can't continue like that. Not if I want to have a healthy life, be a happy, strong mum to my child.

"Not if I don't want to end up…" She swallowed away the darkest of her fears. "If the child is yours, Mario won't dare to cast his shadow near him or her.

"So what I need is for you to create an illusion of standing beside me while I build the life I want.

"Can you do that, Leo? For me?"

Neha's laughter—loud, full-bodied—hit Leo like a sound specifically created to awaken every nerve ending he possessed. His hand stilled with his coffee cup halfway to his mouth. He had convinced her to stay at his family's villa by Lake Como for the weekend because he'd wanted to keep an eye on her.

It was a familiar sound—a glimpse into the funny, witty woman beneath the elegant facade. But so out of context here, in his home, where he had never invited a woman. Silvio's multiple affairs, paraded shamelessly in front of Massimo's mother, had been enough drama to last a lifetime.

He hadn't sought her out in the two days she'd been here, leaving her in Nat's capable and kind hands.

Ignoring his *nonna*'s complaints about the upcoming celebrations for her eightieth birthday in two weeks, he stood up and walked across the vast balcony.

A weak November sun cast a soft, golden glow around the gardens surrounding the villa that were his pride and joy. The villa had been a stalwart presence in his life when he'd been devastated as a young boy—confused, distraught and lost. The centuries-old legacy, the Brunetti name, thousands of people who'd always depended on the finance giant BFI for their livelihood, the tens of thousands of people who'd put their hard-earned income into the Brunettis' hands for safekeeping, an anchor that had kept him going straight.

But it was the gardens that had given him a sense of belonging.

He'd always been able to will the most reluctant, the most stubborn, flower into full bloom with his hands. For a long time, he'd believed this was his contribution to the Brunetti legacy. Well, this and the fact that BFI had flourished under his leadership for the last two decades.

Vaguely, he remembered following a fragile, delicately built woman around the same gardens with a plastic pail and spade in hand. With a sense of delight that hovered at the edge of his subconscious mind. Soft laughter, sweet words…a memory buried in the recesses of his mind.

Another laugh from Neha pulled his thoughts from murky, unreliable memories. More than relieved to leave the past behind, he studied the woman who continued to intrigue him. The same woman who'd rendered him sleepless for the two days that she'd spent under his roof. Roused protective instincts he'd never even known before.

Neha stood on the sloping path that led to Massimo's custom-built lab. Peach-colored trousers hugged her hips and buttocks, the fitted white shirt displaying the outline of her breasts perfectly. Hair high up in a ponytail that swung playfully as she walked, her smile glorious amid the riotous colors of the gardens.

I want you to father my child.

Even now, the fierceness of her expression when she spoke of a child that hadn't even been conceived amazed him. Then there was the very existence of another image in his head—unbidden—of a boy or a girl he'd try to guide and protect while Neha nurtured with unconditional love.

"She looks much happier just after two days of being here," said Massimo, joining him.

"You think so?" Leo had noticed something off with her but had put it down to the strangeness of her request. It wasn't every day she walked up to a man and asked him to father her child.

"You didn't notice?" Massimo wasn't being facetious for once.

"Tell me what you noticed," Leo invited him.

Massimo cast Leo a curious look but obliged. "She has such dark circles under her eyes her makeup can't hide it. I haven't seen her in…eighteen months, but she's clearly lost weight. I know these ridiculous magazines call her fat and plump—"

"Her brand is successful because, like her products, she's authentic, real. She eats like a real person and has curves like a real woman." Leo heard the vehemence in his voice only after the words were out.

Massimo raised a brow. "It isn't just her physical appearance, though. She doesn't have that glow that lights her up from the inside, that genuine quality of hers. Instead, there's a fragility I've never associated with her." Massimo's tone became softer, gilded with worry. "I remember Mama like that, before she left. As if she were at the end of her rope."

Success is a yoke that can stifle every other joy.

"But the two days here seem to have made a world of difference," Massimo added.

Again, true. Each hour Neha spent here in the villa seemed to restore a little bit of sparkle to her eyes. That innate joy.

"She wants to have a child. With me." The words came

easy because somewhere in the last two days he'd come to a decision.

Massimo's sharp inhale jarred alongside his own steady breathing. "I didn't know you two were involved."

"We aren't. Until now."

"You're considering this," Massimo said, astonishment ringing his tone.

Leo's smile dimmed, his chest tightening with an ache that was years old, that he wanted to shove aside as he'd always done. But today, he couldn't. As much as he wanted to leave it there to rot, the past had a way of shaping the future. He couldn't make a decision without making sure no innocent, and there could be two if he agreed, got hurt.

"Go ahead, play the devil's advocate," he said, inviting his brother's opinion on a matter he didn't discuss with anyone.

Massimo turned around and leaned against the balcony. Studied Leo for long moments. "You're considering having a child with a woman who's the one constant in your life, a woman you respect and admire, a woman who's the real thing. I think it's *fantastico*."

Leo tried to swallow the shock that filled his throat.

"Shades of Silvio's ruthlessness and abusive mentality could be in both of us. That does not mean we'll prey on innocents," said Massimo, who preferred computers to people, perceptive when it came to this.

"You had a mother to teach you right and wrong," Leo whispered, the words coming from a dark place he'd shoved deep inside himself. From a hurt so deep he'd tried his damnedest to bury it. "A mother who taught you that it wasn't weak to...feel."

What he'd had instead was a father who had filled his formative years with poison against the woman who had walked out on both of them. Greta wasn't cruel but she hadn't ever been comforting to her grandsons, either. At least, not until she had married her second husband, Carlo, the first person who'd tried his best to teach them what it meant to be a good man.

But Leo had already grown up by then. Had been filled to the brim with bitterness against a woman whose face he didn't even remember.

"But I almost lost Nat with my own hang-ups, *sì*?" Massimo's gaze gentled. "You reached out to me when you discovered what a brute Silvio was, even though he taught you nothing of what makes family. You made him back off, you encouraged me to follow my passion. You believed in me and brought millions in seed capital when I'd have sold those designs for peanuts. There's a reason a smart, level-headed woman like Neha picked you."

Leo had no words to express the gratitude and the indefinable emotion that pressed down on his chest. He hadn't needed Massimo's reassurance, but it felt immensely good to have it all the same.

"The only thing I would worry about in this whole scenario is...how the both of you will make it work." Massimo grinned. "Nat and I will watch from the sidelines, popcorn in hands. She's going to love seeing Neha bring you down a notch."

Leo smiled. His sister-in-law was determined to see him defeated. In something, anything. "All Neha literally wants is to put me to stud, Massimo."

Massimo burst out laughing, then sobered up when he realized Leo was serious. "What?"

"She wants the child because if I'm the father, Mario will think twice before he comes near the child. He's got her all twisted inside out. She doesn't want a coparent. Much less a relationship."

"You're okay with that?"

Leo didn't answer, his gaze caught on the beautiful

woman who had turned his life upside down with a simple request.

He was going to be a father, yes, but he wasn't going to do it all by her rules.

Neither was he going to be tempted into a relationship with a woman he'd share a child with, with his history of relationships. Agreeing to Neha's request meant he could never satisfy the deep hunger she evoked in him.

CHAPTER THREE

NEHA KNOCKED ON the thick wooden door. When there was no answer, she turned the gleaming metal handle and stepped into Leonardo's bedroom. Uninvited.

The suite was twice the size of hers. Hers was thoroughly feminine with soft pink walls and bedspreads; this was a thoroughly masculine domain.

A dark oak desk sat in one corner of the room with a large monitor and papers neatly filed while comfy sofas and a recliner made up a cozy sitting area around a giant fireplace. Original, priceless artwork hung on the cream walls, a casual display of the Brunetti wealth—an overarching theme over the entire villa.

Dusk hadn't fallen completely yet and the high windows filled the room with an orange glow. One portrait hung on the wall—Silvio sitting in a vintage armchair while Leo, no more than six or seven, stood next to his father, dressed in a matching three-piece dark gray suit, his thick curly hair slicked back, his baby-blue gaze full of grief and an ache he hadn't learned to hide yet.

A jarring contrast to the powerful, impenetrable man he was today. Neha traced her finger over the little boy's face, a host of emotions running through her.

She called out Leo's name a couple of times and heard nothing back. Drawing a deep breath, she ventured farther in. There wasn't so much sunlight in the bedroom and there was a coolness to the room, the air filled with that masculine tone she associated with him. The walls were a light gray with light blocking shades on the windows while a massive king bed sat against a high-ceilinged wall.

A huge upholstered headboard and pristine white sheets made the bed look like an ocean of welcoming comfort and warmth.

She could picture Leonardo sprawled in the middle of that bed, taut muscles relaxing after a long day, languid mouth stretched into an inviting smile, waiting for her. Her breaths came shallow, her fingers reaching out as if she could…

Leo walked in through a large door she hadn't noticed, rows and rows of expensive, tailored clothes behind him.

Any sense she did possess before, any air left in her lungs, rushed out.

His magnificent chest was bare, tailored black trousers hung low on his hips. His jet-black hair, thick and wavy, was damp from the shower.

Neha couldn't even pretend to look away. Every inch of him was chiseled to perfection like one of the life-size statues littered throughout the estate. She knew he worked out with that same ruthless discipline he applied to everything else in life, but dear God, she could spend hours just looking at his body, imagining all the things she would love to do to it.

Miles and miles of tautly stretched skin beckoned her touch. The broad sweep of his shoulders, the jut of his collarbones, the solid musculature of his chest, the slab of rock-hard abdomen…he was intensely male, an utter contrast to her soft curves.

His chest was liberally sprinkled with hair, and she imagined the sensation of that rough hair abrading her silky skin, over her sensitive nipples… An ache filled her breasts, narrowing down into her lower belly.

Every inch of him was defined and all she wanted to do was test the give of all that toned muscle with her teeth.

A single drop of water plunked onto his chest from his wet hair and she followed its trail from one neatly defined pectoral to the dip, through the tight planes of his abdomen and into the line of hair below his navel and into the band of his trousers.

"Should I wait a little longer before I put on the shirt?"

His voice—ringing with a husky wickedness—jerked Neha out of her greedy feasting. Heat rushed up her neck and into her cheeks.

Blue eyes danced with a roguish glint she'd never seen in him before. His sculpted mouth was turned up at the corners, his smile—a rare, genuine flash of teeth digging a groove in one cheek—a beautiful thing that could pull her out of the darkest of pits any day.

She looked away and then back, utterly incapable of coming up with a reply that wasn't a *yes, please*. He was flirting with her and how she wanted to retort in kind. But it could lead everywhere *and* nowhere…

"Massimo said you're leaving for Milan again. That you're off to Paris from there. I didn't want to miss seeing you," she babbled, trying to gather a little sense. "We hadn't talked again and I thought I should…"

He waited silently. And that bubble of intimacy pulled her, deeper and deeper.

"I'll wait outside. Can we talk while you walk to the helicopter?"

He leaned against the big bed, his shirt thrown casually onto it. His glorious chest still bare. "I wasn't going to leave without talking to you."

"Oh, okay," she said, suddenly feeling superconscious of her own attire. The see-through cover-up she'd pulled on in a hurry stuck to her damp skin while barely skimming the tops of her thighs. She pulled the sheer fabric away from her skin and his attention, arrested on every breath and movement of hers, made her shaky all over.

"I just wanted to reiterate that—"

"I have made a decision."

She swayed, her knees refusing to prop her up. He reached for her immediately, his long fingers grasping her elbow in a firm grip.

"I'm fine," she said, snatching back her arm. Forcing herself to breathe in long, deep gulps. "I'll let you finish dressing." She'd barged into his room and now she couldn't wait to escape. If he said no…

"I'd prefer to talk here," he said, pushing off from the bed. "And I'll put on the shirt if it makes you uncomfortable."

"Not uncomfortable, no. After all, it's your bedroom. Just distracting," she said in a half-snorting, high voice, panic letting her thoughts out in a rush.

His laughter was delicious, sexy, rubbing against her skin, winding her up. Heat washed over every inch of her, the very idea of licking up that hard chest sending a rush of desire through her.

"As you wish," he said with a devilish smile, and reached for his white shirt.

Neha watched, shameless and bold and greedy, as he raised his arms and let the shirtsleeves slide down his corded arms. A mole on the underside of his right bicep, a small scar under his left pectoral—details she didn't need to know about him and would never forget.

She followed him into the seating area, too agitated to sit.

He took mercy on her and said, "We need to set expectations."

She nodded. "I'll sign any document you put in front of me that I'll never seek financial assistance. I'll never hint, twist or manipulate you for marriage. Or demand that you be involved in the child's life. I—"

He leaned forward in the sofa, all the humor gone from his face. "That's not what I meant."

"I just want to make it clear that I won't be a headache for you, Leo."

He pressed a finger to his forehead, as if he was exercising patience he didn't have. "In doing so, you're insulting me."

"What? How?"

"You want me to father a child, face off Mario, all the while offering no emotional or financial or even moral support?" His taut expression highlighted the rugged beauty of his features. "That makes me such a shining example of what a man should be, *sì*?"

"I'm not sure I follow."

He sighed. "It's a little...disturbing to be thought a man who thinks nothing of fathering a child as a favor and moves on."

Shock rendered Neha silent for long minutes. That was the last objection she'd expected. "You told me once that you innately don't trust women, and when I said that that was horribly sexist, you said you didn't have the slightest inclination to examine it, much less fix it.

"You said...love was for fools who willingly bought into a bunch of compromises and then glorified it. You told that reporter you were ecstatic to let Massimo propagate the great Brunetti line further.

"I assumed from our long association that being tied down isn't in your future plans."

He ran a hand over his jaw. "Being tied down to a woman is one thing, a child, completely another."

"What does that mean?"

"If I father a child, I will *damn well* be involved in that child's life. Our long association should have told you that."

His softly spoken words packed a punch. Neha swallowed the defense that rose to her lips, slowly realizing that this wasn't about her.

It was about *him, his...feelings.* And he was right—in all the myriad scenarios she'd foreseen she hadn't considered his feelings at all. "It wasn't meant as a statement on what kind of a man you are.

"I chose you because you're the one man I know who'd do anything to protect an innocent in your sphere."

His gaze held hers, as if to see through to the truth of that.

After a long time, he nodded and she let a breath out. "What does this mean, then?"

"The child and its well-being is the most important thing in all of this, *sì*?"

"I'll love my child more than anything in the world. I'd do anything for her or him."

The hardness edged away from his eyes. "That's the only reason I've come this far, *bella.* But you need to accept that I will never be an absent parent or a stranger.

"I know what goes through a child's mind when a parent abandons him or her. I can imagine what this child will hear from friends, well-wishers, every cruel, hard word and taunt. I will not willingly put any child of mine through that."

He had every scenario their child would face covered so thoroughly that Neha stared.

How could she have forgotten that Leonardo's mother had left in the middle of one night, leaving her five-year-old son to his father? How could she have forgotten the fact that she knew better than anyone what a wound that had left in Leo's life?

If Leonardo was a father in the true sense of the word...

Mario's shadow wouldn't touch her child. He or she would have Leo's guidance and support, Natalie and Massimo's affection, be a part of a family. Everything she'd always wanted would be her child's.

The prospect of his involvement was such a tempting offer that Neha had to force herself to think of other implications. "Our relationship—"

"Will be defined by the fact that we want what's best for our child."

She nodded, the confidence in his tone building her own. They were rational adults, they knew each other's strengths and weaknesses—they could handle this rationally.

"You said conditions. What else?"

"I want you to postpone the announcement about your retirement. And, if required, your retirement itself. By a few months."

"No, absolutely not."

Her refusal rang around the room. It knocked Leo off axis to see the sudden fear and distrust in her eyes. Addressed toward him when he'd only ever seen respect.

"Neha," he started softly, reminding himself that, for whatever reason, she was fragile right now, "hear me out."

She stayed at the window, the waning sunlight from the skylight gilding her body in a golden outline.

Even in the tense situation, he felt the tug of awareness on his senses that she so easily provoked.

The loose white sheer tunic had a low neckline that presented him tantalizing glimpses of the upper curves of her lush breasts. The sheer fabric showed silky brown skin, and the shadow of her orange bikini, skimming the tops of her long, toned thighs. Pink nails peeked through the sandals she wore, completing a picture of such sheer sensuality that she took his breath away.

From the moment he'd found her standing inside his bedroom—staring at his bed—he'd had the most overwhelming urge to pull that tunic up and away from her body until he could feast on the sexy curves underneath. With his eyes, hands and mouth.

Damp hair stuck to her scalp, highlighting the classical bone structure of her face. He wanted to run his hands all over her, learn if she was as soft and silky as he imagined.

She stood up from the sofa, walked to the door and back, to the windows and then back again, every step conveying restless energy. Without that elegant facade she put on like a second skin, he could see now what Massimo had seen. Shadows hung like dark bruises under her eyes and there was a pinched look to her mouth.

When he went to her, she turned, her entire body trembling. He wrapped his hands over her palms, keeping the distance between them. She smelled like vanilla and sunlight and an intoxicating mixture of both. Against his abrasive fingers, she was silky soft. "Neha, look at me. I would not ask something of you unless it was important."

Her expression cleared. "You're right." She sat down on the coffee table, her knees tucked between his own. "Tell me."

"You already know a little about the cyber-attacks on BCS, right?" He waited for her to follow along. "But the cyber-attacks on Massimo's firm were just the tip of the iceberg.

"We had three deals in our pocket that fell through. Sylvio's colorful, abusive past keeps being recycled by the media and the press, dragging news of his embezzlement, and how he evaded incarceration because I bribed the pertinent officials.

"Alessandra's personal life, her past, her family—they keep getting exposure in trashy tabloids," he said, mentioning his grandmother's stepdaughter. Neha had met the beautiful top supermodel Alessandra Giovanni a couple of times during her long acquaintance with Leo. And for all her harshness and rough edges, Greta was a different woman with her second husband's daughter. Carlo had been gone for a long time, but Alex had become a part of the family.

"But Alex isn't even a Brunetti," Neha said, frowning.

"Massimo and I think she's been attacked because Greta is close to her. All of us have been featured in the news cycles over the past few months—always some sort of scandal or sensationalism attached to our names. Reputations have crumbled, businesses been ruined, for less in the finance industry."

"So everything is connected?"

He nodded. "Natalie was hired to bring down Massimo's security design. The clients' information was left vulnerable to attack, but she didn't steal it."

"That's how Massimo met her?"

"*Sì.* And thanks to the fact that she's crazy about Massimo, she's given us a name. Vincenzo Cavalli. He's bent upon a revenge scheme, determined to cause as much harm as possible to the Brunettis.

"When Massimo's design was hit, only four of us knew. Massimo, me, Natalie—who'd attacked the system—and the man who'd orchestrated it.

"Yet somehow Mario leaked the news of the attack to the BFI board. He's been riling them up, calling for my resignation. That I'm not unlike my father, that in the end, I will bring ruin to BFI like Silvio had done once. Most of the board members remember the destruction Silvio caused."

A shadow of fear crossed Neha's eyes. "So Mario is involved with this man?"

"We found a financial trail between him and Vincenzo. Mario's as power hungry as it gets. He saw a chance to push me out of the CEO position and he's taken it."

"But what does my retirement have to do with it?"

"You are Mario's golden goose. Your retirement is my currency against him."

Her fingers were tangled so tight in her lap that they showed white. "Currency in what way?"

"Will you promise to not freak out first?"

"I'm still here, aren't I?" she said, some of the fight back in her eyes.

"We will pretend to be a real couple, make all those predictions that have been flying about us real. If I know how Mario's mind works, he will hate us taking our relationship to the next level. He won't like it that there could be another man—especially a man like me, arrogant and powerful as you said—who could control you.

"Everything you've told me about how he has tried to manipulate you all these years tells me that he will do anything I ask to make sure he doesn't lose you."

"So you'll use me like a puppet between you two?"

"To create an illusion that I have control over you, yes. To put pressure on him. If that doesn't work, then yes, I'll hint that I'm pushing you toward retirement."

She shook her head, shadows in her gaze. "I can't postpone it. It's not something I decided easily."

"I know that."

"I don't think you do. I don't trust you with this, Leo."

He sat back slowly, trying to digest the shock those words caused. Disturbing him on more levels than he liked to admit to himself. "Then none of this will work."

"You don't take this retirement thing seriously. You think this is some sort of temporary insanity phase. How can I believe that you'll put my well-being before your need to crush Mario or your need to stop this… Cavalli guy?"

True, he had mostly discounted her claims about wanting to walk away from an empire that had been built over two decades. He'd thought it was her need-to-be-in-control nature that was making plans for the future that weren't quite necessary. But Leo had always been willing to admit to his faults. "Yes, I did think that. But I would never do anything to harm you. Especially now, when our future will be tied together forever, when I'm agreeing to have a child with you.

"All I want to do is put the pressure back on Mario, get him to spill about Vincenzo before he does irreparable damage to my family.

"The fact that you and I will have a child together is going to make Mario nuts."

"Do you want to risk infuriating him with the decision to retire on top of that right now?"

"He's not going to like it," she said softly, running her hands over her neck. "Mario's going to be apoplectic at our…new relationship."

Leo took her hand in his and squeezed, willing her to trust him. All he wanted to do was kiss that tension off her mouth, to hold her until he could feel those lush curves against his, until he could calm her down like she had done him so long ago. But…if he did that, it wouldn't stop there.

He would seduce her, and he knew without being arrogant that she would reciprocate.

And then what? What would happen when he lost interest and moved on? When hers was the face he'd have to disappoint?

Neha pulled her hand back slowly. He didn't miss that she rubbed that palm against her hip. Or that she remained wary of the distance between them. "Okay. I agree to your plan."

"Good," he said. He could always count on her to be logical and rational. "What's next for your plan, then?"

"You have to have blood work done. Mine's done. I'll have a couple of appointments with the IVF specialist first and then we can decide the logistics of when and where…"

Embarrassment dusted her brown cheeks a slight pink, but Leo refused to break eye contact. There was something incredibly satisfying to his male pride to see her blush like that. To see that composure of hers falter at such an intimate subject at least.

"When and where I make my *contribution*. Does that work?"

He smiled when she nodded.

"I don't know much about it, but you have to take hormone injections, *sì*?"

"Yes. It's a…little bit invasive and painful but I want to do this."

"I've never doubted your resolve, *cara*. You will call me if it gets too much or if you need a supporting presence there."

"Will I?" she said, a naughty smile dawning in her eyes, unfurling a beauty that made his body hum with desire, ache for contact. "Don't get all arrogant and commanding on me, Brunetti."

"Don't forget this is a partnership, Fernandez," he replied in the way they used to tease each other a long time ago. *Dio*, the woman had always been so strong. And it was the strength that attracted him, that will to keep going on in the face of adversity. "Everything will be all right, Neha. I'm glad you came to me."

"I hope so. I…"

Eyes wide, breath hitching loud enough for him to hear, she came at him. And hugged him. Hard. The press of her body against his was a pleasure of mere seconds, gone before he could revel in it. The scent and warmth of her fleeting heaven. Her hands on his shoulders, she kissed his cheek, and a shiver of anticipation built inside him. Anticipation that would never deepen into more. "I don't know how to thank you," she said, pulling back. "I promise you, Leo. You'll never regret it."

Leo pulled her arms from around his neck and took a step back. Putting distance between her and him. Giving his discipline a fighting chance.

Every muscle in his body flooded with the awareness that here was a woman who was his match in every way. A woman who'd never ask him for more than he could give, a woman who would be the absolute best mother to any child they had, a woman that would always make him laugh and want.

Awkwardness flashed in her eyes before she fiddled with her clutch again.

As he watched her walk out of his bedroom, Leo stayed leaning against the bed. He turned his neck around, tension clinging to his frame.

Cristo, now even his bedroom smelled of her.

The rest of the day, he wondered if he would come to regret his decision. Because he had tied himself irrevocably to the woman he desperately wanted and could not have.

CHAPTER FOUR

NEHA WALKED ONTO the picture-perfect balcony attached to her suite and took in the astonishingly beautiful view of the grounds surrounding the villa and the glittering lights of Lake Como. After a relaxing day at a luxurious spa and lunch at a café overlooking the beautiful canal district of Navigli with Natalie's irreverent companionship, Neha was equipped to face the evening.

Greta's eightieth birthday celebrations—the perfect event for Neha and Leonardo's first public appearance as an official couple. Today, they'd confirm the rumors that had already been whipped into a frenzy by Leo's carefully orchestrated trips to her offices, even at the opening of a new, trendy café in London.

They'd seen more of each other in the last two weeks than they had in the last fifteen years. He was doing it for the press coverage, but she struggled mightily to not fall into the fantasy right out of her head.

Like sending her favorite exotic orchids the day after she'd returned from Milan.

Like showing up at work last night and packing her off to Lake Como so that she could attend Greta's party and get a weekend away in the process. Neha had protested at first—it was a whole extra day she didn't need to bunk.

"You expect me to accept the fact that you want to retire seriously, and yet you won't cut yourself a break after an eighty-hour week," he'd said, his powerful frame shrinking the size of her vast office. The broad sweep of his shoulders had electrified her senses after a long day, the reality of seeing him in her space making everything she'd set into motion achingly real.

The attraction she felt for him all the more painful to deny for he was just as out of reach now as ever. But he'd been right about her needing a break.

The two weeks since she'd returned had been packed with back-to-back meetings, a visit to a newly launched bakery in east London where she hadn't been allowed inside the huge, state-of-the-art industrial kitchen but posed for pictures with delicious treats she hadn't created, and reading hundreds and hundreds of pages of contracts with the legal personnel for a book deal she was going to sign soon.

A cookbook with her brand name but the actual recipes had been created by a team of world-class chefs.

She'd been thrust right into her soul-sucking life and desperate for escape, but Neha had given in. Even as the cautious part of her whispered that running away *with Leo and to Leo* was a dangerous habit.

Every free moment of the last two weeks had been spent replaying that scene between her and Leo in his bedroom. She'd fantasized in the most wicked detail what it would have been like if she'd taken his mouth for a kiss she'd wanted for so long. If she'd asked him to conceive their child by making love to her…

Her cheeks heated. Would he have taken her up on that offer, too? Did he feel this awareness that seemed to hum through her when he was near?

But she was also painfully aware that it was time to bury what had been her heart's desire for so long that it was a part of her.

They could never be lovers now, not with their lives entangled around an innocent life. Not an easy decision but done.

As the horizon shone brilliantly in the evening sky, for

the first time in years she was hopeful for the future. With Leo by her side, she could finally build the life she wanted. And her baby would have everything she had known once—a doting mother, a caring father, a loving family.

"She's refusing to join us?" Massimo asked as Leo walked into the lounge, having spent more than an hour with Greta, who was acting like a petulant teenager instead of the Brunetti matriarch celebrating her eightieth birthday with Milan's upper crest due to appear in less than an hour to honor her.

Leo took the tumbler of whiskey Massimo offered with a grateful nod and downed it. He sighed. "She's not just acting out this time. She's really upset that Alex is not here."

"It's not like Alex to disappear like this without a word to any of us, for months at a time."

Leo agreed. While their grandmother's stepdaughter, Alex—Alessandra Giovanni, one of the top supermodels in the world—had family in the US and regularly disappeared from Milan for months at a time for her shoots, on a given day, they'd always known where she would be. More importantly, Alex never went more than a few weeks without dropping by to visit with Greta.

But this time, even Alex's mother had no idea of her daughter's whereabouts.

Greta, having lived through the path of destruction her son had blazed through her life, had never been soft or loving with Leo or Massimo. But she had stood guard over her grandsons, helped them overthrow her own son when it had been clear Silvio would destroy BFI.

Only with her second husband, Carlo, whom she'd lost after a precious few years, and his daughter, Alessandra, had a different side emerged of Greta.

He knew Alex felt that same love toward Greta, knew she felt like she belonged here with Massimo and him, more than she did with her mother's family. So why disappear like this? Where was she?

He was about to suggest they reach out to Alex's agent when Neha walked into the lounge.

Looking absolutely ravishing in a fetching pink creation that left her shoulders bare, kissed every curve like he wanted to, molded to the swell of her hips. And yet, somehow, she managed to look elegant and stunning, too. Her hair in an updo showcased the beauty of her high cheeks and strong brows. Mouth glistening a light pink, she reminded Leo of a ripe, tart strawberry. A strawberry that he wanted to bite.

She took one look at them and stilled. "Sorry, I didn't mean to intrude on you two. I can come back."

There was a hint of shimmer on her neck and the valley of her cleavage when she stood under the crystal chandelier, beckoning a man's touch. Leo could no more stop watching her than he could stop breathing. *Dio*, he couldn't remember the last time he'd been this mesmerized by a woman. Maybe never. "Of course you're not intruding," he said.

Maybe a little too sharply, because her gaze jerked up to his.

He cleared his throat and went to pour another drink. He needed the extra fortification if he had to spend the rest of the evening with her—looking but not touching, enveloped by the warmth of her, pretending to be a couple in front of the world. But not doing all the things he wanted to do to her.

"I'll talk to Greta," Massimo said.

His younger brother had that mischievous smile that Leo had rarely seen growing up. Massimo stopped in front of Neha, put his hands on her bare shoulders and pulled her to him. An indulgent smile on those pink lips, Neha let him embrace her and then kiss her cheeks. Which he did with quite a relish.

Stepping back, Massimo smiled. "You look utterly enchanting, *bella mia*. If only you'd reciprocated my interest in you, we'd have been something. But alas, I remember you rebuffed me, of course without breaking my heart."

Neha laughed. And the sound of it snuck into Leo's every pore. "*Per favore*, Massimo. Stop flirting with me, you wretched man, and go find your wife."

"Sì," the rogue said with a smile, then bowed elaborately, which made her laugh harder.

That thick silence descended on them again, ripe with tension.

"Are you scowling because he was flirting with me?" Neha said, keeping her distance. As if he was dangerous.

"Massimo has eyes for no one but Natalie. That whole thing was for my benefit."

"Your benefit?" she said, her eyes growing wide in confusion. "What do you mean?"

Leo shrugged. He wasn't going to explain that his brother thought it was hilarious how attracted Leo was to her. Especially when he was determined to not do anything about it.

"You want a drink before the hordes descend on us?" he finally managed in a polite voice.

"Just some sparkling water, please," she replied.

Leo opened a bottle of sparkling water and offered it to her.

She took the glass from his hands, somehow managing to make sure their fingers didn't touch. "You didn't tell me how I look," she said in a soft, quiet voice characteristic of her. Not petulant, not demanding, just a simple, rational question. Maybe he could handle this better, then.

He let his gaze rove over her again. "I didn't think you were the type who needed compliments or a boost in confidence."

Irritation he'd never seen before flashed across her face. "There are two things wrong about that."

"Two?" He raised a brow, liking that he was getting under her skin. "Explain, please."

"First of all, I don't think I've ever met a woman who wouldn't welcome a compliment from a gentleman friend. No matter how gorgeous or successful she is."

"Touché," he said, raising his glass to her. "'Gentleman friend' has such...an old-world ring to it, *bella*? Is that where we're settling for?"

"Define this—" she moved her arm gracefully in the distance between them, distance she seemed determined to maintain "—any other way you want."

"And my second offense?" he taunted back.

"This is uncharted territory for me. So yes, I'd like to know what you were thinking for a change, instead of having to guess what your expression means."

"What is uncharted territory?"

"Playing your piece in front of the entire world."

Something in her tone snagged at him. But for the life of him, he couldn't put his finger on it. It felt like all the safe, neutral ground they'd carefully trod for so many years had disappeared, leaving them in a minefield. Filled with sexual tension and something else.

Were they foolishly, knowingly mucking up a relationship they'd built?

"Why is this so hard, Leo?" she said softly, a beseeching look in her eyes that shamed him instantly. *Dio*, did the woman have any idea how beguiling she looked like that? How much he wanted to remove any and every problem if it meant she'd smile at him like she did with Massimo?

He was man enough to admit that it was his fault. He'd purposely held back the words that had risen to his lips when she'd walked in. Made it awkward by behaving like a randy, churlish youth who had been denied the one thing he'd wanted the most.

He finished his drink and went to stand in front of her. Tucking his finger under her chin, he raised her face. His heart thudded as she met his gaze, his match in every way. "You're the most beautiful, poised, smart, courageous woman I've ever known in my life."

She laughed, swatted at his shoulder with her hand and stepped away. Leo buried the pulse of irritation at her need to put distance between them. "Are there any adjectives left?"

"You don't think I'm serious?"

"It doesn't matter, really." A tightness to her words. "I think I've indulged myself enough for one evening," she half muttered to herself. When she looked at him again, there was nothing but that serenity, that composure, he'd known for so long. "Natalie told me it was you who'd arranged such a lovely day for us. Going as far as to hound her into accompanying me.

"Just as you'd told me that she needed my help in picking a dress for tonight."

"She's got terrible fashion sense. You, on the other hand, never look less than stunning."

She laughed, and he basked in it. "You manipulated us both."

"I saw two hardworking, stubborn women who needed a break."

"It was exactly what I'd needed, and I didn't even know it. So, thank you."

"It was my pleasure. When I arrived last night, you looked like you were ready to drop." He'd been alarmed by how dull she'd looked with dark shadows under her eyes again. "Haven't you been sleeping well?"

She tucked a wisp of hair that wasn't in the way, and

he knew she was going to lie. "I was fine. I just had a brutal week."

"Did Mario say anything about my visits?"

"We had a few meetings scheduled but he… Damn it, I'm nervous. About this whole evening."

He frowned. "Why?"

"I just… I wish we hadn't decided to make this whole thing public today. Although that's probably just me wanting to delay the inevitable." She laughed at herself, turning the glass in her hand around and around. "Now you think I'm a little cuckoo."

"No. But I'm definitely beginning to believe that saying you're stressed is an understatement. Are you having second thoughts about this whole thing?" He carefully controlled his voice, loath to betray the pang in his chest that she might have changed her mind.

This had to be about her, always.

"Of course not!" Her chest rose and fell, the thin chain at her neck glinting under the light of the chandelier. "Not at all." When he just stared at her, she sighed. "If you must know, I mostly avoided Mario this past week. I stayed at my flat the whole week, which I never do because I like to see Mum at least every other day—running away when I knew he might be looking for me, canceling on a one-on-one lunch saying I had a checkup, that sort of thing."

Anger flared in Leo's gut. He took her hand and was startled to feel her long fingers tremble. "Neha, are you scared of him? Has he caused you physical harm?"

"God, no. I'd like to think if he'd ever raised his hand to me, at least then my…" She cringed and snatched her hand back. And he wondered at how much she kept to herself, how little she showed of her true feelings. "If he had, I'd have knocked him down in return," she said fiercely. "Mario thinks too much of himself to stoop to what he'd call vulgar behavior. His tactics are more…insidious. I didn't tell you this, but I had an argument with him before I came to see you about this new book deal we're signing and it just blew up.

"I'm sure he thought I ran to you to complain about it. After leaving it like that, you showing up at work in the last week and me avoiding him, he'll be bursting to have a go at me."

"Then why avoid him? Why not face him today when I'm here, too?"

"It's just that…every time he and I get into it, it's Mum who suffers. It's Papa's birthday next week and she's always extra fragile on that day.

"Usually she and I spend the day together, donate a week's worth of meals at this shelter Papa used to volunteer at…help out the whole day. And then we have dinner with a lot of his friends and family, just remembering him. I prep for it for days, take the entire day off, and it almost feels like…she and I never drifted apart." The wistfulness in her eyes tugged at him before she blinked it away. "If I have a massive row with Mario now, it'll bleed through to her. She'll worry that the both of us are fighting and I don't want to make Papa's birthday extra hard for her."

Leo voiced the question that came to him instantly, his tone a little bit sharp. "And in all this, who looks after you? Even I know that you still miss your papa."

She frowned. "I look after myself. My mother has always been emotionally delicate—I don't think she ever recovered from Papa's death, and yes, sometimes I wish…" Guilt shone in her eyes before she sighed. She fiddled with a ring she wore on her right hand. "I don't like talking about all this with you."

"Why not?"

"I feel guilty for talking about her. And I definitely don't want to lose your respect. I know you abhor emotional drama of this sort."

"Because you have a complex relationship with your mother?" he said, swallowing away the stinging words he wanted to use. Like *toxic* and *harmful* and *soul-sucking.*

"I think you have made a lot of extrapolations from whatever the media reports about my relationships with women." For some reason he couldn't fathom, every time Neha made even a fairly reasonable assumption about him, it riled him. He wanted to be…the perfect man in her eyes.

Cristo! Where was this coming from?

"What did you think raising a child together was going to entail? Whether we like it or not, whether we want or not, our families and our history are going to feature in our child's life."

"And it doesn't bother you?" she said, searching his gaze.

"I forgot *extremely stubborn* in the list of adjectives earlier," he said, taking her hand in his. "Believe me, *bella.* We're in this together. There's nothing you need to hide from me.

"In the meantime, I'm more than happy to play your hero."

She rolled her eyes and laughed. "I don't need a hero, Leo. I just want you to pretend to be one." Her fingers dusted at some imaginary speck on his jacket and his heart thundered under the casual touch. Her gaze ate him up. "But yeah, I'm glad you're on my side."

CHAPTER FIVE

TWO AND A HALF hours into the party, Neha was glad she'd let Leo convince her to stick to his side.

There was a power high in being the woman that Leonardo Brunetti couldn't keep his hands off. Oh, she knew that all the long, lingering looks and touches—she loved the feel of his palm against her lower back—were for the benefit of the couple of journalists he'd told her were present through the crowd.

It was about making a public statement without actually standing in front of a high-focus lens and admitting that yes, after years of platonic relationship, they were taking their relationship to the next level. But she couldn't stop herself from enjoying the thrill of the moment.

The warm, male scent of him was both familiar and exciting. Every time he wrapped his arm around her waist, or squeezed her shoulders, or pulled her to his side, she felt a little tingle pulse up her spine, filling her veins with electric charge.

She loved hearing her name on his lips as he introduced her around to the extended Brunetti family, to the powerful board members of BFI. Clung to his every word, loved the secretive smile he sent her way when someone commented that the most untouchable bachelor had been finally caught.

But it wasn't just the electricity arcing between them.

There was a sense of strength in his mere presence at her side. She'd been self-sufficient, emotionally and mentally, for so long that to have him at her back felt like a luxury. An echo of a need that had gone unanswered. She had someone in her corner finally to face Mario.

Even the sight of Mario's scowl when his gaze landed on Leo's arm around her waist, the way his sharp gaze followed them around, couldn't dilute her enjoyment of the party.

The entire grounds around the villa had been lit up until it was reflected on the waters of the lake. Pristine white marquees caught the overflow of guests from the villa. Cream-colored circular lanterns hung from the ceilings while beautiful white lilies made up exquisite centerpieces on round tables. Strategic ground lights added nightly splendor to Leo's gardens. With the backdrop of Lake Como's lights, the estate glittered.

The only strange thing was Silvio Brunetti's conspicuous absence from the celebrations, and Alessandra's, too, who was close to Greta, even more than her own grandsons.

A small dais had been raised at the center of the marquee where the matriarch, Greta, came onto the dais and delivered a speech in Italian that was too fast for her to follow. She invited her family to join her. Neha sat stunned when Leo walked up to her and reached out a hand to her.

For a few seconds that felt like an eternity, she could feel every single gaze trained on her, the silence deafening. Yes, they were putting on a show for a variety of reasons. Neha had never expected to be counted as one of the Brunetti family.

But even her hesitation hadn't thrown off the resolute look in Leo's eyes. Bending down from his great height, the broad sweep of his shoulders cutting off the entire world, his gorgeous, rugged face filled her vision. The focus of that gaze—all on her—was addictive. "I thought I had made this clear between us. Whatever happens in the future, or doesn't happen—" a twinkle appeared in his eyes "—my child, and therefore you, will always be a part of this family."

"You don't understand," she'd whispered, putting her slim hand in his huge one. Shivering at the abrasive slide of his palm. "They'll think it a declaration neither of us intends."

"I do not give a damn, as you say, *bella*."

After that, she hadn't even cared how Mario was taking the whole thing.

There was an exhilarating kind of freedom in letting Leonardo shoulder her burdens, at least for the evening. She danced with Massimo once and then twice with Leo, and tasted so many delicacies while laughing with Natalie.

After a long stretch of loneliness, life felt good, real.

Having just touched up her makeup, she walked out into the small sitting lounge with full-length mirrors and a soft white leather sofa when she realized she wasn't alone.

Everything in her braced to face the vitriolic attack that would come from Mario. Instead, her mum stood inside the room, her delicate face pinched with worry and distress. Dressed in a cream pantsuit that set off perfectly against her fair skin and pearls at her throat, she looked exquisitely lovely in a frail way. When she'd been a teenager, Neha had wished she'd been more like her mum with her petite, feminine frame, the silky dark hair, the delicate, sharply set features.

But now… Neha was glad she'd inherited her dad's build and his resilient nature.

"Hello, Mum," she said, leaning down and kissing Padma's cheek. A subtle scent of roses filled her nose, instantly plunging her into that twisty, minefield she'd been navigating for too long. "I was hoping we could have a quick catch-up before you left. Especially since I hadn't seen you in a while. Sorry, I didn't come sit by you tonight." She hated this, this distance that came between them, all because of

Mario. "Leo had all these people he wanted to introduce me to, and Natalie dragged me into the photoshoot—"

"I thought you were past this rebellious phase where you do things just to annoy your stepfather," Padma said. Launching directly into attack.

No question about why Neha hadn't come to see her in two weeks. No question about the sudden change in her relationship with Leo. That cold knot in her chest squeezed painfully even as that wet, helpless feeling filled her throat. "Mum, what are you talking about?"

"This…thing with that man."

"What about it?"

"Leonardo Brunetti is your stepfather's enemy. You know he causes all kinds of trouble for Mario. Of all the men in the world, Neha…have you no loyalty for Mario? After everything Mario's done for us, after he made sure we didn't wallow in poverty, after he built this empire with your face, after he's treated you as if you were his own…" A long, rattling sigh shook her slender shoulders, and she reached for the wall behind her, her breathing shallow, her pretty face crumpled.

Panic filled Neha's limbs. "Mum, please don't stress yourself like this. You know it's not good for you. You'll have an asthma attack and I—"

Padma jerked away from her touch. "Then you should've thought of that before shacking up with a man Mario can't stand."

"Mum, listen to me. It's not what you think. I'd never do anything to hurt you. This is something I needed to do for myself…" Neha pushed her shaking fingers through her hair, fighting for composure. Fighting the anger and helplessness rising through her, the selfish need to demand her mum's support when she was weak already. "To build the life I—"

"You've chosen to go against the man who gave you everything. And when Mr. Brunetti breaks your heart, and Mario says he will, who do you think will pick you up again? Who do you think looks out for you in all this?

"Your stepfather, that's who." Her mum took her face in one hand, fingers tracing her jaw tenderly, her gaze taking in everything. "Walk away from this man, Neha." Tears made her mum's words a soft, beseeching whisper. "Come home with us, now, tonight. Mario's generous. He'll forgive you the simple mistake of falling into Leonardo's trap."

Of course he would. He'd riled up her mum to see only an enemy in Leonardo. A selfish woman in her own daughter, a naive fool who fell for a man's sweet words. Still, Neha tried. "Mum, I haven't done anything to be forgiven for. I've stayed all these years even though—"

"No, stop." Padma took a deep, shuddering breath, her mouth trembling. Ignoring what Neha was saying. "It pains me to see you at such cross-purposes with him, darling."

"Mum, I'm doing this for me. No one else. For my future."

"Please stop this before you hurt yourself and us, too."

"And if I don't?"

Padma stepped back from Neha, a resolute look in her eyes. "Then I know that Mario's right that you've never accepted him. That you've never forgiven me for choosing to marry again when your papa passed away. That all these years, you've resented the place he's taken in my life."

The dark midnight sky was a star-studded blanket as Leonardo made his way through the well-worn path to the greenhouse that had been abandoned for more than two decades.

He had engaged a crew to renovate the greenhouse, but apart from stepping in there with the architect for a quick inspection, he hadn't been here again. He wanted the renovated greenhouse, not a desolate, haunting monument with memories that could steal his sleep.

Nothing but Massimo's knock at his door, his face concerned, well past midnight, as he'd been getting ready for bed, could have brought Leo to this place. For years, he had ignored the presence of the abandoned structure, refusing to step foot even in its shadow.

But he'd realized that it was silly to let a child's confusion dictate the rest of his life. An utter waste of time and energy having something new designed when a perfectly old structure was sitting right in his backyard.

He keyed in the security code that had been newly installed and pushed open the glass door. The rise in temperature was instant—a blast of warm, wet air hit him in the face.

Surprise filled him at the progress the team had made. Most of the overgrown shrubbery and vines had been cleared and new temperature-controlling tubing had been installed all over the ceiling. A huge industrial-size porcelain sink sat along one wall with gleaming granite counter space.

That, along with the perfectly placed overhead lights in a crisscrossing design through the center line of the high ceiling, made it eons different from the abandoned shell he'd discovered months ago.

There was one corner of the huge greenhouse where the overgrown, climbing vine had been left in place. The small area stood like a piece of the past he never seemed to let go of.

Cristo, he was in a strange mood tonight.

The lounger he'd ordered in a moment of self-indulgence stood like a throne in an abandoned castle. Her gray sweatshirt lay discarded on the lounger while Neha walked around the long aisles, drifting aimlessly, in deep thought. Even the ping of the door hadn't disturbed her. Leo took the time to just watch her.

The rational part of him wanted to turn around and walk

out, leave her to her midnight rambles. She'd made it clear before the party tonight that she was never going to cross that line that she had drawn around herself and let herself be vulnerable to anyone, much less him.

The loose, sleeveless T-shirt and cotton shorts she had on should have looked anything but sexy. But the slightly damp fabric stuck to the outline of her curves and the shorts—*Cristo*, her legs were long and lean, packed with muscle.

He'd never gone for the delicate, wispy, stick-thin kind of women. He liked curves, and from every glimpse he got of Neha's, it felt like she was tailor-made to fit into his hands.

Her face scrubbed free of the makeup only highlighted the dewy silkiness of her skin. Her wild hair had been braided into submission into a single braid, already half undone and framing her face.

It was only when she raised her gaze to his and gave a soft gasp that he saw the wet tinge to her eyelashes. *Cristo*, she'd been crying?

He pushed away from the wall, all thoughts of leaving her to her own problems fleeing. "Neha?"

She scrubbed a hand over her face. "What're you doing here?"

"That is for me to ask." He tucked his hands into his pockets. She looked crumpled, a little broken, and the last thing she needed was for him to paw at her. "Massimo told me he found you walking out here. That he gave you the code."

"Oh." Her fingers played with the hem of her T-shirt. "I couldn't sleep and was walking the grounds. I can't come down from the high of the evening that quickly, y'know? Especially when… It was a lovely party, yeah?" He didn't for one second believe the glassy, too-bright smile. She looked around herself self-consciously. "I'm sorry for intruding. *Again.*

"Massimo thought it was better if I wandered inside

here. I gathered from what he said this greenhouse…is off-limits to guests. But he wouldn't leave my side until I went in or returned to my bedroom.

"I didn't want to lie down when my head's spinning."

"This apologizing of yours is becoming a bad habit, *cara*. You're welcome to walk into any part of the estate."

"I think I've done enough midnight meandering. I'll wish you good night."

"You are upset," he said, reaching for her arm as she passed him. He kept his grip slack. She didn't pull away and, this close, he could feel the tension emanating from her. All his protective instincts went into overdrive. "Did Mario get to you? I made sure he came nowhere near you. And when I was busy with Greta, I asked Massimo to keep an eye. What did he say? Did he scare you?"

"No, he didn't. It's not that," she said, stepping back from him, trying to hide her face in the shadows.

Leo was in no mood to be fobbed off.

One hand on her shoulder, he gently tugged her toward him until the overhead lights illuminated her face. He clasped her chin. Her eyes were puffed, her nose slightly red at the top.

Dio, the woman gave new definition to self-sufficiency. Usually he was the one who maintained those boundaries in a relationship religiously.

"Keeping the lines between us separate is one thing. But this isn't just about you anymore, even before a child comes into the picture. I dragged you into this battle against him, *after* you told me it's been near impossible to decouple yourself from him.

"So tell me what happened. The last thing I think right now is that you're weak. Infuriatingly stubborn, however, comes to mind."

She bent her forehead to his shoulder, her body shuddering with shallow breaths. Running his palms over her bare arms up and down, he waited. In the damp air, the faint vanilla scent she used mingled with her skin to create a musky fragrance that filled his nostrils. Her warm breath coated his neck. He gritted his teeth, willing his body to not betray him.

"You're right. I've got to talk about this."

When she pulled back, she looked composed, strong again. And he realized how similar they were.

"Mario didn't get to me," she said, her long lashes looking thicker with wetness. "I saw his ugly scowl the moment they arrived and stayed well out of his way. The last thing I wanted was to make a spectacle at Greta's celebration. Even when I saw your exchange with him, I ignored it. But Mario is nothing if not clever."

Leo knew what she was made of, and he knew that the ache in her eyes had its origin a long time ago. He waited patiently, understanding in a way no one could how hard it was to show vulnerability when you spent most of your life making sure there wasn't any.

It only made him respect her more.

"But he got to her."

"Your mum?"

"Yep." A smile that was nothing but a caricature of the usual loveliness twisted her mouth. She ran a hand through her hair, a violent physical energy vibrating from her frame. "Frankly, I'm a fool to be surprised by this. I know the kind of hold he has on her. I know how his mind works. But she…" She swallowed, and then looked up at him. "After a long time, today I realized how nice it is to have someone in your corner. I know it was all for show but still it felt good to belong with people who like and respect me, with whom I don't have to walk on eggshells.

"And bam! She ruined everything."

Leo wanted to tell her that it hadn't been for show, that he did have her back in all this. That inviting her to be a part of his family's celebration while the whole world watched had come naturally, easily. That with every deeper glimpse into her, he wanted her by his side. The strength of the urge was inexplicably overwhelming.

Physical attraction was one thing…this quite another.

"Mario constantly feeds her lies and she swallows it all. Apparently, the only reason you could be interested in me is to get at him. The only reason, after years of a purely platonic relationship, that you're taking this to a new level.

"For so long, I tried to be strong for her. I let him manipulate me, twist me inside out. I let him run my life because I was afraid of hurting her. And the one step I take to build something for myself, to reach out for something I want…

"She actually asked me to leave with them tonight! She thinks I'd…tangle myself with you out of some petty need for rebellion? It's like she doesn't realize I have my own dreams and needs," Neha finished. "She'll never realize that I have my own life to live."

There was anger in her voice now—anger that reverberated within him, a hundred times stronger, calling for action. And Leo knew she would come out of this fine. Anger led to action whereas grief just left one powerless. Under someone else's control.

Like love.

Dio, how could Padma miss the ever-present shadows of anxiety in Neha's eyes? How could she put Mario ahead of Neha?

"Then it's time to remove that toxic presence from your life," he said softly.

Her head jerked up. "What?"

"Mario's not at the root of that grief in your eyes. Your mum is. So don't give her that power anymore."

Her eyes widened. "I can't just cut her out."

"No?"

She sat down on a cement bench, her bare legs stretched

out in front of her. Her gaze turned thoughtful, her chin rising in that stubborn way. "What would've happened if Massimo had decided you should be cut out of his life all those years ago, just when you wanted to build a relationship with him? What if he'd decided you weren't worth it?"

The question stopped him in his tracks.

If Massimo had refused his olive branch...

Leo's isolation would've been complete. Silvio would have succeeded in turning him into a mirror image of the power-bloated monster he was. The idea disturbed him on so many levels that Leo couldn't curb his harsh words. "I'm not the one questioning every choice I've made over the last decade."

Neha fidgeted where she sat, the awkward silence building into something she couldn't break through. His harsh tone shouldn't have surprised her, but it did. Because she'd never been on the receiving end of it.

Her question had disturbed him. And he had shut her inquiry down. Neither was she unaware that they were discussing her own family's shortcomings...but instead of resentment, she felt a sense of kinship with him.

What kind of a man would Leo have been if hadn't been tempered so harshly by the discovery of what kind of a man his father was? If he hadn't had his fundamental beliefs shaken so early in life? If he hadn't had to shut down a vital part to survive another day?

So many years of knowing him, learning him and wanting him...a lifetime of watching him like this, and she'd never have enough.

From the thick slashes of his brows to the deep-set eyes with long lashes he used to hide his expression, the deep scar on the left cheek and the thin-lipped mouth, combined with that weather-beaten quality of his skin—the gardens outside were clearly a labor of love—he was not classically handsome. But the ruggedly hewn features, that sense of calm confidence in his broad frame, the power of aura that radiated from him…the appeal he held had intensified as he grew older.

Where there had been a cocky, the-world-is-mine kind of arrogance to him when she'd met him all those years ago, the fierce discipline with which he ruled those around him, and himself, had entrenched into his features.

Her mum's marriage to Mario had changed the course of Neha's life, too. Carved away her choices bit by bit until this version of her remained. How much longer?

"I've lived almost fifteen years of my life walking the tightrope of wanting something and being afraid of the blowback to her. Afraid that Mario would use my actions to drive a wedge between us. I turned myself into something even I don't recognize."

Leo covered the distance between them, shaking his head. "You're being too hard on yourself."

She swallowed the lump in her throat as he took her hands in his and squeezed tight. She'd been so lonely. But it was Leo's touch that jump-started something that had been dormant inside her for too long. "Yeah?"

"You took the first step toward building the life you want despite knowing what the consequences will be. Not only did you approach me with your…request but you knew what to say to convince me. You didn't let your mum frighten you off today." His gaze searched hers, as if he was seeing her anew. "Despite the emotional toll it's taking on you."

A lone tear tracked down her cheek, the tenderness in his words a balm to her soul, the sheer conviction in his voice a steely source of strength.

He pulled her up to face him, and Neha could have drowned in the emotions swirling in those blue depths. His grip on her hands was the only anchor in a collapsing world, the warmth radiating from his solid body the only reality she could hold on to while she built a new foundation for her future.

With infinite gentleness, he flicked away the tear. “Do you remember the heated arguments we used to have about my opinions of women?”

She nodded, wondering where he was going. “You were a budding sexist.”

He laughed and she watched that stark, serious face bloom into gorgeousness that shook her knees. “You’ve been the biggest, most positive influence in my life, Neha. Like a river carving away at the bedrock of a mountain, you cleared so much anger I’d harbored toward women, just because of what one woman did to me when I was a child. You helped me realize how irrational and hateful I could become if I didn’t let go of it. Watching you become this woman of grace and courage and beauty…helped me in ways you can’t imagine.

“So don’t you dare say you’re a coward because that’s my friend you’re trashing.”

A sob rising through her, Neha threw herself at him. And luckily for both of them, the giant of a man that he was, he caught her. The strength of his arms rocked her as she tried to curb the emotional storm unleashing within her.

She kissed his cheek and whispered a hundred thank-yous. The scent and warmth of him was a cocktail she felt drunk on, the muscled wall of his body a heavenly slide against her own. Her arms vined around his neck, she pulled back and looked at him.

Nostrils flaring, eyes shining with desire, he radiated the same kind of energy she could feel thrumming through her veins.

A ribbon of awareness whipped around them as her gaze fell to the languid curve of his mouth. It was a matter of seconds, maybe, but it felt like an eternity as Neha pulled herself closer. Their breaths were a harsh symphony around them. She moved her hands down to his chest, scrunching her fingers in his shirt.

She'd spent an eternity wanting this man…wanting one kiss, wanting to be the woman he needed. And now she couldn't turn away even if her very next breath depended on it.

After years of living in a prison she'd made for herself, Neha stepped into her own life. And took Leonardo's mouth in a kiss she'd needed for more than a decade.

Lips that were both firm and incredibly soft met hers. That first contact spread warmth through her, unraveling in spools through her limbs, leaving her trembling, stomach tightening with anticipation, standing on the cliff of something new and painfully exciting. He was unnaturally still, not rejecting her, but being a passive participant that was nothing like the man.

She flicked her tongue over his lips next, tracing the defined curve while the rhythmic in and out of his breath coated her skin in soft strokes. A continuous thrill thrummed through her veins as she fit her mouth this way and that, teasing and tasting, tugging on that lower lip with her teeth, licking her way into his mouth and touching the tip of his tongue with hers before she retreated and started all over again. And again gorging herself on him. Breathing him in.

And still, he held himself rigid, his hands not holding her but not pushing her away, either.

He tasted of whiskey and maleness and Neha reveled in the high of having him like this—hers to pet and play with, hers to ignite. Hers to rumple. When she dug her teeth hard into his lower lip, his chest rumbled. Her own need deepened at the utterly masculine sound drawn out of him despite his control.

Dampness bloomed at her sex, every part of her aching to be touched and stroked and possessed. She ran her palms down to his neck and pulled at the lapels of his shirt until the buttons popped and she could sink her hands inside.

Her groan was joined by his, creating a symphony of need and desire.

Defined pectorals and warm skin, the sensation of the springy hair under her palms, the tight points of his nipples—his chest was an endless delight to her questing hands. She touched him all over, loving the hard clench of his muscles, the feral sound that fell from his lips. This time, when she explored the moist cavern of his mouth, she tangled her tongue with his, sucking it into her mouth. Playing hide-and-seek with it. Digging her teeth into the soft inside of his lower lip.

Her breasts ached to be touched. Her hands roamed restlessly over his hard body, across his broad chest, back onto his rock-hard abdomen, her fingers digging into the waistband of his trousers. She dragged her mouth from his, trailing kisses over his rough jaw, down to his throat, and pressed her tongue against the hollow there.

Salt and sweat and incredibly male—he was heaven on her tongue.

The growl that fell from his mouth reverberated up from his broad chest, shaking her with its ferocity. Like an earthquake rearranging everything beneath the ground on which she stood. His powerful body shuddered around her, and then he was jerking her up to him, his fingers sinking deep into her hair, and his mouth crushed hers.

The kiss was raw, fiercely honest, and it whipped her into a frenzy of sensations. Not a single one of her dreams had done justice to what the man could do with his mouth.

There was no exploration in how he took her mouth, no tentative melding to see if it could be anything more than a pleasant experience. No gentle welcome or a soft landing. No initial awkwardness that came with two people kissing for the first time, no searching for rhythm, no place for anything that was remotely rational.

The savagery of the need between them…this need that had been building for a long time, it tossed him around just as it did her.

He devoured her lips with his. Hunger and heat and hardness… Neha drowned in a surfeit of sensations he seemed to evoke so easily with a masterful glide of his lips, or a sensuous nip with his teeth or a rough, needy dance with his tongue. Everything she'd done to him, he paid back a hundred times over—sometimes smooth and slow, sometimes hard and demanding. Leaving her mouth stinging, her nipples taut and needy, her body scandalously ready for his possession.

A needy groan fell from her mouth when his arousal—thick and hard—rubbed against her belly, sending sparks of renewed need. She stole her hands down his body, desperate to trace that, desperate to feel what she'd done to him. He grunted in denial, his fingers arresting her questing hand. *"Basta, cara!"*

Neha felt his soft whisper like a cold lash against her skin. Her body cooling off in a matter of seconds into a frigid cold despite the warm air currents, she stepped away from him. "I'm sorry." She ran a hand through her hair and bit her lip. Which was swollen and tender. The memory of digging her teeth into his lower lip and his answering growl…it was a sound she'd never forget. "I'm… I've no excuse for attacking you—"

"You didn't attack me!"

She looked at him and away, but not before noticing how devastatingly handsome he looked with his hair all rumpled up, by her fingers. The flaps of his shirt open and baring that magnificent chest covered in hair. "I've been so up and down tonight, and I—"

"Look at me, *cara*! I knew what you were doing, and I was a more than willing participant."

"Still, I'm sorry, Leo. I'm—"

"Stop saying sorry. All you did was make the first move. One nanosecond later, I would have been all over you. *Cristo*, do you have any idea what watching you in that wet shirt sticking to your body is doing to me." He thrust his hand roughly through his hair, his breaths harsh. "Do you have any idea how long I've wanted you? *Dio mio*, it seems wanting you has become a part of me. If not for the fact that you're very important to me and my lovers don't last long, I wouldn't have mustered the sense to put a stop to it, *cara*."

The raw emotion in his voice gave her the courage to stop lying. To herself and to him. To face what had been staring at her from the moment she'd gone into his office with her bold request.

Her gaze fell to the swollen curve of his lower lip and something fractured within her at the blazing passion of their kiss. The rightness of this moment between them. The reality of the future she wanted to build with him. Something that took wings and wanted to fly. "I want to do this the real way," she blurted out, one of the biggest decisions of her life falling into place as easily as her next breath.

So easy, yes, but so, so right, too.

"What?" Leonardo looked at her with that penetrating gaze. Giving nothing away. Already retreating from that fracture in his impenetrable self-control.

Wanting you feels like...it has become a part of me.

A new sense of freedom ran through her limbs. There was a high in standing here, staring at him unabashedly, and glorying in it. In acknowledging her desire for this man.

His face one of those bulletproof masks that no one could break through. And that mask was doubled down right now. She was finally beginning to understand the real man beneath the larger than life figure she'd built in her head.

He'd been attentive and filled with concern from the moment she'd walked into his office. Playing the role of a man pursuing her perfectly for the public. At her back the whole evening tonight because he'd decided she needed protection from Mario. And she had no doubt he'd do the same for the rest of their lives with their child and, by extension, her.

Whatever she needed—physically, emotionally, mentally—he'd be there.

But to give her a part of him—to let down that guard that surrounded his mind and his heart, to show a little vulnerability—was unacceptable. To need her even in a small way was unacceptable. It would always remain a weakness.

That admission that he'd wanted her for a long time—had it been too much already?

She wondered if she'd have understood him so perfectly if she hadn't built that same armor around herself for so long that she'd ended up choking herself within it.

The intense loneliness, the craving for connection, the long, silent nights blending into farcically busy days, always alone, even in crowds… She was finally breaking through those chains she'd bound herself with and she wasn't going back into them willingly.

She wanted to live her life. She wanted this man. She wanted to create a child with him doing what would bring them both incredible pleasure.

There wasn't a moment's doubt in her mind that what she was starting tonight had a very definite endpoint. Having that endpoint made it easy to push away her fears. Leonardo and she were rational adults with very clear boundaries.

"I want to conceive *our child* the traditional way."

When he stared back in mute silence, she huffed, "You. Me. Sex, Leonardo."

CHAPTER SIX

LEO JUST STARED, his mind filled up with images of their naked limbs tangled, slick and moving together. The woman he'd wanted forever, finally within his reach.

He shook his head, as if he could simply dislodge those images. "You've had a very emotional evening." He ran the pad of his forefinger gently over the dark shadows under her eyes. Amazed by her resilience and the strength of her resolve. Aroused by the boldness of her gaze. "On top of a manic two weeks. On top of a stressful last decade."

"Leo—"

"Tomorrow, you'll regret it. Tomorrow, you'll panic that we've blurred the lines. I will not take advantage of a weak moment."

She pulled back, a flare of anger in her eyes. "Ah…this is you being all honorable and letting me down gently, isn't it? I'm a big girl, Leo. I can take it."

"I have no idea what you mean."

"Just say you're not interested in sleeping with me. Especially after learning that I'm not as rational and robotically perfect as you thought I was," she said, a flash of self-doubt in her eyes.

"*Maledizione!* You think I could want you less because you stuck to your guns in the face of emotional blackmail from the one person who should be protecting you from that bully Mario? You think years of want goes away in a single evening? If only it were that easy, *bella*."

Silence descended on them, fraught with the energy of

an attraction that was all out in the open now. She licked her lips, the pulse at her neck drumming away madly. "I believe you. Now will you do me the courtesy of taking me at my word?"

"I always have."

"Good. I feel as if the fog I've been living in is finally lifting. I'm sick of living afraid, always calculating risks, always worried about the outcome. I hate that I let Mario win all these years. I hate that I've used him as an excuse to give up so many things that give me joy, pleasure, excitement."

But no more.

"I want to leave all thoughts of ovulation kits and basal temperatures and IVF out of this. I want to conceive our child doing what I desperately want."

Her husky demand carried over the damp air currents in the greenhouse, the naked want in it echoing around them. And Leo knew his reasoning capability was crumbling to dust. That in the face of her bold demand and perfectly outlined reasons and the heat of their kiss singing through his veins, he was going to give in. Still, he looked for reasons to make sure this was exactly what she wanted.

"You can't do this because you're angry with him."

"Let me come closer."

Neha kicked at his feet and he spread his legs apart in response and she moved into the gap, closer and closer until her thighs grazed his hard thighs and the tip of her breasts were a mere inch away from his chest and the deepening scent of his skin filled her nostrils.

She moved her fingers from his chest—his racing heart gave her courage—up the corded column of his neck, to the raw stubble already coming in at his jaw, winding around his neck until her nails were sinking into the rough hair at his neck, scraping at his scalp. Digging for purchase. Determined to stay.

She bent closer, her mouth inching toward his. His hands stayed on her shoulders, pressing lightly, stopping her from covering that last bit of distance between them.

"If you think this is some twisted way to get back at Mario or a petty rebellion against my mum, you've got it all wrong." She shook his hands off her shoulders and pressed up snug against him. Heat and hardness, he was a perfect fit for her, and she shuddered at how good it felt. "I had a huge crush on that hot twenty-year-old who walked into my life that day. In a parallel universe, I grabbed that boy, and planted a kiss on him that sent him to his knees. If I could tell my younger self one thing, it would be to go after that guy."

She wiggled against him, trying to get closer, and he cursed softly. She felt his arousal against her belly, incontrovertible proof that sent shivers up and down her spine. Her lips close to his, she licked at the corner of his mouth. "This is all about me and you, Leo. I want this for no other reason than I need to desperately know how it will feel to have you inside me."

"Let me look at you, then, *cara mia*."

Neha pulled back from him, her heart still racing. Her body already mourning the loss of warmth from his. "What?"

"That damp T-shirt has been tormenting me ever since I walked in." Wicked light filled his eyes—a flash of that Leo he must have been before he'd had to bear the burden of the Brunetti legacy. "I should very much like to see you properly."

"You mean…here?"

"Sì." Unholy amusement curved his mouth. "You said tonight. I say here. Now." He looked around the greenhouse, that hardness that was an intrinsic part of him etched on his features again. Lost to her in those few seconds. "This ghastly place needs new memories, anyway. I can think of

nothing better than walking in here a few years from now and picturing you, all damp and naked and waiting for me."

That glitter in his eyes at his imagined image of her was incredibly sexy. "But—"

"Second thoughts, *cara*?"

Neha shivered at the blatant hunger written over his features. At the dawning resolve in his eyes. At the unspoken challenge in every pore of his body. It wasn't enough that she'd thrown herself at him, was it? He would strip her bare, of clothes and defenses, until there was not even a sliver of doubt that she'd walked into this with every sense alert, every cell desperate for it.

Leonardo Brunetti wasn't a man who would give anything of himself without demanding everything in return.

"I'm more than ready to persuade you, like you did me. Unless you prefer the dark and a bed, then, we will walk back to my—"

Neha tugged the hem of her T-shirt up and over her head in a smooth movement that surprised the heck out of even her. The appearance of the lacy baby-pink bra and how it cupped her breasts, the way his eyes drank her in, pushed away the hesitation that came with baring her body to a man after a long time. To the man she'd always be attracted to on so many levels.

"I forgot there's a reason you've held my interest for so many years, despite my every effort to suffocate it, *sì*? *Dio en cielo*, you're sexy and bold and you will be the death of me, *cara*."

Every word out of his mouth bucked up Neha a little more.

She didn't wait for another order. *In for a penny, in for a pound.* Not that her heart wasn't beating at a pace that might send it careening out of her chest. But Neha had never lacked for guts once she'd set her mind on a goal. Never lacked the gumption to see things through thoroughly.

While the media regularly published articles about how she'd gained weight or that her body type wasn't currently in fashion, Neha had never let the criticism get to her. Thanks to her mum's constant positive dialogue and praise when Neha had complained as a teenager that she was too big, everywhere, she'd developed a healthy appreciation for her body early on in her life.

Reaching her hand behind her, she undid the clasp of her bra. An expansive sigh drummed up her chest as her heavy breasts were freed from the metal underwires of her snug bra. Dark color streaked Leo's cheeks as he watched the gentle bounce of her breasts.

Her spine straight, she threw her bra at his feet, reveling in the naked desire chasing away every other shadow from his face. The damp air currents swirling around the greenhouse kissed her nipples, making them rigid. Her skin was damp, and hot, and felt far too tight to contain her.

Holding his gaze, she kicked off her shoes. The smooth floor was surprisingly cold against her bare feet, a welcoming contrast to her overheated body. Then she peeled off her shorts and stepped out of them, standing in front of him in white lacy knickers. She'd never been more glad of her expensive lingerie habit—her one decadent indulgence.

He made a thorough inventory of her—as if he was determined to not miss an inch of everything she had bared. Her heart thudded so loudly in her ears that she could barely hear herself think.

"I'm glad you waited to take this chance with me, *cara*. I'm glad you decided I wasn't worthy of you back then. That twenty-year-old, he was full of arrogance and ego and vigor. He didn't have enough sense to appreciate—" his gaze touched her everywhere: her bare breasts, the firm and yet soft curve of her belly, her muscled thighs, the white lace barely covering her sex "—everything about you. He wouldn't have known what to do with a bold, sensual creature like you. But me, now… I can appreciate everything you are. I can appreciate what a gift you are."

And just like that, Neha knew she'd picked the right man to do this with. She mock frowned and licked her lips. His gaze zeroed in on the action. "Are you saying the thirty-six-year-old man has all the sense but lacks in vigor?"

A flash of white teeth against dark skin that gleamed with such masculine intent that some places in her body tightened and some loosened. He undid the rest of the buttons on his shirt and shrugged it off those broad shoulders. "Why ask questions when you're about to try it, *tesoro*?"

Between one blink and the next, he was all over her, a violent storm of need and demand that pulled her in.

His mouth crushed hers, his arms were steel bands around her body and his hard thigh was lodged in between hers, almost lifting her up, rubbing exactly where she needed contact. She dug her nails into the bands of muscle in his back and rubbed herself shamelessly against the taut clench of his thighs.

"*Cristo*, you're wet already," he whispered, licking into her mouth just as eagerly as she clung to him.

The slide of his rough chest over her sensitized nipples was a sensation she'd remember to her dying breath. His hands seemed to be everywhere on her body and yet landed nowhere. Not for enough time. Not to her satisfaction.

His hands patted every inch of her back, his teeth tugging and his tongue licking at the hurt, and then moved to her chest. The graze of his callused fingers over her swollen nipples sent a needy moan rippling out of her mouth. Learning her, drawing on her body's cues, he rolled the tight knots back and forth between his fingers, tightening the arrow of need concentrating in her lower belly.

Pleasure flew in rivulets up and down her body, there

one second, fleeing to a new part of her the next, driving Neha to near madness.

When he bent her over the counter that he'd been leaning against and brought his mouth to her breast, Neha jerked at the wet warmth. He licked around the center begging for his attention in mind-numbing circles. Blew hot air, plumped and shaped and caressed the soft weight with such exquisite skill that Neha arched into his touch, begging for more and more. Again and again his clever fingers and his cleverer mouth ministered to her, noting her responses, driving her wild, waiting for the wet lash to reach the place where she needed it the most.

"I've had dreams of touching you like this. *Cristo*, I've brought myself to…"

He stopped when Neha jerked her head up, his words just as arousing as his caresses. "You what?" The thought of Leo taking pleasure in an image of her was like a hot cinder going off in her entire body.

Color streaked his cheeks and those thick lashes hid away his expression. She rubbed his lower lip with the pad of her thumb. "Show me," she said, knowing that he'd always be a man of actions and not words. Never words. Even if every cell in her wanted to hear all the intimate things he'd thought of her through these years. "I'm in your hands, lover. Do whatever you want with me."

"Sì?"

"Sì."

"What do *you* want?" he asked, his hands never stopping in their exploration of her body. Cupping her buttocks, tracing the line of her spine, palming her breasts, nipping her lips. On and on and on, he kept the fever building in her.

"Your mouth, now, here," she demanded boldly, cupping her breast and raising it up to his mouth like a prize.

His nostrils flared, primal male satisfaction in every

carved angle. "*Dio*, only you could demand and yet somehow give, *cara mia*."

She didn't have enough brain cells left to figure out his cryptic remark. All she cared about was that he...

And then he was there. The cavern of his mouth was there, surrounding the hard tip of her nipple. Wet. Warm. Welcoming. First this breast and then its twin, until her nipples were gleaming with wetness and exquisitely sensitive even to his warm exhale.

He licked and stroked the nipple with a thousand lashes of his tongue, pressing up against it in such a cleverly wicked way that each swipe of it sent a current of need down to her sex. And then he closed his mouth around it, and he sucked in deep, drawing pulls that made her sex twitch with growing need.

"*Dio*, you'll climax if I continue this," he whispered against her neck, almost to himself. "You're extra responsive here." He tweaked a nipple and she felt an answering jolt in her pelvis.

Neha nodded, engulfed between ropes of sudden shyness and a desperate desire to climax.

Baring her body to a man she'd known for fifteen years hadn't given her a moment's doubt. But this intimate dialogue between them, the look in his eyes when he so thoroughly studied every inch of her damp skin, every rise and dip of her body, every jerk and twitch when he touched her somewhere new, as if he was cataloging it all away for future reference, this made a fragility she didn't like fill her up. Fragility that would let fears in, that would make this moment into more than what it was right now—utterly perfect.

"Please, Leo." She pulled at his hair, forcing him to lift his mouth from her tender nipples. "I need you...now."

"Not yet, *cara*." The sheer masculine arrogance in his tone scraped at her skin, winding the knot in her lower belly tighter. “Not until I have touched and kissed and learned every part of you.” His palm was on her belly now, inching lower and lower. The tips of his fingers played hide-and-seek with the flimsy seam of her knickers. In and out, in and out, covering more ground every time, stealing her breath on every dive inside.

“Not until I’m inside you and we’re moving together, *sì*?”

She shivered at the rough promise in his words. Drank in the sight of him—damp hair sticking to his forehead, muscles bunched tight in his shoulders, that hard chest breathing harshly as if he’d been running, greedily. “I think that’s setting the bar a little too high for the first time.”

“I like high bars—” a rough tangling of tongues and teeth “—and bold challenges issued by a bolder woman—” a wet lash against her turgid nipple “—and I want to be inside you when you come so hard that you’ll burst out of your skin.”

Neha jerked at the first touch of his fingers against the folds of her sex. Light and soft and oh, so gentle that she was ready to scream, he explored every inch of her. Drew a line around her opening with his finger and brought the wetness up to the bundle of nerves desperately waiting for his touch.

When he rubbed her there in a soft, mind-numbing circle, Neha cried out at the burst of fiery sensation. Heart in her throat, her breath coming in a harsh rhythm, she lifted her pelvis, chasing his clever fingers. He repeated the action, until she thought she would go mad with wanting.

Wanton, incoherent cries fell from her mouth. She was writhing under his careful, crafty caresses, begging him with her body. Reduced into nothing but a shivering, spiraling mass of sensation and pure pleasure.

Every stroke of his finger, every kiss he showered on her breasts, every breath he exhaled into her skin, every word out of that wicked mouth, drove her higher and higher until release was a shimmering mirage beckoning her fast. She gripped his wrist when he'd pulled away, her limbs honeyed, her entire being pressed down under a languorous weight. "I'm so close, please," she said, and his husky laughter enveloped her in its embrace.

"No, not yet." His smile was wicked, his rough tongue-and-teeth kiss purely possessive.

"I hate you," she whispered, sweat dripping into her eyes, her body unwilling or unable to follow her brain's simplest commands.

He pulled her up gently, as if she were a treasure he meant to hoard all for himself, his mouth curved into a dark smile, his eyes dilated, tension radiating in waves from his powerful body. Large hands clasped her chin, pulling her closer. He kissed her softly this time, less lust and desire and more…affection and connection. If her heart had ever been at risk, Neha knew it was then. His desire and his ultimatums and his possessiveness…she could handle all of those. His tenderness, however, would be the ruin of her.

"You trust me, don't you, Neha?"

"Always, Leo."

His face broke into a radiant smile that washed away any misgivings on her part. Washed away the frustration inside her limbs, flooding her with a renewed sense of wonder. She loved seeing him like this—demanding things of her—loved being with him in that moment, sharing this intimacy.

He tugged her with him, and she went without protest.

The lounger she'd noticed earlier came into her vision and dissolved like every other thought that didn't concern her eyes when they could gorge on the supremely male specimen in front of her.

Any thoughts of even intrusive shyness disappeared as he undid his trousers. And his black silk boxers.

A soft gasp built up and out of her chest as her gaze lowered to where he couldn't hide his desire. She could stare at him for the end of time and still not have enough. His thighs were thickly muscled, covered in hair, while his hips were leanly sharp planes, his skin lighter there than the rest of his body.

Neha licked her lips, her gaze once again going to his arousal, and a growl rumbled up from his chest. While she watched him, he hardened and lengthened. Her core dampened, as if in perfect answer.

"Come to me, *cara*," he said in a wicked tone that promised to make every fantasy of hers come true. Flushing, Neha lifted her gaze to find him seated on the lounger, his long legs on one side, utterly confident in his nudity.

Neha went to him, her skin damp, every muscle shivering, her heart overflowing with the rightness of this moment. With the conviction that she was exactly where she wanted to be in the entire universe. Naked, wanton, with the one man she'd wanted all her adult life. Living her life purely, simply, fully, in the moment.

CHAPTER SEVEN

SHE CAME TO HIM, her lush breasts bobbing, her small waist and wide hips calling to be held, her strong thighs and shapely calves utterly feminine. Her light brown skin glinting like burnished gold with a damp sheen, her hair tumbling around her face in a messy tangle, her eyes filled with a deep hunger that mirrored his own. Plump brown nipples shone with the wetness from his mouth. He gripped the lounger on the sides of his thighs, his hands already missing the voluptuous dips and valleys of her waist and thighs.

Her underwear was a narrow, white lace thing that just covered her from him.

He felt painfully hard, desperate to possess this woman who challenged him every step of the way. Who met his desires with her own, who it seemed was determined to carve away a piece of him without asking but by simply giving and trusting and wanting.

Strength and sensuality roped together in an irresistible combination, she was unlike any woman he'd ever known.

Cristo, he'd always known Neha was a force to reckon with. Everything about her shouted incredible confidence and innate sensuality and a strength he found utterly arousing.

She'd knocked him over with her gutsy plan to build a life she wanted, she amazed him the way she'd looked at her own flaws and decided to change her life and now… now she matched him hunger to hunger, demanding boldly and giving everything in return. He had a feeling he'd never hold a woman like that ever again. That he would never forget tonight, whatever juncture life brought them to in later years.

And he wanted to make tonight unforgettable for her, too. Every time she laid eyes on him, he wanted her to remember tonight. If ever she went to another man after tonight, he wanted the memory of this encounter to be the one she measured it against and found lacking. He wanted to be the man she measured every other man against.

His gaze caught on the flash of a thin gold chain around her ankle, a detail he'd overlooked before. And he didn't want to. He didn't want to miss an inch of her gorgeous body, or her smile, or a nuance in those expressive eyes. He didn't try to curb the urgency pounding his every muscle and instinct as she reached him. He knew it would be a useless attempt.

The scent of her hit his nostrils first—vanilla mingled with the smell of her skin, becoming a richer, deeper scent he would always remember when he stepped into the greenhouse. He spanned his hands around the sharp dip of her waist as she came closer, humbled again by the beauty and grace of the woman who was his match in every way. "You're trembling," he said, pressing openmouthed kisses to her soft belly.

"You're the reason I'm shaking like a bloody leaf in a storm," she said, her arms coming around his shoulders, her fingers sinking into his hair. Her nails scraped at the nape of his neck and Leo's body hardened between the slick rub of their bodies. Her voice caught on those words, a smoky quality to them, as if she'd ill-used her throat for a long time. "Make it better, Leo."

Instead of giving her more promises, Leo showed her he would. Worshipped every square inch of her gorgeous body. Set his fingers, his mouth, to working her into a deeper fever, kissing every inch of her silky-smooth skin, palming the globes of her breasts, raking his nails down those turgid nipples, stroking and kneading every inch of her supple flesh. Giving her everything she'd dealt him a thousand times back. Driving her as mad with need as she was doing to him.

"Naked, now," he said in a husky, demanding tone even he'd never heard before, pushing her away from him.

Dutifully, she stripped off her knickers, her brown eyes drugged with desire, her breaths coming in shallow and fast.

One hand on a hip, she stood before him, naked. And it was the honesty in her eyes that undid Leo.

She was the only woman in his entire life that aroused every primal instinct in him. That made him want to rumple her up and bend her to his will and also, in contrast, made him want to protect her with everything he had in him.

Pulling her to him, he filled his hands with her buttocks, dug his teeth into the tight flesh of her hip. When she jerked against him, he held her immobile with his arm around her. "Open your legs for me, *bella*."

She did and he was dipping his fingers into her folds, reaching for that wet warmth that had welcomed him earlier. *Merde*, her damp heat drenched his fingers.

He cursed hard and long, every inch of him shaking with need. He pushed one finger and then two into her and she cried out and rubbed sinuously against his hand. Taunting him. Teasing him. Half mad with the same want, he smiled.

Dio, she was more than ready. And after so many years, Leonardo was ready. For whatever this was. Because he had no doubt that something was beginning tonight. Here, in this moment. Something he didn't even fully understand.

"Leo, enough games. Now, please," she said, half sobbing.

Lust riding him hard, he pulled her on top of him until she was straddling him on the lounger. He sank his fingers into her thick hair, took her mouth in a hard kiss. Adjusting her body slightly, in one smooth thrust, he was inside of her. A filthy curse fell from his lips as she fit around him like a snug glove.

With a soft gasp, Neha stiffened in his arms, her spine bowing back, her nails sinking into his shoulders.

Stars blinked out behind his eyes at how incredibly good she felt. *Cristo*, he'd never felt anything remotely like this before. He'd never had sex in his life without a condom, he instantly rationalized. He'd never let a woman seduce him like Neha did and she had, so thoroughly tonight, even though he'd taken the ropes from her in the end.

As much as he tried to, he couldn't pin down the gloriousness of being inside this woman to some rational reasons. He buried his face in her neck, breathing her in, listening to the racing of her heart, letting emotion after emotion run through him, trying to center himself. Trying to not let it unsettle him.

Or was it the fact that there was an element of the emotional commitment already between them? Something he'd never let enter his relationships with women. The simple fact that while he always made sure there was an expiry date to his relationships, here, in every look and touch and caress, there was that awareness that they were tangling with each other for more than one night and not to just satisfy their desires.

But in an incomprehensible way, it felt more than just good. It felt right. It felt right that his experience with Neha should be different from any other sexual experience he'd ever had. It felt right that the woman who would bear his child should somehow be different. Be more than all the women he'd been with in his life before that.

"Are you well, *cara*?" he asked belatedly, aware that his accent was thick, aware that every inch of his body was drawn tight into a sharp point of need and desire and an unknown quality he didn't want to put a finger on.

When she looked down, her eyes held the same wonder Leo was sure his did. Her face glowed from within, a tentative, slumberous smile touching her pink lips. "You know how there are moments in life you want to use fancy words to describe how…big and grand they are and then you suddenly realize no language has a word that could ever encompass the enormity of everything you feel and yeah…"

He crushed her tart mouth with his, needing the anchor of her taste. Needing to know she was just as lost as he was. The kiss went from soft to devouring, morphed with the sure knowledge of how good it was between them, becoming something neither could corral or define.

Every simple touch turned into a conflagration. Passion ebbed and flowed between them in perfect rhythm, sometimes he the aggressor and sometimes she, and Leo knew he could spend an age kissing her like this, breathing her in, joined in the most intimate way possible.

Soon, he was dueling his tongue with hers, her teeth were scraping at his jaw, their bodies slick with sweat sliding and gliding against each other in an instinctual rhythm that defied something as rational as good sex. Arms vining around his back, she snuggled closer, her breasts rubbing up and down his chest. Pleasure came at him in waves, building up into unbearable pressure in his pelvis, a tingling storm sweeping up the backs of his thighs.

Hands on her hips, he gently pulled her up and down, testing the fit. A spark of sizzling sensation raced up his spine and he closed his eyes, as if he could will the climax coming at him hard to slow down.

A soft cry fell from her mouth as she wriggled in his hold.

"I don't remember it ever being this good, Leo." A bemused, overwhelmed quality clung to her words.

Leo ran his hands over all of her again and again, not getting enough of her supple, sweat-slick skin. All the while, she moved forward and backward, up and down, kissing his mouth when she came closer. The friction was incredible. Sweat beading on his brow, he willed his self-control to last just a little bit more when all he wanted to do was pound into her.

Eyes wide open, she held his gaze as he trailed his hand behind a bead of condensation tracking all over her skin, and reached the curly hair at her sex.

He dipped his thumb and found the slick bud throbbing for his attention. He saw her swallow, her breath coming in shallow bursts. Every time he stroked that bundle, she tilted her pelvis up and down, sending friction down the length of him. Every muscle in Leo's body screamed for release. She was so close he could feel her body clamping down on him, contracting and expanding, and he wanted to push her to the last edge.

"Look at me, *cara*," he said, and she tilted her head down. "Cup your breasts for me." He wanted to give her what he'd promised.

Eyes wide in her face, she raised her breasts to his face. Leo rubbed his stubble against the tender nipple and then flicked the tight knot with his tongue while he kept his finger on her and worked her over and over. Soon, she was writhing and twisting and moving up and down on him and then with a cry that shot shivers down his spine, she orgasmed.

Her muscles spasmed around him, setting off his own climax.

Leo rode the wave of it with her, pushing her down onto her back. Wild and abandoned, she was the boldest creature he'd ever seen. And all he wanted was to lose himself inside her. He pounded in and out of her with a savage need he didn't even recognize. Her eyes flew open, she clasped his jaw, and when she pulled her upper body and took his mouth in a shuddering kiss, she sent him over the edge faster than he'd ever known.

His climax swelled through him, splintering pleasure far and wide. His breath was so deafening in his ears that Leo could see or hear nothing for a long while. He was still shaking with the force of his release when he opened his eyes. Sweat dripped from his forehead and fell on her neck, and the drop pebbled down her damp skin. He followed the drop with his finger, a fierce possessiveness filling him.

Her eyes closed, her head tilted away, she was a study in sensuality. Leo ran his knuckles over her cheek before turning her to her side and joining her on the lounger. She was damp and trembling and warm when he wrapped his arm around her waist. Tenderness filled his chest and he gathered her to himself. For himself as much as her for he needed a physical anchor right then.

It was a long while before the high of his release and the glut of emotions that had overpowered him ebbed. And in its wake an unusual knot formed in his stomach.

Leo couldn't shake off the sense of alarm that he'd gotten more than he had ever bargained for. And yet, as he tucked her into his side and wrapped his arm around her trembling body, he didn't want to leave her.

Not tonight. Not for a long time.

Her body's unfamiliar aches in new places woke Neha up when she tried for a more comfortable position on the lounger. A deep languor thrummed through her, as if her limbs were filled of honey.

The first thing that struck her was the delicious kind of soreness between her legs. Enough to short-track the details of where and what had led to it. As did the scent of what they had done thick in the air around her.

She tried to sit up on the lounger when firm hands on

her bare shoulders pressed her back down. "It's okay, *cara*. I'm here."

Her chest ached at the tenderness in Leo's voice. Neha stretched her neck back. To find herself looking up into that impenetrable gaze that she'd have known in the midst of a dream.

His thick hair formed a wild halo around his face; his mouth was a little swollen, his expression as always hidden. Leo sat leaning against the back with one foot dangling down and the left folded at the knee, while her head lolled about on his thigh. He'd put both his trousers and shirt on, though the latter was unbuttoned. All she wanted to do was sink her fingers into his thick hair and pull him down to kiss her.

She kicked back up into a sitting position. "How long did I sleep?"

"Thirty minutes, at the most."

A shudder of relief passed through her as she noticed that her bare torso had been covered up with the T-shirt she'd discarded. Her shorts hung loosely on her hips.

"You put my shorts back on me?" she said, not quite meeting his eyes.

She was aware of his shrug from her side vision. *"Sì."*

"You should've left me here."

He turned her to face him with a rough grip. "And leave you to find your way to your suite at the crack of dawn? I know you have this idea that I'm allergic to being tied down, but it doesn't mean I treat women like trash."

"That's not what I meant." It was exactly what she meant. Heat washed over her. "I'm sorry for—"

"*Dio mio!* Stop apologizing. It was either cover you up or wake you up for session two. You were exhausted after everything from the evening and that was the last thing you needed."

A rough shove of his fingers through that thick hair.

Which like hers had taken on a life of its own thanks to the humid air. This version of Leo—hair wild, shirt unbuttoned—the intimacy of seeing him all rumpled and sexy, broke the tension choking her.

"I wouldn't have minded session two," she said, tongue in cheek.

His expression didn't relent. If not for the muscle jumping in his cheek, she'd have thought he was already regretting everything. Did he regret admitting that he'd wanted to make love to her again? Or was he wondering if she'd make it all awkward and weird now that it was done?

No, she wasn't going to go digging for things that weren't there. Overanalyze what was there. With a man like Leo—who exercised the utmost self-control and discipline—it was his actions that mattered. What he chose to say would always be more important than what he left out.

She'd gotten more than she'd ever dreamed of having of him. If she lived to be a hundred, this would remain the most extraordinary night of her life. She'd found not only incredible pleasure but an inexplicable joy in what they had shared.

Time to make a graceful exit. Without wondering what could be or what it hadn't been.

"I only meant to stay horizontal for a little while." She looked down and up into his eyes again. "I've read that it's good to prop your hips up after…to increase your chances of conception." He folded those corded arms and waited. "So I didn't immediately get up and then I fell asleep."

"You do not need a reason to not run away as soon as we're finished, *bella*."

She nodded and pushed to her feet. He stood up, too, and all Neha could see was the broad sweep of his shoulders, the delineated line of his muscles, the lean tapered waist, the strong, hard thighs that had cradled her.

Hand on his chest, she rose up on her bare toes and kissed him on the cheek. “Thank you, Leo.”

He took her wrist in his hand and slowly returned it to her. His gaze studied her as if he meant to look beneath the amiable expression she was determined to keep. As if he wanted to know everything she was neatly stashing away to be explored later. Or never.

She tossed around in her head for some mundane topic while looking for her shoes. “What’s going on here?”

His head tilted down, he was buttoning his shirt. A slightly reddish mark above his pectoral winked at her. Furious heat climbed up her cheek when she realized she had raked his skin with her nails.

She watched greedily until the last patch of olive skin stretched taut over hard muscles was covered up. Fisting her hands, she swallowed the longing that rose through her.

Asking him to sleep with her so that they could conceive had been easy. But now there was so much more she wanted, so much more she still didn’t have. Small, intimate things she wanted to share with him—like buttoning that shirt, or pushing that thick, unmanageable hair away from his forehead, or kissing away his frown…those would always be out of her reach.

She looked away barely a second before he faced her. “With what?”

It took her a few seconds to trace back their conversation. She walked around the lounger and ran her hand over one of the vines that had crawled up all the way to the high ceiling. “The greenhouse.”

“I’m having it restored.”

“Why did it get to such a dilapidated condition in the first place?”

There was a tenuous quality to his silence behind her that raised the hairs on her neck. A cold remoteness entered his eyes. Those rough fingers moved over and over on an ancient-looking ceramic pot with two handprints on it—one adult and one child.

"This ghastly place needs new memories."

Realization slammed into her. Her throat closed up, words coming and falling away to her lips.

"It belonged to my mother."

"Oh." There was a violence to his contained stillness, a restless energy that would only singe her if she ventured closer. And yet she couldn't help it. "You must have got your green thumb from her, then. Massimo says there's not a flower in the world that won't blossom in your care."

A shrug that conveyed so much without saying it.

"Do you remember much—?"

"After she left, it went to hell," he said, cutting her off. It was as if a door had slammed in her face. The tender lover of just a few moments ago was gone.

"When I realized I wanted a greenhouse, I asked the architect to build a new one in the same spot." He passed her and opened the door. "He said it would be a waste to gut the structure. He's restoring it instead."

There was no doubt left that he'd preferred to have it ripped out. Maybe remove any sign of his mother in the process, like he'd done in every other area of his life. Like he'd advised her to do earlier.

And yet, Neha intrinsically knew she'd never be capable of that. Removing the bad stuff meant removing the good stuff, too, and she could never sterilize her life of her mum's presence. Before it had all been destroyed with her papa's long illness and death, she had known happiness with her parents. She'd been loved by her mum, before her papa's death had broken her, had changed the course of their lives permanently.

The moment she stepped out of the greenhouse behind him, Neha took a bracing breath. The dip in the temperature outside had her shivering.

Leo tucked her under his arm as they walked, their thighs wedged close all too comfortably for her.

She knew she was dangerously skating over the invisible boundary he'd always drawn around the topic of his parents, but Neha couldn't keep quiet. Couldn't bear to know that it had affected him but had never been addressed.

Because who would do that for him? Not his father, who'd been an abusive man. Not Greta, who knew no tenderness. Leonardo had always taken the role of the head of the family and the burden that came with it whether he wanted to or not…but had anyone ever asked him what his mother's leaving had done to him? Had anyone even wondered?

"I didn't see any pictures of her in the villa."

"I have an early start tomorrow and I'd really like to get to bed now."

"Of course," Neha replied, keeping her tone steady, even as tension swathed them. She wanted to push—she had a feeling he'd talk about it to no one, but the last thing she wanted was to be told it was none of her business.

Physical intimacy didn't equal emotional intimacy. Especially with Leo.

Finally, they reached her suite. He turned the knob but didn't release the door.

"I didn't mean to be so curt," he said, his hand on her lower back, his breath raising the little hairs on her neck. He was a wall of warmth and want behind her.

She nodded, refusing to give in on the issue but accepting his apology. Years of habits couldn't change overnight, and she wasn't even sure she wanted Leo's secrets. That way only lay more blurring of lines and emotional labor she didn't want to pay.

"Everything is okay?"

"Yes." She turned her head and laughed softly. "Don't

worry, Leo. It's not going to be awkward between us. I won't let it be."

She didn't wait for his answer as she went into her bedroom and headed straight for the shower. Even though she wanted to linger in the scent of him still clinging to her skin. She wasn't going to turn what had been a fantastic evening into what could only be a dream made of cards.

CHAPTER EIGHT

IT HAD BEEN three days since Leo, for the first time in his adult life, had woken up late, sunlight streaming onto his huge bed the morning after the party, and felt a strange reluctance to begin his sixteen-hour workday. He had wanted to revel in the complete languor that had filled his mind and body. Three mornings ago, since he'd wandered through the villa only to discover that Neha had caught a lift with Massimo to London.

He had no idea how the woman had found the energy to disappear the morning after what had to have been an eventful, emotional night for her. But then Neha had always possessed a no-nonsense, pragmatic approach to life.

Three days in which he'd thought of her every hour, on the hour, as if someone had set an alarm in his head. Of how pliant and responsive and eager she'd been in his arms. Of how she'd felt around him, her gaze boldly holding his. Of how she'd tried to assure him that he had nothing to worry about.

If he were honest with himself, he hadn't needed that cheeky reassurance. Taking his honesty a step further, he even admitted to himself that he'd been annoyed by her reassurance that she wasn't going to act the part of a clingy lover.

He'd never had a connection like that with a woman even during sex before, the connection that had gone a little beyond the physical.

Whatever the reason, he was finding that one evening

hadn't been nearly enough. If anything, seeing how incredibly good it had been between them, Leo wanted a lot more of her.

He had a million things on his calendar to take care of—he'd been postposing his visit to his father. Silvio's health had taken a rapid downturn in the last month. Alex was still acting strange even though she'd had the sense to call Greta the night of the party, and he had a meeting with Mario. A confrontation that had been coming for months that he needed all his wits for, and yet, here he was thinking of Neha in the middle of the afternoon.

Basta! He'd never been a man to sit and wonder why he wanted something. He'd just gone after it.

He picked up his phone and clicked on Neha's dimpled smile on the screen.

A flurry of voices accompanied her greeting. He heard the click-click of her heels and then quietness. "Hey, Leo."

Just her voice sent memories of remembered sensations rushing through him.

Cristo, she'd openly admitted she wanted him. He didn't have to stand here and moon about that one experience like a teenager. He could simply arrange to see her again. And take her to bed. "I called to see how you are."

"Oh, thanks. I'm good, yeah? Y'know, the usual. Back-to-back meetings, morning to night, but I'm okay." A pause, and he could feel her hesitation through the space. "Did you get a chance to talk to Mario?"

"No," he said, instantly alert to the ragged quality to her question. "Did he confront you again? Did he send your mum?"

"No. I called her, but I haven't heard back." The ache in her words made him feel entirely too powerless. He had the overwhelming urge to hold her close in his arms, to tell her in person that it would be all right in the end. "I just… was wondering where we're at. In the scheme of things."

"I have a meeting with him in two days," he said, and could practically hear the relief in her sigh. "I can't look overeager to wave the proof of our relationship in front of him. Mario's clever. I have to keep him thinking he has the upper hand in all this for now."

"Do you want me to be there?"

"No." The last thing he wanted was to rub Mario's face in it or expose Neha to the man's temper any more than she already was. "If he asks you about us, just say that we've been spending more time together. Don't go into any kind of detail about BFI or even my family. The press coverage tells him enough, *sì*?"

Just as he'd expected, the media was going gaga over the two of them finally heating up the relationship. His asking Neha to join the rest of his family on the dais hadn't been lost on the media or Neha's fans. The only thing missing was a statement from So Sweet Inc.'s publicity team.

"Okay, yeah. I've been trying to keep my meetings with my lawyer on the down low just in case he—"

"You didn't have to sneak out the morning after the party." He finally gave voice to the one thing that had been bothering him.

He could imagine her leaning on her desk, worrying her lower lip, wondering what to say and what not to. "I thought it was better that way, to have some distance. Because, as good as it was, it was also…a bit emotional for me. It's been a while and it came on top of everything. I don't want to make you feel as if I want more than you're willing to give. I never—"

"*Cristo*, Neha! Did it occur to your overthinking mind that I wanted you there the next morning?"

He'd no idea what to make of her silence except that he'd stunned her. "I told you in the greenhouse that I was okay. It would have been just…" A sigh and then the sharp inhale. "Leo, I… The truth is I've been only with two other men in my life and I thought I was going to marry one of them. Sex is emotional for me, and with you, it's like a minor earthquake, both physically and in other ways. I needed the distance. To keep things in perspective."

"I wanted to take you to bed again, a proper bed this time. If you were still willing."

Another silence. Another few seconds wondering what she was thinking. "Oh."

"Instead, you ran away with Massimo."

"I didn't run away, I just—"

"I want to see you this Friday. Be ready, I'll pick you up at work."

Another long pause.

Cristo, he should have just flown into London to see her instead of engaging in this conversation over a ridiculous phone call.

"I have plans on Friday. Saturday, I'm meeting with the publicity department to shoot some pics for the new book, and then in the evening—"

"You're the boss. Take one Saturday evening off."

The urge to ask her to make herself available rode him hard. He held himself back.

Why couldn't he? Was it because they hadn't established that this was a relationship? He had no hesitation to call it that because he wanted her.

"I can't take any more days off because I already flew twice to Milan and..." He heard someone call her name and then she was rushing through her words. "I'll look at my calendar and text you."

"You'll text me a fifteen-minute window where we can conceive our child in the most efficient way possible?" He regretted the words the moment they were out.

Dio, he sounded like a spoiled, privileged, puffed-up man determined to have his own way.

But instead of being offended, her laughter filled the

line. "I like you like this, all grumpy and…frustrated?" When he grunted, she laughed again. "My calendar is full just as yours is, you know that. To beat a dead dog, this is the reason I'm trying to revamp my entire lifestyle."

God, the woman was as graceful as she was beautiful. "My continued frustration because of your unavailability will mean everything will go too fast when you're in my hands, *bella*."

She gasped—that hoarse, throaty sound that played over his nerves as if she'd run those long fingers over his clenching muscles. "Then we'll go fast to relieve your…frustration the first time and then take it slow.

"Now, unless I want to scandalize my team by sprouting more sexual innuendo over the phone and give them enough to sell to a tabloid, I really must go."

"*Bene.* Remember, don't engage with Mario without me."

"Okay."

"Call me any time you need me. If you can't reach me, call Massimo."

"I will."

"Ciao, bella."

"Leo?"

"Sì?"

"Thank you."

"I don't think I've ever been thanked so many times for sex, *cara*. It is annoying the hell out of me."

She laughed and the carefree quality of it made him smile. "No, I'm not thanking you for the mind-blowing sex. Although you give it good. I meant…for checking up on me." A catch in her throat.

He waited, instinctively knowing that this was harder for her to do than ask him to make love to her. Knew that she'd gone so long without leaning on anyone that it had become a way of being. Because he was exactly like that.

"I feel a little less alone than I've felt in a long time, like the future I want is really in my grasp. We work really well as a unit. On so many levels, y'know. I'm just..."

Leo stayed silent, trying to dislodge the unfamiliar tightness in his chest. He didn't know how to give voice to emotions. Even with Massimo, it was only this past year, once his brother had fallen for Natalie, that they'd put into words the divide their father had caused between them and all the steps Leo had taken to build a bridge to Massimo.

Even that night in the greenhouse, all Neha had done was to broach the topic of his mother. Not so out of context because, *Dio*, he'd commanded her to cut her own mother out of her life. He had shut her down so curtly that it was a surprise she hadn't taken it as an insult. But in that moment, like right now, Leo couldn't open up.

Couldn't tell her that he liked hearing her say it so openly. Liked that she'd always been honest with him.

He had a sense of what was right and wrong, though he didn't know where it came from because all Silvio had taught him in his formative years had been how to wield power. Greta had taught him how to do the right thing by the Brunetti name no matter what. Greta's second husband, Carlo, had tried to nurture the little good that had been in Leonardo.

But no one had taught him how to let another human being close, how to process, much less express, emotions like fear and need, so he'd simply buried them all for the sake of survival.

And now, Leo wanted to say something meaningful, but all his energies went into burying the weight he felt on his chest. On fighting the web into which Neha drew him so easily, so effortlessly. So he stayed silent and he sensed her confusion in the pause.

"I have to go now," she whispered softly.

Without a reply, Leo hung up. And for the first time

in his life, he wondered if there would come a day when Neha would ask something of him and he couldn't give it.

Even having been prepared for the meeting, Leo felt a strange reluctance when Mario walked into his office at the appointed hour wearing a self-satisfied smile that Leo wanted to wipe off with his fists. He had never liked Mario—too smooth in hiding the oily nature beneath, even when he'd been Silvio's cohort in any number of activities.

Mario's true nature had been revealed when, at the first sign that Silvio was going down all those years ago, the man had immediately cut any ties and jumped ship. Leo had always wondered how much Mario had known about and hidden Silvio's activities even then, but there had never been any proof of his complicity.

Now, knowing how the older man manipulated Neha, using her affection for her mum, Leo knew his estimation was right. Mario was of the same ilk as Silvio, a man who preyed on weaker people. Except much cleverer.

With a full head of gray hair, strong, sharp features and a fit body, at sixty-five, Mario was considered a handsome man.

"It is a good thing you scheduled this," he said, strolling in and going straight for Leo's leather chair at his desk. The CEO's chair. While Leo stayed at the sitting area. "Ever since the spectacle you made of her at the party, I've been meaning to have a word with you."

"A spectacle of whom?" Leo asked.

"My stepdaughter, Neha, that's who."

"I don't understand."

Mario grunted, coming away from Leo's desk. "Her mother and I worry about her. She hasn't been—" he pretended concern so well here that if he hadn't known his true colors, Leo would have bought it "—well these last few months. She's not operating at full judgment."

"Are you saying something's wrong with Neha?"

"Ah, so she didn't let you see that, did she?" he said with unconcealed satisfaction. "But no, the girl hasn't been well."

"She's not a girl, Mario. She's the CEO of So Sweet Inc. She's the engine that keeps your empire running."

Pure evil glinted in Mario's eyes. "Neha hides it well, even from her mother, but I know something's wrong with her. Clearly, these anxiety attacks have messed with the good sense God gave her."

"Anxiety attacks?" Leo asked, stunned.

"She had one a few months ago, when she was in China. Her assistant told me even though Neha ordered her not to.

"She's not operating properly. Or she'd have realized you're just playing with her. That you're using her to get at me. And that she'll be shown to be a fool in front of the whole world when you dump her and move on." The pure cunning in Mario's shrewd gaze sent a shiver even through Leo. "Maybe I should just wait for this whole thing to play out to its natural ending. Let her learn that lesson publicly, despite her mum's constant worries."

So her mother did worry about Neha. That would be of consolation to Neha, but it wasn't anywhere near enough to cancel the pain the woman caused her own daughter. "What lesson would that be, Mario?"

Mario waved a hand through the air between them imperiously. "She's always had a thing for you. Follows your affairs quite religiously. Thinks the world of you, thinks she has you in her corner, *sì*?"

Fury rose through Leo and he barely stopped himself from turning away in disgust. What kind of a man betrayed his stepdaughter's confidence like this to a man she was in a relationship with to be used as ammunition? What kind of a woman tied her daughter up in such a man's toxic shadow? *Dio*, how had Neha stayed sane all these years?

"She looks like she's falling apart at the seams. That joy, that sparkle of hers is gone."

Massimo's words came at him with a painful clarity he had been missing before.

"I'm not surprised you figured out her little thing for you and decided to use it to advantage," Mario went on, without missing a beat.

Leo held up a hand. "You think I'm using Neha's…admiration for me to lure her into a relationship to some nefarious purpose?" That the man had hit his eventual goal on the nail only made Leo's hackles rise.

Mario shrugged. "It's what I'd have done. Your plan has one big loophole, though. You will tire of her when you realize she gives you no leverage with me and then dump her. The girl will be heartbroken and then she will know where her loyalties should lie. A lesson she needs reminding of."

That Mario would relish Neha's downfall with such glee sent bile through Leo. All his careful plans crumbled to dust in the wake of the fury coursing through him. "I wouldn't be so quick to decide that," he said, the words sticking to his throat like thorns. But a man like Mario only understood his language.

He wasn't going to betray to this snake of a man what regard he had for Neha, how she consumed his every waking thought and how that regard for her was only growing with every glimpse into her life. "There are many advantages to be had in an ongoing association with a successful, beautiful woman like Neha. Especially a woman who would go to any lengths for me, it seems." He mentally apologized to her for it. "I wouldn't make bets on how long our relationship will last, Mario."

Mario's handsome face transformed in a mere moment into something ugly. Somehow, he wrangled his temper back under control to say, "What will it take to…shorten the duration of your relationship with her?"

"How did you know that BFI's systems had been cyber-attacked two times?"

"A rumor."

"Impossible. Only four people knew about it. Me, Massimo, the woman who did the attack and the man who engineered it. Which means the source had to be that man."

"This whole meeting is a waste of—"

"What did Vincenzo Cavalli offer you? BFI's CEO chair? More stock in BFI?"

Mario examined his buffed nails at leisure. "I've no idea what you're talking about."

"*Basta*, Mario! If you know what's good for you, tell me where I can find him and why he's bent on ruining BFI."

"Or what?"

"Your golden goose is in my hands, Mario. I can turn her head whichever way I want."

"What the hell does that mean?"

"You and I both know Neha's tired of it all, *sì*? Of the rat race, of the eighty-hour-week grind, of you running her life... What do you think it would take for me to nudge her into taking a more permanent holiday from So Sweet Inc.?"

A vein dangerously popping in his temple, Mario looked ready to explode. "Neha would never do anything that would hurt her mother."

There it was... Mario's means of manipulating her again and again. "Not the first time a weak woman's so in love with the wrong man that all sense deserts her, is it?" Leo said.

Mario's skin flushed, confirming his own awareness of his wife's sheer inability to see what Mario was doing to her own daughter. "So you're your father's son, eh? You would use a foolish woman for your own power play, then? Is it any wonder Cavalli is out to ruin you all? Don't forget I know all of Silvio's secrets, Leo. Secrets even you don't know.

"I can lead you or Cavalli to them. It's your choice.

"Dump Neha. Walk away from anything to do with her. End this thing publicly. And maybe I'll think about what I can tell you."

Leo stood up from his seat. There was only so much he could pretend before his skin crawled. Only so much he could do to turn a snake like Mario. "I'm nothing like my father. I don't make deals with bullies."

"He's got it in for your entire family, and he's not stopping any time soon," Mario retorted, finally showing his true colors. "Think about it, Leonardo. Think about what your temporary association with Neha will cost you.

"You consider yourself honorable, *sì*? Think about what this association with you will cost her...because both you and I know, in the end you'll move on to the next woman.

"She's already crumbling. Where will she be when you've dumped her and she's all alone in the world?"

With that warning, the hateful man exited his office, leaving Leo shaking with fury and guilt.

It took Leo more than a few minutes to calm down, to bring his mind back to rationality. *Maledizione*, he hadn't meant to throw Neha's retirement plans in Mario's face so soon. But the way the man had spoken of Neha, Leo couldn't regret his loss of temper.

Mario's words only confirmed Massimo's and his suspicions.

Their father was at the heart of all this.

Leo needed to visit Silvio, ask him to remember the Cavalli family, get him to sign the will transferring his stock to Leonardo and Massimo equally.

It was also the only chance to ask Silvio about something that Leo had buried deep down for years. A chance to open up the past again and let it rake its fingers through his present.

Cristo, but he was sick of having to deal with the fallout from his father's actions. *Dio*, all his adult life he'd spent rebuilding what Silvio had destroyed, cleaned up what Silvio had corrupted, had taken on the responsibility of BFI on his shoulders.

No, he wanted to leave the past where it was. He had never wanted less to see the man he'd worshipped for half his life and abhorred the rest of it. He refused to let the past leave a mark on him. Or on Neha for that matter.

She'd had an anxiety attack...

It was the last piece of the puzzle of those shadows in her eyes. But Leo couldn't muster anger that she'd hidden it from him. Could understand the kind of defenses Neha had built around herself after being let down by a parent...

All he felt was a certain resolve that she needed his protection. Especially now that Mario knew of her retirement plans.

From her own stubborn clinging to her self-sufficiency to begin with. From her mother's manipulations.

Their child, whether she retired in a few weeks or not, would always need protection from Mario's hateful shadow. From Neha's own inability to cut her mother out of her life.

And there was only way to achieve it.

The idea of marrying Neha, instead of knocking him back, built in his head like a tsunami, gaining momentum with each passing moment. It was Neha herself who'd made that decision so easy.

She'd never ask him for what he couldn't give. She'd proved in the last two weeks how rational she was. They'd have a solid foundation for a marriage—respect, passion and a mutual desire to do the best by their child.

Suddenly, there was a future he could see when he closed his eyes, a future he wanted for himself. Not just the ashes of the past. Their child would be part of a family unit and have everything Leo had never had and desperately craved for as a child.

* * *

Leo stood inside the grand entrance hall of Neha's Mayfair apartment complex and studied the high, domed ceiling and the dark stained oak curving staircase with pleasant surprise. The expansive cream Nettuno marble floor with the black onyx squares popping the monotony screamed understated luxury.

He'd recommended the property a few years ago when she'd asked him about investment advice, since Mayfair had been on the cusp of rivaling Knightsbridge as the area for luxury residential homes. The value of the two-bedroom flat she'd purchased had only gone up.

After facing down Mario two days ago and still digesting the disgusting lengths the man could sink to, his admiration for Neha grew boundless.

How much of a fight had she had to put up to buy such expensive property in her own name? What had Mario already unleashed in the last week that Leo had been gone?

He had the concierge let her know that he was waiting in the lounge, aware with every breath that the sense of urgency he felt to see her, touch her, was something he'd never experienced before. Now that he had a plan in hand, Leo couldn't wait to put it into motion.

His breath caught when she stepped out of the lift, her hair shining like a silky black curtain.

She was wearing a blouse with a long shawl draped over it and a billowing skirt underneath—all in the same cream and gold silky, flowing material that made her look like some beautiful princess stepping out of a fairy tale.

Large earrings with a cluster of pearls bobbed when she moved her head. A black dot took the pride of place between her eyebrows, and her eyes, lined with kohl, were huge in her face.

Her mouth was painted a light pink shade that reminded him of those decadent, pink confections she had once asked him to taste-test when he'd found her in the industrial kitchen at one of So Sweet Inc.'s branch of bakeries. The bracelets she wore on each arm shimmered gold.

She stilled, her gaze running over him like a physical caress, a warmth in her eyes that he couldn't help but bask in. "Will I do?" she said, reminding him of his pithy text that she should dress up.

He nodded, something primal and possessive rising inside him.

"Will you tell me the surprise now?" she asked, her hand reaching his hair and pushing away at a lock. And, just as fast, snatching it away. The subtle scent of vanilla and something sweet filled his breath, his body desperate for more.

He pulled the tickets out of the inside pocket of his jacket and waved them in front of her. "We're going to a *tabla* concert, although I'm not sure if 'concert' is the right word? By your favorite maestro."

"My God, Ustaad Atif Hussain? That's why you asked me to dress in traditional clothes." Her eyes widened as she grabbed the tickets from him and scanned them. She vibrated with excitement. "I was too late to get tickets for it. Wait! It's a super-exclusive invite-only event because Ustaadji doesn't perform for crowds. He's supposed to be super-private… How did you…? I can't believe you remembered how much I adore his music."

"You told me once you'd always dreamed of taking your papa to see him. That he and you used to spend hours in the bakery working with the *tabla* records on in the background."

Tears filled Neha's eyes. "I never got a chance to bring Papa to see him." She lifted those beautiful eyes to his, and a tightness filled his chest at the emotion in them. He grunted when she threw herself at him and hugged him with all the strength she had in her. He laughed when she kissed his face, sputtering thank-yous in between, with all the enthusiasm of the younger Neha who had stormed into his life one summer.

She pulled away suddenly and stared at him. "Why did you do this?"

Leo didn't hesitate. "I know how upset you were that your mum canceled the whole thing you do for your father's birthday. I know how hard this is hitting you. And it's kind of my fault."

"That's not possible."

"Mario knows about your retirement plans. I knew he was going to come hard at you. I just..."

"You just didn't expect that she'd break such an important tradition at his behest? Neither did I. But there it is."

Leo clasped her chin, guilt coursing through him. "I'm sorry I went off script, *cara*."

She clamped her fingers on his wrist, sinking into his touch. "No, this was going to happen, anyway, remember? But I'm not alone to deal with it, at the least."

"No, you're not." The ache in her eyes was like a fist to his gut. Ache he still felt responsible for. "I thought this would be a perfect way to pay a tribute to your father's birthday...maybe even become a new ritual?"

She nodded, something flashing in her eyes he couldn't recognize. "Time for new things, yeah." Her chest rose and fell with a deep breath, the tinkle of her bangles a sound he'd never forget. "I don't know how to thank you."

"Just enjoy the evening. Mario and your mother and BFI can all wait for a few hours, *sì*?" He ran his thumb over her lips, unable to hold back. "After all these years, I thought we deserved a normal date."

She nodded, that sparkle back in her eyes. "I'm game. No talk of dysfunctional families or careers or vengeful enemies." She tucked her arm through his. "But you don't even know if you like Hindustani music."

"If you can sit through the opera when you hate it," he said, mentioning the time they'd attended the opera at La Scala and she'd barely sat still, "I can sit through this."

"Oh, the opera's got nothing against Ustaadji's fingers on the *tabla*," she said.

"No worries, *bella*. I'll find a way to exact some kind of compensation in return if I do find the maestro boring," he whispered, and laughed when she instantly got his meaning.

Suddenly, the evening ahead felt incredibly long when all Leo wanted to do was to bring her upstairs, slip the ring in his jacket on her finger, find that bedroom and claim her.

CHAPTER NINE

LEONARDO'S PRESENCE STARTED a thrumming in Neha's veins. He walked around her home—her pride and heart and her first big victory against Mario—stopping here and there to study artwork she'd collected on her international travels.

She'd been telling herself that the time in the greenhouse couldn't have been as spectacular as she remembered. That she wasn't that wide-eyed teenager who still nurtured a fragile hope that Leo would want her in his life. But tonight…tonight that hope had come roaring back into life.

Tonight, all the lines between them were blurred. And she wasn't even afraid.

God, he'd been the most amazing companion through the *tabla* concert, going as far as encouraging her to talk to Ustaadji after. Dinner had been a noisy affair at an outdoor café, and she'd talked and talked about the exquisite music they'd heard. And now…now that he was inside her flat, she had no energy to hold herself aloof. No way to stop what the evening had meant to her, what his actions meant to her, from drowning her in a surfeit of emotions she didn't know to handle. Even knowing that it was mostly guilt that had motivated him.

He'd been right when he'd said she'd run away. She had. She'd resolutely buried the longing she'd felt, the insane urge to ask him when she'd see him again on the phone. How was she to fight it now when he was the most perfect man she could've asked for?

While he looked at the gallery wall she'd decorated with

a number of pictures of her and her parents through the years, she stole the time to study him to her heart's content.

He'd shrugged off the charcoal jacket he'd been wearing, and the very breadth of his shoulders made her palms itch. He was a giant of a man and a primal part of Neha loved that he was so big that he made her feel feminine, fragile, sexy.

The sky-blue shirt fit his torso perfectly. With no tie and three buttons undone, he looked less the suave businessman and more the rough and tumble gardener who loved getting his hands dirty. Whose fingers had felt so abrasively delicious against her skin.

She let her gaze traverse to his lean hips and the taut behind. Her fingers curled as the memory of sinking her nails into his buttocks while he'd pumped into her came at her fast.

He turned at that exact moment. His gaze dipped to her mouth and lingered. Awareness enveloped them in a world of their own, taunting with memories of that night.

"I'll change and then we'll talk. I made a list of things to run by you," she added, suddenly feeling incredibly vulnerable, "when you said you'd be coming over."

"You don't need a reason to have my company."

"Or to simply have you?" she taunted.

He caught her wrist, arresting her between his legs in a sudden move. A sensual smile curved his lips. "Or to have me, *sì*."

Rough fingers abraded the plump vein at her wrist, pulling her down, down until she rested her hands above his knees. His thighs were rock hard under her fingers. Her hair fell forward on both sides of her face like a shimmering curtain, blocking the world out.

"I don't have the emotional energy today to walk away when we're done," she said, offering them both an out before she gave in.

"I never asked you to, *cara*." Each word pelted her skin like a caress, drawing a shuddering response. This close to him, she could see the lines carved into his rugged face, feel the heat radiating from his powerful body. "You're so busy acting how you think I want you to act that you're depriving us both of what we really want."

She gasped as he held the *dupatta* in one hand and pulled sharply. It fell away with a silky hiss, leaving the deep neckline of the blouse and, with it, her cleavage exposed. Dark eyes tracked the rise and fall of her flesh like a hungry hawk. His fingers landed on the patch of bare skin between her blouse and the skirt, and she had to fight to not sink into his touch.

His mouth covered hers, swallowing away her confusion and vulnerability and in turn giving her pleasure and joy and warmth. In the beat of a harshly drawn breath, she was in Leo's lap, her legs draped over his, her flowing skirt and all, and his mouth continued to devour hers. Neha sank her fingers into his hair, loving the rough texture of his hair. Soft and firm, his lips laved and licked, his tongue teasing her into such erotic play that she writhed in his lap. He gave her everything she wanted without being asked for it.

It felt like heaven. Like coming home. Like a safe place to land. After that first demanding taste of her mouth, he groaned against her quivering lips. "That's all I've wanted to do for days now."

He explored her mouth softly, slowly, as if he had all the time in the world to learn her anew, as if he was determined to know more of her than anyone ever had. His fingers held her with infinite gentleness, his body a haven of warmth she didn't want to leave.

There was already a sense of familiarity in how they melded their mouths, in the pull and push of their lips and breaths, and yet there was that thrill making her blood rush, her nipples knot, her body melt with each increasingly clever touch of his.

His long fingers left striations of heat on her belly and back, inching up and up under the loose blouse. His hands busily roamed her torso, plumping and squeezing, stroking and pinching. The pad of his thumb unerringly found the tight knot of her nipple and Neha arched into his touch.

She palmed his shoulders with her fingers, exploring every tense muscle in his neck and shoulders and back, while he ravished all her senses. With him so solid in her hands, it was hard to fear the future. So deliciously demanding against her mouth, hard to stay rational, sensible.

She was falling, falling, and yet didn't care about anything but the thrill of his hot mouth and roving hands and warm body.

His large hands encircled her waist, pulling her closer and closer, his desire a hot, hard throb against her hip. All Neha had to do was undo the zipper on her *lehenga* and slide it off her legs, and straddle him until her warm core was notched against that hardness. The world disappeared when he was inside her. She could escape the pain of the increasing rift between her mum and her; she could escape the seesaw of her own emotions when it came to this man.

But when it was done, he would leave and…tonight, she felt too raw to face the rest of the night alone. Lord above, please help her that she'd already conceived, and these were hormones taking over her body and not something else. How many months of this could she take if they didn't conceive immediately?

Would she be able to keep her emotions separate from her desires when it was Leonardo? It was such a scary thought that she pulled her mouth away from his. She buried her face in his neck, willing her breath to even out. Every inch of her shivered with longing and something else she didn't want to identify. "I'm afraid this is getting too hard," she said, opting for honesty. She could never play coy or tease, especially not with Leo.

"What is?"

"This…you and me." She tugged her gaze to his face and felt a tug in her chest that had nothing to do with attraction and desire or dreams she was determined to realize. This was all about the young man she'd adored once and the perfect man she admired so much today. This was about wanting so much more than what she already had. Of him.

His fingers played on her cheek. "Tell me what's going on in your head."

"You'll think I'm changing the rules on you."

"Because you want me for more than one stolen night in a greenhouse?"

"I don't know what I want anymore. Or how much. That's what's scary."

His fingers clasped her cheek gently. "This was never going to stop only at sex and conception, *bella*," he said, shocking her with his perceptiveness, the scent and feel of him a warm anchor in the maelstrom of her emotions. "We've known each other for years and it could never be just that, *sì*? I don't think we established rules in the first place, *tesoro*. Not for any of this. So how about we address it now?"

Neha nodded, her eyes still closed, a rush of warmth filling every inch of her. God, how did he know to say the exact thing she needed to hear?

He crossed his legs with a grimace, and she laughed. A wicked hunger shone in his eyes, making promises that didn't need words. "I have the perfect solution for our situation, but first, let's talk about Mario. That should cool me down like nothing else."

She studied her hands, willing the shaking that began deep in her soul to subside. "I didn't think Mum would cancel our day together for Papa's memorial. When I called, she wouldn't even come to the phone. He's completely cutting me out of her life and there's nothing I can do."

His fingers squeezed her shoulder. "Mario's every bit the monster you said he is. I'm sorry for doubting your fears for even a moment."

She frowned, something in his tone tugging at her. "What did he say?"

"A lot of posturing…but the most important thing was that you had an anxiety attack when you were in China. Why didn't you tell me, Neha?"

"I told you everything but about the attack. And it was a full-blown panic attack actually, the one when I was traveling. It scared the hell out of me, but it was the kick I needed to make much needed changes. I promise, Leo, my health—physical and mental—is my top priority. I wouldn't put our child in harm's way."

"I never doubted that." He squeezed her fingers and Neha had to swallow the lump in her throat. "Have you spoken of it to anyone? Your mum?"

"No. I… There was something to deal with when I came back and—"

"You're struggling with a very serious problem and you hadn't felt like you could confide in her?" He nudged her in that infinitely patient tone.

Neha sat back in the sofa, a tremble in her very limbs. As if a truth she'd been trying to escape hit her in the face.

There was no excuse that she could offer that answered his softly spoken question.

He was right. She should've been able to confide in her mum, draw on her support. She'd been close to falling apart, and still, she'd had to make allowances for her mum, instead of the other way around. That the attacks could be used by Mario as some sort of weapon meant she'd had to hide it from her parent.

Her chest tightened at the pain of that final thread breaking in her heart. She couldn't fool herself that if just given a little more time, her mum would do the right thing.

Her mum might never do the right thing by Neha.

"New things don't grow unless everything that is dead is pulled away at the roots, *sì*?"

Neha flinched, an ache that had been building for years and years settling like an unbearable weight on her chest. "She's hurting me with all this, yes, but she does love me. Neither can I stop loving her, Leo. Love can't be calculated like a transaction."

"Tell me this, *bella*. If you had any inkling that our child was struggling with something like this, for instance, what would you do?"

"I'd fight the entire world to protect her or him. I'd take on anyone. Even you." The fierce quality of her answer was inescapable.

"Tell me what the doctor said."

"That it was chronic fatigue. I know the signs of an impending attack now and I've been trying really hard to avoid the triggers. But it's not going away until I fix the root of the problem. I work eighty to ninety hours a week doing things I have no interest in. I have no life outside of work, no companions, no friends."

"Which is why you want to retire," Leo said, concern in his eyes.

Neha hadn't cried even when she thought an attack had been impending, but hot tears filled her eyes now. And crashed down her cheeks, her control in shreds.

She turned away from him, embarrassed beyond measure, but he arrested her, his arms like steel bars around her, crooning to her as if she were a fragile thing. Whispering to her that she'd never be alone again. That he'd always be there to catch her if she fell. That she was the most beautiful, most courageous woman he'd ever known.

God, she should've had this with her mum. This outlet

to let all her fears out, to sob through the crippling fear, to have the plain comfort of another person's touch…there was nothing to be gained in hanging on to a relationship that only brought grief. "You're right. I need to let her go. But I can't do it overnight. I…just can't."

"I know, *cara*." Arms tightening around her, his mouth warm against her temple, Leo just held her for a long time, his body a haven of tenderness. "Describe the attack to me."

She took the rope he threw her with overflowing gratitude. Words came so easily then, piling on top of each other, as if they'd been waiting to be let out.

"I'd been working without a break for months. We were shooting a segment for my guest appearance in between my tour in Beijing. I'd barely eaten and I still hadn't adjusted to the jet lag. When the lights came on, I froze for a few minutes. I…had no idea where I was or what I was doing. I could hear people calling my name, but it was like I was in a separate world.

"It felt like someone was cutting off my breath. I fell to my knees and stayed on the floor until it passed. I… It was exactly the wake-up call I needed."

He held her like that for she didn't know how long, and Neha stayed there. Long fingers clasped her cheek, fanning out in a caress. "For future reference, I would like for us to not have any more secrets, *sì*?

"Your health, your finances, your business—anything and everything that concerns you, your future, this baby, I want to know. I want you to come to me if you need help. If you need a sounding board. If you—"

Neha placed her finger on his mouth, smiling at the pure arrogance in his tone. "That's a tall order. You can't just order me to open my life up to you with a command."

"I believe I just did."

"It doesn't work that way," she said, fighting not him but her own weaknesses.

She wanted to feel the tensile strength of him beneath her fingers any time she reached for him; she wanted to escape the increasing rift between her and her mum in his arms every night. She wanted to ask him to hold her until all the destruction she had begun was done and she could see the light at the end of it and maybe even beyond. "You don't want a woman completely dependent on you, Leo."

"Do not tell me what I want or do not want, *cara mia.* You shouldn't be under any pressure. Dealing with Mario and your mother is enough to begin with."

"But—"

"Learn to ask for help. Learn to take it when I give it."

Neha nodded slowly, knowing in her heart that he was right. She hadn't even conceived yet—she had resolutely kept away from the dozen or so pregnancy kits she'd stashed in the cupboard under her bathroom sink—and already she was on an emotional seesaw from morning to evening.

She looked down at her hands and then back at Leo. "I've spent years making myself self-sufficient. I can't undo it in a few days."

A nod of concession. "Tell me one of these things you outlined for us."

Neha pulled the laptop forward on the coffee table and pointed to the browser. "I'm going to put the flat up for sale soon."

Leo didn't even look at the browser. "Why? Its value is only going to go up."

"I've been doing my finances, and retirement means my income's going to be fluctuating in the near future. Also, I don't want to raise the baby in a flat. And since I have plans to experiment with some new recipes and start a baking school, I figured it would be a good thing if I buy land and have a house and an industrial-size kitchen custom-built. All that's going to need a lot of capital—"

"If you raise the child outside of London, I'll barely be able to see him or her."

The vehemence of his tone took Neha aback. "I understand that but—"

"Move closer to me. Whatever property you want or capital you need, I'll provide it. Keep the flat."

"That's not a good idea. Everything will get too complicated then and—"

He stood up so suddenly that Neha lost track of what she was saying.

"I made it very clear that I won't play the role of a stud that provides you with genetic material. This is a partnership and you have to start treating it as such."

Neha had never seen that hardness directed at her before.

Her guarded nature, her fears that she'd want more and more, would always come between her and the future she could have with him. And she was sick of living in that fear. She wanted to take more than one step toward him. She wanted to carve a place for herself by his side; it was all she'd been able to think of this past week.

She went to him and took his hand in hers. "It's not my first instinct to ask you for help or even accept it when you offer it but I'm learning to navigate my way through this. I'm learning to find a way to you. Uprooting my entire life, however, just so you can be near—"

"You began uprooting your life before I came into the picture, *cara*. Do you truly have such a full life in London that you can't turn your back on? We can't move forward with our lives with you determined to keep all the lines, Neha."

Neha smiled at the impatience peeking into his tone.

She didn't want to be alone anymore.

She'd need him more and more in the coming months, especially because she wanted his advice on some of the legalese around her retirement and IP associated with So

Sweet Inc. And because her growing hormones would only make her more susceptible to another attack. She couldn't forget that stress could always make her anxiety worse.

He'd already more than proved that she could count on him, that he'd be there for anything she needed. And yet to uproot her life in London and move to Italy on the strength of his words sent her heart palpitating. To see him with another woman down the line, when they called their own affair off, God, the emotional stress of that would be too much…

"What happens when there's another woman in your life? Can you imagine how awkward it will get with me trying to cling to the fringes of your life? I don't want to presume a place in your life—for me or for the child—and then be made to feel that I took more than was mine. I couldn't bear to—"

Leo placed his finger on Neha's lips, cutting off her rambling protest.

"No woman will come before you as my child's mother. I give you my word on that."

"It's not possible, even for you, to predict the future. You might fall for another woman, you might get bored of being a parent, you might want to escape with a—"

He pulled her to him by her shoulders, needing to feel her soft body against his. "None of these scenarios will happen because we will marry as soon as possible."

"What?" She stepped back, her frame radiating emotion. "Marriage is not a small thing you decide on on impulse, Leo," she said, mirroring his own words.

"It's not an impulse. I've been thinking about it for more than a week."

"But…why?"

"Think on it, *cara*. What we have between us—respect, admiration, an attraction that's not going anywhere soon and clear expectations of each other…it's more than most marriages have. We share the common goal of doing everything right by our child. Why not just make it official, then? Why these arguments over logistics when a simple, convenient solution is right in front of us?

"Both of us are too wise to get embroiled in love and all that entails. Instead, we can build something even better."

"But what will it mean between us?"

"It means fidelity and respect. It means we'll build a family, *cara*. Isn't that why you started this?"

Her brown eyes flashed with an emotion he couldn't recognize. "I have to think on this. Will you give me time?"

Leo nodded. He wanted her acceptance more than anything he'd ever wanted in life before.

For now, he decided to be satisfied by the lack of her objection. And really, she was a sensible woman and he hadn't expected her to jump with joy. He knew she would weigh every pro and con just like he'd done. And she would come to the conclusion that they were a perfect fit, just as he'd done.

However, he'd never been one to leave things to chance, either.

He reached for her from behind and drew her into his body. She smelled like the most decadent treat, her body warm and curvy and so soft against his. He shuddered at the press of her buttocks against his front. He caught his hips from thrusting into that behind with the last inch of his control.

Dio, the day she discovered the power she could wield over him with that sexy body of hers…

She didn't stiffen or pull away. Leo leaned his chin on her shoulder, his palms settling on the almost flat curve of her belly. The very idea that she might already be carrying his child filled him with a joy he had never known.

Mine, a part of him wanted to growl. *All mine.* It felt as if a part that had been missing from his life for so long had finally settled into place.

He pushed away the silky curtain of her hair and rubbed his stubble against her soft cheek. Sent his fingers questing up the dips and valleys of her curves until they rested right beneath her breasts. "While you decide whether you want to accept my proposal or not, there's no rule that says we can't indulge ourselves, is there?"

He couldn't see if she smiled or not, couldn't see if those gorgeous brown eyes had flashed with want that she had boldly shown him that night. But he felt the rise and fall of those gorgeous breasts, felt the tremor that shook her luscious body. He trailed soft, slow kisses along the line of her jaw.

She pressed her behind into him, and he hissed at the tight groove he nestled against. "I want to be inside you, *cara mia*. Desperately. In every way possible. And it has nothing to do with business empires, or twisted revenge schemes, or even conception.

"Just you and me and what's been there between us for so long. Say yes to this at least, *carissima*."

Her whispered, "Yes," was barely out before Leo clasped her chin and took her mouth in a kiss that told her he had no doubts about their future.

CHAPTER TEN

SLEEPING WITH A man wrapped around her—a mansion of a man at that—was a sensual feast Neha would never get enough of. As dawn filtered orange light through the windows, her entire body ached with the good kind of soreness; a lethargic sense of well-being, like honey, filled her limbs. They'd spent most of the last two days in bed—after almost a decade of wanting each other, getting the edge off took a long while.

While the attraction between them still amazed with its intensity, Neha was also aware that Leo was very systematically seducing her into accepting his proposal.

The space he created around them was like a cocoon of warmth and laughter and security and thrill. To reach for him in the middle of the night and find solid, dependable, utterly masculine Leo at the tips of her fingers—whether she wanted comfort or closeness or this mind-bending physical intimacy that was so good between them—it was a potent, addictive feeling.

With Leo there would never be a doubt that he had her best interests at heart.

She would always know exactly where she stood. There was a such a sense of security in that and a sense of freedom, too, especially after the minefield of emotional dependence she'd been navigating with her mum for so many years.

A real family with Leo was more than she'd ever even

conjured in her wildest dreams. So why was she hesitating so much?

Why did her heart stutter when he outlined all the rationale as to why they'd be a good fit? Why did doubts engulf her when she was away from him?

Was there still some naive part of her that hoped for the happiness that her parents had shared once? For all the pain her papa's long illness had caused them, she was sure her mum wouldn't trade the number of joy-filled, loving years they'd had together.

If she went into this with Leo, that naive part had no place in her life. She could never hope for more for this relationship than what they had now. And there was something very heartbreaking about that.

She reached out with her hand and found the other side of the bed empty. Burying her face in the pillow, she breathed in the scent of the man who consumed her thoughts to distraction.

She pushed up on the bed just as Leo walked back into the room, his hair gleaming black from the shower, already dressed sharply in black trousers and a neatly pressed white shirt that made him look painfully gorgeous.

His gaze took in her bare torso, and the heat in his eyes stopped her fingers from pulling up the duvet to cover herself.

Any awkwardness Neha would have felt over being naked with a man she'd admired for so many years, a man she'd always told herself wasn't for her in that way, had disappeared after Leo had pushed her to new realms of pleasure with his carnal demands.

Sitting on her sofa with her bum pulled up to the edge and her legs splayed open in shameless abandon, while Leo on his knees pushed her over the edge with his mouth and tongue and fingers, left no place for awkwardness.

Having sex on the rug in front of a cozy fireplace on

her hands and knees, his powerful body thrusting into hers while she urged him on to go deeper and faster, dissolved any self-consciousness.

Being taken care of afterward with tender, apologetic words in lilting Italian, masterful hands wielding a wash-cloth with tender care she couldn't ever have imagined him to possess, did away with lingering doubts.

Laughing about the rug burn on her knees and being fed crisp grapes and apple pieces by a half-naked giant of a man removed every rational defense and argument against not doing this for the rest of her life.

"Buongiorno, cara," he said in a voice that sent ripples down her skin, even though his blue eyes seemed alert, almost distant.

"Hey," she said, nothing more coherent rising to her lips. "You're already dressed."

"I had the chauffeur bring me some of my stuff. I have to catch a flight to Bali. Sorry if I disturbed your sleep."

"Is the honeymoon already over?" she teased in reaction to his curt tone.

"It wouldn't have to be if you agreed to just move into the villa immediately." A pithy curse followed the sharp retort. "The last thing I need right now is to worry about what Mario will do to you while I'm on the other side of the world."

"Stop treating me as if I were another obligation."

"What do you think the future we're building together means, *cara*? I'm obligated to worry about you, and you're obligated to stop being your old stubborn self and make things easier on both of us."

"You know it's not that simple," she said, sticking to her guns about not moving to Italy for a couple more months. Her fingers finally found the loose T-shirt she'd discarded only a few hours ago and she pulled it on. "Is everything okay?" she asked, not liking the sudden distance between them. And yet wary of trespassing where she wasn't wanted.

"Nothing that I can't handle," he said, turning away from her. "But I would sleep better while I'm gone if we make the announcement official. If you refuse to move there, I'd have to simply ask Massimo or Nat to keep you company while I'm gone."

"That's not necessary," she added, trying to understand that behind his high-handedness he was worried for her. That he had felt her fear when she'd described the panic attack.

"What's not necessary, *cara*? The announcement or the engagement itself?" he said in a rising voice that reverberated around them.

The tight set of his shoulders chipped away at her own rising frustration. She wanted to spend her life with him building the family they both wanted; she knew he would never hurt her…so why was she still punishing them both with her stubbornness?

Once upon a time, marriage and a husband and real, messy love were all she'd wanted. But Leo would never offer that. Did that make everything else less real?

Neha went to him and wrapped her arms around his wide frame and pressed her cheek into his back. Uncaring that she was mussing him up. She was slowly realizing she didn't want the perfect, larger than life, arrogant Leonardo that had dazzled her back then. She wanted the real man beneath that—the man that was determined to do the right thing despite the odds, the man who fought every inch of himself he gave. She shouldn't, but Lord help her, she did.

"You insist this is a partnership and yet, when it comes to your personal matters, you push me away. You don't share what's going on with you, you…you keep those boundaries around you so very tight, Leo." Her heart ached at how alone he always seemed, at how much burden he carried on his shoulders. "What is the point of getting married if you won't even share what's on your mind? If you're determined to keep me in the same box after all these years. Talk to me. Please. Share your burden, if nothing else."

"I'm not used to it."

She smiled into his back. "I'm not used to a giant of a man ordering me about in my own flat. But then I remind myself of what the giant can do with his crafty fingers and how he holds me when my mum's breaking my heart and how he finds ways to let me know I'm not alone anymore and I go…okay, I can compromise.

"I can let go of stupid, girlie dreams and reach for what's real. I can have an imperfect but real future instead of fluffy, romantic fantasies.

"I want you to be my husband. I want to make a promise to you that I'm committed to the life we build together. Watching my parents together all those years ago, marriage is the most honorable thing for me. If I make that promise to you, if I agree to be your wife, I take everything that comes with it very seriously.

"We've been good friends, lovers, we trust each other, but being a husband and wife…there's something about that holy bond that changes everything. I want to be the best wife I can be, Leo," she said, trying to articulate some of her fears into words. "But I can't if you shut me out at every turn."

He turned around, pressed a kiss to her temple. It lasted only seconds, but when their gazes met, she saw that her words had registered. That she'd surprised him with both her vulnerability and her opinions about marriage. "For me, marriage is a logical step. A way to make sure history is not repeated with our child."

She nodded. To hide the sudden shaft of pain that pierced her heart. "It is, for us. But it also means a lot more to me."

His frown slowly morphed into a smile and he clasped

her cheek. "Of course. I should've known you won't enter into anything without planning to give it your everything." And then a hand through his hair, his only tell, before he leaned back against the wall, putting distance between them again. "What do you want to know?"

Neha lowered her arms, glad that he was at least talking. "You never even told me what Mario said about that man and what he's up to."

"Just a lot of threats about what this Vincenzo means to do to our family."

"Any light on why he's targeting you?"

Leo shrugged. "Vague hints at how all roads eventually lead to my father."

"To Silvio? This is all connected to your father?"

"*Sì.* All these attacks seem personally motivated. Other than maybe a spurned girlfriend in Massimo's case, we haven't harmed anyone, on a personal or a professional front. That was a conclusion Massimo and I drew weeks ago."

She knew she was venturing into dangerous territory but she had to try. "Then why can't you simply talk to Silvio? Tell him about this Vincenzo's mad campaign against all of you. He can shed light on the whole matter. And you can clear it up with some sort of…reparation to this man, can't you?"

"You think a man who has continually launched attacks on BFI, BCS and on personal fronts on me, Massimo, Greta, even Alex, will accept reparation and move on?

"Not knowing what Vincenzo wants, waiting for him to make his next move while being unable to do anything… it's the most powerless I've ever felt.

"As for Silvio, my father is not one who will willingly come clean about every crime he's perpetrated in his life. The only communication he and I have is the deal we made years ago. He gives me proxy power over his shares, and I let him out of that clinic once a year and let him keep his friends. We've shared nothing more in a long time, *bella*."

"Leo, that's not…healthy. I know what an awful man he's been his entire life, but have you never wanted to ask him about your mother? Never wanted to find out why?"

"And play into the old man's manipulative games again? Do you think he'd tell me the truth, or some twisted version he could use against me? Men like my father only understand power. Do you think it makes a difference to me now? She left me with him, *cara*. I made my peace with it a long time ago."

"Have you, though?"

Blue fire glittered in his eyes. "*Sì*. And you get nothing by excavating a topic better left in the past. You know me better than anyone, Neha. Please don't assume I need a heart-to-heart about all this to get in touch with myself better. I want to solve this Vincenzo thing once and for all and look to the future. Not get mired in the past."

But was anything ever untouched by the past? Could anything new ever grow when everything that was hard, and painful, had been buried underneath? When emotions were stifled because they would bring pain?

Because that's what Leo was doing. Without pain and ache and fear, could there be joy and contentment and peace? Without the risk of vulnerability, could there ever be love?

There wouldn't be. Because Leo had closed himself off to all of it a long time ago.

And yet, she couldn't bring herself to voice those fears. She couldn't push when he wanted to leave it where it belonged. When he was determined to not let it mar the future.

His, and now hers. Their future child's.

"This trip to Bali…is it to find Vincenzo?"

"*Sì*. Massimo and Nat found financial details for an offshore company that originates there from the transaction to Mario."

"What if you can't catch him there, Leo? You can't go chasing this man around the world, can you?"

"But he's not all I'm chasing. Last I heard from her agent, Alessandra has been in Bali this whole time."

A soft gasp escaped Neha's mouth as she thought of the genuinely lovely Alessandra within this… Vincenzo's reach. "You don't think it's a coincidence?"

Worry etched into Leo's brow. "No. Neither does Massimo. Since the last organized dark net attack on BCS, we've been waiting for his next move. It's been months and he's been quiet and then we learn that she's been in Bali this whole time… Greta is going mad with worry.

"I have to find Alessandra and make sure she…stays clear of him." *If it wasn't already too late...* Neha heard his unspoken fear.

And now, after knowing how many things he handled, she couldn't blame him for being short with her. "I'm sorry I added to your worries."

"That's the deal we made, *bella.* But this is an obligation I chose for myself, Neha. Not had thrust upon me. Can you remember that?" He reached her, his fingers sinking into her hair at the nape of her neck. She nodded, her heart jerking in place at the distinction he'd made. "I don't like having to leave right now when Mario's furious with me. He'll manipulate you and use your mum to do it."

"I'm through with her," she said, swallowing the ache in her throat. "She's going to miss our wedding. She's lost her chance to be a part of her grandchild's life. She…" A sob rose through her, but she killed it. She'd shed enough tears over her mum. "There's nothing he can hold over me. I promise you. Go, do this thing and be back soon."

"Bene."

Neha rubbed her face against his chest, loving the solid

musculature of him against her cheek. Knowing that it was useless to deny herself and him. She wanted this future with him. She wanted whatever little he had to offer.

She swallowed away the lingering doubts and pressed her mouth to his. "I want that future with you, Leo. For the first time in so many years, I feel like I'm alive. I wake up with joy and expectations and…yes, I'll marry you."

His kiss said everything she knew he wouldn't say. It was warm and desperate and full of a longing that was more than just physical between them now. The velvet box glimmered in the soft morning light. Her breath lodged in her chest as he tugged her left hand up, and placed a warm, lingering kiss at the center of her palm.

His breath was a symphony against her skin as he took her mouth in a devouring kiss. The platinum set, princess-cut diamond winked at her in the weak morning light, and turned her into an inarticulate jumble of emotions.

"You play dirty," she finally said. *This was for convenience*, she chanted to herself as if it were a mantra, using it to corral her runaway imagination.

"That's a serious accusation."

She laughed at the seriousness of his tone. "You misunderstand. I'm not talking about that diamond. I'm talking about seducing me all night and then springing the ring on me when I have no defenses or rationality left. I'll agree to anything."

Her fingers trembled as he slid the ring on, and it fit perfectly. She kissed him this time, needing the intimate connection that came when they communicated with their bodies. Like every single time, the simple contact flared into something more, so much more, until they were both breathing hard.

When he looked at her like that, Neha could almost trick herself into believing he genuinely cared about her.

No, he did care about her.

"This feels right, *bella.* Everything I do with you feels easy…uncomplicated, in a way I've never expected.

"For the first time in my life, I'm building something for myself. Something tangible and real for the future. You, this child and what we build together…it's mine, all mine. *Only mine.* Untouched by my family's dirty legacy, untouched by the ugly past. A fresh start. There's a powerful quality to new beginnings, it seems, that even I can't resist."

Neha stood leaning against the bed for a long time after Leo left, his words ringing around in her head. On paper, she and Leo could have the perfect marriage. No lofty expectations of each other. No messy emotions. No high highs and low lows.

But life, she knew, was never that simple or easy to be ruled by logic and boundaries.

Even with all her rationale in place, she would always be vulnerable when it came to Leonardo. Already, she was far too invested in his every word, look and gesture. In what he said and everything he didn't say. And for all the distinctions he made, she was another obligation to a man who had spent most of his adult life shouldering numerous ones.

And yet, Neha knew it was too late to walk away from him. Knew her vulnerability to Leo meant her heart was already in danger.

Just as Leo had predicted, Mario walked into her office on Tuesday afternoon, his mouth curled into a sneer. Neha sighed, thankful that he hadn't brought her mum along at the least.

From the moment the news of her engagement to Leo had gone viral, she'd been on tenterhooks, her heart jumping into her throat every time her phone rang, hoping it was her mum. Hoping she'd at least begin to see that Mario hadn't been right about everything.

The glass door to her office barely closed behind her

when Mario erupted. "Have you no loyalty? No shame? Are you that desperate for him, for his attention, that you'd let him manipulate you?

"Have you no shame in selling out your own family?"

Neha let him spew his poison, let him vent it all out, before she said, "Are you through?"

"No. You'll wish you hadn't taken me on when you see what I can do. You think you have it all neatly tied up, don't you? Your retirement, your IP from the company, your engagement to Leonardo…you've no idea how fast he'll dump you when I bring my full might onto his precious company and—"

"Enough, Mario! I've heard enough. For years, I shut my mouth because I was afraid you'd twist Mum against me.

"So many years, so many wasted opportunities…and you know what?

"The worst is done. Despite my every effort, you've created a rift between us. No, she let you create a rift between us. She gave you that power and I'm done.

"Tell her that, won't you?" she said, tears streaming down her cheeks. "Tell her I'm done being the sensible one, the adult, the strong one. Tell her that I'm done putting up with her bully of a husband just for her sake." She swiped at the tears on her cheeks and took a calming breath. Still, her voice reverberated with conviction and strength. Strength Leo had given her.

"And you've lost any leverage you had over me. By threatening Leo, by threatening me, you've lost any chance I might have given you because you're her husband.

"I'm through with you and I'm going to take every penny that's mine from you."

For the first time in her life, Neha saw shock descend into her stepfather's eyes.

She walked around her table and opened the door. "Get out of my office. And if you threaten me like that ever again, if you come near me, I'll let Leo do what he really wants to do to you," she added for good measure.

In the ensuing silence, Neha slumped onto her chair, a sense of relief and freedom engulfing her. She lifted her cell phone with shaking fingers, her vision blurred.

"Neha?" Leo's voice came through clear and concerned.

"I told him off, Leo," Neha whispered, tears clogging her throat.

"Of course you did," Leo said with such conviction in his tone that Neha thought she might have lost a little of her heart to him on that phone call. "You must have been spectacular."

She laughed through the tears. "I was. Truly. But he's not going to go away calmly. On second thought, I don't know if I should've enraged him like that."

"You had every right, *bella*. And don't worry. I'll deal with whatever he brings, *sì*?"

"Sì."

"Will be you okay?" he said with a smile in his voice.

"Yes. But come back soon to me, won't you?" she said, letting the longing she'd always felt for him pour into words.

"*Sì, bella.* Soon."

Neha sat in her chair for a long time, the phone pressed to her chest. She looked around her office but there was nothing she was attached to here.

One chapter of her life was done. And one would begin soon. And she couldn't wait to start it with Leo at her side.

Standing in her underwear in front of her bathroom vanity, Neha checked the small plastic stick resting on the dark marble surface again and again.

Pregnant.

The world seemed blurry and distorted to her tear-soaked vision. She hastily scrubbed her eyes, afraid the word might change to something else.

It didn't.

It was her sixth pregnancy test and none of them had changed the verdict on her. And slowly, the truth sank in, filling every cell and pore in her.

God, she was pregnant.

With Leo's baby.

With Leo's baby...

Pregnant by the man she'd wanted for so long that every time he looked at her with that dark, knowing gaze now, she had to remind herself that it was real and not just a fantasy out of her head.

They were going to be a family, support each other, shower their child with love. After being mired in loneliness for so long, the dream of being a part of something would finally come true.

A shiver swept through her as she imagined the future, an intense rush of emotions and thoughts stealing her breath. Fingers holding on to the marble, she ducked her head, focusing on taking deep, long breaths. As she pushed her hair away from her sweaty forehead, her gaze caught on the diamond glittering on her finger.

It had been a week since the night since she'd agreed to marry Leo, caught up in the warmth of his sexy body and his clever caresses. And ever since that day, she'd been waiting to wake up to some kind of reality check. For some rational voice inside of her to say this was madness.

Instead, the weight of the ring on her finger had become familiar already, an anchor to ground her, a comforting, caring voice in her head when the madness of her unraveling life threatened to overwhelm her.

Like the explosion of media and fan interest after her and Leo's PR team made an official announcement. But in the effusive rush of well-wishes from her fans, Neha hadn't let herself forget that the rushed announcement was more for optics.

He was committed to a future with her and their child, but it didn't mean he wouldn't use it to put pressure on Mario. To show Mario that Leo was in Neha's life and he intended to stay. To push Mario to the edge where he might cough out any information he had on Vincenzo Cavalli.

A stark reminder that Leo was still unswerving and strategic when it came to achieving his own ends, that he didn't forget for one minute that this was a convenient arrangement on so many levels.

She ran her palm over her bare belly repeatedly even though it was too soon to tell. She couldn't wait to share the news with Leo. Couldn't wait to say goodbye to the pieces of her life that brought her pain and nothing else.

In the meantime, she still had to deal with the consequences of her confrontation with Mario, face whatever it was he threw her way.

Just a few more weeks, she reassured herself as she dressed in a white dress shirt and black trousers. She'd just finished her smoothie and put on her jacket when her phone rang.

She frowned as she saw Massimo's face on her screen.

"Massimo?"

"Hey, Neha." His greeting was subdued. "How are you doing, *bella*?"

"I'm fine. Is everything okay with Leo? What happened?"

"Leo's fine, *cara*. He's just busy dealing with things here at the villa…"

"Oh. I didn't know he was back from Bali already," she said, fighting the shaft of discontent settling in her chest. Why hadn't Leo called her as soon as he was back? After being worried that he was leaving her alone to face Mario at that. When they were so close to knowing whether they had conceived or not.

Her practical nature asserted itself in the next minute.

Honestly, she couldn't expect him to remember the dates of her cycle as obsessively as she did. The man not only ran BFI but managed a thousand other responsibilities. Sometimes, she wondered how Leo had sustained it all for so long.

"Neha? Are you okay?"

"Yeah, of course. Sorry, I just wandered off." She frowned as she sensed his hesitation. "Massimo, why are you calling me?"

"Leo had to cut his trip short since we got news the previous night that my father...our father had a cardiac arrest. Silvio passed away late yesterday afternoon at the clinic. Leo has been dealing with all the arrangements and, of course, Greta, and hordes of my father's old friends descending on us.

"None of us have had a moment to process it yet. Natalie reminded me that you probably didn't get the news yet."

Neha pushed away the niggle that Leo hadn't even thought to inform her. This wasn't about her. This was... about Leo. And his complex relationship with his father. This was about being there for a man who'd always been there for her, a man who seemed as if he'd never need anyone. A man who'd shown he was capable of incredible kindness and yet shared nothing of himself.

"When's the funeral?" she said.

"Tomorrow afternoon."

"Can you make arrangements for me to fly out there immediately, Massimo?"

Neha heard Massimo's relief in his long sigh.

"I just... I don't want to deal with Mario right now," she added when he remained silent.

"Of course. I'll have the pilot contact you directly."

"Thank you, Massimo. For remembering me," she added, knowing that for all the dysfunction behind closed doors, the Brunettis had always presented a united front to the world. Whatever his sins against his sons, Silvio Brunetti had been shielded by them. By Leonardo.

"I have my own selfish reasons for hoping you'll come, *cara*," Massimo said, throwing Neha for a loop.

"What do you mean?"

"I want Leo to have someone by his side. Even if my brother acts like he needs nothing and no one."

Neha stood at the same spot for a long time after Massimo hung up, thinking how right Massimo was.

Whether Leo wanted her or needed her or not, she would be there by his side.

CHAPTER ELEVEN

NEHA WALKED AWAY from the last, lingering group of guests as the sky shimmered orange at the end of the day, pleading the excuse of a headache, which was quickly becoming more than real. She'd been up since dawn after a bad night's sleep, and worrying about a showdown between Mario and Leo had stolen the rest of her sanity.

Most of the guests had already left—including Mario and her mum. Just seeing her mum while she had this momentous news to share but not being able to…it had taken everything Neha had to maintain her equilibrium. Not for a moment had her mum strayed far from Mario's side *even if* Neha had wanted to talk to her. With so many guests' eyes on her, in the end, Neha had simply been glad that Mario hadn't created his signature drama again.

But of course, he'd been busy in other ways, as she'd realized the moment she'd arrived.

In the two days since she'd arrived at the Brunetti villa, she'd been mostly on her feet, holding the fort on the home front with extended family and close friends descending on the villa—discussing the meals with the housekeeper, having to arrange rooms for their stay at a neighboring villa, keeping well-meaning but curious relatives away from Greta, while Leo and Massimo dealt with the massive media ruckus following Silvio's sudden death.

By the time the helicopter had dropped her off, the whole household had been in uproar in the wake of a rumor that Silvio had died leaving or selling his stock in

BFI to an unknown third party in the weeks leading up to his death.

Neha had a feeling she knew the source of the nasty rumor that had been making the rounds among BFI's board members. It was clear Mario was still not backing down. For who else would get such a piece of news to go around and around? Especially after the showdown between him and Neha herself.

Couldn't the circling hyenas keep their hungry noses away from his sons at least on the day of their father's funeral? How had Leo dealt with this for so long?

Greta, who'd always come off as the strong, implacable type with boundless energy, had been close to a nervous breakdown when Neha had checked on her upon arrival. Natalie had pulled Neha aside to tell her that the Brunetti matriarch had gotten other distressing news from her stepdaughter, Alessandra, who was still worryingly absent, on top of her son's death. Finally, Neha had called her physician, who'd recommended a mild sedative for Greta.

Natalie herself was young, inexperienced in real-life situations, so Neha took the ropes of handling people at the home front with Massimo's help. For all that Silvio Brunetti had brought BFI to its knees once, he'd still had a huge network. There were a lot of families and powerful figures that wanted to pay their respects to the family, including one cabinet minister.

At least Neha hadn't received strange looks or comments about taking over the hostess duties. Not that she'd give a damn about anyone's opinion except the one man who had maintained an aloof distance the whole time.

She only saw Leo in passing the first day and he'd done no more than acknowledge her presence with a nod. Most of the first night, she'd spent it in a restless slumber hoping he would join her, only to find out that Leo had only retired to his bedroom past dawn.

He had so many things on his mind, she knew that. And she'd never be the clingy, needing-reassurance-for-everything kind of a woman, but oh…she just wished he'd said something, anything, to her.

She'd have had a hint of where his mind was at. Instead, he'd given off the clear vibes that he wasn't available or willing to have even a quick conversation. The last thing she could do was throw the news of their pregnancy at him… in the midst of it all. She hated it but there was even a part of her that was afraid of what his reaction would be to the news in the current situation.

So, she'd acted like nothing was wrong between them and done everything she could to let him know that she was there for him. Having been burned so many times by her mum's fluctuating moods, Neha had stayed out of his way, like a docile puppy. When she was anything but.

That little niggle grew into resentment, with herself that she'd let him discourage her, with him for treating her as if nothing had changed between them, and morphed into a pounding headache.

Her pasted smile and polite words took too much out of her. She grabbed a glass of water and guzzled it down, remembering that she needed to take better care of herself. That tranquil quality she'd cherished so much on her first trip returned to the villa as the guests became scarce, but it couldn't restore her own spiraling mood.

Most of the staff was well trained under the efficient housekeeper, Maria, and wouldn't need further instruction. After thanking her, Neha checked on Greta—who still looked pale but rested— one last time and walked back to her suite.

Wondering all the while what was going on in Leo's head.

She wanted to hold him, and she needed to be held. She wanted to tell him about their child already growing in her belly, day by day, moment by moment. She wanted to see that glow in his eyes when he talked about their future together. She wanted him to tell her what his father's death meant to him, if anything. She wanted to talk about how close she'd come to pulling her mum away from Mario and spilling the news of her pregnancy. She wanted to talk about how scared and alone she felt when she saw that distant, aloof look he got in his eyes sometimes.

As if she were alone again… No, she couldn't tell him that. She couldn't throw her niggles and fears at him at a time like this. As long as he came to her, she'd somehow deal with it.

But would he?

From everything she knew about him, Leo was a man who retreated in times of grief, or pain. That glimpse she'd gotten so long ago was a one-off. Until he processed what Silvio's death meant to him and how little it should, he would hold her at a distance.

Thoughts in a turmoil, she unzipped her black sheath dress and moved to the closet.

And came to a standstill.

Why was she letting him decide how this would play out? They wouldn't have much of a relationship if she treated it like a paint by numbers canvas. Things had changed between them. It wasn't all sex and conception and business between them…wasn't that what he'd said? And when she'd needed him, he'd been there, so why couldn't the reverse be true?

She understood he'd been too busy to call her once he'd returned from Bali, too busy fighting the rumors that he wouldn't stay CEO of BFI much longer to give her two minutes of his time, but enough was enough. He wasn't going to compartmentalize her role in their relationship before it had even taken off.

She wasn't going to wait for his time and attention like one of Massimo's affectionate hounds.

She didn't want to sleep in an empty bed, not when he was only a few rooms away.

Not when she missed him like a physical ache. Not when she was dying to share the most important news of their new life together. And she sure as hell wasn't going to let him go to his room alone. If he was okay with her taking over at the villa, with acting as his hostess, then he needed to be okay with her moving into his suite.

Because that's exactly what she was going to do.

Never again in her life was Neha going to wait for someone to tell her what her place in life should be. Never again was she going to let someone else decide where she belonged and where she didn't. Not even Leo.

Zipping the dress back up, heels hanging from her fingers, she walked out of her assigned suite.

She found Maria, told her she'd be in Leo's suite and begged for a snack. Once in the massive suite, she stripped, showered, fished for something to wear inside Leo's closet and crawled into bed. The sheets were luxuriously soft around her as she sat cross-legged in the center of his bed and ate the bowl of fruits Maria had sent up. Stomach full, she pulled up the shirt and studied the curve of her belly for a few moments.

Joy was a visceral thing inside her chest, a tremendous force of emotion for this child and the man who had given her everything she'd asked for and more.

Her heart felt overwhelmingly full, tears filling her eyes. This house, this family, the man at the center of it…she wanted this for her, this future, so badly that her heart raced at an alarming rate in her chest. She'd do anything to keep it, to hold on to it. To build it.

She grabbed a pillow, buried her nose in it and was rewarded with the lingering scent of the man she never wanted to let go. Beneath the overpowering surge of emotions that took over every time she thought of the child in her belly, there was also a pulse of something else, softly calling her. Something that utterly terrified her.

She closed her eyes, tried to order her thoughts and frantically prayed to God that this was just her hormones already in play, that this seesaw of emotions was just the consequence of having to keep mum about her pregnancy for forty-eight hours. She wasn't resentful because Leo hadn't given her something she didn't even know she'd wanted. She couldn't be.

Her last thought before she drifted off to sleep was wishing he'd come to her for whatever it was he needed. Share a little more of himself with her.

Because she could walk into his bedroom and his life and take what she thought was rightfully her place, but his heart…his heart was always going to be out of her reach unless he gave it to her. Unless he let her in.

Leo walked into his bedroom after midnight had come and gone, his fingers wrapped around the slender neck of a two-thousand-euro bottle of whiskey. Half of it was already in his bloodstream but the liquor hadn't done a thing to numb him so far.

He had maintained his usual implacability in front of Massimo and fobbed him off because the last thing he needed right now was to be studied under a microscope of brotherly concern. Not that he didn't want it, but because he wasn't sure what Massimo would discover if he delved too deep. There was a volatility to him that he didn't want anyone exposed to tonight, not until he had it under control.

Everything felt upside down, and he hated that feeling.

A mere forty-eight hours ago, the news had reached him that Silvio wanted to speak to him urgently. But he'd put it down to Silvio having one of his tantrums and decided not to expend his energy and time on it.

Within a blink of an eye of that decision, Silvio had died of a cardiac arrest.

If not for the coroner's report and his father's physician's diagnosis that Silvio had been having a lot of breathing trouble for the last week, Leo would have expected foul play. Because it was so convenient for his father to drop dead right after he'd decided he didn't want to bequeath his stock in BFI to Leo and Massimo, after all.

Now there would be more investigation while the lawyers picked up the trail to figure out who Silvio had sold the BFI shares to.

For once in his life, Leo realized he couldn't bring himself to even care about who had bought Silvio's shares in the company or who was masterminding the whole thing, or what it would mean for his CEO position.

Cristo, he was bone-tired physically after two nights of practically no sleep and keeping his family's name above the rumor mill. Of course his father hadn't made it easy on Leo and Massimo even in this final step—the bastard. All he wanted was to numb himself until rationality and balance and his composure returned.

For his mind to stop going in circles looking for an answer to a question that was forever lost to him now.

Moving into his bedroom, he shrugged his shirt off, undid the button of his trousers. His eyes—gritty from lack of sleep and out of focus—took a few seconds to get used to the darkness. And then his gaze found her. His heart jolted like a drowning man given a benediction.

In the center of his massive bed, fast asleep.

Everything in him drilled down into a laser-like stream of focus on the beautiful, sexy woman, all troubling thoughts fleeing, all concerns dying, until nothing but she remained. Like walking into a dream where no questions existed, no doubts remained, no possible answers haunted him—only the present mattered. Only she and her sensuality, and her passion, mattered.

Moonlight drenched her body in sweet, pale light, and he fisted his hands, fighting the memory of how soft and responsive she'd been to his slightest caress.

She slept on her side, one arm tucked under her head, long, bare legs flung in opposite directions, her silky hair flying rhythmically with each exhale. Her lashes cast crescent shadows on high cheekbones. The shirt rode up high on her thighs, giving him a glimpse of a pink-lace-clad curve of one buttock, while the collar fell open to reveal her breasts pressed up together in a tempting invitation.

A flood of carnal hunger surged through him, washing away what even alcohol couldn't. Leaving nothing but the primal need to claim her.

Putting the bottle away, he moved to the head of the bed. His breath punched through him as he realized that the shirt she wore was his. It threw him, in his current mood, her clear claim to him, here in his bedroom and outside over two days.

Not for a single second had Leo been unaware of how seamlessly Neha had fit into his life in the past two days. Of how easily she foresaw people's needs and met them with an effortless grace. Of how calmly she'd handled Greta's impending breakdown with no input from either himself or Massimo. Of how strongly she'd faced her mum while he knew it had to break her inside for not being able to reach out to her.

She'd been there all day at the back of his consciousness—a calming presence, a landing place, when he wanted to keep the world at bay, centering him, even when he avoided her, with the practicality of her calm nature. It hadn't been easy to shut down the urge to follow her into that bedroom and let her see the growing void he could feel in himself and ask her to soothe it away with whatever magic she weaved.

Somehow, he'd fought it.

But now, seeing her sprawled like a queen at the center of his massive bed… As if she belonged there. Daring him to face her and the vulnerability he'd never been able to shed within himself. Forcing him to face things he'd rather stayed buried.

A soft moan left her lips and the husky sound went straight to his groin.

He knew he should walk away right then, knew that what he wanted to do to her, with her, was wrong after he'd purposely avoided her for two days. *Dio*, the bastard he was, he hadn't even asked how she was feeling.

Somehow, he pulled himself away and almost reached the door when he heard her throaty, sleep-mussed voice.

"Leo?"

The rustle of the sheets made him think of the soft fabric gliding up and down her body doing what he wanted to do. Giving up the fight, he turned around.

Hair in a rumpled mess, knees tucked together and away, the shirt—his shirt—unbuttoned all the way to her navel and falling off the smooth, rounded shoulder he'd sunk his teeth into the other night, she called to every masculine instinct in him.

"Go back to sleep, *cara*," he whispered.

She blinked, pushed her hair away from her face and looked around. "It's one-thirty in the morning. Where are you going?"

He shoved his fingers through his hair, his entire body thrumming with sexual hunger and the tension that came with denying himself. "I'm not… I don't think I can sleep tonight."

He swallowed the need flaring through him as her gaze swept over his bare chest like a physical caress. So openly she devoured him. Such hunger in that sensual body for him.

Cristo, he felt it a thousand times more. Especially now, when he knew that the fire between them only flared hotter and higher every time they came together.

"Okay, that's fine." Her words were soft, soothing, as if she were gentling a wounded animal. *Dio*, he hated this so much, hated his inability to accept the haven she offered. But he just couldn't bare himself to her now. "We can just talk."

"I'll only disturb you if I stay," he said through gritted teeth, his impatience and need swirling through the air. "And the last thing I want to do is talk."

She tossed the duvet aside, and threw her long, bare legs over the side.

Lifting the bottle to his mouth, he took a long sip. Her eyes followed the drop that fell on his chest with a lingering fascination that corkscrewed through his body.

"You're drunk," she said, her eyes widening, her fingers scrunched tight around the duvet. "But you never drink to that point. You hated Silvio's alcoholic rampages. You'd never willingly give up control like this. Leo, please—"

"You know me so well, *sì*, *cara*?" he said in a mocking tone that rendered her pale. "I'm drunk because I wanted a moment's peace from the million obligations that choke me at any given moment. Which is why I'm going to find a different room."

"I'll be damned if I let you call me an obligation."

God, even spitting mad, the woman was simply magnificent. "I don't really care what you get from that."

"Wait, Leo—"

"*Merde!* Let it go, Neha! Get some sleep. You've been on your feet constantly for two days."

"I didn't think you noticed," she said with a flash of vulnerability that pierced him.

"I notice everything about you, Neha." The words rushed out of him, emotion ringing in them.

"So you kept me at a distance on purpose," she said, the shadow of hurt in her eyes lingering far too long for his comfort.

Maybe it was better that she understood that he'd purposely avoided her. Knowing her and how strongly she prided herself on her emotional self-sufficiency, she would back off now.

"Yes. I had a lot on my mind, and I didn't have time to coddle you."

"Ah… I see now why you shouldn't drink. The ruthless bastard, the arrogant jerk version of Leonardo Brunetti, comes out to play."

Despite the dark mood clouding his better judgment, he smiled. "Now you know. I'm a mean drunk, just like him."

"Are you mad that I snuck into your room? Your bed?"

No, you were born for that role. For my bed. For my life.

The words stuck in his throat, like acid he couldn't swallow or spit out.

Everything he'd wanted with her tilted on its axis in the current state of his mind, everything that had been easy and good now felt as if it could choke him with all its myriad possibilities…everything she made him feel yawned open like a dark pit from which he might not pull himself out if he ventured further.

The Brunettis had a dark history of abuse and dysfunction. Massimo had changed it by reaching for Natalie and he'd wanted to do the same. Because it would take a woman like Neha to break that cycle, to rewrite a new chapter, a different ending.

Until yesterday, he had wanted that new beginning… but tonight, today…

"I'm not mad," he finally said, "but I wanted privacy tonight." He knew he sounded like a petulant boy.

In the blink of an eye, Neha was in front of him, a solemn expression in her eyes.

"I'm sorry about your loss, Leo. I know you didn't have an easy relationship with him. I know he was a beast of a father but—"

"No. Don't give me that. *Cristo*, not you, too, with lame condolences, not when you know how little I care.

"I don't feel anything at his death, Neha. Don't you get it? I don't feel...*anything*. He was a monster who ruined so many lives. When I got the message that he wanted to see me urgently two days ago, I brushed it off as if he were an annoying ant.

"Even knowing what happened after, I don't regret that decision.

"That's how ruthless I'm.

"This is the man you've invited into your body, into your life. I don't feel anything. I can't feel anything. There? Are you happy now? We've talked about it."

Tears filled her eyes and the concern in them almost undid him. "Is it really that simple? Then why get drunk? Why those shadows in your eyes? Talk to me, Leo. Burying your pain does nothing but damage us irrevocably. Believe me, I've done that to myself for so long until nothing but a shadow of me remained. I understand at least some of what you're going through. I want to—"

"*No*, you don't! You can't."

Pain burst open in the void of his chest, everything he'd buried his entire life flooding into this moment, this night cloaked in the dark, into the present he wanted with this woman, poison fouling up the very air between them, running unchecked, messing with his head.

He rubbed his hand over his temple. "You can't imagine what it is to be a five-year-old boy who wakes up one morning to find his mother's room deserted, who frantically searches her closet, every nook and corner of an eerily empty villa, who rifles through her drawers to find her things are gone, who runs around between the villa and the greenhouse and the grounds, panic beating out of his chest, short legs eating up the distance, terrified that if he stopped looking, she'd really be gone, terrified that if he stopped running, his world would crash down around him…who kept running until the physical pain buried the emotional.

"And today, when I face the question I should have asked him once—a single time, over all these years, the question that haunts me, the question that changes nothing of the past or the future or my present…"

And still the words came, into the stunned silence. As if he couldn't lock them away now that they'd been released.

"Why did she leave? Did he drive her away with his rages and his abuse? How could she go when it meant leaving her son with the same monster?"

"What is wrong about wanting to know?" Neha said, her palms on his chest, rattling him, rumbling him, still determined to get through to him. Her tears drew wet tracks on his chest, drenching him, crying for him when he couldn't for himself, her shoulders shaking against him. Grieving for him. Fighting for him, he realized with a strange fascination. "She was your mother! What's wrong with wanting to think maybe she'd had a horrible reason for deserting her son? With being hurt by their selfish actions—either as a boy or a man?"

He pressed his hands to her shoulders, feeling spent. Feeling that void take over again. Feeling the blessed relief of numbness starting to descend on him.

"Would Silvio's answer have changed anything? No.

"No little kernel of truth is going to shine a light in the closed-off quarters of my heart. I will never be vulnerable like that again, because I don't know how to be. This is who I am. Nothing will change the man I've become. Nothing will turn me into that boy again, open to hurt."

Tears poured down her cheeks and even now, when he should walk away from her, Leo reached for her.

"Shh…don't cry, *cara*. Don't waste your tears on me."

"I'm not crying for you."

He bared his teeth in a sneering facsimile of a smile. "*No?* Then do you cry for yourself, *cara*? That you get a damaged man who will never let himself be vulnerable with you? That you made a commitment before you realized what you were truly getting? Are you thinking of going back on our deal now?"

She wiped her face, a resolve in her eyes that threatened to knock the blessed numbness. "I'm not going anywhere."

He raised a brow. *"No?"*

Stepping back from him, she looked up. "No. However, since you've made it very clear that you don't want me here tonight, I'll go back to my bedroom and you can—" her gaze swept over his face and then dismissed him "—continue your drinking binge or whatever you want to do with yourself. When you're in a…better mood, come find me."

His heartbeat kicked up. Even ravaged with the ache she felt for him, her eyes smudged with tears, her mouth pinched and trembling, she was the most beautiful woman he'd ever seen.

And still, he wanted her.

She grabbed the duvet and wrapped it around herself, covering up the lush beauty of her body. "Good night, Leo."

"No," he said, grabbing the edge of the duvet, challenge shimmering in the very air around them. He tugged at it and she came with it, unwilling to give it up, fiery and sexy and every inch his deepest fantasy come true. "I want you to stay."

"Why?"

He needed anesthetizing from whatever she had made him spill. He needed to bury the overwhelming emotions in his head. He needed to isolate the scab and cauterize it forever.

He threw the bottle in his hand carelessly behind him and it fell with a hard thump against the sofa. "You want to make me feel better, *sì*? You want to be there for me? That's why you were here, in my bed?"

She licked her lips, and he tightened painfully at the memory of how she'd licked him up one night. It was a magnificent thing to be with a woman who went after what she wanted.

Sex with Neha wasn't just sex anymore. It was…something else, something that defied definition. Something he was already addicted to. Nothing, it seemed, was simple or easy anymore. And yet, in this, he couldn't make himself retreat.

If he'd expected her to flinch away, he'd have been disappointed. Shoulders straight, gaze steady, she was awe-inspiring as she said, "Yes."

"Then kiss me. Go to bed with me. Give me your body tonight." Arrogant demand reverberated in his voice and Leo hated himself for what he was saying, the reckless cruelty it seemed he was capable of toward the one woman who'd tried to reach the darkness in him.

Maybe the apple didn't fall far, after all.

He braced himself for a slap. For stinging words. For the fury that he could see brewing in her eyes.

The duvet fell to the floor in a silky hiss.

Her fingers went to the last three buttons on her shirt. No hesitation in those eyes or her fingers. She wriggled her shoulders in that way of hers that made her full breasts bob up and down, until the shirt fell off, clinging to her wide hips for a few more seconds and then to the floor in a whispered hush.

Desire hummed through his body, not even the alcohol in his blood curbing the anticipation swelling his desire.

Miles of smooth brown skin stretched taut over supple curves. The slopes of her breasts partially covered by strands of silky hair, the sweep of her hips, the soft swell of her belly, the muscled length of her thighs…she was a goddess he didn't deserve.

But she'd come into his life and he was damned if he'd let her go.

"Sacrificial lamb, *bella*?" he said, even knowing that he'd take her however she came to him.

A soft laugh from that incredibly lush mouth. A fire in her eyes. "I told you. I'm done with living my life for someone else. I came to your bed because I wanted to be here for you, *yes*. But I also came because I didn't want to sleep alone.

"I've already gotten used to having you next to me—hard and warm and solid and real." Such naked need in her eyes that it pinned him to the spot. Such vulnerability she exposed that it humbled him. "I want you. Inside me. Over me. Any way I can get you."

He undid his trousers, pushed them down and stepped out of them. Covering the distance between them, he pulled her to him roughly. One hand around her nape, he held her open for him, while he devoured her lush mouth. Her moans were a balm to his frantic need.

The other hand, he sent it questing—to cup her plump breast, to rub the pert peak, to follow the lush lines of her body, to trace the curve of her hips, to dip into her folds, to stroke and caress her core, to press against the bundle of nerves he loved to taste, to make her ready for his ravenous possession.

And as always, she rewarded him. So quickly, so easily, so generously. Her nails dug into his shoulders, her teeth digging into his bicep, her leg opening around his hip when he slid a finger into her wet warmth.

His heart raced, his body throbbing almost painfully.

He kissed her with a bruising need that showed no sign of abating any time soon. He filled his hands with her buttocks, brought her to the edge of his bed. She wrapped her legs around his hips, her skin damp, her eyes drugged with desire.

Leo took one more look at her face, then another and then another. Pushing her thighs indecently wide, he entered her without his usual finesse, his need far too urgent.

Somehow, from somewhere, he gathered enough sense to help her reach climax, moved her back onto the bed. Urged on by her throaty moans he climbed over her and slid inside her again. Fast and hard, he used her body to race toward their climax.

And finally, on the heels of his own thundering release, wrapped in her arms, her breath stroking his damp skin, came the quiet and calm he'd been seeking for forty-eight hours. And with it came the determination to keep the one good thing that had walked into life with him whatever the cost.

Leo didn't sleep at all. Neha had slept on and off between his urgent demands for more and more of her, as if he could chase away whatever demons prowled after him tonight.

"We're pregnant," Neha said into the quiet, inky depths of the pitch darkness of the dawn, a few hours later.

She was lying on her front, her face to the side, his body covering most of hers. His hand in her hair stilled; his heart might have come to a screeching halt, for all the breathlessness he felt in his chest.

"What did you say?" he said, wondering if he was making the whole thing up.

"I took the test before I left London. And then five more. They were all positive."

With shaking hands, he turned her, with none of the tenderness his mind was screaming she deserved. The shadows under her eyes were even more significant now. But her eyes were alert, studying him. And wary, too, as if she was unsure of his reaction.

Could he blame her when he'd behaved like a beast? *Cristo*, did she think he regretted this, her, them?

"Why didn't you tell me?" The question shot out of him like a bullet.

But of course, there was no answer she could give.

First, he had avoided her, then when she'd confronted him, he'd mocked her concern and then used her body through the night. Had she come to him hoping to share the news? Needing him to share in the happiness he heard in her tone?

Instead, he'd all but bitten her head off.

Cristo, he was a bastard.

"How do you feel?" he asked now, a hint of wonder he was beginning to feel creeping into his voice.

"Good. Mostly good." Her voice caught on the last part. Her gaze held his, asking questions he didn't understand. "You still want this?"

He cursed, instead of giving a straight answer. And still she didn't flinch. "Of course I do. Nothing has changed between us, *cara*," he said, knowing full well that the words were a complete lie.

Something had changed. In him. Between them. He just didn't know what it was or how to handle it or how to bring everything back to how it had been before.

"This is good, Neha. This is *perfecto*," he added with emphasis, and finally the wariness in her eyes receded.

She pulled his palm to her belly and it felt as if he could breathe again. He spread his fingers over the soft, lush swell of it, a sense of wonder and inadequacy surging up inside him.

"This is our future, Leo. All ours. Just ours," she said with a tremulous smile, before pulling his head down and kissing his mouth. A promise in the kiss, a demand in the thrust of her tongue, an anchor winding around him when he felt as if he was drowning.

Leo nodded, and took over the kiss, needing her, needing this. For the first time in his life, he felt as if he didn't know a way forward, but he wanted to let her guide him. He wanted to let her hold his hand and pull him along for the ride, but the gnawing in his gut wouldn't ease.

Tenderness and fear roped together to beat an incessant tattoo in his chest. Gathering her to him, he kissed her temple. Her nose. Her cheek. Her mouth. The crook where her shoulder met her neck. Everything in him shuddered. "Talk to me, *cara*. Tell me your plans for us, for…our child. Tell me your hopes and your dreams and your wishes. Tell me every single thought that comes into your head about our baby. *Please.*"

And as she talked about their family and their future, Leo listened, hoping that her voice and words would wash away the vulnerability that threatened to open up within himself again.

Hoped that the future she so clearly envisioned for them and their baby was all in his power to give.

"Massimo said you're leaving? Again?"

Leo looked up from his computer to find Neha standing at the entrance to his study, a soft, white nightie falling to below her knees, making her brown skin look strikingly gorgeous against the thin straps. She looked incredibly beautiful and utterly rumpled, though he had left her in their bed not an hour ago, her hair a cloud framing her face, her eyes full of that challenge he adored.

"*Sì*, I have to."

"Why? Exactly, do *you* have to, I mean?" Her question exploded into the silent midnight just as the door banged behind her with a loud thud.

He closed his laptop and sighed. Damn Massimo and his big mouth!

"Why are you up at this time, *cara*? The OB-GYN asked you to rest as much as possible after your high blood pressure numbers."

"Resting is all I've done the past week, Leo. And please don't treat me as if I'm a child who would endanger her health. Nothing is more important to me than this baby."

He nodded, greedily taking in the fierceness of her expression. *Dio mio*, she got lovelier day by day, fiercer minute by minute, when it came to the child she carried and Leo didn't know how to stop from wanting that same fierceness for himself, how to stem the desperate need to see the same wonder and adoration in her eyes when she looked at him.

For a few scattered moments here and there, he'd even caught himself being envious of that innocent life they'd created together. Had wondered if his mother had ever loved him like that, for a second. Had wondered if Neha would ever… *Basta!*

He had more than he'd ever wanted in his life and this fixation had to end.

"Leo?"

He rubbed a finger over his brow. He hated disappointing her but until he found some kind of balance in his head, he had to stay away. "What do you want from me, Neha?"

She flinched as if he'd raised his voice to her. "If you maybe take the time to answer my questions properly, instead of playing hide-and-seek with me, I can rest better. It doesn't help that I have to chase poor Massimo through the villa and the lab for information and that you keep enrolling him to be some sort of bodyguard for me while you go chasing shadows across the world."

Despite his reservation, he went to her, as if he was pulled by a magnet. "We still haven't identified who the new stockholder is. Alessandra is still MIA. Mario's rallying board members behind him, using your retirement announcement as some kind of backstabbing play from me. Until I discover who'll be coming onto the BFI board in Silvio's place, every rogue on the board thinks the position of CEO is up for grabs."

"I know all this. What I don't know is why you have to be the one to solve it all." Her fingers tapped at the shadows he'd glanced under his eyes earlier. "Why you have to be the one who shoulders all this. Why can't Massimo go for once?"

Because I need the distance from you.

"Because Massimo hates dealing with bureaucracy and strategic moves. And if it were up to him, he'd let the whole Brunetti legacy burn to the ground with Vincenzo and Mario and the whole lot..." He saw the question in her eyes and answered it. "As much as I hate my father, I can't be that reckless, *bella*. Thousands of people depend on BFI for their livelihoods. I simply can't let a madman with a thirst for revenge tear it up."

"Sometimes I hate that you're so honorable." She looked up at him then. "If you're not going to be here, why can't I just go back to London? I feel like a third wheel with Massimo and Nat, and really, if you're that busy, we should postpone the wedding. I'm really not sure if we should even be having a wedding this soon after your father's death."

He barely kept the bite out of his tone. "It's a small civil ceremony, *bella*. And for the thousandth time, I refuse to let his death have any effect on my life." He sighed, hating the wary look that entered her eyes. "Think of it this way, *cara*," he said, lying through his teeth, hating himself for what he was doing, "the sooner I figure out all this, the freer I'll be when the baby comes."

Her arms vined around his waist, her face pressed up against his chest, she stole the ground from under him. She gave her body, her thoughts, her loyalty, and yet it felt like he didn't have enough. "And that's all it is, Leo?"

"Sì."

He nodded, sinking his fingers into her hair. Wanting to run away from this moment as much as he wanted to stand there and hold her for all of eternity. Wanting with everything he had to tell her about the turbulence inside him.

The solid foundation they'd built with years of friendship was still there. He trusted her more than he had anyone else in his life. And yet…there was a new intimacy between them that scared him. A sense of everything not being in his firm control, himself included. A weight on his chest as thoughts of past and future wrapped up in a vicious cycle.

As if she'd weaved some kind of magic and created a chink in him. As if she'd unearthed a weakness in him, a vulnerability no one else had.

And he hated being vulnerable. He found himself at the oddest of moments wondering at how all this had started. He hated that she'd come to him because he could stand up to Mario, that she'd come to him because he was wealthy and powerful enough to protect their child, that she'd agreed to be his wife only for the child… God, he was all twisted inside out.

And until he figured out how to put himself back together, until he rid himself this ridiculous vulnerability, he needed distance.

CHAPTER TWELVE

See you the morning of the twelfth.

THE MORNING OF the twelfth was the morning of their wedding.

Neha stared at the message on her cell phone, frustration and anger rising like a tide through her throat. She threw the phone onto the sofa, and plonked down next to it, her hand on her belly. Tears prickled behind her eyes. Slapping her head back, she closed her eyes to stem the confusion overwhelming her.

They were going to be married in two days, and he told her over a pithy text that she wasn't going to see him before that? After another week of barely giving her any time and attention? And where the hell was her own self-sufficiency? Her composure?

God, she was too tired of wondering whether she was overreacting. If it was just her hormones or if it was truly Leonardo retreating from her. From their relationship, even before it took off.

The tears she'd been holding back for a long time drew tracks down her cheeks. Already, she felt heartsore from all the guessing, walking on eggshells because she didn't want to upset him, afraid what she might say that would be too much.

It had been three weeks since the day of Silvio Brunetti's funeral and she was at the end of her tether. She had meant to wait before telling him about the pregnancy.

But wrapped in his arms, her body sore from his fierce lovemaking, her heart tender and desperately needing an anchor to bring him back to her, to the common footing they had started this with, she'd blurted it out.

And he'd responded as she'd hoped, in a moment that had clearly been hard for him.

He'd kissed her with a tenderness that had her heart bursting, asked so many questions, kept her on the topic for so long that she'd gone to sleep a little worried about him, yes, but her heart full of hope that things would work out.

But the day after, he'd barely said goodbye before he'd left on another trip.

She'd given Leo time. She'd given him of herself when he'd been so angry and hurting and grieving, when all she'd wanted was to run away to her previously sterile and safe life. Where boundaries were not blurred and he'd been the immovable rock in her tumultuous life, her safe harbor when everything was sinking.

But now, he was the rocky outcropping she'd have to save herself from.

She honestly hadn't even minded that after that emotional outburst, after plainly rejecting her offer to talk, he'd wanted sex. Forget not minding, she'd needed it, too. She'd needed to feel close to him after seeing the pain of his childhood rip him open like that, knowing it was the only way he would let her comfort him. She'd needed to know that beneath the hurting, lashing out, he was still the Leo she trusted above any other man.

If he wanted to use her body in times of ravaging grief, she was more than happy to be used.

Because that's how much he meant to her. Because that's what she wanted this relationship to be—them holding each other through the worst that life threw at them, that was the family she'd always wanted to build.

But the aftermath of that night, the aftermath of her

impulsively whispered admission in the dark of the dawn, nothing had been right.

They hadn't come through that night intact on the other side. Something had been broken. Or reality had changed. For her.

Their lovemaking had a deeper level now, sometimes torrid, sometimes his tenderness brought tears to her eyes, and yet the rift between them seemed to grow increasingly wide, almost insurmountable. If she'd thought giving herself to him freely in his moment of pain would fix anything, it had done the opposite.

He'd retreated from her so far and so fast, as if he'd betrayed far too much of himself that night.

Oh, he was polite, and concerned for her. He watched over her like a mama bear, he granted her wishes before she could even think of them; he was the perfect lover, the perfect companion, and when they married in less than two days, he'd be the perfect husband.

The perfect husband, the perfect father, the perfect provider, and yet it wasn't what she wanted at all. Not anymore.

What he had promised, what she had wanted, was not enough anymore.

Pushing away from the sofa, she walked into the closet where her wedding dress hung. Panic was a bird in her chest, wings fluttering incessantly—night or day, wondering if she was making too much of nothing. Wondering if she was making a huge mistake. Wondering when he would do or say something that would bring her out of this misery.

The expensive, ivory silk rustled with a quiet whisper when she ran her fingers over it.

All the arrangements had been made for a quiet civil wedding, with only family present, but Neha hadn't been able to give up on the wedding gown. The minute she'd expressed a long-buried wish for an intimate wedding with a beautiful gown, Leo had made it come true within hours.

A custom design by an A-list designer specially commissioned for Neha. The straight lines of the dress highlighted her bust, falling into a loose drape from there as her belly was already rounded, to her knees. Stylish and elegant, it was Neha to the T.

It wasn't the traditional style or length but it suited them perfectly, she'd thought then.

Because she and Leo hadn't started in a normal way, either, but their relationship, she'd foolishly hoped, would only go from strength to strength.

A diamond necklace had been delivered yesterday—tiny, multiple diamonds delicately set into platinum wire—so exquisite that Neha was afraid to take it out of its plush velvet bed.

For my beautiful bride, the note had said.

And a week ago it was the tour of the ten-acre smallish estate he'd found on the shores of Lake Como where, if she wanted, he'd have the waiting architect design and build a state-of-the-art, industrial-size kitchen for Neha to play in. Mountains in the background and the lake on the other side, it was the most beautiful place Neha had ever seen. And only ten minutes from the Brunetti villa.

Interviews for nannies, a horde of lawyers to better settle the IP of So Sweet Inc., a twenty-four-hour companion/nurse to stay with her for the duration of the last two months and after—something she'd fought for instead of starting now. There was no end to the number of things he had arranged for her.

And yet…

Will you be at the villa tonight?

She texted him standing in her closet, her chest heavy with a weight she couldn't shift.

If he was there, she could ask him if everything was

okay. She'd let him hold her, like only he could, and they would talk. And maybe she'd tell him that she…

The answer came after a few minutes.

No. I won't be.

I can fly to wherever you are tonight.

There wasn't even that bubble that said he was typing.

We've hardly seen each over the past two weeks.

Her heart crawled into her throat, thudding, as she waited.

Nothing.

She sent another, something in her chest cracking wide open.

I miss you.

Most of her life, she'd spent it on eggshells with her mother, wondering if she was asking too much, wondering if she should be even stronger, waiting to be loved. God, she couldn't spend the rest of her life like that, too.

She didn't want her future to be like that. She wanted to tell him how much she missed him, how much his withdrawal hurt. She wanted to demand he open up to her, she wanted to tell him how much she…how much she loved him.

God, she loved him. She'd loved him for so long. She'd loved from a distance. She'd seen him grow into the most honorable man she knew, and today, she wanted a part of him. She wanted his heart.

She texted again, her fingers slipping on the smooth screen, her thoughts unfurling, her emotions unraveling like the spool of a yarn her mum used.

I want to be near you.

His answer came finally.

Only a few days and then we'll be a family.

A family? But this wasn't the family she truly wanted. This distance between them, this game he played with her, these doubts and confusion, this misery in her heart…

She wanted more, she wanted everything—she wanted his heart.

She jumped as her phone chirped. Fingers shaking, she swiped to answer.

"Neha, what is it? Are you unwell, *cara*?"

"No," she said, the urgent concern in his voice jolting her rationality. "I'm fine. I have an appointment in a week but everything's good."

The silence on the line stretched from relief to tense in that awkward way she hated.

"I just… I'm not feeling good today. In my head, I mean. This wedding and us… I barely saw you the last few weeks. I know, I know, you're busy with figuring out the identity of new stockholder and I just…this doesn't feel right, Leo."

"Are you having an anxiety attack about the wedding? I told you we should hire that companion full-time starting now."

Whatever choke hold had been gripping Neha, whatever second-guessing she'd done over three long weeks—castigating herself, telling herself that she shouldn't demand too much of his time, his emotional energy, pulling herself back, wondering if they'd return to that open, honest place before that night—all of it collapsed into dust at his careless question.

Fury vibrated through her so hard that for a few seconds she couldn't even breathe, much less speak.

"Neha, *cara*, if you're—"

"Will you come if I'm having an anxiety attack?"

"What kind of a question is that?"

"It's an honest question. Answer me, Leo. If I was frothing at the mouth having an attack, what would you do?"

"I would be there as soon as possible."

"Because that falls within the purview of the boundaries you've drawn in this relationship?"

"Neha, you're worrying me."

"I don't want your bloody worry, Leo. I want you."

"What's the distinction?" she heard him say and then sigh. "You don't sound like yourself, *cara*. I'll be there in a few hours. In the meantime, I want you to call Nat and talk to her."

"I'm not having a breakdown here, Leo. So stop. Just stop." A laugh fell from her mouth. "In fact, after a long time, I'm shedding that final shackle around my heart."

"What are you talking about?"

She knew she had to do it like this. Take the coward's way out. Because if she saw him, if he touched her, if he held her, if he looked at her with those beautiful eyes that promised so much and yet gave nothing, she'd never be able to walk away.

She'd spend the rest of her life, loving him so much, waiting for the little crumbs he gave her, wondering what would be too much to ask, wondering what was too little to take, wondering if she was settling again.

She flopped to the floor in her closet, her knees unwilling to hold her up. Her body shaking. Her heart breaking into so many pieces. "I can't do this, Leo."

"You can't do what?"

"I can't marry you. Not like this."

"Not like what? Neha, what's going on? What has got you upset like this?"

"I'm in love with you. So much. I've loved you for so long that you're a part of my soul. A part of me. And you…"

I'll never be vulnerable like that…

The words he'd said that night reverberated in the distance between them, mocking her.

She rubbed at the tears on her cheeks but more came. The silence was so deafening, as if she had said the words into a bottomless abyss and they would never be returned to her. They would only be swallowed up.

"It's so strange, isn't it?" Her voice was unbelievably strong, clear, in contrast to his silence. "I was so determined to keep this all rational and in between the lines. I thought, *I'm prepared for whatever little he gives me*. I have wanted you for so long, from a distance, and there you were, offering me everything, and honestly, I couldn't believe that this dream I had was coming true. But then I realized your everything is really…not much, is it?"

"So you'll walk away from this after all the promises you made? You'll bolt at the first hurdle just like my mother once did, like a coward? Will you make me a stranger to my child?" His voice was piercingly cold, soft. As if he were determined to remove any emotion from it.

"How dare you? How dare you call me a coward? How dare you turn this on me when you can't even acknowledge the hole she left in your life?

"And no, I'm not backing out, Leo. I'm doing what you taught me to do. I'm standing up for myself. Dead things should be cut away, *sì*?

"You're stunted. Your heart is dead.

"Even in your weakest moments, you never reveal yourself to me. Any time I get close, you run away. You will never be vulnerable. You will never go through that pain she caused you again, you won't even risk it.

"A month ago, even a week ago, I was okay with that. I

was going to have this family with you. It was more than I'd ever imagined having…

"But I love you so much and I want to be able to say it. I want to be able to show it. I want so much, and this little, it's not enough.

"This is me doing what's healthy for me and our baby. This is me putting myself first.

"I can't marry you and lose the rest of myself. I can't spend the rest of my life loving you and resenting you for it. And believe me, our child will be better off with two parents who live apart than two who would stay together and destroy each other."

Neha cut the call and in the terrifying silence gave into the sobs crashing through her.

Leo waited in the gleaming white marble lounge the maid had shown him to. It had been three weeks since Neha had called off their wedding. Three weeks since he'd discovered what Vincenzo Cavalli had been up to in the last two months, while Leo's own life had been turned upside down by the one woman he'd trusted more than anyone.

And yet, a day after the realization that Silvio's stock was firmly in Vincenzo's ownership, Leo found he didn't give a damn anymore. The man could raze BFI to the ground for all he cared right now.

"Hello, Mr. Brunetti."

He turned when he heard the soft voice. It was the first time he'd taken the time to study Padma Fenelli. Her hair was cut into a fashionable bob and she wore a beige pantsuit that was expertly cut.

The woman was a complete contrast, even physically, to Neha, from her fair skin to the fragile, almost elfin features to the carefully but expertly applied makeup. She looked like an exquisite doll that might break if handled even a little roughly.

Leo found himself greedily looking for signs of Neha in that beautiful face. But there was not the fire in Padma's eyes that Neha's held, no strength of character in the thrust of her chin, no fierce sparkle to her smile that Neha's crooked one had.

"Mario's not here," the older woman said, a small flash of belligerence in her eyes.

"I know," he said, wondering at the way she squared her shoulders as if she could take him on. "I came to speak to you. About your daughter."

Her fingers fidgeted relentlessly with a napkin in her hand, her diminutive frame shaking with alarming tremors. "What's there to talk about with me? You've ditched her just as my husband predicted, as soon as she's of no use to you. She deserves better. Lord, she's been strong for so long and she deserves better than all of us. And with all the social media sites positing that she's expecting, how could—"

"It's not a rumor. Neha's expecting. My child, yes. That's how this whole thing began." Even to his own ears, Leo sounded infinitely weary. The weight of the past few weeks without Neha had gouged a hole in him. "She wanted to have a child and she thought I would be the only man who'd take on Mario and keep him out of the child's life.

"That's the only reason she came to me. That's why she chose me."

Even as the last words left him, Leo realized how much bitterness he had amassed in the last few weeks at that. Yes, it had started like that, but *Cristo…*

I've loved you for so long...

The older woman crumpled as if she were built of cards, and despite his aversion to theatrics, Leo couldn't help but reach a hand out to catch the woman, couldn't help but feel that her worry was genuine.

"Oh, God, she's pregnant! My darling girl's pregnant? When is she due? How could she not tell me? How could you have abandoned her at such an important time? I have failed her, haven't I? I'll be a *nonna* and she hates me, my own daughter hates me and it's all…my fault. Her father would've been so disappointed in me."

Leo escorted her to an armchair and patiently waited for the woman to find her calm.

Her ramblings were incessant, the sobs rising up through her chest violent enough to make Leo realize how hard it must have been for Neha to walk away from this tiny, weak woman. To understand that for all the years of mistakes she'd made, she could still have a good heart.

Just like another woman who'd abandoned him long ago might have had. A sense of calm descended on him as if the small acceptance had burst through the darkness he'd built up inside him for so long.

He buried his face in his hands and let the pain of that boy steal through him. He'd never be at peace with that piece of the past but acknowledging the hurt lightened his chest. Cleared away so much baggage he hadn't realized he was carrying.

You can't even acknowledge what a hole she left in your life.

Neha had told him again and again and he'd just refused to listen. Because he'd been scared. Because he'd been afraid he wouldn't be enough for her in the end.

The fire in Mrs. Fenelli's eyes when she looked at him had him recalculating his opinion of her. "You're just as despicable as Mario said you were."

Leo shook her head. "I didn't call our wedding off. Neha did."

"Why?"

"It doesn't matter why, does it? Neha's the most courageous woman I know. But she still needs you, Mrs. Fenelli. Especially now. That's why I'm here. She believes that you deserve another chance. That if only you could be made to see how Mario has manipulated her behind your back all these years, you would not let her—"

"It's too late." Fresh tears poured down Padma's cheeks. "I confronted my husband last week. I watched the interview she did for that network, speaking out about her retirement and her anxiety attacks and being so brave in front of so many people, going it alone, again. I did that to her. I was so angry with myself and with Mario. I asked him why he'd hidden it all from me.

"For the first time in all these years, I argued with him, and in a matter of seconds, I could see the manipulative monster I'd subjected my child to for so long. My darling girl needed me, and I let her down. Again and again. I'm so ashamed of myself."

"Then go to her. She still loves you. And more than that, she believes in you. She believes you deserve her love even though you've wronged her. Even after you let her down countless times. Even after you…"

Even after he'd pushed her away again and again, from that night in the greenhouse to the night of his father's death.

I love you so much...

Leo stood up and walked to the French doors that opened up onto a beautifully manicured garden. For all the trust he'd claimed to have in her, he hadn't believed the simple thing she'd told him, had he?

She loved him. And Neha's love, like her heart, was all-encompassing, forgiving, strong. And he'd wanted it from the beginning. He'd wanted everything with her.

And because he'd been afraid of realizing that, he'd avoided her, retreated from her, trying to get a better handle on his own emotions.

On the slow but irrevocable discovery that Neha was the one woman who could make him vulnerable again like that boy. That she could make him hurt again. She'd held him and loved him when he'd been the lowest denominator of himself.

But what he hadn't realized was that it had been too late already.

He'd always loved her—wasn't that why he'd never gone near her?

Because with her, he'd want everything. *Dio*, look how eagerly he'd jumped into the idea of marrying her, of having her by his side for the rest of his life.

The knowledge came so easily now, so freely, as if the huge weight that had been crushing him had been released.

Maybe the past was truly gone. Maybe his father's death meant he was free of the questions he'd never asked. Finally, he was ready, he was enough to love the precious woman that had chosen him, even before he had chosen himself.

Or his happiness.

Now he had to make the same choice. For her, for them. For himself.

CHAPTER THIRTEEN

NEHA HAD WALKED back to her flat from her yoga class and was about to jump into the shower when the doorbell pinged. She frowned, wondering if her mum had already packed up her things at the mansion, even though it had only been yesterday that she had confronted Neha in the street market, tears in her eyes.

A smile curved Neha's mouth now as she remembered how much her papa had loved Mum's dramatic bent as he called it. It might have taken her mum years to realize how much distance Mario had created between them, but damn if she hadn't jumped in a taxi and accosted Neha the moment she had realized.

Not bothering to pull on shorts, Neha walked to the door in the loose, sleeveless pink tee and opened the door, a welcoming whoop on her lips.

The smile dropped from her face and something like a balloon filled her chest, stealing her breath. Sending tremors rippling through her frame.

His shoulder pressed against the door frame, Leonardo stood there. His unruly hair looked even more rumpled, his light blue shirt fit snugly across that chest that had held her so securely, his jeans highlighted the power in his thighs. He looked broad, rugged and painfully handsome at her front door. *Where he belonged*, the stray thought lodged in her head.

Fingers gripping the wood tightly, she stood there, unmoving, staring at him, while her body combusted with myriad chemical reactions. Every inch of her flooded with longing—a desperate weakness she'd foolishly thought she'd buried.

His gaze held hers for what felt like an eternity, unspeaking. A caress running over her face, her neck, her body. Down her bare, clenched thighs, to the gold chain she wore around one anklet, to her pink-tipped toes and then back up again in what felt like a rite in fire to her.

That magnetic gaze lingered on her belly, her breasts and then rose to meet her face again. Heat swept her damp neck and into her cheeks. Her head was dizzy beneath the desire humming into life as if she were a generator that had been plugged into the power socket.

God, all it took was one look from him and she was melting from within…

"I didn't know you were coming to London," she said into the thick silence, just to break the tension.

Because honestly, she'd done everything she could to keep him out of her life. Out of her thoughts. Out of her near present.

Which was damn hard with the fact that he'd sent Nat to her in London at the crack of dawn after she'd broken everything between them on that phone call. Damn hard to do when he called her like clockwork every two days to inquire how she was doing.

She'd been far too miserable to not have expected something like that from him. Just because she'd called off their wedding didn't mean Leo would stop looking after her. Or that she would stop hating it this century.

Keeping him out of her heart was another matter completely.

Because she still wasn't in a good place to deal with him. Still felt this powerful tug toward him. Still harbored anger and resentment and pain over what he wouldn't give her.

She wanted to be rational and clearheaded and reasonable in their partnership. Because he was still the father of her unborn babies…

Her composure nearly broke at the thought of the small clip sitting on her cell phone.

"Hello, *bella*," he said finally, his voice husky and rough, like it got when he was inside her. When he felt some strong emotion he usually buried deep inside. When he was so fiercely pursuing his pleasure that he had no control over himself.

Every inch of her skin tingled in response to that tone, her body loosening itself in some sort of ritual, awaiting the pleasure he gave so skillfully.

"It felt like a good time for a visit. We finally discovered who the new stockholder is."

"Yeah? Who?"

"Vincenzo Cavalli.

"Somehow he's managed to get his hands on Silvio's stock. Massimo is investigating if it will hold up in court."

"What does it mean for BFI, then?" she asked, knowing how much of himself he'd poured into the company.

He shrugged and her eyes widened. "Massimo and I can take on whatever he brings, *sì*? If Vincenzo razes BFI to the ground, we'll just build it bigger and better. I've decided to focus my energies on other things for now."

"Oh," she said, still struggling to swallow the overwhelming urge to throw herself into his arms.

She hadn't seen him in four weeks. She'd imagined how this conversation might go, she'd steeled herself for the impact of seeing him. But God, nothing was ever going to prepare her for the sight of this man. She was never going to look at him and not want to hold him with such force that it was an ache in her belly.

"Can I come in?" His voice was polite while his gaze felt hot, greedy, on her skin. Like in those beginning years when they'd still been learning each other, testing each other, starting to like each other.

She nodded and stepped back.

He passed her and the scent of him—so familiar and wrapped up in so many good things in her life—gripped her hard, like a vise clamping down on her chest. She felt the heat of his body surround her.

His fingers touched her cheek gently, tenderly, and retreated when she stiffened.

"You okay, *tesoro*?" Again, that husky shiver in his tone.

Or maybe she was going mad with longing and imagining things that weren't there. God, he hadn't uttered a word when she'd poured out her heart. She was crazy and hormonal to think something had changed.

"Fine. Great," she added for good measure.

She walked into the kitchen, aware of his eyes on her back. Pouring herself a glass of cold water, she downed it in one go. She walked back into the living room but kept the length of the sofa between them. "I'm meeting Mum for lunch and I don't want to keep her waiting," she fibbed.

"She came to see you, then?"

Something in his tone snagged at her. "Yeah. She… kinda accosted me when I went to the local market, crying. She apologized for years of not realizing what had been right under her nose. Said she was leaving Mario, if you can believe it. She said all those years ago, she'd only even accepted his offer because she knew she was too weak to look after me, because she thought I would need at least one strong parent… All these years, so many times, and for her to realize only now how much Mario harmed me…" Neha gasped, her hand rising to her chest.

"What?" Leo said, his tone urgent. "*Cara*, are you unwell?"

"No. I was so happy that she finally came to me, so happy that she… I never asked her. You…*you* did it. You went to her and told her what's been happening? You went to my mum and told her what's been going on all these years? You told her how much she hurt me? You…"

Her heart beat so rapidly that Neha thought it might rip out of her chest. God, was there no end to this stupid thread of hope?

She reached out to him, and he stepped back, as if he was afraid she might assault him.

"*Sì.* I did. Even before you broke things off, I knew how much pain she was causing. I was so sure you were better off without her. But you…you love her so much and I thought there must be a reason for that, other than the fact that she simply gave birth to you. I thought if Neha loves her that much, then there must be something redeemable about the woman.

"You were right. She loves you just as much as you love her. She's just not as strong as you are. No one is, *cara.* All she needed was some reassurance."

He'd gone to her mum for her. He'd convinced her mum to see the truth even when he didn't like her. Her throat tight with tears, Neha blinked. "Reassurance about what?"

"That I…was here. To protect you against any blowback you might face from Mario when she left him."

And just like that, he shattered her all over again. "Oh, of course. Thanks for that. For everything. You didn't have to come all the way to London to tell me that."

A shadow crossed his face. "What the hell does that mean?"

Her head jerked up. For the first time in her life, Neha saw beneath the polite, calm facade he wore like a second skin. Some emotion darkened those eyes. That flash of emotion exhilarated her, winding her up, breaking the tight hold she had on her own emotions.

"I just don't need a regular reminder that I'm an obligation to you, Leo. One of the million you carry on your broad shoulders."

"Is that what you think? That you're a responsibility to me?"

"Yes. And to be honest, I'm quite tired of it. I know—" she cut him off forcefully when he'd have argued and knew at the back of her mind that she was being completely irrational, but man, she was tired "—I know that I asked for your help. I invited you into my life. I opened the can of worms that's my family. But I'm honestly beginning to develop an aversion to the way you see me."

"And what way is that, *cara*?" His voice went dangerously low, and if she had any sense, Neha would've remembered that the more furious Leo got, the calmer he looked.

"As another thing to protect. Now doubly so, because I'm the mother of your unborn children."

A pulse in his jaw ticked dangerously as he waylaid her. His fingers on her arm were firm, and yet somehow so gentle. "You said children…why children?"

She buried her face in his chest. "Twins. We're having twins. A boy and a girl. I saw the ultrasound yesterday."

"And you didn't call me?"

"I was going to. I so desperately wanted to… But if I had… I was so desperate to hear your voice, to tell you the news, to ask you to…"

"Ask me what, *cara mia*?"

"I wanted to be held, Leo. I wanted to be kissed. Where does that fall in your duties? Will you kiss me out of obligation? Will you sleep with me because I'm extra turned on because of this pregnancy? Where does your obligation to me end? Do you see what I've gotten myself into? Do you think I want you to—"

"Shh…*tesoro*. No more. Shh…" A torrent of Italian flew from his mouth—lilting and gentle and a litany of warmth and joy. He kissed every inch of her face—her eyes, her temple, the tip of her nose, her cheek and then, finally, her mouth.

Her body arched into his, as if he were her homing beacon, her home, her salvation. He kissed her with a desperation that mirrored her own, sweeping into the warm cavern of her mouth, his hands incredibly gentle as they moved all over her body, his mouth breaking into tender words in between. "I love you so much that it terrifies me, *sì*?

"You declared so boldly that you loved me and I ran even from that. I went to talk to your mum and I realized the weight of your words to me…

"I loved you for so long, always, maybe. But I didn't know what love was. I couldn't see it even when you told me. I couldn't see past the fear that if I opened myself up, you might leave me. You might hurt me.

"Loving you…it makes me quake in my handmade loafers." He was laughing and Neha was crying and she didn't know if it was a dream or real.

His rough hands clasped her face, pulling her up, and when she looked into his eyes, Neha knew it was all real. "But loving you also makes me joyous. I'm finally at peace. Like a piece I hadn't known was missing has been slotted in. Like I could finally let go of the past.

"I wake up in the morning and dream about our future. Loving you makes me stronger and yet somehow weaker at the same time.

"But if you will have me—only because I couldn't bear to spend another day without you—I will spend the rest of my life proving to you that I'm enough to love you, *cara*."

Neha pressed her mouth to his and tasted her own tears. "Of course you're enough, Leo. All I wanted was a tiny piece of your heart. All I wanted was a foothold, my love."

"You helped me discover my heart is whole. It is all yours."

Tears overflowed from her eyes again and Leo wiped

them away, his own alarmingly wet. Hands on her shoulders, he held her at arm's length and let his gaze take her in.

Dio, this incredibly gorgeous, strong woman was his. All his. He fell to his knees and placed his forehead on the swell of her belly. Then he kissed it, wonder filling him at the change in her body. Then he looked up into those beautiful brown eyes. "I had nothing until you came into my life. Thanks for loving me, *bella*, for choosing me. For you. And for these babies."

She came into his arms like lightning and took his mouth in a hot, possessive kiss that got his blood thrumming. "I'll always choose you, darling. Always."

EPILOGUE

Three years later

NEHA PULLED THE fresh batch of cinnamon rolls out of the monstrous oven that she still hadn't gotten used to, and placed them with great care onto a ceramic plate. It was a waste of time and effort, she knew, but she still liked seeing her handiwork beautifully arranged, even for a few seconds.

Even if her audience hadn't developed an aesthetic sense along with a palate.

She poured cold milk into the glass carafe and carried the whole thing out into the backyard, which had a view of beautiful Lake Como.

She'd barely put the tray down when two pairs of grubby hands reached for the rolls and her carefully crafted tower was demolished into a blob. When she'd have run after the screeching toddlers with a roll in one hand and a plastic shovel in the other, strong arms gripped her from the back and held her arrested in a cocoon of heat and hardness she couldn't resist to this day.

Maybe never.

"Let them be," Leo whispered at her ear, and then buried his face in the crook of her neck. The press of his warm mouth at her pulse sent shivers spewing over her skin. "Your mum will watch them."

"My mum's a fragile, delicate thing and those children of yours are two monsters. Maya, somehow, you can still reason with. But Matteo… God, Leo, he's already a little terror the way you let him do whatever he wants."

"He's two, *cara mia.* I don't have the heart to tell him to stop digging for treasure or tell Maya she's responsible for her brother. He'll learn when it's time how to behave. Let them be children. For as long as possible."

Neha sighed and swept her arms around his neck, sank her fingers into his hair, knowing that her husband was a marshmallow when it came to their children. And a natural at it, too. "Fine. Don't come to me when he's a moody, spoiled teenager."

Leo's hands pushed up her blouse until his roughened hands reached the skin beneath. He stroked her skin, the fingertips reaching up and up until she heard her breath hitch. "Maybe what they need is company. You wouldn't be up for another set, would you?"

"Another set of what?" Neha demanded, even as she pressed herself shamelessly into the hardness nestled between her buttocks.

"Twins, *cara mia.* We'll ask Massimo and Nat to babysit, go on a proper honeymoon this time and get to working on that. *Sì?"*

"Sì," Neha whispered before turning her mouth for his voracious kiss. "*Sì* to anything you suggest, darling," she whispered, and he laughed, those blue eyes shining with love. And Neha knew that even thirty years later she'd still be shaking at the knees when he looked at her like that.

"Ti amo, tesoro," he whispered before he claimed her mouth with his.

* * * * *

CHRISTMAS CONTRACT FOR HIS CINDERELLA

JANE PORTER

CHAPTER ONE

MONET WILDE WAS in the back room on the fifth floor of Bernard Department Store, searching for a customer's missing gown, which she was sure had gone to alterations but apparently had never actually arrived there, when one of her salesgirls appeared, informing her that a gentleman was waiting for her, and while he was brusque, he was not as irritable as Mrs. Wilkerson, who couldn't understand how her daughter's bridal gown could just disappear.

Monet sighed and reached up to smooth a dark tendril that had come loose from her neat chignon, aware that she dressed more matronly than most matrons, but as the manager of the bridal department it was important to maintain a sense of decorum. "Did he say what he wants?" she asked with a glance at the clock on the stockroom wall. Fifteen minutes until closing. Fifteen minutes to find a very expensive gown for a very irate mother of the bride.

"You." The salesgirl's expression turned rueful. "Well, he asked for you. By name."

Monet's heart fell. "Tell me we haven't misplaced another gown."

"He didn't say. He just asked for you."

Monet's frown deepened. It had been a maddeningly busy day at Bernard's, the kind of busy that characterized Christmas shopping on a weekend in December. The customers had descended in hordes the moment the department-store doors opened this morning at nine, and the queues and demands had been endless. Apparently everyone had decided that an impromptu wedding was in order, and what could be more festive than getting married on Christmas, or a destination wedding for New Year's? Monet had spent hours already on the phone calling designers, other stores, seamstresses, trying to find out what was available, and what could be done with gowns that might be available, and she still had a dozen things to do before closing.

"Does he have a name?" Monet asked.

"Marcus Oberto, or something like that. He's Italian."

Monet froze, even as she silently corrected the girl. Marcu Uberto was the name, and Marcu wasn't Italian, but Sicilian.

"I told him you were quite busy," the girl added. "But he said he'd wait. He said to take your time and there was no rush."

Monet didn't believe that for a second. Marcu was not a man to be kept waiting.

And yet what was he doing here? And why now?

Those two questions circled her brain, creating unwanted anxiety. She hadn't seen Marcu in eight years, and the last time she'd heard from him had been almost three years ago to the day. What could he possibly want this close to Christmas?

"Shall I give him a message?" the salesgirl asked with a cheeky smile. "I don't mind. He's seriously sexy. But then I adore Italians, don't you?"

Sicilian, Monet again silently corrected.

Marcu was Sicilian to the bone.

"Thank you for the offer," Monet said, "but I'll need to handle Signor Uberto. However, you could help me by phoning Mrs. Wilkerson and let her know we haven't forgotten her, and we should have news about the missing bridal gown first thing in the morning."

"Will we?" the girl replied, wrinkling her brow.

Monet couldn't even imagine the fallout if they didn't have good news. "We had better," Monet said firmly, squaring her shoulders and heading from the stockroom to face Marcu.

She spotted him immediately as she emerged through the silver-and-gray curtains. He stood in the center of the marbled floor, commanding the space, which was something since the fifth floor of Bernard's was topped by a glass dome and there was nothing but airy space on the bridal floor.

Tall, and broad through the shoulders, Marcu looked every inch the powerful wealthy aristocrat. Sophisticated and impeccably dressed in a charcoal suit and crisp white shirt—a suit and shirt she was certain from the tailoring had been made just for him. He'd paired the severe suit with a brilliant blue tie to set off his glossy black hair and piercing blue eyes. Eight years ago he'd worn his thick black hair long, but now it was cropped short and combed severely back from his brow while a hint of a shadow darkened his strong, angled jaw.

Monet's pulse pounded, and her mouth dried as she fought back a wave of memories—memories she couldn't bear to deal with on a night like this. Fortunately, he hadn't yet seen her, and she was grateful for small mercies as she fought to control her breathing, and center herself. She'd worked so hard to block the past that she felt wildly unprepared for dealing with Marcu Uberto in her present.

"Courage and calm," she whispered to herself. *"You can do this."*

"Marcu," she said politely, approaching him. "What brings you to Bernard's? Is there a gift, or purchase I can help you with?"

* * *

Monet. A streak of icy hot sensation raced through him at the sudden sound of her voice, a voice he'd know anywhere. It wasn't low or high, but there was a warmth to her tone, a sweetness, that matched her warm, sweet personality.

He turned to face her, half expecting the girl he'd last seen—petite, laughing, unassuming—but that wasn't the woman before him. The Monet he'd known in Palermo had a quick smile and bright golden-brown eyes, but this Monet was incredibly slender with a guarded gaze and firm full lips that looked as if they rarely smiled. She certainly wasn't smiling now, and with her hair drawn back, and dressed in a matronly lavender and gray tweed knit sheath dress with a matching knit jacket, she looked older than her twenty-six years.

"Hello, Monet," he said, moving forward to kiss her on each cheek.

She barely tolerated his cheek grazing hers before stepping quickly away. "Marcu," she replied quietly, unemotionally.

No, she wasn't happy to see him in her workspace, but then he hadn't expected her to welcome him with open arms.

"I've come to see you on a personal matter," he said, matching her detached tone. "I'd hoped that by coming here near to closing time, I would be able to steal you away afterward so we could talk without distractions."

Her already guarded expression shuttered completely, leaving her pretty features utterly blank. Once he'd known her so well that he could read all of her thoughts. He could read nothing now.

"The store might be closing soon," she answered with a small, stiff smile, "but unfortunately I'll be here for another hour. I still have orders to process and missing items to be found. Perhaps next time you're in London—with advance notice—we could have that visit?"

"The last time I was in London you refused to see me."

"Our schedules prevented it."

"No, Monet, *you* prevented it." His eyes met hers and held. "I won't be put off this time. I'm here, and happy to wait until you've finished."

"You won't be allowed to remain in the building after we close."

"Then I'll wait in my car." He glanced around the floor with its sleek silver Christmas trees and elegant decorations. "But why will it take you an hour to wrap things up? There's no one here. Everyone but your colleague has gone."

"I'm the manager and this is my department, so it falls to me to take care of all the pieces." She paused, her gaze lifting to meet his. "Surely you don't really want me to explain all the details of my job to you? I can't imagine you're that interested in bridal retail."

"I'm not surprised you opened and closed."

"It was an unusual day. We're short-staffed." She hesitated. "How did you know I opened?"

"I was here this morning. You were extremely busy so I left, and returned four hours ago. You were also very busy then, so here I am now."

She'd held his gaze the entire time, and while her features remained neutral, her brown eyes burned with intensity. "Has something happened?" she asked, her husky voice dropping even lower.

"There has been no accident, no tragedy."

"I don't understand then why you're here."

"I need your help."

"Mine?"

"Yes. You might recall that you owe me, and I've come to collect on that favor."

She seemed to stop breathing then, and he watched the heat fade from her eyes until they were glacier-cool. "I have much to do tonight, Marcu. This is not a good night."

He gestured to the pair of charcoal velvet armchairs near the platform and the tall trio of gilt-framed mirrors. "Would it be easier to just speak now?"

He saw her indecision and then she gave a curt nod. "Yes. Fine. Let's talk now," she said before walking to the chairs and sitting down on the edge of one, ankles crossing neatly under the chair.

Monet's heart hammered as Marcu followed her to the chairs backed by huge framed mirrors, and then took his time sitting down. The trio of mirrors gave her views of him from all angles as he first unbuttoned his dark jacket, and then sat down, all fluid grace and strength, before adjusting the cuff of his shirt, making sure it fit just so.

This was her workplace, and her floor, and yet he managed to make her feel as if she was the outsider…the imposter. Just as she'd been as a girl, living in the Uberto palazzo, supported by his father. Monet hated remembering. She hated being dependent on anyone. And she very much resented Marcu's appearance and reminder that she owed him.

She did owe him, too.

Years ago Marcu had come to her aid, providing an airline ticket and a loan when she needed to escape a difficult situation. He must have known there would be questions, and consequences, but he'd bought the airline ticket to London for her, anyway, and sent her with cash in her pocket, allowing her to escape Palermo, which is where the Uberto family lived, as did Monet's mother, who was Marcu's father's mistress.

Marcu had warned her as he'd dropped her off at the

airport in Palermo that one day he would call in the favor. Monet was so desperate to escape that she'd blindly agreed. It had been eight years since that flight out of Palermo. It had been eight years since Marcu had told her that one day he would settle the score. It seemed that day was now. He had finally called in the favor.

"I need you for the next four weeks," he said, extending long legs. "I know you were once a nanny, and you were always good with my brother and sisters. Now I need you to take care of my three."

She hadn't heard from him in years. She'd avoided all mention of the aristocratic Sicilian Uberto family in years, the Uberto palazzo was one of the oldest and most luxurious in Palermo, and yet now he was here, asking her to drop everything to take care of his children. It would be laughable if it had been anyone else making such demands, but this was Marcu and that changed everything.

Monet drew a quick breath and shaped her smile, wanting to appear sympathetic. "As much as I'd like to help you, I really can't. This is a terrible time for me to take leave from my work here, as retail depends on Christmas, and then there are my own clients. I'm quite protective of my anxious Christmas and New Year's brides."

"I'm more protective of my children."

"As you should be, but you're asking the impossible of me. I won't be permitted to take any leave now."

"Then give notice."

"I can't do that. I love my work here, and I've fought hard for this position."

"I need you."

"You don't need *me*. You need a caregiver, a professional nanny. Hire a proper, skilled child-minder. There are dozens of agencies that cater to exclusive clientele—"

"I will not trust my children with just anyone. But I will trust them with you."

She wasn't flattered. The very last thing she wanted to do was to take care of Marcu's children. She and Marcu had not parted on good terms. Yes, he'd helped finance her escape from Palermo, but *he* was the reason she'd had to leave Sicily in the first place. He'd broken her eighteen-year-old heart, and shattered her confidence. It had taken her years to build up her self-esteem again.

"I appreciate the vote of confidence," she retorted calmly. "But I can't leave Bernard's at this time of year. I have an entire department that depends on me."

"I'm calling in my favor."

"Marcu."

He simply looked at her, saying no more, but then, nothing else needed to be said on his part. They both knew she had agreed to return the favor. It was the only condition he'd made when he'd helped her leave Palermo. That one day he'd call in the favor, and when he did, she needed to help, and she'd agreed. As the years passed, Monet had come to hope—believe—that he would never need her. She'd hoped—believed—that he was so successful and comfortable that he'd forget the promise he'd extracted from her as he drove her to the airport. She'd grown so hopeful that he'd forgotten, that she herself had almost forgotten, that such a promise had even been made.

But clearly he hadn't, and that's all that mattered now. "This is not a good time to call in the favor," she murmured huskily.

"I wouldn't be here if it was a good time."

She looked away, brow knitting as she looked toward the huge Palladian-style window that dominated the fifth floor, adding to the department's restrained elegance. A few fat white flakes seemed to be floating past the glass. It wasn't snowing, was it?

"I promise to put in a good word with Charles Bernard," Marcu added. "I know him quite well, and I'm confident he will hold your position for you, and if not, I promise to help you find another job in January, after the wedding."

The wedding?

That caught her attention and she turned from the window and the snow to look at Marcu. His blue gaze met hers and held.

Marcu was still Marcu—brilliant, confident, arrogant, self-contained—and for a moment she was that eighteen-year-old girl again, desperate to be in his arms, in his life, in his heart. And then she collected herself, reminding herself that she wasn't eighteen; years had passed and thankfully they weren't the same people. At least, she wasn't the same girl. She wasn't attracted to him. She felt nothing for him.

So why the sudden frisson of awareness shooting through her, warming her from the inside out?

"I'm afraid you lost me," she said huskily. "What wedding?"

"Mine." He hesitated for a moment, then added, "Perhaps you didn't know that my wife died shortly after my youngest was born."

Monet had known, but she'd blocked that from her mind, too.

"I'm sorry," she said, fixing her gaze on the sharp knot of his blue tie, the silk gleaming in the soft overhead light. Of course he was exquisitely tailored. Marcu looked sleek and polished, Italian style and sophistication personified. Perhaps if she kept her attention fixed to the crisp white points of his collar, and the smooth lapels of his jacket, she could keep from seeing the face she'd once loved. It had taken her forever to get over him, and she would not allow herself to feel any attraction, or interest, or concern or affection.

"I need help with the children until after the wedding, and then it will get easier," he said. "I won't need your assistance longer than four weeks. Five, if it's really rough going."

Four or five weeks, working with him? Minding his children while he married again? "Does that include the honeymoon?" she asked drily.

He shrugged. "I have a conference mid-January in Singapore. I'm speaking so it depends on Vittoria if she'd like to make that our honeymoon."

Monet was appalled but it was none of her business. She wasn't going to get involved. "I can't do it. I'm sorry, but I've already paid you back the cost of the airline ticket, and the cash you lent me, with interest. Our debt should be settled."

"The debt is settled, the favor is not."

"They are one and the same."

"No, they are not one and the same. You do not owe me financially, but you owe me for the position you put me in when you left the palazzo, and the speculation you created by abruptly departing without saying goodbye to your mother, my father, my brother and sisters. You put me in a most difficult position, and that is the score that is to be settled now as once again I am in a difficult position and this time you *can* help me."

It crossed her mind that she could argue this point forever with him, but he would never change his stance. Marcu was fixed. He was absolutely immovable. Even at twenty-five he'd been mentally strong, physically strong, a force to be reckoned with. Perhaps that had been his appeal. Monet had been raised by a woman who couldn't put down permanent roots, and didn't know how to make a home, or even make responsible decisions. Monet's mother, Candie, was impulsive and irrational. Marcu was the opposite. He was analytical, cautious, risk-averse. He was reason personified.

The only time he'd ever surprised her was the night he'd kissed her, and made love to her, only stopping short of taking her virginity. And then his regret, and his scorn, had scarred her. In mere minutes he'd gone from passionate and sensual, to callous and cold.

Monet had left less than fourteen hours later, flying out of Palermo with nothing but the smallest knapsack of clothing. She owned very little. She and her mother had lived off the generosity of Marcu's father and Monet was not about to take any of the gifts he'd bestowed on her.

It proved easy to leave Palermo, and yet once she'd arrived in London, far too hard to forget Palermo. Not because she missed her mother, but Monet missed everything else—the busy life at the historic sprawling palazzo, Marcu's younger brother and sisters, and then there was Marcu himself…

In that first year in London Monet spent far too many nights sleepless, agonizing over the evening in Marcu's arms. It hurt to remember his kisses and his touch, and yet they were the most potent, powerful emotions and sensations she had ever felt. She had felt like a flame—flickering, hot, radiant. He had woken something inside of her that she hadn't known existed. And his harsh rejection of her had been confusing…shattering.

She'd worked to forget Sicily. She'd tried to put the entire Uberto family from her mind, and yet she missed the children. They had become the only family she'd ever really known.

She had also been in desperate need of a job, and her father, a man she'd only seen a handful of times in her life, had introduced her to a family in need of a nanny while the children were out of school for the summer holiday. She'd performed the job so well that the family had kept her on for the coming school year. She helped with the children, and their schoolwork, and ferrying them from one after-school activity to another. She'd stayed with that family until the parents divorced and could no longer keep her on, but she'd found another job right away, and then another until she'd realized that she couldn't continue in child care—all the goodbyes were too hard on her heart—and she went to work in retail.

She'd started downstairs at the register in hats and gloves, and then when they were short-staffed in bridal, went to the fifth floor to fill in, and had never left the bridal department. If others thought she was too young to be the manager of the department at twenty-six, no one said so, because despite her age, she had style and flair and an eye for quality. Monet wasn't entirely surprised. She was her mother's daughter after all.

"I know this is a lot to take in so I propose we postpone further conversation until you've finished here, and we can go to dinner and relax and have a civilized discussion." Marcu gave her an encouraging smile. "It will give you an opportunity to ask the questions that I'm sure will come to you—"

"But I have no questions," she interrupted, refusing to fall for his charm, painfully aware that in the past she'd found Marcu nearly irresistible—and he knew it, too. He knew exactly how to play her, just as he'd successfully played her eight years ago. She had no wish to fall in with his plans again and rose, indicating she was finished with the conversation.

"Marcu, I have no interest in this position. It's pointless to continue as I have no wish to waste your time, nor do I wish to waste my own. I'm to return here early tomorrow morning and I still need to find a missing gown before Mrs. Wilkerson descends on us again." She drew another short, tight breath. "I wish I could say it was good to see you, but that would be a lie, and after all these years there is no point in either of us lying to the other."

"I never imagined you to be vindictive."

"Vindictive? Not at all. Just because I can't fall in line with your plans doesn't mean I harbor you ill will. You were important to me once. But that was years and years ago."

He rose as well, and he towered over her now. "You made me a promise, Monet. I'm afraid you can't say no…at least not yet, not until you have heard me out, and you haven't. You don't know the details. You don't know the time frame. You don't know the salary, or the benefits."

She threw up her hands. "There are no benefits to working for you!"

"You once loved us. You used to say that we were the family you never had."

"I was young and naive. I know better now."

"Did something happen after you left Palermo? Did something occur that I do not know about?"

"No. You know everything."

"Then why so much scorn and hatred for my family? How did they hurt you?"

She couldn't immediately answer, not when her emotions bubbled up, her chest too hot and tender. She had once loved them all. She had once dreamed of being part of them, a cherished member of the family. But that wasn't to be. She wasn't one of them. She hadn't any hope of being one of them. Her eyes stung, and her throat ached. Monet fought to speak. "It was good of your family to tolerate me for so many years, especially in light of who I was. So no, I do not hate your entire family. I do not speak of your brother and sisters with scorn."

"So your anger is with me, and my father, then?"

This is precisely what she didn't want to do. Dredge up the past. Relive the old pain. She dug her nails into her palms, fighting for control. "It doesn't matter. I don't wish to discuss it. I don't live in the past, and neither should you."

"Unfortunately, it does matter to me, and unfortunately you are in my debt, so we will discuss it later, over dinner. I shall leave you now to finish up here. My car will be downstairs waiting for you. I look forward to continuing our discussion then." He nodded at her and walked away, heading for the gleaming elevators against the distant wall.

She stood there watching him until the elevators opened and he stepped in. He never once turned around until he was inside the elevator and then, and only then, did he turn and look back to find her still standing where he'd left her. Their gazes met and held, a fierce silent challenge that was only broken by the closing of the doors.

He crossed his arms over his chest and exhaled in the privacy of the elevator. Marcu hadn't missed the challenge in Monet's eyes, or her defiant expression as she'd stared him down until the elevator doors closed, blocking the view. He'd expected some resistance from her but this was ridiculous. Monet Wilde needed to remember that she owed him, and not the other way around.

Further, she hadn't been his first pick for child care.

He hadn't even thought of her until after he'd exhausted every resource, trying to find someone already familiar with his children to take care of them over the Christmas holidays. Their nanny of the past two and a half years had a family emergency and needed to be with her own parents, and he understood that it was an emergency but Marcu was now in a terrible bind because he wouldn't let just anyone be with his children. He was very selective, very protective, and he needed more than a warm body to mind his three young children over Christmas. Marcu hadn't even thought of Monet until the last woman he'd interviewed for the position had exited the room and he'd faced the window, disappointed, and deeply troubled. He didn't want his children to be with a stranger.

He didn't trust strangers.

But then, he didn't trust many people, period.

He was well aware that his lack of trust was a problem. It had been a problem for much of his adult life, resulting in a tendency to overanalyze, which wasn't a bad thing as a venture capitalist, but an issue when it came to his social life. Until very recently he'd refused to extend himself beyond his small, trusted inner circle, but when it became obvious that his inner circle would not provide him with a replacement wife to mother his young children, he'd been forced to go further afield. After a series of excruciating dates he'd found a suitable prospect in twenty-nine-year-old Vittoria Bonfiglio, and it was his plan to propose to her on Christmas Eve, but first, he needed some time alone with her, something difficult to achieve when his children were running wild while their nanny was at home in England with her family.

Which is when Monet came to mind. He hadn't thought of her in years, and yet once he'd thought of her, she seemed to be the perfect solution.

He knew her, and she'd never once betrayed his trust. She'd always been good with his younger brother and sisters—why wouldn't she be as patient and kind with his three?

And once Marcu set his mind on something, it was relatively easy to make things happen. It took him less than fifteen minutes to locate her—she lived in London, and worked at Bernard Department Store. She wasn't married.

She might have a boyfriend. Marcu didn't care. He needed her for four weeks, five weeks tops, and then she could return to her life in retail and he'd have his new bride and his child-care issue would be permanently sorted.

It didn't cross his mind that she'd say no, because she owed him. She'd left Palermo in his debt and he was calling in the favor.

Even after Marcu was gone, Monet couldn't move. She was too stunned to do anything but wish the ground would swallow her whole.

All she'd wanted today was to go home after work, take a long hot bath, change into cozy pajamas and curl up on her couch and stream her favorite television programs, lost in the pleasure of diverting entertainment.

She wouldn't be going home anytime soon now.

There would be no long hot bath or a satisfying hour or two of her favorite program.

Slowly she turned, her gaze sweeping the fifth floor. Over the years this elegant, luxurious space had come to feel more like home than her own flat. She was good at what she did. She knew how to soothe the nervous bride, and organize the overwhelmed one. Who would have thought this would be her gift, never mind her skill set?

The illegitimate daughter of a struggling French actress and an English banker, Monet had a most unusual and Bohemian upbringings. By eighteen, she had seen far more of the world than her peers, having lived in Ireland, France, Sicily, Morocco, and three different American states.

She'd spent the longest stretch in Sicily, Palermo being her home for six years from the time she was nearly twelve until she'd turned eighteen. Even after she'd left Palermo, her mother had continued to live with Sicilian aristocrat Matteo Uberto for another three years. But after leaving,

Monet never returned to Sicily. She didn't want to see any of the Uberto family, and she'd rebuffed Marcu when he tried to visit her in London three years ago, just as she'd rebuffed his father a year earlier when Matteo appeared on her doorstep with wine and flowers and a delicate negligee more appropriate for your paramour than your former lover's daughter. It was that visit by Matteo that ensured she finally closed the door on the past, locking it securely.

She had nothing in common with this family she had lived with for six years of her life. Yes, they'd shared meals together, and yes, they'd gone to the movies, and various plays, ballets, and operas together, as well as shared holidays at the beach and Christmases at the palazzo, but in the end she was not one of them, not a member of the family, or a member of Sicilian aristocratic society.

No, she was the bastard daughter of a careless British banker, and a French actress more famous for her affairs and her wealthy lovers then her acting talent, and therefore to be treated as someone cheap and unimportant.

Monet could live with cheap. She couldn't bear to be unimportant, though. She didn't need to be valued by the world, but she'd craved Marcu's love, and respect.

Instead he'd been the first to shame her, but Monet was a quick learner, and she vowed to never be dependent on anyone again, and she hadn't been.

Determined to be different from her mother in every way, she not only rejected all things scandalous, but also pushed away her colorful, Bohemian past. She was no longer Candie's daughter. She was no longer vulnerable, or apologetic. She was herself, her own creation and invention. Unlike her mother, Monet didn't need men. It might not be fair, but it was easier to view them with suspicion than be open to their advances.

It didn't stop men from pursuing her, though, and they

did. They were intrigued by her very French cheekbones, pouting lips, golden-brown eyes and long thick dark hair, but they didn't know her, and they didn't realize that while she might look like a siren on the outside, she was British on the inside, and not about to indulge in meaningless affairs. She wasn't interested in sex, which is why at twenty-six, she was still a virgin, and quite possibly frigid. Monet didn't care if she was. She wasn't interested in labels, nor did she care what men thought, aware that to most men, women were just toys—playthings—and she had no desire to be anyone's plaything. Her mother, Matteo, and Marcu Uberto had made sure of that.

CHAPTER TWO

AN HOUR LATER Monet was outside, and the black car was where Marcu said it would be, parked in front of Bernard's front doors. The driver appeared the moment she stepped outside, and he opened a large black umbrella to protect her from the flurries of snow. She murmured her thanks as she stepped into the car.

She glimpsed Marcu and held her breath, careful to keep a distance between them.

"So what exactly do you do here?" he asked, as the car pulled away from the curb, sliding into the stream of traffic.

She placed her purse on her lap, and rested her hands on the purse clasp. "Manage the department. Assist brides finding their dream gown. Keep mothers from overwhelming their emotional daughters."

"An interesting choice for you, given your background."

Her chin notched up. "Because my mother never married?" she asked, a dark elegant winged eyebrow arching higher.

Of course he'd find it ironic that she'd work as a bridal-gown consultant, but most people didn't know her background. In fact, the only ones who knew her background were the father who'd never been part of her life and the Uberto family.

"Any problems closing?" he asked a moment later, his tone one of excessive politeness.

She nearly rolled her eyes. Surely they were beyond such superficial pleasantries. "No."

"Were you working at Bernard's when I reached out to you a few years ago?"

"I was. I've been there for four years now."

"Why wouldn't you see me when I reached out to you?" he asked.

Her shoulders lifted, and fell. "There was no point." She turned her head, her gaze resting on his hard masculine profile illuminated by the streetlights. He had a perfect face—broad brow, straight, strong nose, wide firm lips, angled jaw, square chin. And yet it wasn't the individual features that made him attractive, it was the way they came together—the quirk of his lips, the creases at the corner of his eyes, the blue gleam in his eyes. She steeled herself against the curve of his lips and the piercing blue of his eyes now. "Was there?"

"I don't understand," he answered simply.

"You were a married man. I was a single woman. I didn't see what good could come of us meeting."

"I wasn't coming to you for sex."

"How was I to know? Your father did."

"What?"

She shrugged again, exhausted by the day, and his appearance. Her exhaustion made her careless. Why keep all these secrets? Why not tell the truth? "Your father approached me a year before you did. He came bearing gifts."

"Your mother had just passed away. He was just being kind."

"Then perhaps a casserole would have been proper. But roses? A pink satin robe? It was wildly inappropriate."

"He gave my sisters a similar robe each for Christmas one year—pink, even. Why must you make his gift sound scandalous?"

Because he didn't like me, Monet thought, turning her head to stare out the window, regretting her words. Why share such a thing with Marcu? Of course he wouldn't believe her. He'd always worshipped his father. Matteo Uberto could do no wrong.

Silence stretched. They sat forever at the next stop light. The snow was heavier, wetter, and it stuck to the glass in thick clumps.

"I wasn't interested in making you my mistress," Marcu said roughly, breaking the tense silence. "I came to see you as my wife had just died and I needed advice. I thought you could help me. I was wrong."

His words created a lance of pain. Her stomach knotted and her chest grew tight. "I'm sorry. I didn't know."

"But you did know I'd married?"

She nodded. He'd married just six months after she left Palermo. She hadn't wanted to know but it was splashed across the tabloids as well as the internet as the Uberto family was wealthy, glamorous, aristocratic, and very much darlings of the media.

Marcu's wedding was held at the cathedral in Palermo, a place she knew well as that was where the Uberto family attended church services every Sunday. Marcu had married an Italian countess from northern Italy, although her maternal grandmother was Sicilian. Galeta Corrado was an only child and stood to inherit all the ancestral homes and estates of her family, a family that could be traced back hundreds of years. Marcu's family was considerably older, his ancestors Sicilian royalty dating back five hundred years, a fact the tabloids mentioned ad nauseam in their coverage of the Uberto-Corrado wedding, sharing that Marcu's great-grandfather had been a Sicilian prince, and Marcu could probably claim the title, but he was far too egalitarian.

He wasn't.

Monet could scarcely stomach that one.

Marcu and Galeta's wedding had been lavish, with Galeta's bridal gown costing close to forty thousand euros. The silk train stretched for yards, with the hand-crocheted lace veil equally long, the delicate lace anchored to a priceless two-hundred-year-old pink diamond-and-pearl tiara. The bride had been a stunning vision in white, her slender form showcased by the luminous silk. The first baby came not quite nine months later. There was gossip that Galeta was pregnant at the time she married, and it was then Monet had refused to read the tabloids ever again. She was done. Spent. Flattened.

She didn't want to know anything else. She didn't want to live on the fringes of Marcu's life. She didn't want to know about his wife or children. She refused to look back, refused to remember, unwilling to feel the pain that washed through her every time his name was mentioned.

The pain baffled her, too, because when she left Palermo, she'd convinced herself that she hadn't loved him, she'd merely been infatuated. She'd told herself she felt curiosity and desire, but not true love. So why did his name hurt? Why did his marriage wound? It wasn't until he'd married Galeta and they'd had that first baby together, that Monet realized her feelings for him were stronger and deeper than she'd previously allowed herself to acknowledge. She couldn't possibly hurt so much if she'd merely been infatuated. She wouldn't miss him so much if she'd just been curious. No, she hurt because she loved him, and he was only the second person in her whole life she'd ever loved.

Monet turned back to Marcu again, still not quite able to believe he was here, beside her. She felt so many different things, and her chaotic emotions weren't improved by his close proximity. Marcu had been handsome at twenty, and twenty-five, but now, at thirty-three, his face was even more arresting. He'd matured, the bones in his jaw and cheekbones more defined, the hollows beneath his cheekbones more pronounced, his skin lightly tanned, glowing with health and vitality.

"How did she die?" Monet asked, trying to organize her thoughts, never mind her impossible emotions.

"She had a stroke after childbirth." He drew a breath. "I'd never heard of such a thing but our doctor said that while it's uncommon, strokes cause ten percent of all pregnancy-related deaths." He was silent another moment. "I wasn't even there when it happened. I'd just flown to New York, thinking she was in good hands at the palazzo with the nanny and night nurse."

"You don't blame yourself, do you?"

"I don't blame myself for the stroke, but I can't forget that she died while I was on a plane over the Atlantic Ocean. It wasn't right. It shouldn't have been that way. If I'd been there, maybe I could have gotten her help sooner. Maybe the doctors could have saved her."

Monet didn't know how to respond and so she sat there with the distressing words resonating around her, listening to the soft rhythmic sweep of the windshield wipers moving back and forth, clearing the glass, even as her heart did a painful beat in her chest.

Of course Marcu would feel badly. How could he not feel partially responsible? But at the same time, that didn't make his situation her problem. He needed help, yes, but why from her?

"Does your late wife have no family who could help with the children?" she asked as the traffic thinned. They were approaching London's commercial financial hub, and during the week the streets bustled with activity but now the area was quiet and dark. "What of Galeta's parents? No grandparents to lend a supportive hand?"

"Galeta was an only child, and her parents are both gone. My father is gone. I have my brother and sisters, but they all are busy with their own lives."

"Just as I am busy with my own life," she retorted lightly, unwilling to escalate things in the close confines of his car.

"I'm asking for a few weeks, not years."

She glanced out the window and watched the grand Bank of England pass by. Lovingly referred to as the Old Lady of Threadneedle Street by some, Monet was always awed and reassured by its history and size. "It's simply not a good time," she answered, glancing from the bank to Marcu.

"Would any time be a good time?" he countered.

The car turned at the corner, passing more historic buildings that formed the heart of the city of London, making Monet wonder where they were going to eat in this particular neighborhood before her attention returned to Marcu.

"No," she answered with a sigh, even as she reached up to tuck a long tendril behind her ear. She was tired and uncomfortable and she wanted out of her slim dress and heels. She wanted the delicate underwire bra off and the smoothing undergarments off so that she could climb into pajamas and eat warm comfort food and sip a big glass of red wine. Merlot. Burgundy. Shiraz. "I have no desire to work for you, ever."

"I know," he answered even as the driver pulled over in front of one of the big dark buildings, parked, and exited the driver's side, again wielding the umbrella. He opened the back door and Marcu stepped out and then reached in to assist her. She avoided his hand, neatly stepping away to make sure there was no contact between them.

He shot her a sardonic glance but said nothing as the

driver walked them to a plain wooden door. Marcu reached out and touched one gray stone. There was a long pause and then the door silently opened. They stepped inside a dimly lit, severe-looking entrance hall. The door closed behind them and Monet gazed around, curious but also confused by the stillness and emptiness of the impersonal cream-and-gray space. There were stairs at the back of the hallway and a service elevator to their right but that was all.

"I normally prefer the stairs," Marcu said, "but you've been on your feet all day, so I suggest we take the elevator."

They did, traveling down, but it was impossible to say how far down they went, before the doors silently opened, revealing a black-and-white marble parquet floor, massive columns, and what looked like the entrance to a huge bank vault. Walls glimmered gold and silver on the other side of the vault entrance. She glanced at Marcu, an eyebrow lifting in silent enquiry.

He gestured for her to proceed through the open vault door, where they were greeted by a gentleman in a dark suit and black shirt. "Mr. Uberto," the man said. "It's good to have you back."

They were ushered past an elegant bar of stainless steel and thick glass where a bartender was mixing drinks, then through another archway to a dining room dotted with chandeliers. The chandeliers were an eclectic mix of styles and time periods, and hung from a silver ceiling casting soft pools of light on pale lavender velvet chairs and upholstered booths. There weren't more than a dozen tables in the room. There were men at some tables, and couples at others. Monet and Marcu were taken to yet another room, this one small and private, with just one table. The chandelier was all pink glass, and the upholstery on the high back chairs was gray.

Monet sank into her well-upholstered chair with an appreciative sigh. It felt even more welcoming than it looked. "This is quite a place," she said, as waiters appeared in quick succession with bottles of chilled mineral water, olives, and pâté with slivers of toasted baguette.

"It was once part of the Bank of Sicily. It's now a private members' club."

"I suspected as much." She reached for an olive and popped it in her mouth, suddenly ravenous. "Let me guess, your father used to have a membership here, and they extended an invitation to you?"

"My grandfather used to own the bank, my father closed it, and when he couldn't find someone to buy the building for its proper value, I took it on and turned the Vault into a private club five years ago."

"What happened to the rest of the building?"

"It's now a members-only hotel and spa."

"Do you use the same door to access the hotel and spa?"

"No, there is a different entrance."

"Why?"

"Because membership to the hotel doesn't give one automatic membership to the Vault."

"Is this where you stay when you're in London?"

"The top floor is my apartment, yes."

"It's quite spacious."

"You don't make that sound like a question," he replied, leaning back in his chair.

"It's not," she answered, before thanking the waiter who presented her with a silver menu. She glanced down at it, scanning the delectable offerings. She could have been perfectly happy with just pâté and toast but once she spotted the flat-iron steak she knew what she wanted.

After ordering, Marcu got straight to the point. "I do need you, urgently. I would have liked to leave tonight, but obviously it's too late now. So I'll organize travel for the morning—"

"Marcu, I haven't said yes."

"But you will."

She rolled her eyes, frustrated, and yet part of her frustration was based on the truth in his words. She did owe him. "January would be so much better for me."

"I've already told you, I have a conference in the Far East in January, and I would like to have things sorted by then."

"Sorted as in…?"

"Married, with Vittoria at home with the children. I worry more about the children when I am far away. This way they'd have their nanny, Miss Sheldon, who's on leave at the moment, and a mother—"

"But they don't have a close relationship with this new mother, do they?"

"They've been introduced."

She felt a bubble of incredulous laughter. "I don't know who to feel more sorry for, your future wife, or your children. Where is your sensitivity—?"

"Oh, that's long gone. I'm as hard as they come now."

"Your poor future wife."

"I'm not romantic. I never have been."

"So says the man who loved opera? Who'd listen to Puccini for hours?"

"*You* loved opera. I simply supported your passion."

She eyed him, trying to come to terms with this new version of Marcu. He was so hard to stomach. "You do know you'd be better off hiring a new nanny, or even two, to job-share than trying to fix things by acquiring a wife. Wives do come with feelings—"

"Not all women require extravagant gestures. Vittoria is quite practical. And I'm hoping you can be practical, too. I'll pay you one hundred thousand euros for the next five weeks," he added. "Hopefully that will adequately cover any lost wages from Bernard's."

"And if they don't take me back afterward?"

"You will continue to earn twenty thousand euros a week until I find you a new position."

She was intrigued and appalled. "That's a lot of money."

"My children are worth it."

"So you are still consumed with guilt over your wife's death."

"I'm not consumed with guilt, just determined to make amends. They are very good children, but they are also in need of a mother. I do not, and cannot, meet all their needs, which is why I'm determined to marry again. A mother will be better equipped to handle their ups and downs and various emotions."

"This mother you speak of will be practically a stranger to them."

"But they will form a relationship. I don't expect it to happen overnight, but I do believe it will happen eventually, and I imagine when a new baby arrives, the children will be excited to have a new brother or sister."

Monet studied him for a long moment. Did he really think his children, who had already been deprived of a mother, would welcome the competition of a new baby for their father's attention? "I remember you studied finance at university. It's a shame you didn't study more psychology. Creating a new family isn't an easy thing, and children who have been through loss and heartbreak don't always welcome more change."

"I don't expect them to understand immediately. They are still very young but their innocence is also to their advantage. They will be grateful for a permanent mother figure. As it is they are very attached to their current nanny, and I fear the day Miss Sheldon leaves us for good."

"I thought your nanny was only on temporary leave?"

"So she is, but I see the writing on the wall. It's only a matter of time." He hesitated. "Miss Sheldon has fallen in love with my pilot. They've been secretly dating for the past year. They don't think I know, but neither of them are as discreet as they imagine."

"Your nanny couldn't marry and continue working for you?"

"They will want to start a family of their own. She's in her thirties. I know how these things go. She's not our first nanny, nor will she be the last."

"But she hasn't left yet—"

"I don't care to discuss Miss Sheldon with you. I'm simply informing you that you will not lose any wages while you work for me."

His brusque tone put her teeth on edge. His arrogance was beyond off-putting. The very idea of working for him made her nauseous. She'd had so many feelings for him, but none of them involved being his employee. She didn't want him as her superior. The idea of having to answer to him made her want to stand up and storm out. She'd thought she'd loved him once—desperately, passionately—but he'd deemed her unsuitable. Unworthy.

Suddenly she flashed back to another conversation, one between Marcu and his father as they'd discussed how inappropriate Monet was for someone of Marcu's stature. That Monet might be sweet and charming but she was the kind of woman you took as your mistress, not as your wife.

To hear this at eighteen. To be so painfully and thoroughly dismissed, reduced—*marginalized*—at only eighteen. It had changed her forever.

"I can't work for you," she said in a low voice. "I can't be at your beck and call."

"I won't be around after the first few days. I'll only be

there to get you settled and then I'm taking Vittoria to Altapura for Christmas. She loves to ski. She's a very good skier, too, so unless something unexpected happens, we'll return just after New Year."

"You won't be spending the holidays with your children?" she asked, confused.

"No. That's the whole point of me seeking you out. I won't be with them this year, but you will be."

Monet felt another welling of pity for his children. It was also difficult to believe that Marcu had become such a cold, pragmatic man. He'd been so warm and kind when he was younger. He'd been a very loving, and much-adored, big brother. "Do they know this?"

"They know that it's going to be a different kind of holiday this year. I haven't told them more than that. I didn't think it appropriate until Vittoria accepts my proposal."

"You worry me, Marcu, and you make me worry for the children, too."

Marcu's eyes met hers and held, the light blue gaze heavily hooded, and assessing. "They are not mistreated in any way."

"They'll miss you."

"They won't. They might even be relieved to have me gone." He hesitated. "I know they have more fun with Miss Sheldon when I'm away."

"And that doesn't bother you?"

"I never asked to be both mother and father."

"But leaving them altogether seems exceptionally unfair—"

"It seems you want to fight with me. Does it give you pleasure? I've already told you I'm not good at this parenting thing. I have not been a rousing success. What more do you want from me?"

The raw pain in his voice silenced her. She sat still for

a moment, feeling his deep anguish echo in her ears. She waited another moment until she was sure she could speak calmly. “I don’t want to fight with you, but I’m not comfortable with the way things ended between us. And while I’m sympathetic to your children’s situation—they’ve experienced loss and grief and they need stability—I also recognize that I’m not the right person to fill in for your nanny.”

“Why not? You’re very good with children.”

“I only did child care temporarily, until I found permanent work. Further, I can’t leave Bernard’s on such short notice. I was down two saleswomen in my department today. It’s impossible for my department to run without anybody there tomorrow. I must speak with management. I must clear things—”

“I already have,” he interrupted flatly. “I had a brief conversation this morning with Charles.”

“Bernard?”

Marcu’s dark head inclined impatiently. “He was sorry to hear of my emergency, and agreed that you would be the best help for me—”

“Emergency? What emergency?” She exhaled hard, battling to keep her temper in check. “You’ve decided to go skiing with your girlfriend during the same time period your nanny needs a break. That’s not an emergency.”

“I have no dedicated help for them.”

“Then do what others in your situation do—hire a replacement through a professional service. You refuse to, but that doesn’t constitute an emergency.”

He shrugged. “You’re wrong. Charles agreed that young children cannot be left with a stranger. Once he understood your connection with my family, he thought you were the best answer.”

Such a power play. What arrogance! Monet was shocked at how manipulative Marcu had been. “I can’t believe you went to my boss and told him some ridiculous sob story. I'm sorry that your nanny needed a break just now, and I'm sorry you had plans to ski—"

"It's not about the skiing. I'm going to propose—"

"Regardless, that's not my problem, and I'm livid that you've spoken to anyone about me, much less the CEO of Bernard's."

"I didn't think it'd hurt you in any way for Charles to know that we have a close family connection. If anything, it will help your standing on your return. I'm quite certain you will see more promotions, and more salary increases."

"Did you happen to tell Charles just what our close family connection was? Did you explain to him that my mother was your father's mistress? Charles is quite conservative—"

"He knows our connection, just as he knows you are Edward Wilde's daughter. Your father is on the board at Bernard's. I suspect your rapid promotions have had something to do with that."

Her mouth opened, closed. She had no idea that her father was on the board. She hadn't spoken to him in years... not since he'd provided references, helping her get her first nanny job. "I earned my promotions through hard work, not through family connections."

"Your father is quite respected in the banking world."

"That has nothing to do with me. I've seen him less than a half dozen times in my life. He had no interest in me, and only gave me those references I needed because I went to him, and told him I needed his assistance. He balked, at first, but came around when I threatened to introduce myself to his wife and children."

Marcu lifted a black brow. "You don't think they already knew about you?"

"I'm sure they didn't, and that's fine. Everyone makes mistakes and my mother was Edward's mistake."

"You call him Edward?"

"I certainly don't call him Father."

"You're more defensive than ever."

"I'm not defensive. He didn't want me, and he paid my mother to get rid of me. Instead she took the money and went to the States and then Morocco and you know the rest. Edward tolerates my existence because he has no other choice. Just as your father tolerated me because he had no other choice. As a young girl I had to accept that I was barely tolerated, but I don't anymore." She drew a quick breath. "This is why I can't do this favor for you. I won't be treated as a second-class citizen any longer. It's not acceptable. Not from you, not from anyone."

"I never treated you as a second-class citizen."

"You did at the end, you know you did."

"What are you talking about? Does this have something to do with the kiss?"

Heat flashed through her, making her shake. "It was more than a kiss."

"You welcomed my attention. Don't pretend you didn't."

"You did not force yourself on me, no. But what I thought was happening was quite different from reality."

"I don't understand."

She drew a breath and then another, battling to hang on to the last thread of her composure. Crying would be a disaster. Losing control would be the final humiliation. She refused to endure any more shame. "We were not equals. You let me imagine we were. But we weren't."

"I still don't understand."

"It doesn't matter. It's no longer relevant. But what is relevant is my answer today. It's a no. If I had wanted to be part of your life I would have stayed in Palermo, but I left for a reason and I have no desire to spend time with you. Ever. Which is why I'm demanding you forgive the debt, forget the favor, and let me let leave now with us both closing the door on the past, once and forever."

Marcu froze, her words catching him off guard because yes, they probably both needed to close the door on the past and yet, it was the last thing he wanted.

And in that moment he realized something else.

Marcu hadn't been honest when he told himself Monet wasn't his first choice for a backup nanny. That was a lie. He'd interviewed plenty of candidates, but none of them had been right for the job, because none of them had been Monet. He'd been dismissive of the other women, finding fault with each, precisely so he could come to Monet today and say, *I need you.*

Because he did.

He needed her to come help him stabilize things at home while he figured out how to give his children a better life.

His children needed more than him. He wasn't patient and tender, or particularly affectionate. He loved his children but he didn't know how to meet all their needs, which is why he needed a partner...a better half. He needed a wife, someone maternal, someone to create stability in their home. He traveled too much. He worked too long. He was constantly at war with himself, juggling his business commitments while trying to be present with the children—not easy when his main office was in New York and his children were being raised in Sicily. He'd fly to New York for three days, but inevitably he'd have to extend his trip by a day, and then another, and another. Sometimes his brief trips became a week long and then two weeks, and he not only worried about the kids, but he'd also be filled with guilt and self-loathing.

Guilt that Galeta had died.

Self-loathing because he didn't want to remarry and it's why he hadn't proposed to someone sooner.

Galeta had been a kind, loyal wife, and while they didn't have a passionate marriage, they became friends and partners, with Galeta creating a warm loving home for him and their children in the main apartment at the palazzo. Her death had been a shock, and it had taken him years to wrap his head around the tragedy. Why hadn't he known that a woman was still so vulnerable after delivery? Why had he thought that once she was home from the hospital everything was fine?

The guilt. The agony. She had deserved better, and so did their children. He wasn't the father he'd thought he would be. He wasn't good enough at all. And so while he didn't want another wife, he would remarry, and he'd make sure that his new wife understood that her first responsibility was to the children.

"I can't forgive the favor because I need you," he replied now, his rough tone betraying his impatience. "You needed help from me eight years ago, and I helped you, and now I'm asking for you to return the favor. You understand this, I know you do. You lived with us long enough to understand our Sicilian view of these things."

Monet gave her dark head a faint shake. Two bright spots of color stained her cheekbones, while her large golden-brown eyes glowed, burning with emotion.

"I also know that you could choose to be magnanimous and forgive the debt."

"If my children weren't involved, then yes, perhaps I could. But this is about my children, and they need you, which is why I need you."

She slowly sat back in her chair, her slim frame practically vibrating with fury. She was both beautiful and fierce, and it struck him that he'd never seen this side of her before.

In Palermo she'd been quiet and sweet with a deliciously dry sense of humor. She rarely spoke when his father was present, but when she was with Marcu and his brother and sisters, she had plenty to say, and inevitably she made everyone laugh. He should have known that underneath her sweet persona she had backbone. He was pleased to see it, finding it something of a relief. His world was filled with people who acquiesced to his every desire simply because he was wealthy and powerful. But it was hard to trust people who claimed they always agreed with you and only wanted to please you. Those people were dangerous. They could be bought.

"I don't like you," she said quietly, carefully, the lushness of her lower lip quivering before she pressed her mouth into a firm line.

Her words hung there between them, coloring the private dining room. He let them hover, too, even though his first instinct was to remind her that once she'd followed him everywhere, had been absolutely devoted to him, and was always the first to defend him even though he'd never needed her defense. No, he'd never needed it but her loyalty had always touched him, and in return he'd kept an eye out for her, been protective of her even when he'd been away at university. He'd paid one of the palazzo staff to report to him because he worried about her in his absence. Her mother was oblivious to her existence and while his father would never hurt her, he only tolerated the girl for Candie's sake.

It was never good to merely be tolerated. Monet was too smart, too sensitive not to have been aware of her position in the Uberto household.

"Now," he said, breaking the silence. "You don't like me *now.* We both know that wasn't always the case."

"But that dislike should be enough for you to not want

me to be with your children. That dislike should make you reject me as a suitable caregiver."

"Your dislike is at least honest. I respect such honesty, and I also know that you are far too fair to allow your personal feelings for me to prejudice you against my children."

"But you don't know me. I'm not the girl who left Palermo eight years ago with nothing but a knapsack on her back—"

"And five thousand of my euros in your pocket."

"Don't you understand?" she blurted, rising swiftly to her feet. "I didn't want your money then, and I don't want it now."

She would have fled if he'd allowed it. He wasn't going to let her go, though. His hand snaked out and wrapped around her wrist, preventing her from leaving.

"Sit down," he said quietly. "Have a conversation with me."

"There is no point," she said hotly. "You don't listen. You're not hearing what I'm saying." She tugged to free herself. He didn't let go. "Why can't you offer a compromise? Why can't you meet me partway? I can't leave my job now. I would be willing to do it in January—"

"I don't need you in January," he interrupted, releasing her, hoping she would sit. She didn't. She continued to stand there at the table, furious and indignant. "Miss Sheldon will be back then," he added. "Once she's back, I won't need you."

"I can't leave my work for up to five weeks. It's mid-December now. That means I'd still be gone in the middle of January."

"Four weeks then." He suppressed a sigh. "Will you sit, please?"

"That's still the middle of January."

He was silent a long moment before countering. "Three weeks from tomorrow, but only if you sit down. This is uncomfortable, and we're drawing attention."

"There is no one else in this dining room. It's exceptionally private."

"I'm in this dining room and you're making me uncomfortable."

"Heavens, we can't have that, can we?" she retorted mockingly, before slowly sitting back down. "Two weeks."

"Three."

She reached for her wineglass and took a sip, hoping he wouldn't see how her hand trembled. "I wouldn't want to remain after you and Vittoria return after New Year's."

"You wouldn't have to."

"I'll be on a flight home that first weekend of January."

"I'll send you home on my plane. I promise."

Her gaze met his. "Or sooner if you and Vittoria return sooner. I've no interest in being present while you integrate Vittoria into your household."

"Understood."

"And one more stipulation," she said after a long pause. "I need to go to work in the morning. I must find a missing wedding gown—"

"We need to return to Italy."

"*You* need to return to Italy. I don't." Her eyebrows lifted as her brown eyes flashed indignant fire. "*I* need to find Mrs. Wilkerson's daughter's missing gown, and then I can go with you. Give me until noon. I've made Mrs. Wilkerson a promise and a promise is a promise."

He digested her words for a moment before brusquely nodding. "Fine. My car will be at Bernard's at noon. We will leave straight for the airport."

The corner of her mouth curled up. "You're not worried that I'll try to run away and escape you?"

His body went hard at that saucy curl of her lips. Thank God he wasn't going to be spending much time with Monet. Thank God he was taking her to the *castello* and leaving promptly. Monet had always tested his control. She still tested his control.

"No," he answered roughly. "Because a promise is a promise."

CHAPTER THREE

MONET KEPT HER eyes closed during the flight over the jagged peaks of southeastern France lit by the setting sun. She wasn't afraid of flying, but this afternoon her stomach thumped, queasy with anxiety and dread.

She couldn't quite believe this was happening.

Christmas in the Italian Alps. Christmas with Marcu—correction, Christmas with Marcu's children, as Marcu would be elsewhere, wooing his future wife.

As a girl she'd dreaded the Christmas holidays. There had been years where she and her mother didn't celebrate Christmas at all, and then there were years where they celebrated someone else's holiday traditions, and when she was little Monet had found it confusing. So many people seemed to love Christmas but for her it was often incredibly painful.

She didn't really experience a proper Christmas until she and her mother moved to Palermo. Her best Christmas memories had been with the Uberto family at their palazzo. The Ubertos celebrated Christmas in a grand way, their December filled with music and food, gifts and sweets. But even in Palermo, Christmas had been about the Uberto children and their father and their aristocratic Sicilian heritage. Monet had merely been that odd French-English girl who kept to the background to avoid drawing unnecessary attention to herself. It was better for her, and better for her mother, who didn't really want to be a mother but loved

Monet just enough to keep her daughter with her, but not enough to do what was right for her.

Uneasy with the memories, Monet stirred and opened her eyes to glance out the window. As she looked up her gaze briefly met Marcu's. He was still at his table, working on some pile of paperwork. Obviously he wasn't so engrossed in his work that he was oblivious to her, and Monet wasn't sure how that made her feel.

"This is a terrible idea," she said huskily. "We will both regret this."

"I won't regret it. I need help, and I know my children will be in good hands with you."

Monet regarded him from beneath her lashes. He was so arrogant and self-assured. As well as shockingly handsome. He had been incredibly good-looking as a young adult, but now as a mature man, his face was all strong angles and planes, slashing cheekbones, broad, strong brow, firm mouth, firmer chin. His thick black hair was swept back from his face, framing piercing blue eyes, and a counterbalance to straight white teeth. His face alone would turn heads, but paired with his tall, lithe, muscular frame, he was beautiful indeed.

It would be easier, sitting here, if she didn't find him physically appealing. It would be easier if her heart didn't jump every time he glanced her way.

She'd forgotten that she could even feel this kind of fear and anxiety flooding her. It was the fear she'd felt as a girl, the fear that made it hard to breathe properly and therefore her head would spin, feeling light and dizzy.

She felt dizzy now.

She felt angry, too, that he'd forced her into this job. She wasn't a nanny anymore. She had a career. She had responsibility and work she enjoyed and yet he'd insisted she drop everything for this stupid "favor."

She closed her hands, fingers curling into her palms, nails digging in sharply to try to contain her crippling anxiety. The tension was almost unbearable. This was such a terrible mistake and there was nothing she could do it about it.

"Did you find your customer's missing wedding gown?" Marcu asked suddenly, his voice surprisingly close.

She opened her eyes and shuddered to see that he'd left his desk and was seated opposite her now in the pale cream leather chair that matched hers. He was by no means sprawled in his seat and yet his long legs seemed to fill up the space, and his imposing shoulders drew her attention up to his face, and those cool blue watchful eyes. He felt far too relaxed for her peace of mind. She hadn't heard him approach or sit down. She should have. Her skin prickled with unease. She wasn't afraid of him, but rather, was afraid of all he made her feel—the anger, the shame, the heartbreak.

"I did, yes," she answered. "It was in alterations, but had been mislabeled. Crisis averted."

"Your customer must have been very relieved."

"Not as much as I was. It was a very expensive gown."

Marcu lowered his blind partway, blocking the glare from the setting sun. "I'm still trying to come to terms with you as a bridal consultant."

"Is it really so shocking?" she asked, aware it had never been her goal or dream to work with brides, but it turned out she had a knack for finding the right dress for the right woman who wanted nothing less than spectacular for her wedding day. It seemed that Monet had somehow absorbed her actress mother's knack for the theatrical, and coupled with her own artistic flair, as well as with the hefty measure of patience required when working with emotional, temperamental brides, Monet had worked her way up from fetching gowns from the back room to managing Bernard's entire department.

"There is a great deal of theater in a wedding," she added thoughtfully. "My mother was an actress. I understand what is needed and wanted—the wedding, like any great production, is to be magical and meaningful, and the show is to go off without a hitch. No one must know about the work involved. Fortunately those heavy red velvet curtains hide the stagehands and the frantic activity in the wings."

"You're the stage manager."

"I understand this is not my play or my production. I am simply there to make people happy."

"Very much like your mother then."

She felt a hot lance of shame. "Except I don't sleep with people to make them happy," she flashed, voice hardening.

"That's not what I meant."

"No? Then what did you mean?"

He regarded her from beneath heavy lids, his black lashes nearly concealing the piercing blue of his eyes. "I think you want to take offense. You've been harboring this resentment for years."

If she'd been anywhere else she would have bolted from her seat and raced away, but seeing as they were thirty thousand feet in the air on a small private jet, there was nowhere to go. No way to escape. "Resentment against what, and whom? I am not a victim, Marcu. I am satisfied with my life, pleased by what I have accomplished. Everything I own, and everything I've achieved, has been through hard work, not gifts, or handouts."

"I wasn't implying that you've slept with anyone to get where you are—"

"Good, because I haven't."

"All I was saying was that your mother's…success… was due to her ability to give people what they wanted."

"Can we not discuss my mother? We don't constantly reference your mother, and I know her absence wounded you."

His broad shoulders shifted carelessly. "At least I knew her. The younger ones have no memories of her."

"You were how old when she left?"

"Twelve."

"The same age I was when I arrived at your family's palazzo."

"Do you remember being twelve?"

"I do," she answered. "And you?"

"I do, too." His long fingers casually drummed on the leather armrest. "Mothers are important. It's why I must remarry."

"Do your children like Vittoria?"

"They've only met her a few times, but there were no problems, and Vittoria seemed quite taken with Antonio." He hesitated. "It's easier to adapt when the children are very young, and Antonio is little more than a toddler."

"How old are they?"

"Three, five, and nearly seven," he answered. "Antonio is my youngest, Rocca, my only girl, is five, and Matteo will be seven just after the New Year."

"Matteo, like your father."

"Yes."

She said nothing for a long moment, and it was then that Marcu filled the silence. "My father liked you, you know. He was always quite protective of you."

She'd always thought so, too, until that last night when he'd said such terrible, hurtful things to Marcu about her. *She is not the sort you get serious with. Remember her background. Remember who she is, and where she comes from. A dalliance is delightful, but she is not one you keep.*

And then Marcu's brutal reply: *Of course I know. I do*

not need the reminder. When I marry it will be to someone suitable.

Marcu didn't know she'd inadvertently overheard the conversation. He hadn't even known he'd wounded her, and yet even then, he'd been more than happy to see her leave Palermo, buying her one-way airline ticket to London with startling alacrity before driving her to the airport himself.

She'd been numb on the flight to London, and she'd been numb as she collected her luggage at Heathrow. The only thought circling her exhausted brain was that he couldn't wait to see her gone, and he hadn't been able to get rid of her fast enough. Their passionate night wasn't meaningful at all to him. Instead it was a mistake. A colossal embarrassment.

As she searched for a place to live, Monet consoled herself with the fact that at least they hadn't consummated their lovemaking. At least she'd only given him her heart, and not her innocence. It wasn't that she cherished her virginity, but she certainly didn't need to give Marcu more than she already had.

Monet gave her head a faint shake and forced her attention to the present. The next three weeks would be difficult. She wasn't worried about the children, as she'd cared for children in the past, but she dreaded even a few hours in close proximity to Marcu, never mind a few days, because memories were flooding her and the memories created pain. "He really gave your sisters pink robes for Christmas one year?"

"Yes."

"You don't think it was inappropriate for him to give me a satin bathrobe?"

"I am certain he didn't mean to make you uncomfortable. Knowing him, I'm positive he meant well."

She bit the inside of her lower lip to keep from contradicting him because if Matteo had meant well, he wouldn't have poisoned Marcu against her. He wouldn't have talked about her as if she was little more than garbage.

Marcu shot her a narrowed glance. "You don't believe me."

"I don't know what I believe anymore," she answered simply, and that was the truth.

Their private jet landed twenty-five minutes later at the executive airport in Milan, where Marcu's gleaming black Maserati was waiting. A steward stowed the luggage in the boot of the car and Marcu opened the passenger door for Monet. The interior of the new car was as sleekly designed as the exterior, the black leather plush, and still smelling new. They left the airport immediately for the drive to the *castello*, a drive that should take less than two hours if the weather was good, and the weather was good.

She and Marcu were mostly silent as he drove them up into the mountains. Snow blanketed the hills but the road was clear and free of ice. Monet struggled to relax but it was difficult in the close confines of the luxurious sports car. Everything about Marcu overwhelmed her—he was both familiar and not, changed by time and yet even more ruggedly appealing than before. She wanted to be indifferent to him but everything in her felt far too sensitive and aware of the way he sat, and the way his hand rested on the stick shift, and how his other hand looked against the black leather steering wheel. He had strong hands, beautiful hands. Just like his profile was strong, and beautiful. More chiseled and beautiful than it had been eight years ago.

"Do you have snow tires on the car?" she asked as Marcu took another sharp curve with ease.

"I do, and I also have chains if needed." He shot her a

mocking glance from beneath dense black lashes. "Nervous?"

"No," she lied, crossing her legs.

"You're wringing your hands."

She unknotted her hands and smoothed her heather-gray skirt, then made a conscious decision to at least fake appearing relaxed, even if she didn't feel it on the inside.

Marcu wouldn't be around much longer. He'd be leaving for his holiday with Vittoria soon. It would just be her and the children by the end of the week, and she'd be fine with the kids. Even if they were little beasts, she'd be fine. She could manage just about anything…except her reaction to Marcu it seemed.

"I'm sorry we're arriving so late," he said. "It's a beautiful drive in daylight."

She turned her head to look out the window, the soaring peaks of the Alps hidden now by darkness. "I would imagine you have good views from your *castello*?"

"Breathtaking," he agreed.

And that was the end of their conversation until they reached the Aosta Valley, where Marcu's *castello* sat just outside the village of Aosta. She'd been many places in her life, but she'd never been to the Italian Alps and she was looking forward to exploring someplace new. Hopefully the children would have a sense of adventure, too.

"Here," Marcu said abruptly as they left the highway to turn off the main road, passing through huge iron gates and stone walls into a groomed winter wonderland. The road cut through the middle of an ancient park filled with soaring trees frosted with snow and just when Monet was certain they'd be driving through woods forever, the trees cleared and before them rose a castle. It could be called nothing else with its stone-and-stucco facade, and soaring towers and turrets.

"This isn't a new construction," she said under her breath.

His lips curved faintly. "It was built at the end of the twelfth century."

"So I'm sure it's warm and cozy inside."

"Fortunately, Galeta's family updated the heating. We don't just rely on drafty fireplaces. And should you be cold at night, there are small space heaters you can plug in as well."

Marcu slowed as they traveled up a narrow cobbled road and then parked in front of the entrance to the *castello*. Staff appeared on the front steps. Men in dark gray suits claimed the luggage while a woman in an austere black dress nodded her head as Marcu ushered Monet through the front door. "Welcome back, Signor Uberto," the woman said.

"Thank you," Marcu answered. "Are the children still up?"

"No, *signor*, they are already in bed and asleep. The housemaid, Elise, took them for a walk to help them burn off their energy earlier and they were ready for bed tonight."

Monet heard the wryness in the housekeeper's voice and glanced from the housekeeper to Marcu to see how he'd interpret her words, but Marcu's stern features revealed nothing.

"Were they difficult to manage without Miss Sheldon?" he asked.

"Not at all, sir. Elise enjoys spending time with them."

"Tell her I'm grateful for her help," Marcu instructed, tugging off his leather gloves and then his coat.

"She knows, *signor*. Do not worry."

The butler was there to take Marcu's coat, and then he turned to Monet, ready to collect hers, but she smiled and shook her head. "I'd like to keep mine, if I could," she said.

"Of course." Marcu glanced up the stairwell to the floors

above. “I’ll give you a quick tour now and then tomorrow you can have a proper look around.”

“That’s all right,” Monet said quickly. “I don’t need a tour tonight. It’s been a long day and I’m happy to just call it a night. But I do look forward to meeting the children in the morning.”

“Your suite of rooms is next to the nursery on the third floor,” Marcu answered. “I’ll walk you there.”

They climbed three flights of stairs before Marcu opened the door on the third floor to a sitting room with a dark beamed ceiling.

The walls were a creamy plaster over stone. The pale stone floors were covered with plush Persian rugs, and a rich burgundy velvet couch faced the fireplace, with a pair of peach brocade upholstered chairs on either side. There were small tables scattered about, one round table topped with hand-painted burgundy-and-gold tiles, while another had a hammered silver tray that reminded her of a table they’d once had in Morocco. A Venetian glass mirror hung on one of the smooth plaster walls while an antique peach, green and gold tapestry hung on another.

“The children are next door,” Marcu said. “Their nursery and bedrooms take up the rest of the floor. They have a playroom, and two bedrooms. Matteo and Antonio share a room, and Rocca has her own. Miss Sheldon used to sleep in the nursery in Palermo to be near them, but once Antonio turned three, we moved the boys in together and now Miss Sheldon has a bedroom adjacent to the nursery like here.”

“If they have a bad dream, what do they do?”

“They know you’re here, next door.”

“They don’t come to you?”

“You are closer. I’m on a floor below and the stairs are steep.”

“I see,” she said, careful to keep the judgment from her

voice as she crossed the living-room carpet to peek through the open door to the bedroom. The apricot-and-burgundy color scheme was repeated. The bed was a four-poster with apricot fabric panels. Wooden shutters were at the windows but heavy curtains framed the shutters, adding an extra layer of protection against the frigid night temperature.

Marcu gestured to a large wardrobe in the corner. "You'll find a mini kitchen outfitted in the wardrobe with a coffeemaker, teakettle, and a small refrigerator. I believe housekeeping has stocked it with milk and some fruit and snacks. I know we had dinner on the plane, but if you're hungry for something more substantial—"

"I'm not," she said, cutting him off. "But thank you. I think I'll have a cup of tea and call it a night. I imagine the children will wake early and be ready to go."

"Elise will look after them until you're settled."

"I'm settled now," she said firmly.

"I'll send for you once they are up and dressed and fed. There is an intercom button inside the wardrobe, and another on the wall near your bedroom light switch. You can call the butler at any time—we have a night attendant available—and request food, drink, or anything else you might need."

"The children have one in their room, too?"

"Yes. But they don't use it. Normally they get Miss Sheldon and then she handles their requests."

A light knock sounded at the bedroom door. Marcu crossed to open her door. A castle steward was on the doorstep with Monet's luggage and silently entered the room, carrying her suitcase and smaller bag into the bedroom.

Marcu looked at her. "Any other questions?"

"No." She suddenly felt exhausted and disoriented. What *was* she doing here? "I'll wait for you to send for me tomorrow."

* * *

It took Marcu hours to fall asleep. He was too keyed up, too restless to switch his thoughts off so he could sleep.

Now that Monet was here he could focus on his trip with Vittoria. He'd already looked at rings in Milan and his assistant at the Palermo office had booked the top floor of the resort Altapura for him and Vittoria, as well as making several reservations at the best restaurants. Vittoria was far more extroverted than Galeta had been and she enjoyed the social scene. It was one of the reasons he was taking her to the Alps. She loved showing off her prowess on the slopes during the day, and she enjoyed dressing up at night. Christmas for her was about parties and people, and he was trying to muster enthusiasm for a holiday that sounded dreadful.

He didn't want to be away from the children. He didn't want to be in some damn hotel. And he didn't want to propose over Christmas—he hated this time of year—but Vittoria had made it clear that she wanted a commitment from him, and she wanted it by the New Year.

Vittoria wasn't the perfect solution to his wife problem, but she came from a well-respected family, an old, powerful, wealthy Sicilian family, and she was beautiful and outgoing, which he thought would be good for the children. Proposing to Vittoria wasn't an impulsive decision. They'd been seeing each other for the past year and she'd handled herself well when she'd been with his children. Of course the children were a little standoffish because they didn't yet know her, but they would grow to care for her, and Vittoria would care for them. With time, everything would fall into place.

The hard part was done. Details had been organized, and everything problematic was sorted. It hadn't been easy, but Monet was here now and she'd take care of things for the next few weeks while he was gone. The children would be fine. Vittoria would accept his proposal. There was no reason to worry.

And yet, sleep still eluded him.

All because Monet was here, just one floor above his.

CHAPTER FOUR

MONET WAS AWAKE long before her breakfast tray was delivered to her room along with a folded card.

> The children and I will meet you in the music room at nine. The music room is one floor down, and the second door on the left. Marcu

She'd already had two cups of tea and a biscotti when the breakfast tray of yogurt, juice, and warm fragrant rolls arrived. She'd thought she was hungry until she read the note and then her stomach did nervous flips.

She wasn't ready to see Marcu again. To be honest, she found him rather terrifying. There was no boy left in his handsome face, and no softness in his personality. The loss of his wife had hardened him and made him intimidating and ruthless.

Years ago she would have said he'd be an amazing father but now he struck her as impossibly cold. She hoped he wasn't truly that cold with his children.

One minute before nine she left her room, headed down the stone stairs and counted the doors on the left, opening the second door as instructed.

The music room looked like a formal sitting room with antique chairs and oil paintings on the walls. The baby grand piano near the tall leaded window was the only instrument in the room. On closer inspection Monet discovered that the oil painting hanging over the fireplace was of a young woman playing the harp, while the painting near the piano was of a man playing the violin. So she was in the right room—this had to be the music room—but where were Marcu and the children?

She glanced at her watch. It was a minute past nine now. Perhaps they were still at breakfast.

She walked to the piano and lightly ran her fingers over the keys, not pressing hard enough to create sound. The keys were smooth beneath her touch and she was tempted to sit down and play something—she'd never had formal lessons but she'd learned to play by ear—but wasn't sure if Marcu would frown on her playing the piano here. He'd once played the piano. He'd been a serious musician, taking lessons and practicing for an hour or more every day. At the palazzo she'd creep into a corner and listen to him practice, amazed by his gift. When he played, he made her feel so much. Maybe it was music that had made her fall in love with him.

"Sorry to be late," Marcu said in English, as he entered the room, looking sophisticated and impossibly masculine in a black turtleneck sweater and black wool trousers. He didn't wear the clothes, they wore him, hugging his broad shoulders and narrow waist, while outlining his muscular torso and thighs.

Heat washed through her, and Monet bit down into her lower lip, hating the sudden weakness she felt as Marcu ushered his three shy young children toward her.

The children all had dark glossy hair, but it was the smaller boy, the one who must be Antonio, that was the spitting image of Marcu. The resemblance was so strong it nearly made Monet smile. *"Buongiorno,"* Monet said huskily in Italian. *Good morning.*

"These are my children," Marcu said, switching to Italian as he lined the children up by age. "Matteo, Rocca, and Antonio."

"It's nice to meet you," Monet said, approaching Matteo first and shaking his hand. "I am Monet."

"Signorina Wilde," Marcu corrected. "I can call you Monet because I have known you many years, but the children must call you Signorina." He clapped Matteo firmly on the shoulders. "And they will be good for you. They have promised to be obedient and polite and not make things difficult while you are here with them."

Marcu couldn't see how the little girl's face tightened, or how young Antonio blinked hard to hide the fact that his eyes were watering. She felt a pang of sympathy. The children were even more anxious about the change in their child care than she was. "I am only temporary," she reassured them. "Signorina Sheldon will be back before you know it."

"I have a great deal to attend to," Marcu said. "Can I leave them to you, Signorina Wilde? You're welcome to stay here or go upstairs to the nursery. I'm certain the children will be happy to show you around."

"We're fine. Please, don't worry about us," Monet assured him, giving him a bright smile. "See you later."

"We'll all have dinner tonight," he answered, heading for the door. "I'll see you then."

After Marcu left the music room, there was just silence. The three children gazed at her, clearly uncertain, as well as more than a little curious.

It had been a long time since Monet had spoken Italian but she was sure it wouldn't take long for it to come back as it was a language she'd spoken daily for years. "Do any of you play?" Monet asked, pointing to the piano.

The children shook their heads.

"Mamma used to play," the little girl said. "This was her music room."

"Your father plays for you, doesn't he?"

They looked at each other, puzzled, before shaking their heads.

"He used to play really well," Monet said, but this was followed by more silence. Monet gazed back at the children, lips curved, uncertain as how to proceed. She remembered from her past work that if she was too friendly the children would think her weak, and someone to be ignored, but if she didn't appear somewhat friendly and kind, then they would fear the worst.

"Did you really use to live at our house?" the little girl, Rocca, asked after a moment.

"This one?" Monet asked. "No—"

"No, not here," Rocca said quickly. "This isn't our home, this is Nonno and Nonna's house. Our house is in Palermo."

"The palazzo?" Monet clarified.

The children nodded.

Monet sat down on the edge of one of the chairs upholstered in gold silk. "I did. I knew your father when I was much younger, and I spent six years at the palazzo. It's a very beautiful place to live, isn't it?"

"It's very old," Matteo said. "I like more modern houses."

Monet's eyebrows lifted. "Are you interested in design?"

"No, but you can't get good Wi-Fi in the palazzo, at least, not in parts of it," Matteo said mournfully. "And it's even worse here. Here there is no internet. I can't play games with my friends."

"But you won't be here forever, and then you'll be back in Palermo," Monet replied. "Surely there are fun things about being here. Tell me some of your favorite things to do."

For a moment no one said anything, and the children looked at each other before Matteo shrugged. "We mostly do nothing. Everyone is very busy."

"And what about your father?" Monet couldn't help asking the question.

"He is very busy with work," Matteo said with a sigh, sounding resigned.

"Papà is important," Antonio added forlornly. "Everybody needs him."

The three faces before her looked so woebegone that Monet immediately wondered how much of their father they actually did see. "Well, I hate sitting around doing nothing so the four of us will do lots of fun things. We will need to make a list." Monet glanced from one young face to another, not certain why they weren't more enthused. "I would think this is a magical place to spend Christmas."

"Maybe," Matteo said, shoulders shrugging. "We used to come in summer. This is the first time we've come for Christmas."

Monet hid her surprise. From the way Marcu had described taking her to the children in the Alpine *castello*, one would have thought this was their annual tradition. "I didn't realize. I thought you came here every year."

"No. But Papà says it's going to be a different Christmas this year," Rocca said, before glancing at her brothers. "We don't know what that means."

Monet felt a heavy, sinking sensation in her chest. Had Marcu not yet told them that he was leaving them for the Christmas holidays? But she couldn't bear to think of that, not yet. "When were you last here? In the summer?"

"No. It's been a long time," Matteo said.

"I didn't even remember it," Rocca said.

"Me, either," Antonio said.

"That's because you've never been here before," Matteo said to Antonio before glancing at Monet.

"Papà didn't want to come here after Mamma died. It

was her house. We inherited it when Nonno and Nonna died. They are all gone now."

"Inherited means it's ours now," Rocca said gravely.

Monet folded her hands. "It must be very hard for you, not having your mother."

There was a beat of silence. "We don't remember her very much," Rocca answered. "I should because I'm five, but it's been too long. Papà says she loved us."

"I am sure she did." Monet scooted over in the upholstered chair and patted the golden silk cushion. "Won't you tell me about her? The parts that you remember… Or the parts that you have been told?"

"She was beautiful," the little girl said, taking a seat on the couch but leaving space between her and Monet. "I look like her. Papà said we have the same eyes, and the same nose and smile. There are pictures of her in the gallery. We can show them to you."

"Oh, I'd like that very much," Monet answered. "Could we do that now? I'd love to explore your *castello*. It's very big and I'm afraid without your help I'll get lost."

The children escorted her down the long corridor lined with ancestral portraits. Monet half smiled at the portraits, nearly all with long hair, black curls on both the men and women, and lots of velvet and ruffles, along with rings and necklaces, brooches and headbands, but what was one to expect when the family in question dated back centuries?

As the children led the way down the hall, the portraits became more modern, and the clothing became contemporary, until at last they came to a gold-framed oil of an elegant young woman with dark blond hair and wide brown eyes. She had a pale, creamy complexion, high cheekbones and a long aquiline nose. Her honey-colored hair was drawn back and her expression was rather aloof, and Monet wondered if that was really her personality or if the portrait painter had chosen that cool, detached expression for her.

"Mamma," Antonio announced.

"She is very lovely," Monet said. "I just wish she was smiling here. I'd love to know if she had a dimple like Rocca's."

"She didn't," Marcu said decisively, his deep voice coming from behind them.

Monet hadn't realized he'd joined them in the corridor and she stiffened in surprise, wondering how long he'd been standing there listening to them.

She glanced over her shoulder at him, her gaze again taking in his soft turtleneck and the well-tailored black trousers. He looked incredibly physically fit, as well as handsome and wealthy and altogether too powerful, which made her pulse race, and her stomach tighten with knots of apprehension, but also knots of something else.

She didn't want to contemplate the something else.

She wasn't here for something else.

He'd essentially forced her to come do a job so that he could be with yet another woman that wasn't her. She shouldn't respond to him. And she most definitely shouldn't care for him. After all these years, she shouldn't care that she wasn't the right woman for him and that she would never be the right one, and yet still, it stung. She didn't know if it was her pride, or that something else, but the fact that he could so easily dismiss her as someone valuable, and worthy of being kept and cherished, still made her ache.

She turned away as he approached, focusing instead on the children's faces, curious to see how they'd respond to his surprise visit. They didn't rush toward him, but then, Marcu and his brother and sisters hadn't rushed toward their father, either. They'd always greeted each other with kindness and civility, but control and discipline were always evident, just as they were now.

"I'm surprised you are still on this floor of the *castello*. You haven't made it very far in your tour," Marcu said.

"We have weeks to discover everything," Monet said lightly. "It's nice just to chat and get to know each other." She looked at him. "And I thought we weren't going to see you until dinner. Have you decided to join our tour?"

"My office is on the other side of that wall. I'm finding it difficult concentrating with all the chatter."

Monet saw Rocca's expression fall and it made her angry. Marcu seemed determined to disappoint his children. "Or maybe you were hoping to join us on our tour." She looked at the children. "Where should we go next?"

"The ballroom!" Rocca said.

"We're going to the ballroom," Monet said to Marcu with an arch of one eyebrow. "Would you care to join us?"

Rocca glanced up at him hopefully but he gave a swift decisive shake of his head. "I have too much work to do," he said.

Again Monet felt a wash of anger. Did he really have that much work to do? Or was he simply avoiding his children? It seemed to her, from all he'd told her, that he wanted as little to do with them as possible. It made no sense. Marcu had once been the most loving, considerate, and selfless of all the Ubertos. He'd been so patient with his younger brother and sisters, generous with his time, always available for a game or to listen and give a bit of advice.

"You're smart not to go with us," Monet flashed back, giving him a sunny smile. "We're going to the ballroom to dance. So, no waltzes for you, Signor Uberto."

"I'd prefer the children to go outside for their morning walk," Marcu said.

"Is that what they usually do, *signor*?"

"Yes. Exercise every morning after breakfast."

"Is there a certain number of push-ups they are to do, too?" she retorted.

He growled something indecipherable under his breath. "Don't challenge me," he said in English, "and never in front of them."

"Why don't you join us for a bit? You can tell me your rules and expectations that way."

"The children know."

She bit back her protest. He might still be gorgeous but he'd become incredibly unlikable. She executed a quick curtsy. "Very well, sir. Have a good day, sir."

"Monet." His voice held a hint of warning.

She stepped closer to him, and dropped her voice, ensuring that the children wouldn't hear as she replied in hushed English. "I've only been here a few hours, Marcu, but it seems to me that the children don't need a new mother, but rather they need a new father."

His hand reached out to clasp her arm. "Not acceptable."

She lifted her chin and her eyes met his. "Don't like it? Fire me."

"That's what you want, isn't it?"

"No, what I want is the kind Marcu. The one that loved his family and didn't punish them for loving him." Their gazes locked and held, his blue eyes glittering with anger. He was beautiful and cold and frightening, but she was just as tough, and just as fierce, and she wasn't going to let him intimidate her. He was the one who demanded she come here. He claimed he needed help—her help. Well then, he was going to get it, whether he liked it or not.

Suddenly the hard pressure of his hand wrapped around her arm eased. A shadow darkened his eyes. "I'm not a monster."

"No? Then don't act like one," she said as his hand

dropped. Her arm tingled from his touch, but she ignored the crazy sensations ricocheting through her and turned to the children, holding out a hand to Rocca, and then to Antonio. "Lead the way. I'm anxious to see what a ballroom would look like in this magnificent *castello*."

The children obliged, walking her out of the picture gallery, and down two floors, through the main entrance of the house, and down a side corridor, where they passed through a stone archway into a stunning room with a gold-stenciled ceiling and fresco-covered walls. The floor featured a marble parquet pattern and three enormous chandeliers lined the ceiling and tall windows filled the room with sunlight.

"Ooh, this is beautiful," Monet said. "I have a feeling this room has hosted some glorious parties, don't you think?"

"Mamma's coming-out ball was in this room," Rocca said proudly. "And Nonno's mother's ball, too. Papà said the balls are usually in the summer because the weather is so beautiful then."

"Well, I think this is beautiful any time of year," Monet answered. "But maybe we should fetch your coats and get some fresh air. It's sunny and beautiful right now."

"And cold," Rocca said. "I miss Sicily."

"You'll be back to Sicily before you know it," Monet countered cheerfully, "which is why you should make the most of your visit here while you can. What could we do later after we go for a walk? Is there anything you've been wanting to do?"

The children glanced at each other and shook their heads.

Monet led them from the ballroom so they could head upstairs to change for their walk. "What about the Christmas market?" she asked. "The Marché Vert Noël in Aosta is supposed to be one of the best in Italy."

"I don't think we can go," Matteo said gruffly as they reached the second floor.

"Why not?" Monet asked, pausing on the landing to wait for Antonio to catch up. "There's delicious food, and bands that play music at night. We could look at the handicrafts and sample sweets."

Rocca scrunched her nose. "We'd have to get permission from Papà and he only ever says yes to us walking and hiking and doing sporty things. He believes the two best things for us are reading and exercise." She huffed a breath. "I hate it, though."

"Reading and exercise?" Monet asked.

"Yes, because I can't read very good yet, and Antonio can't read at all. He doesn't even know most of his letters."

"But he will when he's older. You will all be excellent readers," Monet said, "because reading is fun—"

"Papà says life isn't mean to be fun," Matteo interrupted. "Life is serious, which is why we must be serious, too."

Monet had to hold her breath to keep her frustration in, and it crossed her mind as they reached the nursery door that maybe she really was needed here for Christmas, and the reason had nothing to do with Marcu needing a wife, but everything to do with Marcu embracing his children.

Although they were all to have dinner together that night, Marcu couldn't join them at the last minute and Monet had dinner with the children in the dining room. They'd finished the meal and were now enjoying their dessert, a delicious *budino* with salted caramel, and the children were happily dipping their spoons into the custard layer topped with a salty-sweet caramel sauce.

"I did some reading while you were reading this afternoon and I discovered that during the Middle Ages, this valley was one of the main passages through the Alps, and you couldn't pass through without paying a toll, which gave those who lived here power and money," Monet said, reaching for her coffee. "Castles like this one were built overlooking the valley so the nobleman could see who was approaching, and then he could stop the traveler and demand a toll. Savvy nobles could earn a lot of money monitoring traffic in and out of the valley."

"Our *castello* is really old," Antonio said, licking his spoon. "So old."

"It was built around the original square tower," Matteo said. "You can see the tower if you look carefully. Rooms were added to the tower to create more living space."

Suddenly Marcu was there in the dining room with them, drawing his chair out at the end of the table and taking a seat. "Not just living space," he said, "but public space for conducting government business. The ballroom you visited today was originally a public meeting room, where the locals could come petition the nobleman for help."

Surprised, but also pleased by Marcu's appearance, Monet bit her lip and let him take over the conversation.

"Where can you see the original tower?" Marcu asked his children.

"The kitchen," Matteo said promptly, "because it's all stone, everywhere, and the walls are very thick."

"The main entrance," Rocca said, smiling shyly at her father.

"Your study," Matteo added, "your bedroom and then the *signorina*'s bedroom. They all have the same beamed ceilings, fireplaces, and windows, too."

"That's right," Marcu said, before thanking the steward who'd appeared almost immediately with a coffee and dessert for him. "You can tell the original tower from the newer additions by the change in building material, as well as the thickness of the walls and how the windows are placed within the wall." He paused and glanced at his children, and then at Monet. "Did you have a good day today?"

The children nodded.

"What did you do?"

Monet noticed the children weren't in a hurry to answer so she gave a quick recap of their day. "We walked a lot, and went to the village to look at the Roman theater, and then we came back for lunch, and read, and played games." She lifted her coffee cup and gazed at Marcu over the rim, finding it impossible to look at anyone but him. Marcu had always been fit, but he was downright virile now. She wished he wasn't so appealing. She wished she could sit here and feel nothing. Instead she sat here and felt everything.

Thank God she'd grown up these past eight years. She might still be physically attracted to him, and she might still be awash in emotions, but at least the past eight years had taught her self-control, and discipline. She would never let him know how she felt, unwilling to let her emotions or her inexperience make a difficult situation impossible. "What about you?" she said with a faint smile. "How was your day, Signor Uberto?"

"A busy day," he answered in Italian. "I had a very full schedule of calls and meetings."

"The world markets never sleep, do they?"

"No. And the New York Stock Exchange is proving to be very volatile this week, requiring extra calls and consultations." His gaze swept the children, who were beginning to droop, and he switched to English. "They're looking tired."

"I think it's your mention of the stock market. It's enough to put anyone to sleep."

"Unless you're a financier or economist."

She glanced at the children. The custard desserts were gone, or nearly gone, but they'd stopped eating. Antonio's shoulders slumped and he was yawning broadly. "They do look sleepy," she said, "but I hate taking them away now. You've only just arrived."

"They're used to it."

"That's not a good thing, Marcu—" She broke off, flustered to have slipped and used his first name in front of the children. "I'm sorry. I meant, Signor—"

"You can call me Marcu. It's uncomfortable hearing you call me 'mister' and 'sir.'"

"But Miss Sheldon...?"

"She's my employee. You're..." His voice faded. He frowned and gave his head a sharp shake. "I don't know what you are."

Monet flushed, growing warm all over. Her cheeks suddenly felt too hot, and her skin too sensitive. "A friend of the family?"

"Yes," he said gruffly. "That would work." And yet there was an indecipherable emotion in his eyes that made her feel as if he was saying something altogether different.

"It's late," he said abruptly, rising and abandoning his coffee and dessert. "You should take the children up before they fall asleep in their custard cups."

"Of course." Monet rose from the table. "Come, my lovelies," she said to the children. "Let me walk you up and we'll get ready for bed."

The children kissed their father good-night and then Marcu added as she reached the doorway, "When you've finished putting them to bed, please come join me back downstairs in the smaller of the drawing rooms. I'd like to discuss my travel plans with you."

CHAPTER FIVE

MONET HATED THAT her pulse quickened as she headed down the stairs to meet Marcu in the drawing room. She hated that butterflies filled her middle even as she fought down a sense of excitement and expectancy. She shouldn't be feeling excited, or expectant. What did she think would happen? What was she hoping would happen? Ridiculous. This whole thing was beyond ridiculous. She was beyond ridiculous.

One of the housemaids had told her where to find the drawing room that Marcu favored for the evenings and she quietly opened the door and spotted him sitting in a chair near the fire reading from his stack of papers.

He looked up as she entered the room. "They are in bed?" he asked.

She nodded. "All sleeping soundly."

"Was it difficult?" he asked, folding the newspaper and adding it to the pile at his elbow. "It was your first time putting them to bed."

"They were talkative at first, so I let them talk and then I told them a story, and then we said prayers, and they fell asleep."

"They are in two separate bedrooms—did you tell two separate stories?"

"I brought them together for the stories and then we said the prayers together before I tucked each into his or her own bed."

"There wasn't a lot of resistance?"

"Is there usually?"

He hesitated. "When I put them to bed, yes."

Monet clasped her hands in front of her, feeling rather like a governess in a historical novel being called to explain her actions to her employer. She didn't like the feeling. She didn't like having to answer to Marcu. "May I sit?" she asked, "Or does Miss Sheldon not sit when asked to present herself to you?"

Marcu stared at her a long moment before the corner of his mouth lifted in a faint, wry smile. "You are not Miss Sheldon."

"No, I'm not."

"Please sit. Anywhere you like."

She glanced at her choices and saw that there were overstuffed armchairs near his, next to the fire, and then another seating area at the opposite end of the room. She obviously couldn't go sit at the far end of the room so she took one of the upholstered chairs by the fire. The fabric was soft, the cushions comfortable. She immediately felt better. "I could tell you why I think the children don't want to go to sleep when you put them to bed, but maybe you don't want to hear my opinions."

"You've only been here one day," he said mildly.

"I know, but I've had a lot of time today to think about what I've seen and heard, and I think the reason they are resistant to being put to bed when you do it is that they want more time with you, and they're not ready to let you go."

He was silent a moment before he shrugged his broad shoulders. "I love them and yet I can't give them everything they need. It feels like a losing battle. No matter what I do, it will never be enough."

"They don't require your soul. They do want your time, they want consistency, and they want love."

"You can say that because you have no children of your own."

"True. I don't have any of the guilt or anxiety you have. I have a job to do, and I know what I need to do. If I am doing my job to the best of my ability then I don't rake myself over the coals. There would be no point in that."

He got to his feet and glanced at the fire, and then her. "Would you like a drink? Sherry or maybe a glass of port?"

She started to shake her head, and then thought yes, she really would love something to drink. She could use a drink tonight. The children had not been difficult for her and yet it was still a long day, a tiring day, and she could feel the ache of tension in her back. "That would be lovely."

She watched as he crossed the room, going to a table against the wall with crystal decanters and bottles with pretty labels. He was still wearing his black wool trousers and the cashmere sweater that lovingly wrapped his muscular chest and biceps. His skin was burnished and his black hair looked glossy in the overhead light and she was fascinated by each of his movements as he reached for one of the liqueur bottles, then a small glass, which he filled for her.

"I think you will like this," he said, before filling a glass for himself and carrying their drinks back to where she sat by the fire.

His fingers brushed hers as he handed her the small glass. She felt a leap of warmth at the simple touch, and something electric jolted through her, making her heart do a painful double beat. Panicked that she was too open and transparent, Monet dropped her head and inhaled the port's sweet rich fragrance. Cherries and chocolate and sunbaked fruit.

One sip of the rich spicy sweet port and she flashed back to early years in Morocco, and then with another sip, she flashed back to a summer spent outside Taormina with Marcu and his family. His father had rented an enormous marble villa just above the water. The house had an even bigger pool. She'd spent every day, all day, in the pool, or on a chaise-longue chair, soaking up the sun. It had been a blissful summer for a thirteen-year-old girl, especially as Marcu had joined them for three weeks and he'd been like a god to her—bronzed, muscular, handsome, charming. She couldn't look at him without feeling love and longing. He spoke carelessly of the girls he dated, girls he took on motorbikes for rides, girls he took out to special romantic dinners. She'd wanted to be one of those beautiful girls he took out at night on his motorbike. She'd wanted to be his girl and there was a time she would have given anything to make that dream come true.

The heat from the port mingled with the bruised sensation in her chest. There was nothing good about remembering the past. Nothing good would come from looking back. She couldn't do this…not to him, or herself.

"So Vittoria," Monet said, forcing her mind to the present. "How did you meet? What are the juicy details?" she asked, deliberately keeping her tone light and teasing.

He arched a black brow as he dropped back into his chair by the fire. "There are no juicy details. It's a rather businesslike proposition. I'm marrying for the children's sake, and so it's a practical arrangement rather than a romantic one."

Her brow creased. She hesitated. "So you don't…love her?"

"We both have a strong feeling of regard for each other."

"What does that even mean?"

"It means there is affection, and attraction, as well as respect for each other's families."

"That sounds dreadful. I pity her, and I pity you. To go

from loving Galeta to a marriage of, well, convenience, it's horrible. You're shortchanging Vittoria and yourself."

"It was no different with Galeta. It was the same sort of marriage, except that time there was the understanding that children were important and her number-one responsibility was to provide children. Which she did," he added flatly.

"So Vittoria's number-one responsibility is to take care of the children Galeta gave you."

He gazed at her steadily. "Is there a question in there?"

She felt a pang for him, and the man she remembered, because Marcu had been lovely…warm, kind, smart, witty. She missed him, because that was the man his children needed for a father, not the man he'd become.

"I wish I could say that I was amazed that women sign up for this life," she said carefully, "but we both know women do. My mother would have loved to have married a wealthy man. Instead she spent her life as the side piece, and perhaps she thought she had power that way, or some form of independence, but we both know she didn't. She was utterly dependent on the men that sought her out. Her acting jobs disappeared as she grew older and eventually she had no income other than what men like your father provided."

"My father took care of her until the day she died."

"She only lived another year after they broke up." Monet exhaled hard, and closed her eyes, aware of the rapid staccato of her heart. She hated that he could arouse her emotions so easily. She hated that they were connected through their parents' relationship. "I'm sorry. I shouldn't have said any of that, and you didn't invite me here to discuss your relationship with Vittoria, or our parents. I'm here to be instructed in my duties, and your travel plans."

He grimaced. "You're suddenly more formal than my very formal Miss Sheldon."

"As I should be. I'm here to help you manage things, not complicate matters. So tell me, what is your travel schedule? When will you leave? What should I know?"

"I'm leaving the day after tomorrow for a meeting in Palermo, followed by an overnight in Rome and then I should be back Thursday."

"That's a great deal of driving, or will you be flying?"

"My helicopter will arrive in Aosta helipad tomorrow afternoon, and once the sun is up, we'll be gone early Wednesday morning. If the weather holds, I'll be back late afternoon Thursday by helicopter. If the weather turns, I'll drive up from Milan. But I'll use my helicopter rather than my jet for this trip as I can land right at the palazzo and also on top of the Uberto Financial office tower in Rome. Saves a great deal of time not needing a runway."

"So we should plan for your return on Thursday."

"Yes. I'd like to have a day here with the children before I travel back to Rome Friday afternoon to pick up Vittoria for our holiday."

Monet held her breath, wanting to tell him that he wasn't even giving his children twenty-four hours before leaving again. Instead she inclined her head to show she understood. She had to be careful not to overstep, much less challenge him on every aspect of his parenting. These were not her children. This was but a temporary job for her.

And yet despite her best effort to bite her tongue she must have revealed something of her thoughts because Marcu's brow creased and he sat forward in his chair. "What have I said now?"

"It doesn't matter."

"But it does. I'd like to understand. I need to understand. Once I understood you."

That made her flinch, and she stiffened. "No," she said,

quietly contradicting him. "You didn't understand me. You just thought you did."

His jaw tightened and his eyes narrowed. "I knew you better than anyone in my family."

"But that doesn't mean anything. Because if you'd truly known me, you wouldn't have—" She broke off and pressed her lips together, fighting all the recriminations that were bubbling up. Being near him had thrown the door open on the past and she was finding it impossible to live in the past and the present at the same time. It didn't work. She couldn't bear all the anger and pain. Anger was toxic. Pain created fresh pain. These emotions made her feel once again like the odd little girl with the odd mother with no home of their own.

"I wouldn't have what?" he finished for her.

She shook her head, determined to say no more. Determined to move forward. Determined to get through the next few weeks so she could be done with Marcu Uberto forever. "It's been a long day," she said, folding her hands together. "I'd like to get some sleep so I'll be rested for my day with the children tomorrow."

"Of course." He rose.

She rose, too. "Will we see you in the morning?"

"Probably not, but we'll have dinner together."

"I won't say anything about dinner with you to the children, so they won't be disappointed if it doesn't happen. It's better to not get their hopes up."

Heat flared in his eyes. "Is that a reprimand?"

"No, it's a statement of fact. Why make them promises that won't be kept? I think it's better to keep expectations low at this point."

"I have done my best."

"In this instance your best isn't good enough."

He closed the distance between them. "You don't know

what it was like, losing Galeta, being left with a newborn and two young children. It changed everything. It changed me."

"So I see, but as someone who was once your friend, they need more from you than a surrogate mother. Marcu, they need you. They need you to care—"

"I care!"

"Then don't leave them for Christmas. Stay—"

"Vittoria wants a Christmas proposal. She's made it clear she's expecting a Christmas proposal."

"Then bring her here. Have a family Christmas with her here."

"We will return, after the trip, and it's just one Christmas. It's only this year—"

"What if she demands you go skiing with her every Christmas? What if she wants to have a romantic Christmas with just the two of you every year?"

"She wouldn't."

"Are you sure? What do you really know about her? How do you know she will love them? You've introduced her to them, but there is no relationship, no bond, nothing to reassure you that she'll give them the tenderness they need."

"You have no children. What makes you an expert?"

"Because I know what it's like to constantly play second fiddle to your parents' romantic relationships. It hurts, Marcu."

Her voice cracked and the sheen of tears in her eyes made him want to rage against the injustice of the universe, because fate was harsh and life could be brutal and the only way to survive was by being hard. "Can't you see that I'm trying," he said, wrapping an arm around her back, holding her securely.

She blinked as she looked at him, cheeks flushed, eyes

brilliant with fierce tears. “Are you?” she demanded. “Or are you hiding from them?”

“What does that mean?”

“The children don’t even know you can play the piano. They don’t know you love music and art and beauty—”

“I did. I don’t anymore.”

“Pity, because everyone needs beauty and art in their life. Children need beauty—”

“Why? It’s just going to be snatched away.”

“Beauty helps us through times of pain. Beauty, like love, heals and redeems—”

“I am certain there is plenty more you’d like to say,” he growled, “but I’ve heard enough from you for one night.”

His head descended and his lips covered hers. Monet stiffened with surprise, and panic, but the panic faded the second his lips touched hers.

Monet felt yanked back in time the moment she’d felt his arm circle her, his body pressing against hers, his frame lean and hard and so very male.

The brush of his lips and scent of his skin overwhelmed her with longing, and memory, and she was eighteen again, and in Marcu’s spacious, luxurious bedroom suite at the Uberto palazzo. As the Uberto heir, he had the largest suite after his parents, gorgeous rooms that seemed to go on and on—living room, study, bedroom, en-suite bathroom, huge walk-in closet. He’d first kissed her in the doorway between his living room and study, and then they’d ended up on his bed, his large body pinning hers, their hands clasped, fingers entwined, her body arching against his, desperate for him.

This kiss eight years later flamed hot, and desperate. It was as if they had left off exactly where they’d stopped… the emotion, the need, the craving, so fierce, so insistent, and yet, so punishing. She had wanted him then, and she wanted him now, but want wasn't an easy thing, not with their history. The want created pain and anger, because he didn't care about her, not really. He desired her, the same way his father had desired her mother, but the Uberto men took different women to be their wives. They chose different women to be the mothers of their children. Rage and hurt welled within her, making her burn hot and cold. He'd make love to Monet tonight but then fly out tomorrow to propose to Vittoria.

She'd never be anything more than a side piece. Something used to satisfy one's carnal desire. Heartsick, she pushed against Marcu's chest, hard enough to free herself. He, too, was breathing heavily as his arms dropped, but he didn't move away. She took a frantic step backward, pulse racing, body trembling, even as something inside of her urged her to return to his arms, return to his warmth.

My God, she was stupid. She hadn't matured at all. He was still so dangerous and destructive, at least to her heart, never mind her self-control. She shot him a fierce look before leaving the study, fleeing for the privacy of her own room.

Marcu was as shocked as she was. He heard, rather than saw, Monet leave, even though his gaze followed her to the door, but he couldn't see as much as feel.

He felt stunned, his body hot and cold, but also, strangely alive. Energy coursed through him, hot primitive desire pumped through his veins. His muscles contracted, his heart thudded.

He wanted her.

He wanted her more than he'd ever wanted anyone.

Why?

Was it because she was forbidden? Was it because she represented youth and the last of his innocence?

Why did he crave her when he had never craved any other woman…ever?

His gaze lingered on the closed door, aware of how still everything had become. The room suddenly felt empty and cold without Monet.

He felt empty, and cold, but not as cold as he usually did. She'd lit a flame inside of him and the small flickering flame had the potential to burn brightly. If he let it.

He couldn't let it.

He couldn't give in to sensation, or emotion, or impulse. Not when he'd spent the past three years teaching his children that life wasn't about fun or pleasure. It was about duty, and discipline. It was about reason and intellect.

The flame inside of him was the opposite of logic. The flame was passion and fire and hunger, and it couldn't be allowed to burn. He had to snuff it out. He had to remember the lessons he'd been teaching the children. Order. Predictability. Self-control. These were the virtues and values he respected, and this is why he structured their world as he did. It was a conscious attempt to protect them from chaos. He believed that discipline and control would serve them well as they grew into adulthood. Discipline and control would allow them to make good decisions, logical decisions, so they wouldn't be disappointed by life, or worse, hurt by it.

He'd been hurt, repeatedly, until he'd finally learned what life was trying to teach him: emotions were not to be trusted, whereas a cool head, and sharp intellect, prevailed. Which is why he didn't teach his children about hope, or faith, and why he wasn't looking for love in marriage. He'd been brought up to believe that love was somehow redemptive. It wasn't. Everything he'd been taught was a lie. His childhood was one fabrication on top of another, and after Galeta's death, Marcu had resolved to parent differently.

His children would be guided by knowledge and truth, and that was all.

Kissing Monet had been a terrible mistake and it wouldn't happen again.

CHAPTER SIX

Good God, what had happened downstairs?

Monet frantically paced her private sitting room, her steps muffled by the thick peach-and-cream Persian rug, the peach and cream echoed in the glamorous Italian silk curtains at the windows and the apricot silk panels on the four-poster bed in the adjacent room.

She couldn't believe she'd let him kiss her. She couldn't believe she'd kissed him back, because she had, she most definitely had.

Horrified, she went into the bedroom to stare at her face in the Venetian mirror hanging above the dressing table. Her cheeks were flushed and her eyes looked feverishly bright. Her full mouth looked plump and very kissed… because she had been *very* kissed.

She pressed a hand to her lips, feeling the warmth and sensitivity, thinking it had been forever since she'd felt anything so good, or felt so alive.

She'd wanted the kiss, too. How she'd wanted it. There was no way she could blame him for reaching for her because she'd spent the past few days wondering what it would be like to kiss him now…and if his kiss could wreck her the way it had upended her world eight years ago.

For the past eight years she'd wondered if his kiss had been as overwhelming and wonderful as she remembered, or if it had simply been the fact that it was her first real kiss, and in her inexperience she'd made it out to be more than it was.

Eight years ago his kiss had stripped her bare, stealing her heart, making her his, and all this time she'd wondered why he had so devastated her. And now she knew. It wasn't inexperience. It wasn't innocence. It was *him*. There was something powerful, something electric, in his touch.

His lips on hers just now had made her feel so many things, awakening the past, as well as jolting her from complacency. She wasn't immune to him. She wasn't in control of herself here. She wasn't confident, either. From the time she arrived at the *castello* she'd been certain he was as aware of her as she was of him, and it wasn't a casual awareness, but the taut, aching awareness of heat and memory and barely suppressed desire.

The kiss downstairs had burned with desire.

The kiss downstairs—

A firm knock sounded before the door to her outer room opened. Monet moved from the dressing table to the middle of her bedroom and Marcu was there, closing the door and holding a finger to his lips.

"Let's not have the children in here as well," he said tersely, his gaze sweeping her cozy sitting room with the beamed ceiling and stone fireplace.

"I don't recall inviting you in," she said.

"I wouldn't have had to chase you down in here, if you had stayed downstairs so we could have had a conversation—"

"There's nothing to discuss." Her teeth chattered slightly and she felt cold and hot all over again. She longed for a thick sweater, or blanket, to wrap herself in. She wanted to hide. She wanted to savor the kiss because she knew it would never happen again. It couldn't happen again. "We both know it was inappropriate."

"Yes. You're right. The kiss *was* inappropriate, which is why we must talk, because I can't propose to Vittoria, not if I'm kissing you."

His words sent a shudder through her. She needed him to propose to Vittoria so she could escape Marcu and the *castello*. "I can forgive the kiss if it doesn't happen again," she said quietly.

"It was a mistake."

"It absolutely was."

His blue gaze skewered her, burning all the way through her. "And I won't kiss you, or touch you again—"

"Good."

"—while I'm pursuing another relationship."

"Exactly."

"But should I choose to pursue a relationship with you, it's a different story."

Monet froze, and blinked, dumbfounded. *What had he just said?* "You're about to propose to Vittoria," she said unsteadily. "Let's not confuse things, shall we?"

"I'm looking for a mother for my children. That is my goal."

"I understand that, and I also understand that when you're in Rome Wednesday night, you'll be with Vittoria, and then again with her on Friday, and I want you to go knowing that things will be calm and happy here. I can assure you the children will be safe with me."

"I have no doubt. My children seem happy with you."

"Good. So from now on focus on Vittoria and I will focus on the children and we won't need to speak of this again as we both have agreed it's a mistake."

"Yes."

"And we're both agreeing now that it will not happen again. There will be no further contact between us, and no physical intimacy." She hesitated. "Will you tell her what happened? Will you tell her about the kiss?"

He didn't answer immediately, then he nodded abruptly. "I should, yes." And then he walked out, leaving her even more shaken then before.

Kissing Marcu had been a horrendous mistake and the memory of his warmth and touch and taste haunted her all night, making sleep almost impossible. Every time she began dreaming, it was of him, and being in his arms and in his bed and completing what had begun between them so many years ago.

By the time morning came, Monet was exhausted and tense and wishing she was back in London, in the safety of her flat. She wasn't safe here—not because Marcu would force himself on her, but because she didn't trust herself anymore. Not with him.

That kiss last night…

That kiss had stirred something dark and dangerous and altogether too unpredictable awake within her, making her feel things she didn't want to feel, things she'd only ever felt with Marcu.

He needed to go. He needed to leave Aosta as soon as possible and settle things with Vittoria so she could leave the Italian Alps, too. London had never been so appealing.

Midmorning, Monet and the children walked to Aosta village again, the children's snow boots tramping snow and crunching ice as they talked about nothing and everything. Their chatter made Monet smile because it was sweet and they were so kind to each other. Marcu might be strict and distant but his children were definitely loving.

"Oh, there's the Christmas market again," Rocca said,

pointing to the stands and booths in the middle of the Roman theater. "I really do wish we could visit it."

"I'll ask your father," Monet answered.

"I don't think that's a good idea," Matteo said. "He will just say we can't come to town anymore and I like coming here."

"Why won't he approve?" Monet persisted.

"Because he doesn't like Christmas," Rocca said bluntly. "It makes him mad. He thinks it's better to not make such a fuss at this time of year, and focus instead on winter sports."

Monet tugged on her gloves, pulling them higher. "Is that why the *castello* isn't festive? I've noticed there are no decorations, no Christmas tree."

"We don't *ever* have a Christmas tree," Rocca added.

"Not even in Palermo?" she clarified, and was dismayed when the children shook their heads. This didn't make sense. In Palermo, at the palazzo, Christmas was important, special. In the six years she had spent in Sicily, the Uberto family celebrated Christmas in a big way, kicking off the season on December eighth when family and staff came together to decorate the house. The Uberto family celebrated both Italian and Sicilian traditions, and it was the highlight of the year.

"Since when?" she asked. "Because when I was living with your father's family in Palermo we most definitely celebrated Christmas. Your grandfather Matteo adored Christmas. It was his favorite time of year."

The children just shrugged and gave each other swift glances, but this time Monet saw the worry, and the secret they were keeping. "What are you not telling me? I can see it in your eyes, and your faces. You're not very good liars—which I might add is a good thing—so come on, tell me. You can trust me. Remember, I've known your father for many, many years. Why don't you have a tree and do festive things?"

"It's because this is when my *mamma* died," Rocca blurted.

Matteo nodded grimly. "She died December sixteenth."

"After Antonio was born," Rocca added.

"Me," Antonio chimed in.

December sixteenth had been yesterday. Galeta had died three years ago yesterday.

Monet held her breath, overwhelmed. "Antonio, you must have just had a birthday," she said.

"Last week," Rocca answered for him, giving her brother a little pat.

Monet's heart went out to the children. So much had happened in their lives. There had been so much loss and pain. And then she thought of Marcu, and their conversation last night, and she understood him a little better, understood his pain and desperation better. For three years he'd been grieving and he was desperate for the grief to end. He was desperate for some kind of normalcy for his children, even if he was going about it the wrong way.

"It's cold," Rocca said, clapping her hands.

"Let's keep walking," Monet said, "before you turn to icicles."

Antonio laughed and took Monet's hand but Matteo walked ahead, shoulders hunched. Monet let him walk ahead for a while and then stopped him as they neared the village. "What are you thinking about?"

"I remember when we did have a Christmas tree," he said quietly. "We still do have a *presepi*, but it's not out yet. Maybe we didn't bring it from home."

Monet knew the *presepi*, or Nativity, was the most important element of every Italian home at Christmas. The *presepi* at the palazzo was over a hundred years old, had been hand-carved in Naples, and the gorgeous figurines had filled her with wonder every year.

"What if we do a few festive things together? Just because your father doesn't enjoy the holiday as much as he once did, doesn't mean you can't." She was silent a moment, then added, "Maybe we just have to remind him how beautiful Christmas really is."

"He won't like it," Rocca answered quickly. "We tried once to decorate a little tree in the nursery at the palazzo and he threw it away."

"Well, he can't throw away something that I buy, not if it's mine," Monet answered.

"Papà will make you."

"No, he can't. He won't. I might work for him, but he doesn't own me."

The children gave her a pitying look, which didn't sit well with her at all, and not only because she wasn't the least bit afraid of their father, but also because they didn't realize that it was the Uberto family that had taught her how magical Christmas could be. And it would be magical for these children, even if she had to give them the magic in little bites.

"I understand your concerns," Monet said cheerfully, "but what about me? What about *my* holiday? I can't be expected to go through Christmas without fun, can I? In London everything is so festive and beautiful right now. There are gorgeous lights and decorations everywhere, and all the stores and restaurants have dressed up their windows. Even the store I worked in had Christmas trees and decorations on every floor. My department was silver and white, with a huge silver Christmas tree with thousands of white lights just across from my desk."

"But that was London," Matteo said regretfully. "And this is Italy."

"And Italians love Christmas. Sicilians love Christmas."

"But not Papà, and we really think you'd better ask our father." Matteo glanced at his siblings and gave them a sad look, before looking back at her. "He *hates* surprises."

"I will, because *I* hate being disappointed."

Marcu made it on time for dinner and Monet really wished she could have been excused to let Marcu and his children eat together without her, but Marcu seemed to think a nanny's presence was necessary for everything.

She did make a point of saying little during the meal so the conversation could be between the children and their father, but Marcu didn't ask them very many questions and the children volunteered very little information and conversation petered out before it really began.

It was a relief when they were dismissed for bed but then Marcu stopped her as she rose, saying he expected to see her after she'd finished putting the children to bed.

She nodded that she'd heard and then continued ushering the children out, even as she processed the fact that he never hugged them or kissed them, or said anything loving and tender when saying good-night. You'd almost think he was running some form of military school. It hurt her heart, not just for the children's sake, but for his as well.

A half hour later she came back downstairs and joined Marcu in the smaller living room, having already learned that this was the room he favored in the evenings because the wooden shutters could be closed against the cold glass, keeping out the chill, and a fire could be laid in the stone hearth, making the room warm and cozy.

The ceiling was vaulted and lined with dark beams, and the fabric on the chairs and sofa was a lovely burnt pumpkin brocade, with vivid blue tiled end tables with a matching cobalt-blue wash on the inside of the huge hearth. One wall was lined with glass book cabinets, while another wall featured vivid modern art in pinks, oranges and blues. The room, centuries old, exuded elegance and money and style. No one knew how to layer fabrics and use color like the Italians.

"I'm concerned about the children," she said abruptly, taking the same chair she'd sat in last night.

"What was that?" he asked, glancing up from the book he was reading. It was the same book that had been on the table last night, and she'd glimpsed the title, something to do with politics, economics and world currencies. She couldn't imagine reading a huge book on such a subject matter but then, she wasn't an investment banker or venture capitalist, either.

"Your children shocked me today."

He closed the book. "How so?"

"They told me they don't celebrate Christmas, and I didn't believe them, telling them Christmas was always a special time at the palazzo in Palermo—"

"That was before," he interrupted, placing his book on the table at his elbow. "We don't make a fuss about Christmas anymore. It's not appropriate in light of things."

Monet decided to feign ignorance. "What things? Has the church stopped celebrating the birth of Christ?"

"No, of course not."

"They why would you not celebrate Christmas with your children?"

"We go to Mass."

"And?"

"And what?" he retorted impatiently.

"Where is the Nativity scene? Rocca and Antonio are the perfect age to enjoy the *presepi*, and you always had such a beautiful one in Palermo. In fact, there were three at one time, each set up in a different room of the palazzo."

"But we're not in Palermo," he said.

"You couldn't bring one with you? Or buy one for your children to enjoy here?"

"We're here for just three or four weeks, it seems silly to drag something like that all the way here."

She studied him a long moment. "Is that also why there are no Christmas decorations? No tree? No pretty lights or greenery around the doors, or windows? I understand you dragged skis and skates here, but nothing to celebrate the season?"

He stirred uncomfortably. "We don't make a fuss over Christmas."

"Why? Christmas was a gorgeous, special time in your family."

"That was before," he retorted curtly, rising from his chair to go stoke the fire. "Things have changed. We have different traditions now."

"But to eliminate the wonder of Christmas for your children? There are so many lovely, festive things you could do and enjoy as a family—"

"I've chosen not to."

"They miss it, though."

He added a log to the fire before turning to face her. "How can they miss what they don't know?" he demanded. "They can't."

"Matteo remembers. He was telling me about how Christmas used to be. The younger ones were all ears. They'd love to experience some of the fun and traditions that other children their age enjoy."

"No." He clasped his hands behind his back and stood tall and resolute. "It's not something we do in our family. Not anymore."

She looked at him steadily, her gaze meeting his and holding. "Well, I do. Christmas is important to me and I'm not going to give it up for you. That's not part of our deal, so I'm going to make the most of the next few weeks and have my tree, and decorate it, and go listen to carols, and do my holiday baking and anything else that makes this season so special to me."

"You can do what you want in your time, but you're not to include the children."

She couldn't help her gurgle of laughter. Was he serious? And just what time was her time?

Her laughter made his expression darker, grimmer. His jaw jutted and his mouth tightened and he truly seemed to believe he could give her orders and have them obeyed.

Not happening.

"Marcu, you're not thinking this through," she said more gently. "You've brought me here to take care of the children. There is no backup nanny. I don't have time 'off.' I don't have areas that are only mine—"

"You have your own suite of rooms. You can do what you want in there, but not in the nursery, or their individual bedrooms."

"So I can decorate my suite?"

"It's your own room." He hesitated. "But you can't bring the children into your room, and they can't know about your decorations—"

"Stop. Listen to yourself. You're being ridiculous, you are. When did you become such an ogre, Marcu?"

"I don't like Christmas," he said sharply, "and I'm not going to have you confusing the children. We enjoy this month, we do, but we enjoy it the way I think is best, which is with little fanfare and drama."

"So there is no Christmas miracle for you?"

He gave her an almost savage look, blue eyes glittering beneath black brows. "There is certainly no miracle."

"You've lost your faith."

He picked up the poker and jabbed the logs furiously, sending sparks shooting up into the chimney. "You know nothing about it, and you'd be wise to drop the whole subject now."

The words were as sharp and hot as the sparks, and Monet let them swirl around her a moment before she answered. "I think I understand a little bit," she said quietly before drawing a quick breath for courage. "This is about Galeta. You lost her before Christmas."

"I didn't *lose* her. We were not careless with her. She wasn't misplaced, or lost. She was at home, with her family, with her newborn. She was where she belonged." His hard voice cracked. "And then God took her."

Monet drew another breath. "God didn't take her. Galeta was mortal. Her body failed her—"

"Che palle!"

The oath was mild but his expression was pained.

"To take a young mother from her three children," he gritted, tossing aside the poker. "Children who were just babies. A newborn just days old. My wife had a family that needed her, and loved her, and I don't know how to do this without her. I can't do this without her. So don't talk to me about faith, because you'd question yours, too, should you lose someone so fundamental to your life."

And then he walked out.

Marcu was gone in the morning when Monet woke up, leaving a note for her that he expected her to follow his instructions and if she wasn't clear on his expectations, all she had to do was call, and he'd scribbled his phone number.

After dressing, Monet headed to the nursery to oversee breakfast. As the children ate, they discussed their day.

"I was thinking we could talk to Cook and see if she'd let us visit the kitchen later and make some Christmas cookies. I don't know if you have a favorite kind but I remember the delicious *cuccidati* we used to have at the palazzo, filled with figs, dates, walnuts, spices and a hint of orange."

Elise, the housemaid, had just entered the room to collect the morning dishes and smiled as she heard mention of the Sicilian cookies. "*Cuccidati* are a lot of work, and I'm not sure Cook has all the ingredients right now, but I am certain you could make *canestrelli* or even *pizzicati* without too much effort. Would you like me to ask Cook?"

The children answered with a resounding yes and then after Elise had gone, Monet helped Antonio dress. Matteo and Rocca didn't need or want help from her. Once hair was brushed, and teeth were clean, they resumed discussion about what to do after they were done with cookies—if Cook would allow them into the kitchen.

"Any ideas?" Monet asked them, buoyed by their eager faces. "Suggestions?"

"What could we do?" Matteo asked.

"Well, I suggest we go to the Christmas market in the village tonight," Monet said. "We'll go have dinner there and shop and see if we can't find some pretty ornaments and trinkets to decorate our own Christmas tree."

"But we don't even have a Christmas tree," Rocca reminded Monet.

"Then that is the first thing we'll do today. We'll go find a tree, and have someone help us cut it down and bring it in to the nursery."

Matteo looked skeptical. "I don't think this is a good idea. Father won't like it."

"We're not putting it in his bedroom. Or his study. Or his living room. It's going in your room." Monet studied their suddenly pinched, anxious faces. They really were nervous and that wasn't her intention. "Or," she added thoughtfully, "we could just put it in my room. I would love a Christmas tree. It'd make my room so cozy at night and it'd make it smell wonderful during the day."

"But then when we will see it?" Antonio asked. "I want a Christmas tree. I want a tree with pretty lights and ornaments and things."

She drew Antonio onto her lap. "You can always come into my room. In fact, we can have evening stories and prayers in my room. It will be quite festive. Cookies and stories every night before bed." Monet glanced from one face to the next. "How does that sound?"

"So nice…" Rocca said with a wistful sigh.

But Matteo looked troubled. "I still don't think Papà will like it. He'll say we're being sneaky."

"Then let's not do it," Monet said. "The last thing I want you to do is get in trouble. This is supposed to be a fun time of year, not a time for you to be troubled or anxious."

For a moment no one said anything and then Antonio whispered, "So you're not going to have a tree, Signorina Wilde?"

"I'd like one," she answered truthfully. "Even if it's just a very small tree. I could put it on the desk."

"Or on that table by your couch," Rocca said. "That way you could see it from your bed, too."

Monet smiled. "That is a good idea. I'd like that."

"Can we help decorate it?" Rocca asked.

"I want to, I want to," Antonio cried. "Please can I help?"

"And help pick it out? We could all go look for it together." Rocca looked hopeful. "We could even help cut it and carry it—"

"No, I think we'll leave the cutting to someone else," Monet interrupted with a smile. "But I don't see why you couldn't give me some advice. I can always use advice."

"And then we will put it in your room. There's no reason we can't go there just at night and say good-night to the tree. It's not being that sneaky. We're just saying a quick good-night, and that shouldn't make Papà too mad at us." She darted a swift glance at Matteo, and then at Monet. "He'd just be mad at Monet."

"But we don't want Papà mad at Monet," Matteo said irritably. "It's not fair for her to get in trouble for something we want."

"That's true. If we really want a tree, then we should just tell him so," Rocca said. "And if he shouts, he shouts."

Matteo shook his head. "Papà doesn't shout. He just frowns a lot and gets that expression that makes you think he's never going to smile again."

"I've seen that expression," Monet said. "It wasn't always that way, though. He used to smile a great deal. When he was younger, when I knew him before, he smiled all the time."

"He smiled before Mamma died," Matteo said quietly. "I remember our last Christmas here, before Antonio was born." He looked at his sister. "Do you remember? It was the best Christmas. It was so happy. Like a fairy tale."

The children fell silent. Monet's chest suddenly ached and her eyes felt hot and gritty.

It was the best Christmas.

Like a fairy tale.

Their innocent words pricked her heart and made her want to wrap her arms around them and keep them safe.

What a hard time they'd had of it. How impossible to lose their mother, and their father, because they had lost Marcu, too. He'd lost all joy, and love, and tenderness. It was a tragedy on top of tragedy. She exhaled slowly, letting out some of the bottled air, and said quietly, "It can be that way again. It will be that way again, one day, I promise."

"How?" Rocca asked.

Monet reached out to stroke the girl's dark silky hair,

and Rocca leaned into the caress and Monet gave her head another comforting touch. "Maybe it's time we started reminding him of just how beautiful and special Christmas really is."

It was an extremely busy day, packed with activities from baking cookies to sampling cookies, to dressing in winter gear to tramp through the snow-dusted garden in search of a tree somewhere on the grounds that would be the perfect tree. It took them nearly an hour before they found one they could all agree on, and then they went in search of a gardener to cut it down and bring it inside for them.

There was much discussion about where the tree should go in Monet's room, and they moved it from spot to spot, all while Antonio begged to let them put it in the nursery. But Matteo was adamant that his father would be livid if he found it there and Monet agreed with Matteo. "We don't want your father livid," Monet said.

Once they had the tree positioned in its metal stand, they discussed how they should decorate it. The children made paper snowflakes and colored some stars, and just before they hung them on the tree, the butler appeared with a box of Christmas decorations he'd found in the attic. The children carefully went through the box, oohing and aahing at the old, and very fragile glass ornaments, and the wooden hand-carved ornaments depicting angels and wise men and shepherds and animals from the manger. They were still looking through all the ornaments, deciding which ones were small enough and light enough, to go on their little tree, when the butler returned with a long string of white lights.

The children abandoned the ornaments to help her wind the lights through the tree branches and then hang the ornaments they'd selected from the box, along with the white snowflakes they'd made. They were delighted with their finished product and begged to eat their dinner in front of the fire in her room so they could enjoy the tree. Cook made them a special meal of pizza and they all sat around on her living-room floor with their pizza and their homemade cookies, proud of everything they had accomplished today.

Monet smiled as the children chattered, telling herself everything was fine, but secretly, she had knots in her stomach, and her stomach cramped with anxiety.

Marcu wasn't going to be happy when he returned.

Marcu would probably be livid.

This was exactly the kind of day he wouldn't approve of, and yet the children were beyond thrilled. As they prepared for bed, they were positively giddy, reliving the day, and how they'd found the tree and picked ornaments from the box.

But fortunately, he wouldn't be home just yet. Fortunately they had another full day before he returned late tomorrow afternoon, or tomorrow night.

CHAPTER SEVEN

THE WINTER STORM warnings worried Marcu, and he wrapped up his meetings early, and was in his helicopter flying north, when it became apparent it was foolish to try to land in Aosta. Snow had begun to fall and the wind was howling and the only way he'd make it to the *castello* tonight would be to drive from Milan. Fortunately, his assistant had booked a car for him, and the car was waiting at the Milan airport when the helicopter landed.

Relieved to be behind the wheel, Marcu left the city, and tried to relax as he got on the open road, but the sky was dark and ominous and the news reports indicated foul weather for the next few days, with this new storm being the worst so far this year.

As he drove, he wondered what the children had been doing, and he hoped Monet had gotten them outside for fresh air and exercise. He tried to think of the children but not Monet, which was impossible. The more he tried to block her from his thoughts, the more she consumed them.

He'd been so preoccupied with her even last night when he'd taken Vittoria to dinner. He hadn't wanted to be at dinner with Vittoria. He sat across the table from her thinking that maybe Monet was right, maybe he was making a mistake, and not because he needed a warm wife, but the children needed a warm, tender mother. Only as he listened to Vittoria discuss the ski trip, and the people who would be there, and the parties they'd been invited to, his chest tightened, the air bottling in his lungs. Not once did she ask about his children. Not once did she express concern that it might be difficult for the children to be left behind for the holiday.

What if she was as cold and hard as he was?

What if the children suffered more if he married her?

"I have to tell you something," he'd said, putting down his fork. "I kissed Monet, the woman who is staying with the children while Miss Sheldon is gone. It shouldn't have happened, and it won't happen again. I'm sorry—"

"If it was a one-off, and it won't happen again, why are you telling me?" she asked, coolly. "Was there a reason for me to know?"

"I feel badly about it."

She gave him a long level look before shrugging. "I have never imagined you to be a saint. You will do what you want—"

"But I don't, and I wouldn't when we marry." *If we marry*, he silently added, before wondering where that came from.

He wasn't having serious doubts, was he?

He couldn't let Monet turn everything inside out.

"Men have affairs," Vittoria answered matter-of-factly. "Women do, too. It's human nature."

"I never cheated on Galeta. If we married, I wouldn't cheat on you," he said grimly.

"If," she said, head tipping, long hair spilling over her shoulder. "You are not so sure now, are you? A few days with this nanny from your childhood, and you kiss her, and then question our relationship. Perhaps you have feelings for her."

"I did," he said, "when I was younger, before I married Galeta."

"Perhaps you still do now."

Dinner ended soon after that, and he drove Vittoria back to her apartment, and he left her after seeing her to her door.

Back in his car he'd felt wildly out of sorts. Kissing Monet had changed everything. It shouldn't have because the kiss was brief. It had lasted less than a minute. There had been no touching, no exploration of skin or curves… and yet he might as well have stripped her bare because her body was so imprinted on his mind and imagination.

He'd felt her soft breasts against his chest. He'd felt the shape of her hips, and the indentation of her waist. He'd felt the heat of her slim body and the vanilla-and-orange-blossom scent of her hair and skin.

She'd smelled like summer and her fragrance had stayed with him long after he'd gone to bed, making him think of home, and a past that was long gone.

On the one hand she was vastly different from the girl she'd been, and on the other, she was exactly the same girl—strong, smart, authentic, original.

He'd never met anyone like Monet. She was so opposite him in every way and yet somehow it had once felt right.

Now…

Now…

But there was no now, he told himself tersely, tension weighting his limbs. He still needed a wife, and Vittoria had met the children and it could be a good marriage. He hadn't married Galeta because he'd loved her, but he'd respected her, and he respected Vittoria. Love was inconsequential. Security mattered. Stability mattered. He wasn't going to risk the future—or his children's mental health—on something as temporary, and unstable, as romantic love.

Not that he'd ever loved Monet, either. But there had been desire. Fierce desire. Desire that had destroyed a six-year relationship and created a serious chasm between him and his father.

He had to smash the desire now. He had to get control of himself immediately. There was no way he'd allow an impulse to wreck his plans. He knew what he wanted, and he knew what he didn't want and his decision had been made.

Exhaling, Marcu turned the windshield wipers on higher, needing the increased speed to clear the falling snow from the windshield. The snow was coming down harder. The wind was blowing sheets of snow across the road, turning the world beyond his car a blinding white. It was going to be a long drive to the *castello* tonight.

By the time he arrived home, the children were in bed, asleep—he knew, because he checked in on them and they were all in their beds, tucked in against the night's chill. Marcu went to Monet's room and knocked on the door, wanting to see how things had gone while he'd been away.

It took her a few moments to come to the door and he wondered if she'd also gone to bed. He was just turning away when her door opened and she peeked out, her long dark hair tumbling free over her shoulders, her eyes lovely and luminous in her pale oval face.

"Did I wake you?" he asked, feeling guilty for disturbing her, and yet it wasn't that late, not even quite nine.

"No, I was just in bed reading."

"How was everything here? I didn't hear from you so I hope things went smoothly."

"Very smoothly," she answered. "We get along very well. So well, that the time just flies by."

There was something in her cheerful answer that sounded a little forced. "What did you do to pass the time?" he asked.

"We made cookies, and played in the snow." She smiled brightly up at him, still holding the door close so that all he could see of her was her head and part of her shoulder.

"We had lots of fresh air. I've put your winter coats and boots to good use."

"You're making me suspicious," he said.

"Why?"

"You seem determined to be happy—"

"But I am happy," she interrupted. "I really enjoy your children. We have a lot of fun together."

And that's when he spotted a bit of sparkle behind her shoulder. It was a gleam of light, reflecting off something silver and shiny and then he took a breath and smelled fragrant pine.

Marcu reached above her head and gave the door a push, forcing it open. In her sitting room on the table near her hearth stood a shimmering tree with white lights and colorful glass ornaments. It was small but beautifully decorated and the fresh smell filled her room, making him immediately feel nostalgic.

For a moment he couldn't speak, and then he drew a slow, measured breath, fighting to remain in control. "I thought we agreed there would be no decorations, no tree, none of this nonsense—"

"I didn't agree," she interrupted hotly, arms crossing over her chest. "*I* never agreed, because I completely disagree with you—"

"That doesn't matter. Your opinion doesn't matter. You're here to do what I tell you."

"Wrong. You're here because you trust me to take care of your children, and I am."

"I don't celebrate Christmas, Monet."

"Fine, but must you deprive the children? Are they no longer allowed to experience the beauty of it? I understand you are grieving, and they also continue to grieve, but you are turning their loss into a greater punishment. You are taking the loss of their mother and turning it into the loss of all hope and beauty—"

"Rubbish!" he snapped, silencing her again, his voice growing louder, his temper hotter. She was trying his patience and he didn't like it. Marcu stepped all the way into her room and closed the door behind him.

"You have spent too much time in England now," he added, stalking toward the hearth, which glowed with red embers. He circled the table with the tree, feeling emotions he didn't welcome. "You have bought in to this very commercialized idea of Christmas," he said, looking back at her. "In Sicily, Christmas was never about trees and decorations and presents. I give my children presents on Epiphany. You will see that my children eagerly await for the arrival of Le Befana and the sweets they've hoped for. They will receive little toys and treats if they have been good, and that's our heritage, our tradition, and they don't need your British Christmas."

For a moment there was just silence and then she shook her head, making her long hair dance. "Fine. Have your way. They don't need it. You don't need it. But *I* do. I need my Christmas. You called in a favor, but that favor did not include stripping me of all the things that give my life meaning, and I want to celebrate Christmas. I want to have magic and fizz and joy. So if you don't like it, please send me away now. I would love to return to London and my friends and my life there. Let me leave right now, because I am not going to battle with you on this. I think you are wrong, I think you are actually dreadful—"

"Dreadful?" he practically roared.

"Yes, dreadful," she repeated, stepping close and jabbing a finger in the air, "and hurtful."

He took a step back, affronted. "I am neither."

"Yes, you are, and you enjoy being a beast, too. Now

I realize you were left with three children and a broken heart, but face life, and face the pain and let your heart heal. Let your children's hearts heal. Move forward without this anger, because right now I feel sorry for Vittoria. I pity any woman you want to bring into this family because you are not ready. You are not ready for a new wife, and you are not ready to let go of the past."

"The children—"

"This isn't about the children! This is about *you*. This is about you being angry at God, and angry with yourself, because you are not God and you couldn't be there and you couldn't save Galeta. Heavens, you have serious issues and you need to deal with them."

Rage swept through him. His hands balled at his sides. "How dare you talk to me this way?"

She threw her head back, her eyes flashing fire, not in the least bit intimidated by his roar. "How dare others *not* talk to you this way? They do you no favors. They're hurting you by keeping the truth from you."

"I've had enough. In the morning you will remove the tree—"

"No. That will not happen."

"If you don't dispose of it, I will."

"If you touch my tree, I am gone. And if you choose to fire me, that's fine, too, because I never wanted to be in your employ in the first place. I came here to do you a favor, and whether you like it or not, I am your equal in every way."

"You're being paid. That makes you my employee."

"Keep your awful money. I don't want it. I never wanted it. The only thing I ever wanted from you was respect, and it was the one thing you have refused to give me."

"You're hysterical!"

"Not hysterical, just honest. I'm done holding back. I'm

done worrying about your ego. You have far too much ego. Marcu, you are a man, not a god, or a demigod. You are a human being, and because you're human you make mistakes, and you are making mistakes right now, and that would be okay if you could recognize it and work on it but you won't."

"Are you finished?" he gritted.

"No. I'm not going to tiptoe around you, and I'm not going to pretend that you are right, when you're not. I'm not afraid of you, and I don't care what you think of me. It's not as if I'm going to lose your good opinion. Marcu, I know what you think of me. I know exactly what you and your father have always thought of me. It's why I left Palermo. It's why I left all of you. I wasn't good enough. I wasn't *worthy*."

The words came faster and faster and he sensed she'd been keeping them bottled up for years, and now she could no longer hold them back.

"I know that I was kind of woman you'd take to your bed," she added, "but you'd never respect enough to marry. I was the kind of woman who'd fulfil your physical desires but never win your heart—"

"You're talking nonsense now," he snapped, his own patience tested, his own control threatened.

"*No.* I heard you. I heard you and your father the night he found us in your bedroom. I heard what he said when he pulled you out into the hallway. He asked if you were being careful, and if you'd used protection, because you couldn't be stupid and fall for my schemes as I was not the kind of woman you'd ever marry." Monet's voice quavered and she reached up to press a trembling hand to her forehead. After a moment she continued. "I heard every word he said, just as I'm sure he intended me to. He wanted me to know that

I was not the kind of woman you could take out socially. He wanted me to hear that I was a whore like my mother—"

"He did *not* use the word *whore*," Marcu interrupted gruffly, stunned that she'd heard the conversation in the hall all those years ago. He hadn't known she'd heard what his father had said, hadn't realized that his father's voice had carried so clearly. No wonder she was so hurt and angry. She'd bottled up the pain for years and now it was spilling out of her in a torrent of words.

"You're right. He used a different word, a Sicilian swear word that implied almost the same thing, but what it boils down to is that I wasn't acceptable due to being a bastard."

"My father wasn't trying to hurt you, he was trying to protect me as I was the oldest, and his heir."

"He was your father. He was doing what he thought was best," she said, lips curving up, contradicting the bright sheen of tears in her eyes. "I guess it was a blessing in disguise. It proved beneficial to hear his thoughts—and yours—clarifying many things for me, and allowing me to make a break from you."

"He hurt you, and I'm sorry."

"*You* hurt me, and you're not sorry." Her chin jerked up and tears clung to her lower lashes. "But in hindsight, I'm glad you didn't defend me. It was important to hear that conversation and discover you had no feelings for me. It was a giant wake-up call, one that I desperately needed as it was time for me to stop living my life to please the Ubertos. That conversation freed me, which is why I can stand here and look at you and not feel inferior."

Marcu didn't know what to do with her. He didn't know how to stop these words because they were barbed and brutal and coming at him so fast. Is this why she'd left first thing in the morning? Is this truly the reason she'd fled the palazzo?

"You should have told me you'd heard him," he said tautly. "You should have confronted me—"

"And what would you have done? Denied it? Told me I'd misheard? That I didn't understand? Marcu, I understood perfectly then, and I understand now, but none of that matters. What matters is the family here, in this *castello*. It's time for you to deal with your grief so you can take care of your children. *You* need to love them. You need to love them so well that you don't need a woman to come in and fix things for you. Because you don't need a wife. You don't need a new mother for them. You just need to forgive yourself for not being there when Galeta died. And you could be an amazing father if you stopped looking back and just focused on the present. Your children are adorable. They're smart and kind and funny. They are perfect. And they are still *so* young. All they need is someone to love them and laugh with them. Why can't that be you?"

Her words were relentless, sharp and heavy, and they were piercing the armor he wore to keep from feeling too much. "I think you've said enough for one night," he growled.

"Then leave. This is my room. You're free to go at any time."

"You're trying to provoke me."

"You're refusing to see what's in front of your face!"

He stalked toward her. "You, you mean?"

Every time he took a step forward, she took a step back. "No, your children," she snapped.

She was skirting the furniture now, and moving closer to the wall, but he wasn't about to let her escape. "You're making this about the children, but it's not," he answered. "You're angry with me, angry that I didn't defend you to my father that night—"

"I was angry then, and hurt, but that's behind us. I'm

here trying to help you now. It's what you wanted. It's why you insisted I come."

"To follow my instructions," he said, finally cornering her. There was nowhere for her to run and she stood facing him, her back to the plaster wall, her expression mutinous. "Not challenge me at every turn."

"That's because you've become lazy, and soft—"

"Soft?" he repeated incredulously.

Her golden-brown eyes flashed at him, her lips twisting scornfully. "Yes, soft. You don't want to do the hard work. You want an easy fix, but you're going to be disappointed. You're going to regret this down the road."

"I'm already regretting having you here."

"Send me home in the morning then. We'll both be happier."

She was tiny, barely reaching his shoulder, and she practically vibrated with fury and emotion and he, who avoided emotion, felt drawn to her light and heat just as a moth was drawn to a flame.

He wanted to touch her...kiss her...possess her...and yet he'd promised her he wouldn't. He'd promised her that as long as he was pursuing another woman, he wouldn't touch her, and he was determined to keep that vow. But that didn't stop him from moving closer, and leaning in, his hands against the wall over her head, and his body angling over hers. There was space between them. A sliver of space. Just enough to honor his promise, but not enough to give either of them peace of mind.

There was no peace of mind with her here.

There was no peace of mind since she'd left him all those years ago.

"You promised you wouldn't touch me," she said breathlessly.

He heard the catch in her voice, as well as the quick rise

and fall of her breasts. She wasn't immune to him. No, she was just as aware of him as he was of her.

"Not going to touch you," he said, dropping his head a quarter inch, her mouth so close now that he could feel the heat shimmering between them. The heat was intoxicating. *She* was intoxicating. He felt almost drugged. "Just standing here."

Monet swallowed hard. He could see her smooth column of a throat work, and the muscle in her jaw tighten. Her eyes glowed, flecks of gold against a darker amber. Her lips were full and soft and far too tempting.

To kiss her properly, to kiss her thoroughly…

"I know what you want to do," she said, her voice pitched low, the tone so husky he thought immediately of sex and sin.

He craved sex and sin.

He craved the forbidden.

"So do I, but I haven't, have I?" he answered, a carnal rasp in his voice as he bent his elbows, lowering his body, dropping his head so that his mouth hovered over hers, feeling the warmth of her breath on his lips, and smelling the scent of her shampoo and skin. This was torture. There was no other word for it. He stared at her mouth and the soft lushness of her lower lip, fascinated by the shape. It was decadent and sensual and he wanted to claim it… and her.

His body felt taut and hard, his senses flooded with her scent and heat. Why was she the only one who made him feel this way? Why did she drive him mad? It made no sense. This desire wasn't logical and yet it was the most compelling thing he'd felt in years.

Her cheeks already flushed, darkened to a luscious rose. She chewed on her lower lip. "You're not abiding by the rules," she whispered.

"What rules?"

She closed her eyes, and drew a slow, unsteady breath before exhaling just as slowly. "Exactly my point."

Marcu's body was so hard he ached. He pressed his knuckles to the wall. He craved her mouth. He craved her taste. It was all he could do to just hold his position. "This isn't working, is it?" he muttered.

She gave her head a very slight shake.

"What do we do?" he asked.

She dragged in another unsteady breath. "One of us needs to leave."

"Leave? Your room?"

"No. This place. The *castello*." She opened her eyes, and looked straight into his. The gold-brown of her eyes was dark with emotion. She looked as if she was in pain, and it sent a lance of white-hot agony through him.

He flinched and ground his knuckles against the wall.

"We can't both be here," she whispered. "Nothing good will come of it. You know it."

He did know it, and he hated what she was saying, but she was right. This wasn't good for either of them. This was beyond torturous. He hated feeling so much. He hated feeling helpless. But to leave her…

To lose her…

Again.

And yet she wasn't his. She'd never be his. Why couldn't he accept it?

But no, he could. He did. He was an adult, a man who understood responsibility. He understood ramifications.

"You need to be here. I don't," he said brusquely, before peeling himself away from her and taking a step back. The effort had drained him. He felt almost beaten as he put space between them. "I'm leaving tomorrow."

"Good, because if you don't, I will."

* * *

Monet sagged as Marcu left her suite. Her heart was still racing so fast that she could barely cross to the chair by the fire before she collapsed into it.

She'd never wanted a kiss so badly.

She'd never wanted anything as much as she'd wanted him to throw caution to the wind and just kiss her…

And not a sweet, tentative kiss, but mad passion. Her hands itched for his, her body trembled with longing. If only he'd clasped her hands and pinned them over her head and held her there against that wall as he claimed her mouth, and then claimed her.

She'd wanted the weight of his body, and the heat and pressure. Her body felt so unbearably sensitive. Monet wrapped an arm over her chest, pressing against her breasts, against the tingling in her nipples.

She'd wanted his hands there, and she'd wanted his mouth on her skin, and she'd wanted him…

My God.

This was everything she'd felt in Palermo, and yet more, because she was older now and more confident and she didn't want him because she had some big emotional hole inside of her, but rather she wanted him because he set her body on fire and torched her senses and she loved it.

Loved it.

And she wanted more.

Monet's head fell back against the back of the chair and she sighed heavily. Obviously she wouldn't be kissing Marcu, or taking him to her bed, but the desire burned within her and it wasn't going to be easy to forget just how hungry and fierce he'd made her feel.

Marcu stood at his bedroom window watching the snow fall in white sheets beyond the thick beveled glass. It was after midnight and he hadn't even tried to go to bed, knowing it would be impossible to sleep when his brain still raced, struggling to process everything said tonight.

All these years he'd thought Monet had left Palermo because she'd been disgusted by the kiss. He'd thought she'd wanted to escape, because she was filled with regret over what they'd done. He'd agonized over his actions, thinking he'd let her down, betrayed her trust. Had she viewed him as a surrogate brother, someone who would look after her instead? If that was the case, no wonder she'd given him a look of repulsion when he'd returned to his room after speaking to his father.

He'd misread the situation and violated her trust.

For years he couldn't even think of her without self-hatred, disgusted with himself for taking advantage of her and making her feel unsafe in her own home.

But she hadn't said any of that tonight. No, she'd flung different words at him instead…an altogether different accusation.

She'd been hurt by his father's words, and devastated that Marcu hadn't defended her.

He hadn't known she could hear the conversation—a conversation he remembered quite differently.

His brow creased as he stared out at the swirling world of white.

Either way, it was problematic being under the same roof with her again. He wasn't sure how he had thought this would play out. Had he imagined that he wouldn't be attracted to her any longer? Had he hoped that by bringing her to Aosta, he would finally feel free of the past? Of her?

Except that he wasn't free of the past, or her. Being near her now was even more difficult than before.

Being near her made him feel, and a dark dangerous hunger seemed to fill his veins and heat his skin. He wanted her. He wanted to possess her…to touch her and taste her, to take her, and know her, and make her shudder and come apart for him.

And yet despite the desire, and despite his body being hard and his pulse thudding with demanding need, he had a ring for Vittoria in his travel bag. He had a suitcase packed for his departure tomorrow. His head told him that Vittoria would be the right one. His head said he needed someone suitable, someone who didn't threaten his calm, and control. He preferred a rational world, a world of order and reason. Not passion. Or hunger. Or volatile emotions that weren't to be trusted.

Now if only his body would listen, and his pulse would slow, and his uncomfortable aching erection would ease.

He put a hand to the cold glass, pressing his palm against the chill, trying to freeze the heat within him.

Monet wasn't for him. She was never meant to be his. But at the same time, there was no one he trusted more with his children. They'd be safe with her.

There was no one he wanted more…

But marriage wasn't about passion, or desire. Marriage was duty, responsibility. He couldn't confuse the two.

He'd leave first thing tomorrow. He'd leave before he did something rash, something illogical…something that might change all their lives forever.

The snow was falling thickly in the morning when Monet dragged herself from bed. Her head ached and her eyes felt dry and gritty. She'd tossed and turned all night, her dreams tormenting her almost as much as Marcu had tormented her with the promise of something he had no intention of delivering. He'd been pretty ruthless last night, and she'd been aroused by it, wanting him more than ever.

Monet wrapped herself in her thick robe and went to the

sitting room, where a breakfast tray waited on one of the small tables. Even better, there was no note from Marcu.

She plugged in the lights on her little tree and sipped her *caffe latte*, and tore apart the warm fragrant roll, liberally spreading butter and jam on it. She'd forgotten how much she loved *prima colazione*. Even though she was in the Italian Alps, not Sicily, a part of her felt as if she'd come home.

She was just finishing the last of her breakfast when a knock sounded on her door. She closed her eyes, said a swift prayer—*please don't let it be Marcu*—and then rose to open the door.

It was Marcu, dressed, in winter travel clothes.

"I've said goodbye to the children," he said flatly. "They're just waking, but I didn't want to leave without speaking to them."

"It's early," she said, thinking that just moments ago she wanted him gone and now that he was leaving, she felt strangely deflated.

"If I have any hope of getting out of the valley, it's now. It's only going to get worse later."

"You're not trying to fly, are you?"

"No. The helicopter can't land in these conditions. I'm driving. Once I reach Milan, I'll be able to fly."

She glanced out the window and couldn't even see the massive pine trees for the thickly falling snow. "How will you be able to see? And won't the roads be icy?"

"The roads won't be icy yet. I agree it's not ideal driving conditions, no. But if I don't go now, I'm here all weekend. The storm is supposed to continue for the next couple of days."

"Be safe then."

"I will." He hesitated. "There is something I need to say before I go. Something that I should have said years ago." He hesitated again. "I helped you leave Palermo all those years ago because I thought you were…disgusted…by my attentions. I thought I had taken advantage of you, and—" he broke off and sucked in a breath "—forced myself on you. I thought that was why you were in tears when I returned to the bedroom after speaking with my father." He dropped his head and stared at the floor. "I have hated myself for hurting you. I have always wanted to make amends. It's why I came to see you after Galeta died. I thought perhaps God was cursing me—"

"No."

He made a soft, rough sound under his breath. "I am sorry if I—"

"You didn't." She rushed toward him, hand outstretched to stop his words. She was just about to put her hand to his chest when she remembered herself, and curled her fingers into a ball instead. "God wasn't cursing you, or punishing you. Nor did you take advantage of me. You did nothing improper, nothing that I didn't want. I was upset that night, but for different reasons, reasons that had to do with my eighteen-year-old heart." She struggled to smile. "I had a massive crush on you. I'd had a crush on you forever and my feelings were hurt that you didn't feel the same way about me—"

"Obviously I had feelings for you. I wouldn't have kissed you otherwise."

"Yes, but I wasn't the one you could keep, remember, and while I understand that now, it was…bruising…back then."

"I wish I'd understood better."

"It's fine. I was eighteen, and a romantic. I took the kiss too seriously, imagining possibilities that weren't there. I was wrong, and I survived." She took a step back and did a little bow. "Look! I'm here. I'm fine."

His head lifted and his gaze locked with hers. "One last thing, before I go."

She swallowed hard and forced a smile. "You're making it sound like this is the last time I'll see you. You're not intending on driving recklessly, are you?"

"Of course not. I have three children who need me."

"Exactly right," she retorted. "Don't ever forget it."

"I don't." He reached up to run his hand over his mouth, and jaw. "The favor I demanded of you. It wasn't fair of me, seeing as I put you in that position in the first place."

Monet flashed to Marcu's bedroom suite and how she'd been virtually naked in his bed, her shirt off, her bra off, just her panties on when Marcu's father had barged in. Marcu had covered her so his father hadn't seen her, but it had been obvious that Monet had little on. "It is what it is, Marcu. No one grows up without getting a little emotionally banged up."

"You were so angry with me," Marcu said quietly. "You told me you never wanted to see me again."

She nodded, remembering. "Yes."

"You meant it, too."

"I did." Her shoulders twisted. "I needed a change. And I needed to figure out my life without the Ubertos in it."

He turned to the window and looked out at the fat thick snowflakes falling steadily, relentlessly. "That's why I made you promise me that you'd return the favor one day. I was worried you were cutting me off, and I wasn't ready to lose you entirely. It was my way of letting you go, but not letting you go. The favor was my last tie to you. It represented one more conversation, one more visit, one last bit of connection."

His words put a pang in her chest and she sucked in her lower lip, biting on it, to keep from making a sound.

He'd always known how to get to her.

He'd always known the right words to say…at least until she'd left and he'd married and become someone else, someone she didn't like and didn't want to know. But it seemed that the old Marcu was still in there. The Marcu she adored wasn't entirely gone.

"I'm glad," she said simply. "It would have been tragic for us to go the rest of our lives without speaking again. I'm glad I was able to help you with your children. They are such lovely little people. You are lucky to have them."

The ache in her chest expanded, pressing into her throat, making it hard to talk and swallow. Life had a funny way of turning on itself, upending everything.

Last night she'd gone to bed, body on fire. This morning her heart felt as if it had broken free of her chest and was flopping around at her feet on the floor.

He nodded once. "I need to go."

"Yes, you do." She shot a glance out the window. "It doesn't look good, though. I'm concerned about the drive."

"Once I make it over the pass, I'll be fine."

"You mean, *if* you make it over the pass."

Marcu suddenly smiled, one of the careless, self-deprecating smiles she knew from years past, a smile she'd thought she might never see again. "You have so little faith in me."

"Not so, but with all that you have here, dependent on you, I don't know why you'd want to tempt fate."

He gave her a long look, his smile fading. "You might think I'm not listening, but I am. I have heard every word you've said."

Her chest seized, burning. She blinked hard to keep her eyes from filling with tears. "We will miss you," she said quietly. "Be careful."

"Always," he answered, after a moment's silence, before turning and walking out.

CHAPTER EIGHT

MONET AND THE children spent the morning playing card games and then helping the cook make pasta in the huge stone kitchen that had managed to marry medieval and modern.

The cook was showing the children how to gently fold the pasta and pinch the seams when the butler stepped into the kitchen and gestured for Monet to follow him.

"I just received a call from the police," the butler said quietly. "*Signor*'s car was found. It went over the embankment—"

"Over the embankment?" Monet interrupted, heart faltering. "What do you mean?"

The butler frowned, as if not sure how to make it more clear. "Off the road, over the edge."

Suddenly her grasp of Italian seemed inadequate. "Off the road, over the edge…of the mountain?"

"He wasn't in the car. They don't know where he is. But he wouldn't be able to walk away if he wasn't okay," the butler reasoned.

Or, he was injured and concussed and wandered away from his car to freeze to death in some ravine. Monet swallowed hard. "Was there blood in the car? Had the air bag deployed?"

"The police didn't say. They are looking for him now."

She walked to the tall window overlooking the summer herb garden, a garden currently buried by three feet of snow. All you could see in the walled garden was white—white everywhere—and the snow just kept falling.

Where was Marcu?

Was he hurt? Or had he been plucked from the road and was right now traveling to Milan, courtesy of some kind stranger?

But if that was the case, wouldn't he call? Send word?

She chewed on a knuckle, heartsick. He shouldn't have gone. It was foolish…dangerous… Stupid man.

Rocca pushed the kitchen door open and peeked around the corner. "Signorina Wilde, you're missing all the fun!"

Monet forced a smile. "I'll be right there. Give me just a minute."

The door closed and Monet turned to the butler. "How will the police track him in the snow? I'd think the snow would be covering up his footsteps."

"I don't know."

She held her breath, scared for Marcu, scared for the children. "Do you have the phone number for someone leading the investigation?"

"No, I don't, and I'm not certain it's reached the investigation stage yet."

"Even though Marcu Uberto's car has been found down in an embankment and he's not in it?"

"We're in a very rural area. This isn't the city."

Monet bit her lip and looked over her shoulder to the kitchen door, thinking of the children inside making pasta. This was the last thing they needed.

The butler must have read her thoughts as he asked, "I wasn't sure if you wanted to say anything to the children."

Monet was at least adamant about this and gave her head a firm shake. "No. Not until we know something conclusive."

* * *

Monet was reading stories to the children when a snowplow could be heard outside, scraping the road leading to the *castello*.

She went to the window to watch the huge plow clearing snow. The children joined her at the window. The snowplow stopped not far from the entrance, and a door opened and the driver got out, and then the driver helped a passenger out.

"Papà!" Antonio cried, tapping the glass.

Monet watched as the snowplow driver aided Marcu to the front door. Staff were now spilling out of the house, rushing down the stairs to help.

"I'll be right back," she told the children before racing downstairs, where Marcu was now in the entrance hall.

He looked soaked through, but he was home. The staff continued to swarm him, and Monet pressed forward as well until she remembered her place—she wasn't his girlfriend, wasn't a friend, wasn't family, and wasn't even really staff—and she fell back a step, allowing others to see to him. But even then, her gaze swept over him, intently studying him from head to toe.

He had abrasions on his face, a cut on the bridge of his nose, and another on his cheekbone, plus the makings of a fine bruise on his brow.

He was standing, but just barely, and he gratefully accepted the help of the butler and steward as they each wrapped an arm around him, supporting him as they ushered him to the staircase, heading up to his room. The cook was given instructions to prepare a hot drink and meal, and housekeeping went to build fires in his rooms.

Marcu passed her on the staircase and his gaze met hers. His expression was one of utter weariness. "I should have listened to you," he said.

"You're safe. That's what's important," she answered.

He appeared to want to say something else and then he changed his mind and he continued up the staircase to his suite of rooms.

Monet didn't see Marcu until much later that night. After coming home, he'd showered and gone to bed and stayed there for hours. It wasn't until dinner that he emerged from his room and joined his family at the table in the dining room.

The children were subdued as they took in his cuts and bruises. He told them he'd had an accident driving, and after crashing he'd set off on foot to get help. After forty-five minutes of walking in what he feared were circles, he'd come to a rural house, and met a farmer, and the farmer attached a snowplow to the front of his tractor and slowly drove him all the way back to the *castello*.

The kids had dozens of questions, which Marcu patiently answered. Yes, the cab was small, but it was high up with pretty good visibility. The cab was also new so there was heating. Yes, they were squished but he was so grateful for the farmer's help that he didn't mind being in such cramped conditions. He also mentioned that the tractor had a snow-blower on the back, and they were using that but it had stopped working partway.

Cook had made a delicious almond cake with spiced pears and *crème anglaise* for dessert and after the children had eaten, Monet whispered that they should go give their father a hug and kiss good-night because they were lucky to have him home in one piece.

Marcu seemed caught off guard by the hugs and kisses. He returned them, a little awkwardly, but the children seemed pleased and Rocca gave her father an extra squeeze and kiss.

"You'll come back down afterward?" Marcu said to Monet as she shepherded the children out the dining-room door.

She nodded, returning almost an hour later because the children had so many questions about their father's accident and if he was still going to leave them for Christmas or if this meant he'd be with them after all.

Monet couldn't answer their questions, and encouraged them to ask him themselves tomorrow, after they'd had a good night's sleep.

"Was it hard to get them to settle tonight?" he asked as she entered the room. Marcu was lying on the sofa, his arm over his eyes.

"Does the light hurt your eyes?" she asked.

"I've a headache I can't shake," he answered.

"Can I get you something?"

"I've taken some tablets. I'm sure it will be better tomorrow."

"You probably have a concussion."

"Probably," he agreed. "It was a hard fall."

"The air bag didn't help then?"

"It did. I hit my head when I was trying to climb out of the ravine. I hit a patch of ice and went down, face-first." He dropped his arm and dragged himself up into a sitting position. "Serves me right for thinking I could handle the roads. There was no one else out there."

"You're alive, and that's what matters." Monet realized how trite that sounded and quickly added, "Well, that's what the children were saying. They said extra prayers for you tonight, grateful you were home with them."

Marcu grimaced but said nothing.

She sat down on the edge of a chair facing him. "I think you should join the children for their prayers and stories," she said. "They need you. They want you."

"I don't want to do prayers."

"Let them say their own prayers and you can read them a story." She hesitated. "The point is, they crave time with you, and the bedtime routine is an important ritual. It makes them feel safe, and they need to feel safe with you."

"They are safe with me. I will always protect them."

Monet picked her words carefully. "But part of feeling safe is being emotionally secure. It's having the children comfortable with you, and secure in the knowledge that you want to know them for who they are, not who they should be. And that happens when they can share their thoughts and feelings, and bedtime is perfect for that. It's a lovely time, an informal time, and takes just a half hour. I understand when you are out of town it makes sense for a babysitter to do this, but if you are here, you should be the one in there, hearing their thoughts and validating their feelings."

He closed his eyes and rubbed his temple on the side without the bruise. "You certainly have a lot of opinions."

"I never had my mother's attention at bedtime. By bedtime she was already with your father. I used to wish someone was there to hear my thoughts." Her voice suddenly cracked, and Monet felt mortified for saying so much. She didn't like talking about how lonely she'd been growing up. Life before she and her mother arrived at the palazzo had been chaotic, and tumultuous. It had been a relief to arrive in Palermo and stay put in one place for as long they did.

"You must have resented us," he said quietly.

She shrugged. "Not really. If I resented anyone, it was my mother. I loved your family. You gave me my first taste of family life. I told your children I never experienced a proper Christmas before I lived with your family. You had traditions and customs and I loved it."

He was silent a moment. "And then I took that all from you."

Her breath caught, and she stammered, "I would have had to leave sooner or later."

"Later would have been better for you, wouldn't it?"

She glanced down at her hands, her fingers knotting. "I wasn't going to live with my mother forever," she said before looking back at Marcu. "We'd agreed that I'd support myself once I turned eighteen, and I'd turned eighteen, so it was time."

"I wish I wasn't the reason you left, though."

She dragged in a slow breath, wondering how they'd even ended up here, on this topic. "I thought we were discussing the children," she said huskily, "and how much they'd enjoy you tucking them in at night."

"I will do it tomorrow night," he said. He glanced at her, lips twisting. "I hope that makes you happy."

"It does, because it will make them happy."

His gaze locked with hers, the blue irises bright. "And what would make you happy, Monet Wilde?"

Monet felt heat wash through her, rising up to sweep her cheeks. "I don't know how to answer that. It's an awfully open-ended question."

"Is there nothing that would make you happy?"

"Knowing you were closer to your children would make me happy. Knowing that they come before all else—"

"They do," he interrupted, "and this isn't about them. This is about you."

She said nothing. She didn't know how to answer him, in part because she didn't know her feelings. She'd been torn ever since she'd arrived in Aosta Valley. Being near Marcu was puzzling…bewildering. She wanted him, but she couldn't have him. She wanted him to want her, and then she was terrified of his touch because she knew she couldn't resist him.

"I've ended it with Vittoria," he said abruptly, rising from the couch to pace the length of the carpet before the fire. "I told her it's not going to work, and that I'm sorry if I had misled her."

Monet opened her mouth, closed it, still unable to make a single sound.

He faced the fire as he spoke. "She said she wasn't surprised. In fact, she sounded almost…relieved. Apparently she had some serious qualms about taking on another woman's children."

"She didn't say that!"

"She did. And more." He shrugged wearily as he turned to face her. "She had worried that the children might impact our social life and all the travel she'd imagined we would do."

"I'm sorry."

"I'm not. You were right, about so many things."

"Like what?"

"Marriage has to be more than just a contract. Marriage must have some emotions, somewhere. She felt nothing for me, or the children."

"Then why be with you? Why date you?"

He laughed without humor. "I'm rich."

"And handsome."

He gave her a swift glance. "Am I?"

Monet didn't know whether to laugh or cry. "You're impossible."

"So you've been telling me."

"You've had a horrible day," she said, even as her heart galloped. It was ridiculous, still carrying this torch for him. He wasn't a beast. He was just a man who had suffered terribly.

"But it's ending the way it should. I'm here, with my family, and out of a relationship that wasn't a good one, and might have proved disastrous for my children." His lips curved faintly. "I suppose I owe you my gratitude."

"You can keep it. I don't want it."

"Why not?"

"We go back a very long way. Despite what happened at the end, you were my friend when I needed one, and I am simply trying to be a friend now, as it seems you need one."

He made a rough raw sound. "You are so much more than a friend."

Monet found herself watching him, feeling like a girl again, impossibly infatuated with someone out of her reach. Marcu intrigued her, fascinated her, spoke to her in a way that no one else did. It was easy not dating when no one appealed to you. Monet wasn't attracted to most men in her sphere. She simply wasn't interested. The idea of trying to find "someone" for her left her cold. But Marcu made her feel. Marcu made something in her warm, and quicken. She was so alive in his company. It made no sense. But then it had never made sense.

Suddenly he was focused on her again, and their eyes locked and held.

For once she didn't try to hide her raw emotions—the good, and the bad—and she stared back at him, feeling the full weight of her awareness, as well as her bewilderment that he could still impact her so.

She shouldn't still want him. She shouldn't still long for a night with him. She ached for all the things she hadn't ever known. Her body tingled, her skin prickled, her pulse drummed. He had taken so many women to his bed and yet he never taken her there. It was good, she told herself, she shouldn't be there. But on the other hand, she wasn't eighteen anymore, she was an adult. A woman. And she could make love to whomever she wanted.

And she wanted Marcu.

If she was going to belong to anyone, it should be him.

"I should go to bed," she said hoarsely. "It's late and it's been an exhausting day."

"What are your plans for tomorrow?"

"To play with your children, to keep them busy and cheerful so they don't feel lonely."

Marcu's black eyebrows lifted. "Why would they be lonely when they have each other?"

"Because they don't have enough time with you. They'd love to play with you. Cards, chess, checkers, tag."

"I haven't done that in years."

"Exactly my point. Maybe it's time to be a little less distant, and a little more playful.

"Surely, you can remember what it was like to be a boy. You have two little boys who would love it if you'd build a fort with them, or pull out their box of toy soldiers and wage a battle. They'd love to run through the halls and have a sword fight—" She noticed his expression, her lips twisting ruefully. "No, not a real sword fight, but a battle with wooden spoons or broom handles. Better yet, the three of you can make your own swords together. Matteo and Antonio would be over the moon."

"And Rocca, what of her? How shall I entertain her?" he answered mildly.

"A tea party, or a puppet performance—"

"Excuse me?"

"Or a sword fight. Lots of girls like pretending to be sword masters."

"Did you ever once see my sisters run around with swords?"

"That doesn't mean Rocca couldn't." Her eyebrow lifted,

matching his expression. "Or do you have fixed ideas about what is proper play for girls and boys?"

"You're trying to be provocative."

"I'm trying to do what you brought me here to do—make sure your children are truly your first priority." She rose and gave him a crooked smile. "Good night, Marcu. I'm glad you're home safe. Sleep well."

She could feel his gaze burning through her back as she headed for the door. He didn't speak until she was reaching for the doorknob.

"I was on my way home to Aosta when I crashed. I'd already ended things with Vittoria and was coming back here to you—"

"You were not coming back to me," she interrupted firmly, ignoring the quickening of her pulse.

"But I was. I ended things with her because of you."

"No." Monet's heart did another hard double beat. "No, don't say that, because it's not true."

"It absolutely is." He faced her, arms crossed over his broad chest. "I told you I wouldn't touch you again as long as I was in another relationship, and I didn't. But I'm no longer involved with Vittoria—"

"You really hit your head hard today. I think you should lie down."

"You feel the same thing I feel. This attraction isn't one-sided. It killed me keeping my hands off you—"

"I think we should ring for a doctor. You need help."

He rolled his eyes. "Don't be a coward. And don't make me prove my point. There is something between us and I realized a lot of things today. The accident forced me to confront not just my mortality but the future. Why be with someone I don't care about, when I could be with someone like you—"

"No." She flung her hands up, trying to stop him. "We

won't ever be together. We don't have a relationship, nor will we ever have one."

He crossed the room, approaching her. "We've had a relationship for years. We've just ignored it. And I'm not going to ignore it anymore."

She edged the other way, moving behind the couch. "What relationship? Marcu, eight years ago I was an eighteen-year-old virgin who idolized you! I had no life experience. I had no sexual experience. Yes, I adored you. I was impossibly infatuated, but that's not the basis for a mature relationship now."

"Why not?"

"One-sided adoration is pathetic."

"I told you, this isn't one-sided. I wouldn't have broken things off with Vittoria if I had no feelings for you—"

"You don't have feelings for me! And you didn't break up with Vittoria for me. I am absolutely inconsequential."

"If that was true, then why did my father fear you so? Why was he afraid of your power over me?"

She leaned on the back of the couch, hands gripping the crushed velvet. "You're not making any sense. You should sit down. You need to rest. I'm worried about you."

"Monet, I have a headache, I haven't lost my mind."

"Then why say your father was afraid of me? How could he be afraid of me? I was almost nineteen when you got married. I had no power."

"My father knew how I felt about you. He knew how upset I was when you left, and that I was conflicted in those months after you'd gone, so conflicted that I booked a flight to go see you in London but I never actually got on the plane, as he kept finding ways to stop me."

"Your father obviously knew best. Galeta was the right one for you."

"I shouldn't have allowed my father to influence my judgment. I've never forgiven myself for that—"

"You say these things as if you're certain I had feelings for you. You say this as if you coming to London would have changed the outcome—"

"Wouldn't it?" he interrupted. "If I had shown up in London in those first few months, and told you how much I cared about you, you don't think it would have had any impact? You don't think we might have had a real relationship?"

She picked up a cushion from the couch and threw it at him. "*No.* You were never serious about me. You wanted something easy, convenient, and I was there at the palazzo, easy and convenient. But then when I was no longer easy or convenient, I was too much trouble." She grabbed another pillow and threw this one at him, too. He sidestepped the second pillow, just as he had the first.

"I'm not judging you, Marcu, just clarifying facts," she said, wishing there was another pillow to throw. "We were never meant to be. You and I have very different ideas about life, and struggle, and identity. Your whole identity is that of being Matteo Uberto's eldest son. You are the heir. You have royal blood in your DNA—"

"This has nothing to do with us."

"It has everything to do with it. Your ancestry matters to your family, just as your wife's ancestry mattered to your father. I don't come from a family where we brag about our lineage, and I've spent the past eight years trying to carve my identity out, creating one far from my mother's shadow."

"Your mother was a good person, and a beautiful woman."

"And insecure as hell." Monet made a face. "She had a desperate need to be loved—not by me, but by others. She needed your approval more than mine. She needed your brother and sisters' affection more than mine. Why? Because I was hers, and I had to love her. Your family…that was the challenge." She grimaced again. "But why are we talking about the past? It's always about the past. I'm tired of the past. I'm only interested in the present, and the future, which is why I love London. In London everything is new for me. I have interesting work, and a fulfilling life. I never look back, and I never feel like a second-class citizen."

"You've never been a second-class citizen."

She forced a mocking smile to her lips even as she held back the sting of tears. "When it comes to the Ubertos, I've always been a second-class citizen. To quote your father, I'm only 'good enough to bed, but not to wed.' Good night, Marcu."

He followed her out, catching up with her on the stairs. "Monet, wait."

"This isn't a good time for us to talk, Marcu. You've gone through a great deal today. It's been so stressful—"

"I know the kind of day I had today, and it was rough. Twice I thought I make not make it home, but that was also a much-needed wake-up call. Life is short. We're mortal. We don't really have time to waste."

"I'm glad you had an epiphany. But that changes nothing between us."

"I don't want Vittoria. I want you."

"No. *No.*" Her laugh was incredulous. "I'm not a replacement for Vittoria. I'm not easy, or convenient. I'm not an option in any way."

"The kiss we shared—"

"Shouldn't have happened."

"But it did, and it made me question everything." He climbed yet another step so that he was just one stair below her now. "I've been determined to go through life without feeling, but that's obviously not working, not for me, or anyone." He took the next stair so that they were side by side. "The children have no idea how much I love them, when everything I do is to ensure their well-being."

He lifted a long tendril of hair from her shoulder, the silky strands sliding through his fingers. "And you—you imagine that you're someone I wanted to use for my pleasure because I had nothing else to do, and no one else to turn to, and that's not true. It's not ever been true."

"Please, Marcu, I'm not a fool. You married Galeta only a few months after I left Palermo. She must have already been on the horizon when you were making love to me in your bedroom."

"We'd dated. We weren't serious."

"Just like you weren't serious with me."

"I never hid anything from you. You knew I was socially active."

She averted her face, features tightening. "This walk down memory lane isn't helping anyone."

"My point is, I've always been honest with you, even when it wasn't easy or comfortable. I am being honest now when I say that kissing you changed something inside of me. It woke something—"

"No."

"But it did, it has." He reached out, tipping her face up, his finger beneath her chin. "I haven't felt anything in years. I've been numb, and then you come back into my life—"

"Because you dragged me back into your life!"

The corner of his mouth lifted. "Okay, that's fair. I did drag you, but I think I finally understand why I had to call in that favor. I needed you."

She drew away from him and climbed a step. "For the children."

"No, not for the children, but for me. I just didn't know it yet."

She climbed another step. "How convenient to realize that after I was here, hostage."

"You're not a hostage. You could go anytime."

Monet turned to face him fully, eyebrows rising, dark wings above brilliant golden-brown eyes. "So if I asked you to let me return home, you'd allow it?"

"Yes."

"If I said I wanted to go tomorrow, you'd be fine with that?"

He felt a pinch in his chest—sharp, hard, deep. "Yes," he said after a moment, uncertain how they'd come to this place already. He'd fought to come home, fought to return to her, and now she wanted to leave him.

Marcu took a breath, "Yes," he repeated, "but you wouldn't be able to leave tomorrow. You won't be able to go anywhere until the storm passes, and that's another few days."

"Then I want to leave, as soon as I can." Her gaze met his. "Will you agree to that?"

The pinch was even stronger this time, stealing his breath. He didn't want to answer. He had to answer. "Yes."

She seemed to think this over and then she nodded. "Thank you." And then she leaned down and kissed him. "I don't hate you," she whispered against his mouth. "But I can't stay. It's not good for either of us."

And just like that, heat exploded between them, and her light kiss became fire, and the fire was bigger than either of them.

He pulled her to him, holding her firmly while he kissed her deeply, parting her lips with the pressure of his. She made a soft groaning sound, which just whetted his hunger, and his tongue teased the softness of her lower lip before stroking the inside of her mouth. She tasted of almonds and cinnamon and her…how he loved the taste of her. No one had ever felt so right in his arms. No kiss had ever made him feel like this, either.

She reached for him, her arms wrapping around his neck, and the kiss was a mutual give-and-take, the hunger binding them together. Her fingers threaded in his hair, and he shuddered with pleasure at the feel of her fingertips across his nape.

"Take me to your room," she breathed. "Let's not do this where everyone can see."

He swung her into his arms and carried her up the remaining flight of stairs to his suite. She was light in his arms, her body soft and warm, and he tried not to get ahead of himself. She hadn't offered herself up. She hadn't promised anything. This was just a kiss, and he could be satisfied with that because he wanted her to be happy. It was time he made her happy.

She felt like she'd waited for this moment—and him—for her whole life, and she had no fear as he undressed her.

He was the one for her, and the one she wanted to be with now. She wasn't going to think about the future, or the past, she was simply going to give herself over to the pleasure of being with Marcu, the man she adored. Life was complicated and hard and she should be able to have this moment for her, to remember forever.

Stripped bare, he studied her a long moment and then kissed her mouth, and the side of her neck, and beneath her ear in that delicate hollow where every nerve ending seemed to be.

His mouth traveled down the length of her neck, his tongue flicking her collarbone—more nerves, more tingling sensations that made her tremble and ache.

He took his time exploring her curves and shape, lips and tongue and teeth on her nipples, then strokes of his tongue to soothe the light bites. Her breasts felt full and ripe, her nipples strained. She struggled to catch her breath, dazed by the sharp hot sensations filling her veins, coiling in her belly.

He continued his exploration, moving lower, dropping kisses to her belly button and on each hip bone, fingers light across her pelvis, grazing her inner thighs.

She closed her eyes, panting as he parted her thighs, pressing her knees down, open, revealing her most private place. It was terrifying and exhilarating all at the same time because this was so new and yet it felt so good, and it was him, Marcu, who was making her feel this way. Hot, alive, glorious.

His hands parted her thighs wider and then his mouth was there, and his tongue traced the delicate folds. She shuddered at every light lick, unbearably sensitive, her insides feeling like hot thick honey. She was wet and growing wetter, and his fingers slid into her even as he teased her clit, his breath warm, his tongue cool. He lifted his head to watch her as he stroked her with his fingers, burying himself in her tight heat, and it was strange, but wonderful. She bucked as he dropped his head to kiss her nub as he continued stroking her, the incredible sensations flooding her, building, rising higher and higher until she went over an edge, and shattered into a thousand bright pieces.

She lay boneless, heart still pounding, body still tingling, her skin still exquisitely sensitive. It took her a moment to collect herself. “That was nice,” she said huskily, “but I want you.”

“We don’t need—”

"No, we don't need to do anything, but I want everything. I want you. I've wanted this since I was eighteen."

"You're sure?"

"Absolutely," she answered, reaching out to clasp his thick erection, savoring the feel of his hard silken shaft in her hand.

He reached for protection and rolled the condom down before moving over her, his knees holding her thighs open. He lowered himself on his elbows, and kissed her even as the head of his shaft pressed against her slick entrance.

She nearly told him to take it slow, and then she held the words back, because she didn't want to make this about her virginity, but about him, *them*.

He was sliding into her, and the fullness was overwhelming. She had to force herself to breathe and relax, as his body pressed deeper into hers. She wasn't sure she liked it, he felt too big, and too uncomfortable, and just when she didn't think she could do this anymore, the pain eased, and the fullness was less overwhelming and as he moved, she felt a fluttering sensation, a lovely fluttering sensation that made her want to feel it again. She arched her hips against his and he withdrew slightly, stroking back in. The lovely fluttery sensation was amazing and she urged him on, loving the heat of his body, the feel of his warmth within her, surrounding her, making her safe...making her his.

He kissed her the way his body loved hers—deep, hungry, commanding—and she loved it all.

And when she climaxed again, he was there with her, too, and it was bliss. No matter what happened next, no matter what happened in the future, she was grateful to have had this time in Marcu's arms, in his bed, in his life.

Monet woke slowly, trying to get her bearings. It was extremely early in the morning and the sky was still dark outside. And then she shifted and bumped into Marcu's shoulder and it all came back to her.

She was in Marcu's room. They'd made love last night. He'd given her two orgasms and she was most definitely no longer without experience.

She also needed to use his bathroom, desperately. Monet slid from the bed and went to his en-suite bathroom, returning quietly, hoping that Marcu was still asleep. Instead he was frowning at the bottom sheet on her side of the bed.

"Did I hurt you?" he asked gruffly, exposing the red stain.

"No," she answered, mortified.

"But I made you bleed."

"I'll get a washcloth and some soap—"

"I'm not worried about the stain. I'm worried about you. I didn't realize I was so rough with you."

She didn't know how to tell him, so she just blurted the words. "You weren't rough. I was a virgin."

"What?"

She ignored his growl of shock. "Everyone has to have a first time. It's not a biggie."

"You should have told me!"

"Why? How did it matter?"

"I would have been far more careful."

"You were wonderful. I have no complaints." Her lips curved. "Honest."

He left the bed naked, and stared at her, expression incredulous. "I had no idea."

"That I was a virgin? Why does it matter?"

"It doesn't. But I just assumed—" He broke off, scowling. "I would have thought by now you'd have more… experience."

"No. I don't date very much, haven't been interested.

But I have no regrets, giving up my virginity to you. It only seems fitting that my first time be with you."

He covered his face with his hand. *"Mio Dio."*

"Stop with the dramatic curses. Why does it matter that I was a virgin? I wanted to sleep with you, and I'm glad I did. It was amazing for a first time. You've set the bar very high."

His hand fell from his face and he glared at her from across the width of the bed. "What does that mean?"

"I've lacked confidence since I am—was—inexperienced, but maybe now I'll be more confident, and comfortable. Maybe dating won't be such a big deal. Hopefully I'll be more open to meeting new men."

"That doesn't make any sense," he snapped, heading to the bathroom, and returning in a black thick robe. He was knotting the sash as he emerged.

"Maybe not to you, but it does to me. It's time I let go of the past and move forward. It's time I gave others a chance—"

"No."

She arched a brow as she sat back down in bed and pulled the covers up to her chest. "You can't tell me no."

"I don't want you to give others a chance. I want you. I want you to stay with us."

She watched him give his sash a second angry knot. "It doesn't work that way."

"Why not?"

"You're being ridiculous now. Don't ask questions like that. Because I don't belong here. This isn't my home. You're not my family. And I have no desire to be your glorified child care for the rest of my life!"

"I still have Miss Sheldon as a nanny. You aren't meant to be child care."

"You wanted a wife to handle your children so you could

focus on work. I've no intention of touching any of that. Find another woman who wants that responsibility because it's not going to be me."

"You're not even giving me a chance!"

"Marcu, I just spent the night with you. I gave you my body. I gave you my virginity. How have I not given you a chance?"

"Marry me."

Now he was just being cruel. Or was this his idea of being funny? Sighing, she tossed back the covers and began to gather her clothes. "Never mind. I can't listen to this. I need to go."

He blocked her, catching her hands in his. "I'm serious. Marry me. Stay with us. We need you."

His words did weird things to her insides—both good and bad. "Marry me, stay with us" made her heart jump, but "we need you" filled her with mistrust. She struggled to shake him off, desperately wanting to be dressed and in her own room. "That is the worst proposal I've ever heard and I'm going to pretend you didn't say any of it. Now give me space, so I can dress and get out of here."

Instead he pulled her into his arms, and kissed her, a hot, hard punishing kiss that sent a molten wave of longing through her. His hand was low on her bare back, making her body tingle, and as he swept his palm up over her spine, she shuddered with pleasure. He made her feel so sensitive and alive, and when he cupped the back of her head, holding her still so that he could deepen the kiss, all she could think about was him, and having him inside her again, filling her, making them one. When he was with her, making love to her, she'd never felt more connected, or more loved—

And suddenly she flashed back in time, to when she

was just a little girl and she'd accidentally walked in on her mother in bed with a stout older man.

She'd been shocked and confused.

She didn't understand who the man was, and why he was in her mother's bed. She didn't understand why her mother spent more time with strange men than with her.

Desire squashed, Monet pulled back, and Marcu released her, letting her take one step back and then another until there was ample distance between them.

She struggled to regain control, struggled to calm her breathing. Marcu's eyes were narrowed, his expression inscrutable. Monet felt stupid tears burn the back of her eyes. "I hate your proposal. I hate how it demeans me," she choked.

"Because I don't have a ring? I didn't get down on one knee? I wasn't going to get down on one knee with Vittoria—"

"I don't care about Vittoria. Or about Galeta. I don't care about any of your women. I care about me, and what you're offering me and it's nothing—"

"How can you say that? I would take care of you, and provide for you, and you'd never want for anything."

"But love." She blinked hard, fighting the scalding tears. "Because where is the love? There is no love in any of this. There is desire and want and the physical attraction between us is incredible. The sex was unbelievable. I will never regret that you were my first lover. It was right." She reached up to swipe away one tear, and then another. "It's what probably should have happened eight years ago so I could have gotten you out of my system. But now we have been together and we've come full circle. I can move on. We are good."

"We are not good," he snapped. "We are most certainly

not good. I did not take your virginity only for you to walk away—"

She laughed and kept laughing, and it was making him mad but she couldn't help it, and she couldn't stop. Her laughter turned into helpless giggles. "Oh, Marcu, what did you think would happen? That sex with you would make me give up my whole life? My dreams—"

"Of working in a department store?"

"It's actually something I enjoy so don't you dare mock me!"

He rubbed his hands over his face and growled with frustration. "I'm not mocking you, I'm trying to understand how you could choose that life over one with me and the children?"

"I realize marriage for you is a business deal, but it's not my idea of marriage, and I don't need a man. I need independence. I need self-respect. I need my own path."

"So what was this? What happened here?"

"I wanted you. I have wanted to be with you since I was eighteen. And so I slept with you, and I did it mostly for closure. I slept with you so that—" She broke off abruptly, unwilling to say what was burning in her heart.

So that I would always have this moment with you. So that I would always have this memory.

This was her secret, not his. Her memory for her to cherish, and she would cherish it, but he didn't need to know that making love with him was bittersweet. He didn't need to know that being so close to him had been heaven, and it would hurt like hell to walk away, but far better to leave and hurt and heal, then stay and be overlooked day in and day out.

"Finish your sentence," he said curtly. "I'm hanging on your every word. I'm trying to understand."

"There is nothing to understand. I wanted to be in your

bed. I wanted to make love to you. I did. We did. And now I'm ready to go as soon as the storm lets up."

He crossed his arms, and his jaw jutted. "I don't like any of this."

"I know you don't, but you'll be fine the moment I'm gone and you reach back out to Vittoria, or you set your sights on the next appropriate woman. I'm just convenient, Marcu. Don't forget that."

"That's a terrible thing to say."

"But true," she said, tugging her sweater over her head, and crumpling the rest of her clothes into a ball. "This isn't complicated between us. We both had an itch to scratch, and we scratched it, freeing you to find the next aristocratic young woman with the bloodline you desire." And then she tried to put on her knit slacks but Marcu scooped her into his arms and carried her back to the bed.

"Then why isn't my itch scratched?" he asked, pinning her to the bed. "Why do I just want even more of you?"

"Because you like what you can't have."

"But I can have you. I know if I told you how much I wanted you right now, and how much I ache to be inside of you, and how much I want to taste you, you'd welcome all of it." He pressed her hands open, and placed his palm flat against hers in a slow caress. "And if I'm wrong, tell me right now, and I'll let you go and we will be done with the itch and the scratch and all of it, because I do want you, but I want you to want me, too."

There was so much heat and energy zinging between them. Just the press of his palm to hers made her want to arch up against him.

Was it bad that she loved being pinned to the bed like this? Was it bad that the sheer strength of him made her shivery and excited?

"I do want you," she answered, throwing her head back,

which resulted in him dropping his head, and kissing the side of her neck, his lips setting her on fire.

“Then stay,” he said huskily. “Because I want you here, *la mia bella ragazza*.”

His beautiful girl.

She closed her eyes as he kissed her, and gave him the rest of her heart because there was no one else she’d rather give it to. There was no one she’d rather be with. She’d never wanted anyone but him. But she just couldn’t let him know she loved him.

She couldn’t ever give him that power over her.

CHAPTER NINE

A FEW HOURS later Monet was woken by the most lovely sensation of his hand stroking her side, and then up her rib cage to cup her breast. Of course her nipple pebbled and he stroked that, too, all while she pretended to still be sleeping, wanting to just focus on how he made her body feel.

He made her body feel amazing.

But it was harder to feign sleep when he tugged on her nipple and flooded her with warmth, making her ache between her thighs, making her want him deep inside of her again.

And still, she kept her eyes closed, focusing on his warm palm against her breast, and the thick length of his erection against her backside.

Her body was waking everywhere and it was almost painful not responding. She wanted to turn over and give him all of her…well, all but her heart, because she didn't trust him with that.

"I know you're awake," he murmured, his breath warm against her neck.

She smiled into her pillow. "Mmm…?"

"You're a faker," he answered, sliding his hand lower, down over her hip, the curve of her butt, before slipping between her thighs. "So wet," he said, stroking her.

She gasped as he touched her; she was wet, and ready for him. She rolled onto her back and reached for him. He kissed her, and moved between her thighs but didn't enter her. Instead he leaned back and reached for a condom and sheathed himself before burying himself inside of her.

Monet sighed with pleasure as he filled her. He was big and the fullness was somewhat overwhelming and then it was perfect.

She linked her hands behind his neck and pulled him down to her, so she could kiss him as he thrust into her. This was exactly what she needed—him, all of him. It wasn't just sex, but joy at the deepest level. To finally know him, to finally be able to express her love for him…if not in words, then in actions. The climax was shattering, and even more bruising for her heart because the more she cared, the more the pleasure hurt.

Afterward she lay across his chest, in the hazy afterglow, thoughts drifting, emotions still not quite in control.

Leaving him would be so brutal.

Forgetting him would be impossible.

"This is why I came back," he said quietly, playing with her hair, the long strands slipping through his fingers. "I came back for you."

"Marcu," she protested huskily, a lump forming in her throat. "Let's not talk about that again."

"Why not? It's true. You're here because I needed you, and not for the children, but for me. I didn't see it before, but it hit me as I was leaving the *castello* yesterday. I didn't even want to get in the car, and once I was driving away, I felt almost sick. I didn't want to leave you, nor did I want to spend Christmas away from all of you. This was where I wanted to be—with you, and my children."

She sat up to see his face. "Don't mistake desire for love, or affection. It's not the basis for commitment, nor will it provide stability for a family of young children."

He said nothing for a moment. "Are you afraid of commitment?"

Her cheeks flamed with heat and her pulse thudded hard. Her body still felt treacherously warm, and aware. *"No!"*

"Then why can't we discuss us?"

"Because that's not why I slept with you!" She left the bed and reached for the soft cashmere throw on a chair near his hearth, and wrapped it around her. "I slept with you because I found you appealing, and yes, I was curious as to what making love with you would be like, and it was wonderful. But at the same time, I have no interest in pursuing this further. What we did together was lovely, and I have no regrets about losing my virginity to you, but once I leave, it's over."

"Why?"

"Why wouldn't it be? I came to Aosta to take care of your children, not play the part of your mistress. I might be my mother's daughter, but I have too much self-respect to go down that path."

"Our parents loved each other."

She let out a strangled laugh and pulled the fuzzy blanket closer to her bare shoulders. "I wouldn't ever call it that," she said hoarsely, remembering the inequality in their relationship. Matteo Uberto had all the power. Her mother had none.

"My father proposed to her twice. She turned him down both times."

She'd heard this before, from her mother, but she hadn't believed her. Monet had thought her mother was telling her what she thought Monet wanted to hear. "And yet he replaced her with a younger model when she turned forty."

Marcu sat up, the covers falling low to his hips, revealing his lean, muscular torso. "Because your mother was ill and she kept the news from my father, not wanting him to see her sick. She left him, not the other way around."

"That's not true!"

"But it is. My father loved your mother. And he didn't replace her with a younger model. There was never anyone else for him, not after she died."

His words caught her off guard and Monet stiffened, before turning away. Was that true? Or was Marcu twisting the past, changing facts into something less unsavory? She gave her head a shake, unsettled.

"It doesn't matter," she said after a moment, crossing the room to stand at Marcu's bedroom window. He hadn't closed the shutters last night and in the early morning light one could see the snow still falling, piling high on the stone ledge and coating the thick glass. "You brought me to Aosta so you could spend time alone with Vittoria before you proposed to her. That was our understanding. It's why I dropped everything to come to Italy. I'm here expressly to manage the children, and that agreement has not changed." She paused, and turned to look at Marcu, her gaze meeting his. "Nor do I want it to change. Despite the incredible lovemaking."

"So what happens now?" he asked grimly.

"I shower and dress and prepare for a day with the children, and you do what you would ordinarily do."

"I'd like to spend it with the children."

Again, he'd caught her off guard. She nodded approvingly, even if she felt somewhat off balance. "Good. They'd love that."

"And I'd like to spend the day with you, too…all of us together."

"They need time with you, without me there."

His mouth opened, then closed. He nodded. "You're right. Take the day off."

"You mean the morning, or the afternoon?"

"No, I mean the whole day." He paused. "You do get days off at Bernard's, don't you?"

"Of course I do."

"Then enjoy having some time to yourself."

She did enjoy having the morning to herself, but by early afternoon Monet was bored and restless. She couldn't stop thinking about last night, and how she'd spent it in Marcu's bed.

She might be conflicted about some things, but she had no confusion about how he made her feel, especially when she was in his arms, her body pressed to his. There was something magical about his skin against her skin and his mouth on hers. She loved his warmth and his strength, she loved the way he smelled and how incredible his touch made her feel. She came alive in his arms—everything within her screamed to life at the brush of his lips. There were moments when she thought she would give up everything for more of this, and more time with Marcu. She'd sacrifice future security for more happiness right now, but inevitably reason would intrude, and reality would return and she'd scold herself for being foolish. She couldn't afford to be a romantic. Couldn't afford to be stupid. She might want Marcu more than she'd ever wanted anyone, but he didn't love her. He only wanted her, and when the physical desire eventually faded—and it always did, just look at her mother—what would she be left with? Nothing.

Marcu took the children outside after breakfast to build snowmen, and then they had a snowball fight, with Matteo and Antonio battling Marcu and Rocca. The snow had stopped falling for the present, but the storm wasn't over and clouds hung low in the sky.

After the snowball fight they all took warm baths and changed into dry clothes before having lunch, and then relaxed in the music room, where the kids took turns playing the piano. Only Matteo had had lessons but the younger ones wanted to try to play, and Marcu sat down with Antonio and listened to him pound on the keys for a bit until Marcu said he wanted to play something. The children looked so shocked that it jolted Marcu's complacency and it crossed his mind that Monet was right. His children didn't really know him, not anymore.

"You know I play piano," he said, playing a simple melody with his right hand.

The children all shook their heads.

"I used to play a lot," he added. "I loved music. I wanted to study music but your grandfather said it wouldn't pay the bills. So I gave up my music studies when I went to university."

"Play us something then, Papà," Antonio said, still perched on the piano bench next to him.

Marcu thought a moment and then began to play something he'd learned years ago, and even though he hadn't touched the piano since before Galeta died, his fingers remembered the notes, and he just let himself play, lost in the song and the moment, because it was a special moment, having his three children with him, all riveted to the medieval Italian Christmas carol.

Marcu smiled at his children when he finished. "What did you think?"

"Beautiful," said Rocca.

"I didn't know you knew Christmas songs," Matteo said.

"I'd forgotten that one," Marcu answered truthfully, aware that once again Monet had been right. She was opening his eyes and he didn't like what he was seeing. Despite his best intentions, he had failed his children.

"Can you play us something else?" Rocca asked.

He thought for a moment and then began to play an aria from Puccini. Monet had loved Puccini. She'd discovered a passion for opera when she'd lived at the palazzo, and Marcu had gone out and bought DVDs for her of all the great operas, but Puccini remained her favorite composer.

When he finished, the children begged for another song but he shook his head and stood up. "Maybe later. Now I think we go up to the nursery and let you have a short rest before dinner."

"Will you read to us while we rest?" Rocca caught his hand and held it while they left the room. "Signorina Wilde always reads to us."

"She's been reading us *The Nutcracker*," Antonio added. "I like the Mouse King."

"And I like Clara. She's lovely." Rocca skipped next to him as they started up the stairs. "And she gets to have a Christmas ball. I wish we could have one."

"A Christmas ball?" Marcu's brow creased as he glanced down at his daughter. "You don't even know what a ball is, do you?"

"It's where everyone dresses up and they dance and have a huge party, and we have a ballroom here, so we could have one."

"We do have a ballroom," he agreed. "But who would we invite? We know no one here. Everyone in our family is in Palermo."

"But there are lots of people in the village, and we have everyone who works here, and their families. Why don't we invite them to come to our party?"

"It sounds like a lot of effort, and a lot of money," Marcu answered, more to himself than her.

"But it would be fun, and you have a lot of money," she retorted, giving his hand a squeeze. "And it would make everyone happy. Don't you think it would make them happy to come here for a big party?"

He smoothed the tip of her ponytail. "I don't know. That's a good question."

"Well, I think they'd be happy. Especially if we had a big tree like Clara had, and toys and lots of cookies and music." She hesitated, then added in a rush, "And Signorina would like it, too. She said she loves Christmas and in London everything has lights and pretty decorations. Wouldn't it be fun to surprise her and make it look like London here?"

Marcu choked back a laugh. "Well, we couldn't make it look like London, but we could probably organize something in the ballroom and celebrate the holidays with our staff."

"And everyone in the village."

"A few people from the village."

"And the farmer who brought you home."

"*Va bene*, and the farmer who brought me home."

Rocca smiled delightedly. "I can't wait to tell Signorina!"

"What if we don't tell her? What if we make it a surprise?"

Rocca frowned and looked at her brothers and then back at her father, a deep crease between her brows. "That's a terrible idea, Papà. She has to be dressed up, too. How can she come to a ball without a special dress?"

He couldn't stifle the laugh this time. "You make an excellent point, but let's not say anything to her yet because I'm not sure if we can make this happen."

"Why not?"

"We'd need the staff's help and I'm sure they're busy getting ready for their Christmas, too."

"So let's do it before Christmas Eve."

"That's only days from now."

Rocca was not easily discouraged. "Or Christmas day?"

Marcu checked his smile. "Let me ask the staff. If they are to be our guests, shouldn't we find out what day they'd like to come to a party?"

That evening Monet wasn't able to hear what Marcu and the children were talking about in the nursery, but she knew he'd gone up with them to put them to bed and he'd stayed in the nursery for forty-five minutes. She wondered if the children said prayers, or if he'd told them a story. She was glad he was with them, though, and glad she'd decided to accept their invitation and join them for dinner as everyone had looked happy and relaxed, and the children had teased Marcu and he'd teased them right back.

She hadn't stayed for dessert but went up to her room to take a bath and get ready for bed. She tried to read but couldn't focus on the words, and then she took out a bottle of nail polish and touched up her toenails. Monet glanced at the clock on the wall every now and then, noting that a half hour had passed, and then an hour, since Marcu had left the nursery and gone down the stairs.

She waited until another half hour passed before leaving her room to go downstairs to his bedroom. She wasn't sure what he'd say when he opened his door. Fortunately, he didn't keep her waiting. He simply opened his door wide and stepped back. That was all the invitation she needed.

After closing the door behind her, he swept her into his arms and carried her to the bed, where he slowly undressed her, taking time to kiss each inch of skin he bared.

She sighed and shivered as he kissed his way from her throat, to her collarbone, to her breasts, and tummy, and then finally between her legs. He settled there, too, and kissed and sucked and licked for an impossibly long time, making her arch and cry his name until he finally gave her the release she craved.

They made love twice, and she fell asleep curled against him, but now it was almost morning and she was wide-awake and still lying in his arms, but she felt restless and anxious and as she struggled to not think, or feel too much, tears started to her eyes.

This was madness coming to his room. She shouldn't have done it, but she couldn't stay away. She'd wanted him, and this, and he'd more than satisfied her last night, but now she felt sad, as well as strangely empty.

Monet pressed her cheek to his warm chest and blinked back tears. If only she didn't care for him. If only her feelings for him had been purely physical and making love with him could have satisfied her. Instead it had teased her heart, opening her to emotions she wasn't prepared to face.

She'd loved him since she was just a girl. She couldn't imagine ever loving anyone but him. But Marcu didn't love her back. Marcu would be able to take care of her, and give her enormous pleasure, but he'd never give her what she needed most—love. Endless, boundless love.

"What are you thinking about?" Marcu's deep voice broke the silence.

She wiggled closer to him. "Nothing."

"I can feel the weight of your thoughts. You can talk to me. Tell me what is worrying you."

But she couldn't talk to him. She didn't want to change what was between them—the intimacy was lovely, and special, as well as fleeting. It wouldn't last. Which is why she wanted to treasure it as long as she could. "I think I'm just tired. We don't sleep much when we're together."

He laughed softly, and stroked her hair, and then her back, his caress a comfort and a pleasure. "Then sleep."

It had taken her a while, but Monet was sleeping now, curled close to his side. Marcu was glad she slept, but he couldn't. He was lying on his back, an arm behind his head, staring at the ceiling, chest tight with bottled air.

It hurt to breathe. His head ached. He couldn't ease the pressure in his chest, while the difficult conversations with Monet played endlessly in his head.

She said he'd never mentioned love to her, and it was true. Love. Such a difficult concept for him.

He'd spent the past few days trying to figure out what love would look like, feel like. He loved his children, but even that was restrained and controlled. For him, love was duty and responsibility, love was loyalty. Had he ever truly been in love?

He'd married Galeta because it was a smart decision, a good decision, and so it had proved to be in that they suited each other and had a strong marriage. He had been prepared to marry Vittoria because he'd considered that she would make a good wife and mother. He'd never felt any desire for Vittoria. She was a beautiful woman but he felt nothing resembling need, hunger, passion. The only person he had ever truly wanted like that had been Monet. But had that desire, that craving, been love? Or was it, as Monet said, just lust?

He tried to think back, tried to remember who he'd been eight years ago. He'd changed so much it was hard to think back without some scorn because he'd been so much softer then, so unrealistic. He'd wanted Monet badly. He wanted her not just in a sexual sense but in a keep-her-close, and keep-her-safe way.

She'd felt like his. His family, his home, his heart. No one knew him better. No one had talked to him more, or listened more. No one had smiled the way she'd smiled when he entered a room. Her face would light up, her eyes would grow bright. She'd radiated warmth and sweetness, energy and light. She'd made him think of orange blossoms and honey and sunshine.

Had that been love?

Had what he felt then been love, but he hadn't known it? And yet how could he not know?

How could he go through a life without love?

How could he not know how to express love?

Did his children not feel loved by him?

What was his problem with love? Was it the word, or the action?

Or both?

Marcu eased away from Monet, put his robe on and went upstairs to the nursery to check on the children. They were all sound asleep, each in a different position. Rocca slept sideways, Matteo was straight as an arrow, and Antonio was a little ball.

He went from bed to bed, straightening covers, pressing a quick hand to a small warm head, and each time he felt a twinge in his chest, adding to the ache already there.

What had happened to him since Galeta died?

But also, what had happened to him before he married Galeta to make a practical marriage so appealing to him? Surely it wasn't just his father's influence? His father had only had so much influence over him.

Then what?

Marcu knew he was more reserved than his younger brother and sisters. He was old enough to remember the day his mother left, and yet young enough to miss her profoundly. But he'd always been more reserved, hadn't he?

Or had losing her at twelve changed him? Hardened him? Numbed him? Made it more difficult for him to feel—and give—love?

He wished he knew, and tonight as he went back around

the nursery once more, to kiss each child on the forehead, he felt as if his chest was full of hot sharp shards of glass.

He did love his children, very much. He simply struggled to show the depth of his feelings.

Worse, he struggled just feeling feelings.

But that didn't mean he couldn't try to express them. And he would. He had a plan—it'd take some work…but he could do it.

He would do it.

Monet woke up to blinding sunshine. Warm golden light flooded the room, illuminating the floor and warming the bed. For a moment she couldn't get her bearings and then she realized she was in Marcu's room, and from the light pouring through the window, it was late.

She sat up, and glanced around, discovering Marcu in sweatpants and a knit shirt, reading in a chair by the fire. "What time is it?" she asked, running a hand through her long hair, trying to smooth the tangles.

"Almost nine."

"Nine? The children!"

"Elise is with them. We're sleeping in and in moments we'll be having a lovely breakfast here together."

"In your room?"

"In my bed."

She blushed. "It's daylight. I can't be here. If I'm caught having breakfast here, then the staff knows we've been together."

"And you don't think they've known you slept in here the last two nights?"

"No," she said, thinking they'd been quite clever and stealthy.

"There are cameras in the corridors," he said, "for security."

"Oh."

"And then there were the sheets."

Monet closed her eyes, mortified. It was embarrassing to realize that everyone knew what she and Marcu had been doing. "I can't imagine what they're thinking."

"I don't really care."

"But I do," she said, throwing back the covers, to get her robe and gown, because the vexing thing was, she really did care. Having grown up listening to people whisper about her mother, Monet didn't like being the subject of anyone's conversation. She'd spent her whole life trying to avoid gossip and speculation.

He rose from his chair and peeled his sweater off and carried it to her. "Put this on instead, it's warm and will cover you as breakfast will be arriving soon."

She frowned at him but did it, and crawled back into bed. "Is this your normal routine?"

"No."

"Have you had many women stay over here?"

"None."

That gave her pause. "What about in Palermo?"

"No one has ever stayed over at any of my family homes. I conduct my private life elsewhere."

"You mean in hotels?"

He sighed. "Monet, you're not like other women. And you are not convenient. You are actually most inconvenient as you demand things of me that no one else demands. You want things I have stopped believing in. You force me to rethink everything I have viewed as truth."

For a moment she couldn't reply, was too busy processing his words and wondering what they truly meant. Was he trying to placate her? If only she didn't doubt him.

They were interrupted by a knock on the door, and Marcu pulled on a shirt and went to open the door. One of the kitchen staff carried in a huge tray and placed it on a side table before leaving. Breakfast was cappuccinos and a basket of warm rolls and fluffy scrambled eggs. Monet didn't think she was hungry and yet she ate everything on her plate, and then had an additional roll with butter and jam.

"This was most indulgent," she said with a sigh, stretching. "Thank you."

He took her hand and carried it to his mouth, kissing her knuckles, and then turned her hand over, his lips brushing the inside of her tender wrist. "If you were my wife, we could do this every weekend."

"Marcu, don't start on that again."

"Why not? I think we should discuss it, seriously—"

"No. It's not right, and it's not real, and to be perfectly honest, this isn't even about me. You don't really want me—"

"But I do. I want you. I don't even know what that means other than I want you in my life, I want you in my home, I want you to be part of my future."

"And your children? How do they play into this?"

"You like my children."

She drew her hand away, and pressed it to her chest, trying to slow the wild beating of her heart. "I *adore* your children, Marcu, but the last thing they need is confusion. And our relationship would confuse them, just as you confuse me." She drew another short painful breath. "You told me in London you didn't even want a wife. You told me you were marrying Vittoria just because you needed someone for the kids—"

"And you said that was the wrong reason to marry. You said, hire better child care," he said.

"Yes."

"And you're right. I don't need you for my children. I

need you for me. I need you, Monet. I can imagine a future without you, but I don't like it. I don't want that future. I want a future with you."

She climbed off the bed and shook her head, feeling trapped and cornered and overwhelmed. "I have to go," she said under her breath. "It's time to go."

"The roads aren't clear yet."

"They will be, soon."

"It'll take a day, maybe two."

"What about your helicopter?"

"They have to plow the roads to get to the helipad. That's still a fifteen-to-twenty-minute drive from here."

She closed her eyes, hands in tight fists. "As soon as the weather permits, I would like to leave."

"Understood."

"I also ask that you say nothing to the children. They do not need to be part of this."

"Agreed."

"And when I do go, you must reassure them that I loved spending time with them, and that I am only going so that their Miss Sheldon can return."

"If that is the script…?"

She hated his mocking tone. It only flamed her temper. "You dragged me into this."

"Yes, I did, and I'd keep you here, kicking and screaming, if it was the Middle Ages, but it's not, so I will return you to London as soon as I can."

"Good." She found her nightgown and robe and picked them up. "And we won't do this again…we can't. The children won't understand, and it would only confuse them if they discovered me here with you."

"Whatever you think best," he said, watching her from his side of the bed.

"I don't appreciate your sarcasm."

"I'm sure you don't. Monet Wilde is clever and independent. She needs no man, and she's certainly no pushover."

She stiffened in outrage. "I don't need a man, no. And I don't need a minder, or a keeper, or someone to think for me. I'm not my mother—"

"Mio Dio," he snapped, flinging back the covers and leaving bed. "Not this again."

"You seem to think—"

"*No!* You seem to think, or fear, that you are like her. You are not like her. You have never been like her, and that's neither criticism or praise. It's just a statement of fact. You are you, and Candie was Candie and I would never ever confuse you for her, not for a second."

Monet bit into her lower lip to keep it from quivering. "I think the less I have to do with you until I leave, the better."

"Fine."

"I'll go see to the children now."

"I wish you would."

CHAPTER TEN

MONET SAW NEXT to nothing of Marcu for the rest of the day, as well as much of the following day, which was Christmas Eve and yet one wouldn't know it from the lack of festivities.

Monet had done her best to keep the children entertained and happy. Yesterday they'd built snow people—because Rocca didn't believe they should be called snowmen when she only made snow girls—and this morning they'd gone sledding. After lunch they'd bundled up again and returned outside to go ice skating on the frozen pond behind the *castello.*

They'd just laced up their skates when Marcu suddenly appeared at the pond, with his own skates. He looked dashing in his black parka.

Monet's heart jumped at the sight of him, and her hands shook as she finished tightening Antonio's skates.

"I've got that," Marcu said, lifting Antonio's skate to adjust the knot.

Monet silently moved away, leaving him to tie the other skate.

Rocca clapped her hands with pleasure, thrilled to have her father with them. The children swarmed Marcu as he got on the ice with them and Monet kept her distance, letting Marcu and the children play.

Everyone skated for an hour before Marcu said it was time to go back to the *castello* and warm up. As they entered the *castello* they discovered that the staff had prepared a treat—hot chocolate and cookies awaited them—and again Monet hung back, feeling strange. She'd told him yesterday that she didn't want to have anything to do with him, and yet she'd thought of him endlessly and missed his company. It was even worse when he was near and they weren't speaking, or looking at each other.

"Time for you to bathe and change," Marcu said to the children. "It's Christmas Eve and we'll have our traditional dinner in two hours in the dining room."

The children smiled hopefully at each other as Monet steered them from the room. "You're welcome to join us," Marcu said casually. "But if our traditions make you uncomfortable, I understand."

Monet turned in the doorway. "I spent six years with your family in Sicily. Six Christmases and never once was I uncomfortable."

"*Bene*. I'll see you with the children in two hours."

The Christmas Eve dinner was exactly as she remembered from Palermo—the same dishes, the same aromas, the same flavors—stirring past memories, and making her think of Sicily, and the lovely times she'd had there, as well as memories of her mother. She'd loved her mother, but it had been such a complicated relationship. Maybe that was okay. Maybe love was complicated and that was okay, too.

She sipped her wine and listened to Marcu and the children talk, and then after the dessert—again, an Uberto favorite from Palermo—they went to the music room and Marcu shocked her by sitting at the piano and playing songs for the children, and not just any songs, but Christmas carols.

The children didn't seem surprised to see him at the piano. They gathered around him and Antonio leaned against his father as Marcu's fingers moved deftly over the keys. And then he began to sing, and she blinked hard, fighting a wave of emotion, thinking she hadn't heard this song in years and years. It was an old carol, a haunting Italian carol, and it filled her with tenderness.

Marcu and the children would be fine. Marcu loved his children. She didn't have to worry about any of them.

And then it was time for bed, and Marcu said he'd walk his children up to the nursery and tell them a story and listen to their prayers.

Monet nodded, and smiled, happy for them. "Good night," she murmured. *"Buon Natale,"* she said as they parted at the nursery door.

"Buon Natale," the children chorused.

Marcu gave her a peculiar look but said nothing and she went to her room, and prepared for bed, and then fought tears for the next hour before she finally fell asleep.

Monet's breakfast arrived on a tray the next morning, carried to her room by Marcu. She hastily dragged a hand through her messy hair, smoothing it. "Good morning," she said huskily.

"Buon Natale," he said, placing the tray on the table in front of her couch. "I see you have the lights on your little Christmas tree plugged in."

"I've enjoyed my tree very much."

"I'm glad." He hesitated. "We're having a party here, later this afternoon," he added carelessly, as if it was nothing out of the ordinary. "The guests will be arriving at four. The children have party clothes in the nursery if you don't mind helping them dress before."

"Of course I don't," she answered, astonished. "And when did you decide to have this party?"

"Over the weekend."

"You never mentioned it before."

"I wasn't sure if the weather would hold, and I didn't want them disappointed."

He gave her a pointed look. "This was Rocca's idea. Apparently you've been reading *The Nutcracker* to my children, and Rocca very much wants to be Clara."

Monet's lips curved in reluctant amusement. "I do sometimes read the story two or three times a day."

"And she's learned it by heart. Trying to create a Russian fantasy in this *castello* in the midst of the worst winter storm in years hasn't been easy."

Monet couldn't believe what she was hearing. "And yet you're doing it."

"Trying. I don't know if anyone from the village will come, but they have all been invited, and my staff have been invited, along with their families, and I think it should be fun."

Fun. He'd just used the word *fun*. Last night he'd played the piano and sung carols. Today he was throwing a party and talking about fun. "The children know, though," she said slowly.

"The children know I've invited people, and they know the staff have been cleaning and cooking, but they haven't seen the ballroom yet. We've tried to spruce it up a bit, and add a little festive color."

Monet's chest grew warm and she felt a pinch of sharp emotion. "The fact that you tried to do something for them is wonderful. You will have made your children happy, your Rocca most of all."

He fell silent for a moment. "She adores you, you know."

"I adore her, too."

He gave her another long look then walked from the room. Monet exhaled slowly, painfully, as she heard the door close behind him.

The day passed slowly for everyone, but finally it was midafternoon. After helping the children dress in new clothes that had arrived for them, Monet glanced at the clock and saw she had fifty minutes before the party. Fifty minutes to try to pull something together for herself. She returned to her room to see what she could do, and stopped short at the sight of a stunning strapless red silk ball gown hanging from the frame of her four-poster bed.

For a split second she couldn't breathe. Marcu hadn't forgotten her, either.

She blinked and tried to take another breath. It was the most beautiful dress she'd ever seen, the boned bodice and gleaming silk skirt embellished with embroidered white flowers and green beaded leaves. The skirt was cut narrow and featured a dramatic train. Monet could recognize the designer from the construction of the exquisite bodice, and the shape of the skirt. This was old-school glamour, Italian couture, a gown that probably equaled half of her annual salary. If not more.

Silk heels sat on the floor, just beneath the long silk gown, the shoes red, perfectly matching the dress.

"What on earth?" she whispered, lifting the hem of the gown to feel the luxurious fabric.

A little girl giggled behind her and Monet turned to see Rocca standing there, beaming with pleasure. "Papà bought it for you," Rocca said happily, pressing her hands to her own silk dress, the red of her gown darker, deeper, like the color of burgundy wine. "He had it flown in from Milan. It's by a famous person." She ran over to pick up one of Monet's high heels. "These match your dress, too!"

"It's incredible," Monet said, so overwhelmed she didn't know what to think.

"Do you need help dressing?" Rocca asked.

"No, my love, I'm good. Why don't you keep an eye on Antonio so he doesn't get his handsome suit dirty before everyone arrives?"

Marcu had said he'd invited everyone from the village, and everyone from the village came.

He'd also said that he'd tried to make the ballroom festive, and he'd done far, far more than that. The ballroom had been turned into a winter wonderland with a huge Christmas tree dominating the middle of the room, easily fifteen feet high, and covered in thousands of tiny white lights.

Fragrant green garlands were swagged over the doorways, and framed the tall windows. Ornate gingerbread houses filled a banquet table, the houses created by the Swiss chef who'd come to lend the Uberto cook a hand. Tables groaned beneath the weight of all the food and drink and candles. It was just as Rocca had wanted, a glittering holiday party with music and dancing and much laughter.

Entering the ballroom, Monet felt overdressed as no one else had such a formal gown, but after enough guests arrived, and the music was playing, she forgot her self-consciousness, and enjoyed watching the children play with the children from the village. Now and then Rocca would run to Monet and give her hand a squeeze. "Isn't this fun?" she'd say. "Just like in *The Nutcracker*!"

Each time Monet would squeeze her hand back, and say, "Yes. And isn't it wonderful?"

More than once her eyes would fill with tears because it really was a gorgeous party, and everyone was so happy, and this was what Marcu's life should be like—busy, warm, loving, filled with friends and music and laughter.

Monet felt fortunate to be part of the Christmas celebration. It felt a bit like a miracle and she would always be grateful she was here to witness it.

During the party, Marcu couldn't keep his eyes off Monet. She was dazzling in the red silk ball gown, her bare shoulders gleaming, her dark hair swept into a half-up, half-down style that made her look like a fairy-tale princess. She was the most beautiful woman he'd ever seen in his life, and he loved her. All she needed was a tiara to finish the vision. A tiara, and his ring on her finger.

He loved her.

He'd never loved any woman but her. No woman had ever felt so right in his arms. No woman's kiss or touch had ever affected him so strongly. There had been plenty of women in his life, women he'd desired and cared for, but no one that mattered to him like Monet. No woman made him want to throw caution to the wind. He'd only ever lost his head once, and it was with her, eight years ago. And fast-forward to the present, she still had that same power over him. It didn't make sense, either. He had analyzed his actions in the past, analyzed his response to her then and now, and there was no rational answer for why he felt this want and need for her. The desire wasn't logical. There was nothing logical about the attraction, or the emotional connection between them, which was so deep he didn't know how to articulate it. Truthfully, his need for her, his desire to have her in his life, at his side, forever, was baffling if only because he couldn't find words to explain it. It simply was. And she mattered that much.

And why her?

He didn't know the answer to that, either, only that her smile gave light and life to his heart. Her eyes—so expressive—revealed so many truths, and he needed them. He needed her. He needed her honesty, and her ability to stand up to him, and confront him when he was wrong. So many people tried to impress him, and court his favor, but she wasn't one of them. She never had been.

The guests were all gone. The children had been taken to bed and would be tucked in by Elise while the rest of the staff moved through the *castello*, blowing out candles, extinguishing lights, locking doors in all rooms but the ballroom as Marcu had given them instructions to leave the ballroom alone. And now Marcu had Monet alone. His heart pounded and he felt like a boy—shy, nervous, ridiculously tongue-tied—as he drew Monet closer to the soaring Christmas tree, still glittering with lights and delicate glass ornaments, and the beautiful hand-carved angels.

"It was a beautiful party," Monet said.

"It was."

"I think everyone had an incredible time," she added, as they gazed up at the tree.

"Yes."

"I've never been so surprised," she said, glancing at him with a smile. "Who knew that Marcu Uberto, who doesn't celebrate Christmas, would throw the most magical Christmas party I've ever been to?"

"It was Rocca's idea," he answered, pulse thudding.

"Rocca is an incredible little girl."

"She is," he agreed, before drawing a deep breath. "And you are an incredible woman. I don't know how you've done it, but you've changed everything in a matter of days. You arrived here nine days ago and somehow saved all of us."

"Not so."

"It is so." His voice dropped, deepening with emotion, emotion that filled his chest with warmth. "I'm so grateful to you, Monet, for so many things, but maybe I'm most grateful for your love, and your faith in me. Even when you're angry with me, you still somehow believe in me, and that has made all the difference."

He reached into his pocket and pulled out the delicate gold ring with the two-carat ruby he'd bought for her ten years ago, when she'd turned sixteen. "This is temporary," he said, rolling the ring between his fingers. "Just until I can get you the perfect, forever ring, but I've held on to this all these years, and it's my promise to you, that I will always take care of you, and love you, for the rest of our lives." And then he kneeled down, in front of her, and reached for her hand. "Monet, would you please marry me? I love you, and I can't imagine my life without you."

Monet stood frozen in shock as Marcu slid her ruby ring on her finger, specifically on her ring finger on her left hand.

It was a ring she hadn't seen in eight years. He'd given it to her for her sixteenth birthday, but she'd chosen to leave it behind when she'd left Palermo.

Monet's mouth dried and she struggled to speak, but words wouldn't come and her emotions were beyond chaotic, flooding her with shock and then grief, because she couldn't say yes to him, she couldn't. "Marcu, please," she whispered, tugging on his hand. "Please get up. Please stand."

"You haven't answered me," he said.

"Because I can't answer you. You don't really love me."

"I do. Very much."

She shook her head, and struggled to get the ring off her finger. "How can you? You don't even know me—"

"You are smart, and kind, as well as fiercely loyal," he interrupted, rising, and yet he remained close. "You wouldn't be here now if you weren't. But you're also independent and demand respect, and I do respect you, very much, and I want what's best for you."

"And you think you are what's best for me?" she asked, voice strangled, still frantically trying to get the ring off, and yet it seemed stuck, already.

"I think I could be. With your help." His voice deepened. "I'm not without flaws, and I need to work on things, but with you, I can be the man you deserve—"

"Marcu, stop. Please stop. This is too painful, *please*." Her eyes shimmered with tears and she knocked them away, giving up on the ring to fight the tears. "You will forget me as soon as I go. You will move on quickly. It's what you do, and who you are—"

"Because I married Galeta?"

"Yes! Within months of me leaving. And you didn't come find me, and you didn't try to reach out to me. You just dropped me at the airport and we were done, and that's not love. Nor have you changed. You're here because Vittoria was on the other side of the mountain—"

"Not true. Not even close to being true."

"So you didn't marry Galeta months after I left?"

"Yes, I did. I'd gotten her pregnant and she was a good person. I'd known her forever, since we were children. She left to go to boarding school right around the time you and your mother arrived in Palermo. I didn't see her again for years, but she was easy to like. You would have liked her—"

"I doubt that!"

"No, you would have. She wasn't your typical heiress. She was the opposite of a socialite. Galeta didn't enjoy public attention or the spotlight. In fact our biggest source of tension was the media, and controlling the paparazzi. She was as livid as I was that our wedding was in the tabloids. We'd both wanted a private wedding and she wondered who'd sneaked all those personal photos to them and demanded I investigate and fire those who had betrayed our trust."

"Did you investigate?"

"Yes."

"Who was it?"

"It was my father. He leaked his own son's wedding

photos, wanting you to know I was married, and no longer available."

"He loved my mother but despised me."

"He didn't despise you, but he was old-fashioned in that he wanted a Sicilian daughter-in-law, so that his grandchildren would be Sicilian." He shrugged impatiently. "I don't blame him, though. I blame myself. He didn't fail you. I did. I should have gone after you. I should have protected you. I should have been the man you needed."

"I was just eighteen, and not ready to marry. Everything worked out the way it was meant to work out." She took a panicked step backward, feeling foolish in the stunning ball gown. She'd been overdressed from the start. She wasn't a princess. She wasn't even Cinderella. She was nothing… nothing at all…and she just wanted to go home now. She wanted to return to London more than she'd ever wanted anything. "I'm sorry to disappoint you, but I must leave first thing in the morning. I want to leave quickly, quietly, without fuss."

He said nothing.

"You promised me," she said, voice trembling. "You promised me—"

"I'll take you to the helicopter," he said flatly, cutting her short. "It's still here. I'll make sure you're on it early in the morning."

"And the rest of the way? You'll get me a ticket home?"

"My plane will be fueled in Milan, waiting for you."

She nodded, and glanced down at the ring on her finger. The band was delicate and elegant, and then there was the rich red ruby gleaming in the middle. "Twice you've given this to me," she said, once again trying to tug it off, "and now twice I give it back to you—"

"No." He caught her hand, and pushed the ring back down. "It's yours. It was something I had made for you for your sixteenth birthday. It's yours, and I ask you to take it with you. Once you're in London you can do what you want with it, but please don't leave it here. I've held on to it all these years, but I can't do it anymore."

She nodded again and then glanced at the tree, with the lights and beautiful decorations, and then at him, so still, so hurt, so proud, and blinking back tears, she hurried from the ballroom.

Monet couldn't get out of the ball gown fast enough, and she scrubbed the makeup off her face, before splashing cold water over it to stop the tears.

She couldn't cry.

She couldn't think.

She couldn't feel.

Just go to bed. Just get through the next eight hours and she'd be gone. Away. Free.

Monet crawled into bed, shivering. She buried her face in the pillow, trying to hold the emotion in.

Marcu had proposed to her…he'd gotten down on one knee and asked her to be his wife, and he'd said the words she'd longed to hear but she didn't believe them, which was why she couldn't accept the proposal.

She finally broke down, and cried, hard, before falling asleep, but she couldn't stay asleep, tossing and turning all night, until she left the bed and went to sit in a chair by the window, wrapped in her duvet, and watched the sun rise over the mountain, painting the white valley floor pink and gold.

She didn't think she'd ever seen such a beautiful sunrise. She tried to drink it in, despite the fact that her eyes were dry and gritty from too little sleep.

Out there somewhere was the helicopter waiting for her.

Marcu had said he'd make the necessary travel arrangements and she knew he would.

Once the sun was all the way up, she made a pot of tea and focused on packing, determined to leave before the children woke. She left the ball gown and shoes that had arrived via helicopter yesterday in the wardrobe. She would never wear them again, nor did she want to take them back to London with her. They'd just serve as a painful reminder of her time here.

Bags packed, Monet straightened her room, returned a damp towel to the en-suite bathroom, put away the teakettle and began to make the bed. They were silly tasks but tidying her room gave her a sense of closure.

"What are you doing?" Marcu's deep voice sounded, startling her.

She hadn't heard her outer door open, and she jerked upright, pulse pounding. She hadn't seen him, or spoken to him, since she'd gone to bed last night. "Making the bed," she answered, forcing herself back to action, smoothing the bottom sheet before drawing up the duvet.

"Before you leave?"

"I can't leave a messy room."

"We have staff here," he said, approaching. "You're not a maid."

"I'm more comfortable doing it myself. I grew up this way." She glanced at him, trying to keep her pulse steady, not easy when he stood impossibly close to her, and the bed. He looked grim, and tired. She suspected he hadn't slept very well last night, either. But she couldn't dwell on that.

"We had staff and help at the palazzo," he said.

"Yes, you did, but my mother and I took care of our own rooms, and we always did our own beds. The staff would wash our sheets and return them folded, but we did everything else."

"I had no idea."

"My mother worried that the staff would think less of us if we put on airs." She managed a tight smile. "She might have been your father's mistress, but she never forgot she was just another member of his staff."

"Monet!"

His sharp tone drew tears to her eyes. She curled her fingers into a ball, feeling the press of the ruby ring. She hadn't taken it off. It was her own ring after all, given to her by him years ago. At the very least, she could leave with it. "It's how she felt," she said quietly, defensively. "I'm sorry if it hurts."

"I don't think you're sorry it hurts. I think you want to hurt me now. You want to draw blood because you're refusing what you want—"

"That's ludicrous!"

"You love me. I know you do. I know you have always loved me, just as I have always loved you, but because I haven't expressed my love correctly, properly, to your standards, it's not enough."

"That's not true."

"No? Then why refuse me? Why not give me a chance?"

Her mouth opened, and then closed without making a sound because she didn't have an answer for him. She didn't know why she couldn't consider his proposal. She just couldn't…there wasn't enough trust left inside her. "I'm all ready to go," she said. "I just have those bags there."

His gaze swept the room, stopping on the wardrobe with the open door. Her red ball gown was on a hanger inside. "I'll take your bags," he said curtly.

"I'll meet you downstairs."

Marcu tried not to think as he drove Monet to the helipad in the valley. His chest felt bruised, as if he'd taken a hard blow on the left side and he kept having to hold his breath to keep the pain at bay.

He felt as if he was in Palermo driving her to the airport eight years ago. He'd hated that day, and he hated this one. The last thing he wanted was for her to leave, but he had made her a promise that when she asked to leave, he would let her go. He was letting her go.

As he pulled up to the gates he could see his helicopter and pilots waiting. He ground his teeth together. His chest was already on fire and pain filled him, making every nerve and muscle hurt.

He loved her and she didn't believe him. He loved her and had tried to show her, organizing a festive party to demonstrate that he would try to be a better man. That he was willing to change. That indeed he was already changed.

He didn't need her for the children. The children were actually fine. They had a kind, devoted nanny who'd return soon from England, and they had a father who loved them.

He was the one who needed her. He was the one whose life had never been the same after she'd left Palermo, and now she was leaving again. Leaving him again. And it burned within him, the pain and the need and the disappointment with himself for not being able to convince her.

He slowed, and then shifted into Park, as they arrived on the tarmac.

He hated to let her go. He hated that he had failed her not once, but twice. For a moment Marcu felt sick, nauseated by the past, and then he made a deliberate decision to let the past and the painful emotion go. He wasn't who he'd been, and even though this was ending just as badly as it had in Palermo, he knew without a doubt this time that he loved her, and that there would never be anyone for him but her.

Monet didn't just own his heart. She was his heart.

CHAPTER ELEVEN

SHE WAS BACK at work for the huge sales going on after Christmas, sales that continued into the New Year, and through the second week of January. During the week the store was less frantic, but on weekends the traffic always picked up and today was no exception.

Monet was grateful that work had been so busy because it kept her from thinking too much, and prevented her from falling apart. Every day she questioned her decision to reject Marcu's proposal. Every day she kicked herself, angry that she'd been so quick to refuse him instead of asking for more time.

She'd been proud and stubborn, impulsive and frightened, and she had just possibly destroyed her last chance for true love, and happiness.

Maybe if the time she'd spent with Marcu had been different. Maybe if it hadn't been such a whirlwind trip she could have been more objective. Instead she'd felt swept into an Alpine fantasy, complete with adorable children and a handsome profoundly sexy bachelor father, with snow and snow and more snow, as well as that glorious Christmas proposal before the towering Christmas tree in the ballroom—and it was fantastic and impossible. It was fiction, just like *The Nutcracker* that Monet had read to Rocca every day.

And so she'd turned Marcu down to make a point—she was fine, she was strong—but Monet feared she'd cut off her nose to spite her face.

Marcu wasn't prone to grand romantic gestures but he'd tried that Christmas night. He'd organized the party and sent everyone away so he could propose before the tree. It had been romantic, and she'd been wearing a perfect princess gown, but she wasn't a princess. She'd never be a princess.

Monet's eyes grew hot and gritty and a lump filled her throat. She was so upset that her hands shook as she adjusted the delicate lace wedding gown hanging next to the cash register. She had to keep it together. There would be no breaking down at work. Which was why she couldn't let herself think of him anymore. Easier said than done when everything in her missed him and had loved being with Marcu and his children. He did feel like home. He was the only home she'd ever known and she'd given it all up again because she had to be strong. She had to be—

She turned at the sound of a violin, recognizing the first haunting notes, but not yet certain it was what she thought the song might be. And then as a voice began to sing, shivers coursed up and down her spine.

Puccini's *Gianni Schicchi*. Her favorite opera.

Voice after voice joined in. But was the song playing though the department's speaker? Or was there a performance taking place in the store?

She crossed the marble floor and discovered the musicians were on her floor, seated in folding chairs in front of the big arched window.

Stringed instruments, a harp, wind instruments—the musicians were filling in from the sides.

A woman stepped toward her, singing. It was the woman she'd just spoken to fifteen minutes ago, about mother-of-the-bride gowns. Monet's mouth dropped open as she realized that half the people singing and playing instruments had been customers moments ago, or had at least been pretending to be customers…

And these "customers" weren't just singing any song, but *"E Lui,"* in which Gianni Schicchi refused to allow his daughter, Lauretta, to marry her boyfriend, Rinuccio, and everyone was fighting and arguing and the couple was distraught.

Monet's heart pounded as music soared, and the superb voices rose, overlapping, echoing off the ceiling, and filled the high domed ceiling of the fifth floor.

Monet had used to attend the opera in Palermo with the Ubertos, and this had been her favorite. She'd spent hours listening to the recording in Marcu's room, playing her favorite aria, *"O Mio Babbino Caro,"* over and over.

As *"E Lui"* ended there was a beat of silence before a lovely young woman in a red dress—the bride Monet had been helping earlier—began to sing, the lyrics so familiar to Monet, with Lauretta pleading with her father to let her marry her beloved because she couldn't live without him.

Every great soprano had sung *"O Mio Babbino Caro,"* and Monet was moved to tears.

Lauretta was poor. She couldn't marry her Rinuccio because she had no dowry. And yet she loved Rinuccio so much that she told her father she'd die without him…

The heart-rending aria filled the great glass dome with sound, the acoustics perfect, and Monet cried harder, wiping away tears but unable to catch them all.

Only one person knew how much she loved this opera and this aria. Only one person knew she'd once compared herself to Lauretta, a girl from humble origins who'd never be accepted by her beloved's wealthy family as she came without a dowry…

As the soprano reached the end, the fifth floor was overflowing with people, the crowd spilling off the escalators and out of the elevators to watch, and listen. Then it was over, and there was a moment of rapt silence before thunderous applause.

Monet clapped, and tried to dry her eyes, but she was a mess. This had to be Marcu's doing. It had to be, but where was he?

And then he was there, walking through the crowd, sophisticated and dashing in a black suit and black shirt, the shirt open at the throat, revealing his lovely lightly tanned skin. His gaze met hers and held as he approached, and she didn't know what to think or feel, not when she was already feeling so much, undone by the music and the memories and the past that she couldn't ever seem to come to grips with, even though she'd tried. How she'd tried.

"What have you done?" she choked, as he crossed to her, and took her hand. "Have you seen all these people?"

"Yes."

"This was crazy. I'm shaking."

He put an arm around her and pulled her close. "You loved that aria, remember?"

Fresh tears filled her eyes and she couldn't speak, and so she nodded her head. "Why?" she whispered when she could.

"I needed to get your attention. I hope I have."

She cried harder, and she didn't know why she was crying, only that it felt so good to be in his arms. She'd missed him so much. Too much. It had been awful these past few weeks and she'd wanted to go to him so many times. "How did you manage this?" she said, cheek pressed to his chest.

"Not easily. Hit a few roadblocks until I reached out to the English National Opera."

She laughed and blinked back tears. "It's incredible, but also not private."

"Not at all private. Some might say it's a spectacle."

"Indeed. You've put on quite a show, *signor*."

"I'm not finished, either," he said, taking a ring box from his pocket and kneeling in front of her. "I want the world to know I love you, and have only ever loved you, and I will spend the rest of my life trying to make it up to you—"

She reached down and clasped his hands. "You don't have to do this here, and you don't have to say these things—"

"But I do, because I love you, and I'm once again asking you to marry me, not because I need a wife, but because I need *you*, and only you, and if you're not ready to accept me now, then I'll wait, and I'll ask you again in six months, and then again in another six months."

Monet straightened and clasped her hands together, pulse pounding.

He looked up at her, his expression serious, his light blue eyes intently holding her gaze. "If you say you need six years, I'll give you that, too, but there will never be anyone else for me. It is you, and only you." He opened the ring box to reveal a stunning emerald cut diamond—that was huge, easily three or four carats in size—with smaller baguette diamonds on either side. "I will wait for you, because I love you, and life isn't complete without you. In fact, life isn't even life without you."

She glanced from the ring to his face. "I do love you," she whispered. "Very, very much. But I'm scared—"

"I know."

"I've been alone for so much of my life."

"I know that, too."

"I don't trust easily."

The corner of his mouth lifted. "Yes."

"But I can't imagine life without you. I don't want to do this without you anymore." She flexed her left hand, where she still wore her sixteenth-birthday ring. "I haven't taken this off, because it's been my last connection to you."

"Ring, or no ring, I'm not going anywhere."

"We can wait on setting a wedding date?"

"As long as you want."

She smiled. "Then, yes. I accept your proposal. Yes."

He stood and slipped her birthday ring off, and put it on her right hand, before sliding the engagement ring onto her finger, and then he kissed her, a long searing kiss filled with heat and love, as the crowd applauded, and someone whistled, the sound echoing off the domed ceiling with its incredible acoustics.

EPILOGUE

SHE DIDN'T NEED six years or even six months to know she wanted to marry him. They decided to continue working and then spend weekends together, and after just a month of Marcu bringing the children to London to see her, followed by her traveling to Sicily to see them, she knew the sooner they came together as a family, the better. The children did need her and so did Marcu, who worried more and slept less when she was in London on her own.

The wedding took place the first weekend in June at the great cathedral in Palermo, the one the family had always attended. The weather was perfect for a wedding, too, the sky a stunning azure-blue with just a few wispy clouds overhead. It was warm but not too warm and the cathedral's bells rang joyfully as Monet and Marcu stepped from the cool interior into the glorious sunshine, her hand tucked in the crook of Marcu's arm.

Man and wife.

Married.

She looked up at him, and he smiled his dazzling heart-stopping smile, before his head dropped and he kissed her thoroughly, making her tingle from head to toe. *"La mia adorabile moglie,"* he said huskily. My lovely wife.

She couldn't hide her blush, or her smile, as he lifted his head. Wife. She was his wife.

The children came running toward them then, Matteo,

Rocca, and Antonio, all throwing themselves at the bridal couple, and there were hugs all around.

"I love you," Monet said, kissing each of the children, one by one. "You are mine now, forever and ever."

"And you four are all mine," Marcu said, wrapping an arm around her waist. "I have everything now, love and family. I am, without a doubt, the luckiest of men."

* * * * *

MILLS & BOON

Coming next month

SECRETS OF HIS FORBIDDEN CINDERELLA
Caitlin Crews

She hadn't seen him clearly that night in September. That had been the point. She had been bold and daring, and he had responded with that brooding, overwhelming passion that had literally swept her off her feet. Into his arms, against a wall. And then, in a private salon, still dressed in their finery, with fabric pushed aside in haste and need.

Too much haste and need, it turned out.

Even though she had watched him roll on protection.

But now, he wore nothing to cover his face. And he wasn't smiling slightly, the way he had then. Those dark eyes of his weren't lit up with that particular knowing gleam that had turned her molten and soft.

On the contrary, his look was frigid. Stern and disapproving.

It made her remember—too late, always too late—that he wasn't simply a man. He was all the men who had come before him, too. He was the Duke, and the weight of that made him...colossal.

A decade ago, on the very rare occasions that he had looked at her at all, he had looked at her like this.

But it felt a lot worse now.

"This is a surprise," Teo said, with no preamble. "Not a pleasant one."

One of his inky brows rose, a gesture that he must have inherited from the royal branch of his family tree, because it made Amelia want to genuflect. She did not.

"Hi, Teo," she replied.

Foolishly.

"You will have to remind me of your name," he said, and there was a gleam in his eyes now. It made her feel quivery in a completely different way. And she didn't believe for a second that he didn't know who she was. "I'm afraid that I did not retain the particulars of my father's regrettable romantic choices."

"I understand. I had to block out a whole lot of my mother's marriages, too."

A muscle worked in his lean, perfect jaw. "Allow me to offer a warning now, before this goes any further. If you have come here in some misguided attempt to extort money from me based upon an association I forgot before it ended, you will be disappointed. And as I cannot think of any other reason why you should intrude upon my privacy, I will have to ask you to leave."

Amelia considered him. "You could have had the butler say that, surely."

"I will admit to a morbid sense of curiosity." His gaze swept over her. "And it is satisfied." He didn't wave a languid hand like a sulky monarch and still, he dismissed her. "You may go."

Amelia ordered the part of her that wanted to obey him, automatically, to settle down. "You don't want to hear why I've come?"

"I am certain I do not."

"That will make it fast, then."

Amelia could admit she felt…too much. Perhaps a touch of shame for having to come to him like this—especially after the last time she'd shown up here, uninvited. Her pulse kicked at her, making her feel…*fluttery*. And she was, embarrassingly, as molten and soft as if he'd smiled at her the way he had in September.

When he hadn't ventured anywhere near a smile.

"Never draw out the ugly things," Marie had always told her. "The quicker you get them over with, the more you can think about the good parts instead."

Just do it, be done with it and go, she ordered herself.

And who cared if her throat was dry enough to start its own fire?

"I'm pregnant," she announced into the intimidatingly, exultantly blue-blooded room. To a man who was all of that and more. "You're the father.'

Continue reading
SECRETS OF HIS FORBIDDEN CINDERELLA
Caitlin Crews

Available next month
www.millsandboon.co.uk

JOIN US ON SOCIAL MEDIA!

Stay up to date with our latest releases, author news and gossip, special offers and discounts, and all the behind-the-scenes action from Mills & Boon...

millsandboon

millsandboonuk

millsandboon

It might just be true love...